D0437447

STAR WARS™

LEIA

Princess of Alderaan

For information address Disney • Lucasfilm Press,
1101 Flower Street, Glendale, California 91201.

Printed in the United States of America

First Edition, September 2017

3 5 7 9 10 8 6 4 2

FAC-020093-17257

ISBN 978-1-4847-8078-7

Library of Congress Control Number on file

Reinforced binding

Design by Leigh Zieske

Visit the official *Star Wars* website at: www.starwars.com.

THIS LABEL APPLIES TO TEXT STOCK

STAR WARS

LEIA

PRINCESS OF ALDERAAN

Written by

CLAUDIA GRAY

PRESS

LOS ANGELES • NEW YORK

CHAPTER 01

The Day of Demand had been announced months before. Guests had already arrived from worlds across the galaxy, and delicious aromas from the banquet being prepared wafted through the palace halls. The weather had failed to cooperate with the celebration plans—low dark clouds hung heavily over the city of Aldera, threatening a downpour—but even the impending storm felt dramatic and grand, in a way.

It was the perfect setting for a princess to claim her right to the crown of Alderaan.

"Ow." Leia made a face. "That pulls."

"And it's going to keep pulling," promised WA-2V, Leia's personal attendant droid. Her bluish metal fingers swiftly wove one final braid in the complicated traditional style. "Today of all days, you must look your best."

"You say that every day." As a little girl, Leia had only ever wanted to tie her hair back in a tail. Her parents had said she was free to do as she liked. But 2V had held firm. Her programming demanded that she present the princess in grand style, and not even the princess herself could say otherwise.

"It's true every day," 2V insisted, coiling the braid in a loop and pinning it in place. "Standards are even higher for special occasions!"

Leia felt a small quiver in her belly, equal parts nerves and anticipation. This was the biggest day in her life since her first Name Day, when her parents had taken her into the throne room and declared her their daughter by adoption and by love—

She shook off the thought. That time all she had to do was be a baby in her mother's arms. This time she'd have to stand up for herself.

Once the hairstyle was done, Leia gratefully slipped into the clothing she and 2V had compromised on: a simple white dress for her, bold silver jewelry for 2V. Just as she toed into her satiny slippers, the orchestral fanfare swelled from the throne room, echoing through the palace's corridors. It felt as though her parents were personally knocking on her door.

"One more thing!" 2V pleaded. She rolled to the cabinet on the small sphere she had for a base, then swerved back with a silver headband, which she neatly fitted into the braids so its pearl charm hung at the center of Leia's forehead. "Yes. *Yes*. That's it. You look absolutely stunning! I work miracles, I really do."

Leia shook her head in amusement. “Thanks a lot.”

Oblivious, 2V shooed her charge toward the door. “Hurry! They’re all waiting.”

“It’s not like they can start without me, TooVee.” Still, Leia picked up the tail of her gown and hurried into the corridor. She didn’t want to be late. The princes and princesses who had made their demands in ancient times had sometimes had to fight their way to the throne room. It was meant to be a moment of strength and command—in other words, not a moment to prove you couldn’t even show up on time.

Alderaan’s royal palace had been the work of more than a millennium. Their monarchy was one that dedicated itself to serving its people, so they’d never built high spires or commanding towers to dominate the landscape. Instead, new chambers were added every few decades, creating a sprawling labyrinth where modern data centers and holochambers existed side-by-side with ancient rooms hewn from stone. Leia knew each hallway, each door by heart; as a small child she’d reveled in exploring some of the most shadowy, out-of-the-way passages. Sometimes she thought she might’ve been the only person in centuries to have found every single room in the palace.

Fortunately she knew the shortcut through the old armory, which got her to the antechamber of the throne room in plenty of time. The royal guards smiled when they saw her, and she grinned back as she straightened the cape of her gown. To the taller guard, she whispered, "How's the baby?"

"Sleeping through the night already," he replied. Leia mimed applause, and he ducked his head, almost bashfully.

Really she didn't know much about babies, except that parents were very proud of them even though they kept everybody up at night. But if the guard was happy to have a sleepy baby, then she was happy for him.

"We're lucky on Alderaan," her father had said as they sat by the library hearth. "We are loved by our people. We have their loyalty. That's because we love them and are loyal to them in turn. If we ever cease to appreciate those around us—from the highest lord to the humblest laborer—we'll lose that loyalty. We'll deserve *to lose it."*

Leia was jerked back into the moment by the rustling of the velvet curtain at the door. Swiftly she went to the wall where the Rhindon Sword hung, grabbed it by the hilt, and took it in hand. She'd practiced with it a few times, but its weight surprised her every time.

Position: doorway center. Sword: both hands on the hilt, arms close to body, blade upright. Speech . . .

I remember the speech, she told herself. *I definitely remember it. I'm just blanking on it at the moment and it'll absolutely come back to me when I'm standing in front of hundreds of people—*

The curtain was tugged to the side. Brilliant light, tinted by vast panes of stained glass, fell on her. Two hundred guests turned as one, all of them standing on either side of a blue-and-gold carpet that traced a line directly through the room to the golden thrones where Breha and Bail Organa sat.

Leia marched forward, sword held high. A low rumble of thunder made her grateful for the candledroids projecting light through the windows; otherwise, the room would've been nearly pitch-black. She'd practiced this but didn't think she could do it with her eyes closed.

I don't know, it might've been easier if I couldn't see all the guests staring at me. Leia had spent her entire life appearing before crowds, but today was the first time they would hear her voice in an official capacity, as their future queen.

Breha Organa wore a dress of bronze silk, her hair piled high atop her head in braids woven through with strings of beads. Next to her, Bail Organa wore the traditional long jacket of the viceroy. The crown itself had been brought back from the museum to sit atop a marble pillar, illuminated by a candledroid of its own. Her parents looked even more regal than usual—almost forbidding. Were they enjoying the charade?

Leia thought she was, or she would be if her parents had invited fewer people. Usually only a handful of offworlders would be present, but this time her father had asked many of his diplomatic allies in the Imperial Senate—Tynnra Pamlo from Taris, Cinderon Malpe of Derella, and both Winmey Lenz and Mon Mothma of Chandrila. Mon Mothma smiled wider as Leia passed her. Maybe she meant to be encouraging.

As long as she didn't think Leia looked *cute*. The Day of Demand wasn't about being an adorable little kid. It was about growing up.

When she reached the front of the throne room, only a few meters short of her parents, Breha called out the first line of the ceremony: "Who is this, who disturbs the queen in her seat of power?"

"It is I, Leia Organa, princess of Alderaan." Sure enough, the speech had come back on cue. "I come before you to hear you acknowledge that on this day it is known that I have reached my sixteenth year."

The "it is known" was an addition to the simplest form of the ritual, one used only when the eldest child of the king or queen was adopted. Leia had turned sixteen three or four days ago; she didn't know her birthday for sure and didn't much care. She'd become a princess of Alderaan on her Name Day, and that was the anniversary they were marking.

"We acknowledge that you are of age," said Bail. Only the slight crinkling at the corners of his eyes betrayed the smile he was working to hide. "Why then do you come before us armed?"

"I come to demand my right to the crown." Leia knelt

smoothly and held the sword overhead in one hand. Distant thunder rumbled, sending a small tremor through the floor. "On this day, you will acknowledge me as heir."

Breha's voice rang throughout the throne room. "The crown of Alderaan is not merely inherited. It must be earned. The heir must prove herself worthy in body, heart, and mind. Are you prepared to do so?"

"I am, my mother and queen." It was a relief to stand again and lower the heavy sword. "I have chosen three challenges. When I have undertaken these challenges and succeeded in them, you must invest me as crown princess of Alderaan."

"Reveal these challenges, and we will decide whether they are worthy," Bail said, as though he didn't already know each one. For a moment, she was tempted to make something up on the spot. *I'm going to learn to juggle and take to the stage as a feather-fire dancer. Aren't you proud?*

But she'd practiced her speech so many times that it poured forth almost automatically. "For my Challenge of the Body, I will climb Appenza Peak and reach its summit." That mountain was visible from her bedroom window, spectacularly silhouetted against every sunset. "For my Challenge of the Mind, I will no longer merely assist my father in the Imperial Senate but will also represent our world in the Apprentice Legislature. And for my Challenge of the Heart, I will undertake missions of charity and mercy to planets in need, paying all costs from my share of the royal purse. Through these challenges, I will prove my right to the crown."

Breha inclined her head. "The challenges are worthy." She rose from her throne, and Leia stepped up on the dais and brought the sword back into position in front of her. Breha's hands wrapped around the sword hilt, their fingers overlapping for the instant before Leia let go. "May all those present bear witness! If my daughter fulfills these challenges, she shall be invested as crown princess, heir to the throne of Alderaan."

Applause and cheers filled the room. Leia curtsied to her parents, who were beaming so proudly that for a moment it felt as if everything had been put right. Like the ceremony really had made them *see* her again—

—until the guests crowded closer with congratulations and her parents turned away to greet them instead of congratulating their daughter.

Bail was in conversation with Mon Mothma and her fellow Chandrilan senator, Winmey Lenz. Breha had taken the hands of Senator Pamlo, clearly thanking her for her presence.

Already, Leia was forgotten.

"Leia, my dear girl!" Lord Mellowyn of Birren came to her, smiling beneath his bushy white mustache. They were cousins through intricacies of Elder House lineage nobody bothered tracing any longer. "You were wonderful."

"Thank you." She returned his smile as best she could.

It's true. I'm not imagining it. They don't pay attention to me anymore.

Did I do something wrong?

Or do they just not care?

•◆•

She didn't think she'd made them angry. They hadn't turned from her in one moment of displeasure. Instead they had . . . ebbed away these past six months.

Leia had never had very many friends her own age. As egalitarian as the Alderaanian monarchy was, there would always be a dividing line between those within the palace and those outside its walls. She'd gamboled around on the rolling grounds with some of the cooks' children, but for the most part, her companions had been her parents.

Bail and Breha Organa had waited a long time for a child. They had told her that many times, often as she went to sleep, as part of the story about when her father came home from a mysterious mission to surprise her mother with the baby girl in his arms. Leia would've known it even if they hadn't told her, though. No matter how many questions she asked, her parents never tired of looking up answers. When she had bad dreams in the wee hours of the night, they never left her to a human nurse or caretaker droid; one of them always came to her, sometimes both. Every time she entered a room where they were, they smiled. She felt as if she made them happy merely by existing.

Many children would've become hopelessly spoiled. But Leia always wanted to be helpful, especially to those she cared about, and she loved her parents more than she could imagine ever loving anybody else. So she tried to interest herself in everything they did. Breha planted Malastarian orchids; Leia planted orchids and learned to care for them so they sent forth pale pink blooms. Bail liked dancing; Leia studied dancing and would practice with her father until her feet were sore.

With her mother's queenly work, she hadn't made as much progress. Breha Organa had charge of the royal books, balancing the many accounts and personally overseeing funding of all public works on the planet. Leia had gamely tried to get the hang of basic accounting, doing well enough but hating it the entire time. Within a week her mother had released her with a hug and a laugh.

"But don't I need to learn, if I'm going to be queen?" Leia had protested.

"Not if you fall in love with someone who likes bookkeeping." Breha had winked. "Then you can make your viceroy do it."

Her parents had arranged their duties so her mother tended to matters on Alderaan itself while her father represented Alderaan in the Imperial Senate and handled their diplomatic efforts. In the Clone Wars, he'd been their military leader as well, and as a little girl Leia had thrilled to his stories of adventure—and as she matured, she heard some of the darker, sadder stories that formed the largest part of any great war.

But there had been no major wars in a generation. The galaxy was unified in the worst possible way, under the tyranny of Emperor Palpatine. As a representative of one of the most influential Core Worlds, Bail Organa served as one of the few voices in the Imperial Senate that could moderate Palpatine's autocratic rule. Politics involved its own kind of battles, and Leia discovered early on that she liked a good fight. Interning in her father's Senate offices the past two years had meant proofreading his speeches, practice-debating with him on various issues, and unwinding after sessions as they traveled home on the royal yacht or the *Tantive IV.* She'd felt she wasn't only a daughter to Bail Organa but also a partner in his work, and that had made her prouder than her crown ever could.

She'd done her part. She'd been a good daughter. So why had they stopped caring about being parents?

It wasn't like they hit her or were mean to her. It was worse than that.

They ignored her.

Her father began having more and more private sessions in his offices, discussions with senators from Uyter or Mon Cala that Leia couldn't take part in. There had always been conferences like that, but they went from a few each month to sometimes several a day. Afterward Bail would be distracted for hours. If Leia tried to sound him out about them, he'd sternly tell her to attend to her own duties. It was as though power-brokering had become more important to him than anything else, including his own daughter.

Her mother was even worse. She'd suddenly turned into a society hostess, inviting dignitaries from around the galaxy to sumptuous banquets where the revelry lasted until nearly dawn. Sometimes Leia would even catch Breha dozing over the account books the next day. Her responsibility to her people didn't matter anymore, not compared to throwing a fabulous party.

Leia felt her corner of their world shrinking tighter and tighter until she could hardly breathe in their presence. Nothing she said or did seemed to affect them in the slightest. Although she was too old to call out for her parents when she had a bad dream, every once in a while she wanted to do it anyway.

But she never called for them. She never wanted to find out for sure that they wouldn't come.

•◆•

"Come away from that window," 2V scolded as she rolled to Leia's bed and spread the silk coverlet over it. "You could be struck by lightning."

Leia didn't budge from her seat. The open windows let the stormy breeze blow through, stirring her long hair as it hung loose down her back. Her billowy white nightgown covered the knees she hugged to her chest as she watched the horizon flicker bright with another thunderbolt.

2V rolled toward her, jointed arms on the stiff apron that passed for her hips. "Your Highness, please! It's not safe."

"I'm not going to be struck by lightning," Leia said. "Besides, I like the storm."

2V rolled ominously close. "My programming allows me to forcibly remove you from any major physical risk."

"All right, all right. I'm going. See?" Hopping down from the window seat, Leia went to her bed. It was one of the artifacts of a grander age, carved of priceless Glee Anselm hardwoods and inlaid with thin, curling lines of pure gold and silver. Royalty no longer wasted money on splendor like this, but Breha always said it was silly not to use a perfectly good bed, or tiara, or palace.

"The protocol droids inform me you were splendid today." 2V tidied up the vanity table, putting each brush and comb back in place. "I'm sure your appearance was much admired."

Leia had to smile. "Everyone saw what good work you did, TooVee. You should be proud."

Gleaming with satisfaction, 2V did a little half bow,

then rolled out of the room. As soon as the door was shut, Leia threw back the coverlet and returned to her window. Another lightning bolt struck the ground, half-hidden by Appenza Peak; for one second, the mountain was sharply outlined against the brilliant light.

It was so beautiful, she imagined saying to her parents over breakfast—though of course they never breakfasted with her any longer. They were already busy planning their next party before the sun even rose.

Leia threw open the window again and let the wind flow through the room. Her cheeks and arms felt the coolness of a few small raindrops. The ceremony hadn't lived up to her childhood dreams, but a storm like this could never disappoint her. She liked the wildness of it, the unpredictability, even the distant danger. This was something she'd only discovered about herself recently, her love of storms, and she treasured it because it was one of the few things she hadn't shared with her parents. This belonged to her alone.

Still, she wanted to tell them someday, once things had finally gone back to the way they used to be.

Tomorrow, she promised herself. *Tomorrow I'll take up my first challenge. I'll prove myself.*

I'll do something too great for them to ignore.

CHAPTER 02

Three weeks remained before the next session of the Apprentice Legislature would begin. Leia ought to have been preparing—reviewing top issues, drafting potential bills to introduce. That was what her father always did before returning to the Imperial Senate; she'd helped him for two years now, more than long enough to know how to handle the work on her own. So she should've been holed up in the study, surrounded by political materials.

Instead, she was dashing through the principal Aldera spaceport, 2V whirring along at her side.

"You need to show respect for the Imperial officials there," 2V insisted as they swerved around a Gozanti freighter where worker droids levitated crates of cargo into the hold. "You're traveling as a diplomat on a humanitarian mission and must present yourself accordingly. A princess must always dress for the occasion."

"I will, I will," Leia sighed. It had been years since she'd protested wearing dresses or putting her hair up, but 2V remained convinced that as soon as she let her charge out of her sight, Leia would immediately change back into her childhood play coveralls and a ponytail. "This occasion is providing rations to starving refugees on Wobani. So I don't need to braid my hair with pearls."

2V pulled back her upper torso in a move Leia could only describe as *prim*. "There's no need to be ridiculous. Pearls are so passé."

The royal family preferred to use Aldera's central public spaceflight facility. Countless times, Leia had come here with one or both of her parents to be ushered aboard, but this was the first time she'd ever personally commandeered a vessel for an interplanetary trip. Putting the request through the palace majordomo, Tarrik, had felt almost routine. When she saw the *Tantive IV* waiting for her, however, the ship's size struck her anew. The thought of it being at her disposal—the knowledge that more than two dozen crewmembers awaited her orders—thrilled her to the core. For months, even years, she'd been eager for some real responsibility. That began today.

She recognized the gray-shirted man walking toward her, so she drew herself up and clasped her hands together within the wide bell sleeves of her dress. "Captain Antilles. Thank you for readying the ship so quickly. When can we be under way?"

"Within the hour, Your Highness." He smiled down at her, his head tilted slightly to one side. "You can count on us." With that, he gave her a sharp salute and strode back to his work. Leia was left standing there wondering why she didn't like that reply. Captain Antilles had been polite, deferential, even friendly. She had no doubt of his loyalty and willingness to serve. But the tilt of his head—

He doesn't think of me as a leader. He still thinks of me as a little girl. She frowned. *He thinks I'm* cute.

It was silly to be surprised by that, much less offended. The captain had known her since she was a toddler, and she'd only just had her Day of Demand. Leia hadn't grown to her full height yet, either . . . she hoped. As her mother liked to say, *Authority can be given, but leadership must be earned.*

Today, she would begin to earn it. Soon neither Captain Antilles nor her parents would doubt what she was capable of.

•◆•

The trip to Wobani was swift and uneventful. Leia spent her time in the cargo holds, making sure all the rations were stored correctly and that the officers had clear instructions for distribution. When they reached the planet, she'd only need to look over the layout of the resettlement station to decide precisely where to set up.

"Easy as dunking a Mon Calamari," she murmured to herself. (It was an old saying, but she'd learned by playing with Mon Calamari children at the senatorial complex pools that the real trick was getting them to surface first. You couldn't dunk anyone who was still underwater.)

Wobani would require no special climate gear; it was a temperate Mid-Rim world, humid but otherwise unremarkable, and they'd be close enough to the equator not to have to worry about snow. The planet had never been especially prosperous or heavily populated, supporting itself primarily through basic manufacturing of small parts and armor, and growing grains and spices that thrived in marshy conditions. Like many other worlds across the galaxy, it was prosperous just past the point of subsistence, engaged in intragalactic commerce only to a modest degree, and ambitious for no greater position in the galaxy.

Then, six years ago, Palpatine had begun the "Commodities Enhancement Program," which promised better market access galaxy-wide for food and other organic raw material. Like so many of the Emperor's other promises, it was a lie designed to conceal other plans; her parents had taught her how to see through such things. Wobani was given impossible quotas to fill, and when the planet's farmers fell short, they were fined. Large areas of common land were instead parceled out to various Imperial officials who would, supposedly, "put them under better management." Really this meant they could now profit while the native Wobani became ever poorer and hungrier.

Every world targeted by the commodities program suffered, but Wobani had entirely collapsed. Famine was now widespread. As the agricultural sector faltered, the factory cities became overcrowded with desperate migrants in search of work, which in turn meant that the factories could pay lower wages and force people to labor in more dangerous conditions. By now the Wobani would do anything to stay alive. There was talk of building Imperial work-camp prisons on the planet; that was virtually the only industry it could sustain any longer, and the populace was demoralized enough to accept such prisons in their midst. Free movement between star systems was the norm, but the Empire had put Wobani under strict travel restrictions, to "prevent its exploitation." In the Senate, it was widely believed the restrictions were primarily an attempt to cover up how bad the situation had become.

Leia thought that was ridiculous. Every senator and staffer knew about the mess on Wobani, but they didn't say so. If people had just spoken the truth, the news would've spread to everybody on every planet, everywhere, and then there would've been no point in covering things up in the first place.

Even her father had remained quiet. His silence angered her even more than the blockade.

So she hadn't told her parents where she was going on

this mission. Leia, familiar with travel protocols, sought diplomatic landing clearance first. For someone representing the royal house of Alderaan, approval was very nearly automatic. Captain Antilles might think of her as a child, but he'd never question her commandeering the *Tantive IV* for a preapproved mission. Probably he assumed her parents had put in the request, but his assumptions weren't her problem.

She imagined herself returning to Alderaan, strolling into the palace's dining hall, and casually explaining to her parents that she'd been to Wobani herself, yes, that political hotspot even members of the Senate—like her father—hadn't dared to speak out on. *That* would show them. . . .

But Leia didn't really want to show them up. She only wanted to make them see her again.

This melancholy turn of thought vanished when Captain Antilles's voice came over the comm: *"Your Highness, we're beginning our landing approach."*

"Thank you, Captain. I'll be right there." With that, she brought the hood of her dress up over her braids and headed for the boarding ramp. Only moments stood between her and her first, maybe boldest, humanitarian mission, and she felt nothing but the burning desire to do something that would matter, both to her parents and to the entire galaxy, and the confidence that she could.

That lasted until the *Tantive IV*'s doors slid open to reveal hell.

Leia's lips parted in shock as she walked out. The rolling countryside, which once would've been covered with fresh green stalks of spring grain, now was only mud and a few yellowing stalks of plants that could no longer thrive. Wobani's sky had taken on the dingy tint that came only from pollution, a haze that might never clear again. However, the desolation of the planet itself didn't come close to that of its people.

Surrounding the landing field, stretching out to the horizon in every direction, were cheap, prefab shelters, like what someone might take on a long hike to sleep out in the wild. They weren't meant for daily use, but from the looks of things, thousands of people had been living in these for months. Deep ruts scarred the muddy pathways that served as roads between the shelters. Every single one of those ramshackle shelters housed a family, or perhaps two. Surrounding them stood gaunt people with stained, worn clothing and a febrile neediness in their eyes that scared Leia as much as it moved her. Even before she stepped off the platform, people had begun to shout and call, pleading for help.

Yet not one stepped forward, because the platform was surrounded by stormtroopers, blaster rifles in hand, their white armor grimy and mud-splotched.

An Imperial official climbed the short ramp that led to the *Tantive IV*. His eyes were as dead as his tone. "The 'humanitarian' mission from Alderaan?"

"Yes." Leia had prepared a few things to say—some lofty, some defiant, depending on their reception. Any of those careful speeches would've sounded so hollow spoken in front of this hungry crowd. "We, ah, we're ready to get started."

The official shrugged. "Fine." With that he made a swift hand motion, and all the stormtroopers went into resting stance.

What happened next seemed to Leia like an avalanche in the Grindel Range, or maybe a flash flood. A rush of people, vaster and faster than she'd ever imagined, surged toward the landing platform, cresting at the edges where they climbed or jumped or pulled others up. Within seconds she and her crew were surrounded by wide eyes and outreached hands. She could hear nothing but their shouts—"We need food!" "Water purification systems? Do you have those?" "Anything, please, give us anything!"

Captain Antilles was trying to push them back. From the corner of her eye she saw another crewmember struggling to set up the first of what would've been her many orderly distribution tables—and at the ramp, the Imperial official standing like a stone amid the struggling crowd and smirking at the melee.

It was the smirk that got her. Leia's fear burned to ashes in a blaze of anger. She leapt onto the table and shouted, at the top of her lungs, "Everybody *STOP*!"

Everybody did. Probably that was only due to their surprise at a tiny teenaged girl giving orders, but Leia would take what she could get. Captain Antilles snapped a loudhailer module from his belt and handed it up to her.

"Listen to me," she said, module set to full projection so that even the crowds in the far distance would hear. "You don't have to rush. You don't have to fight. We have food here for everyone."

Barely. She'd thought the rations they brought might feed people for a season or more; this community was so large and so impoverished that they'd devour these supplies within a couple of weeks at most. Still, it was better than nothing . . . and nothing was all these people had.

She continued, "Give us a few moments to set up our distribution platforms. Maybe—maybe you could spend those moments finding the people in the most need, like the elderly and the sick. You could bring them forward so they can go first and not have to stand around waiting, because you'll still get everything you need. Everything we have. Got it?"

Murmuring went through the crowd, and at first Leia wondered if they would storm the *Tantive IV* after all. Then the closest individuals began shuffling back to give them space. In the distance, she spotted people bringing forward a few small children and an elderly woman, with more surely to come.

"All right." Leia hopped down from the table, skirts flying in a way 2V would certainly have called inelegant. Shouting at the top of her lungs on top of a table would count as inelegant too; it wasn't exactly how she wanted to be perceived as a leader.

But as she handed the loudhailer module back to Captain Antilles, he looked at her differently. There was no more tilt to his head. Apparently, every once in a while, leadership meant abandoning decorum and yelling as loud as you could. The captain said, "We'll be set up within minutes, Your Highness."

Leia acknowledged him with a nod and got to work.

They could've programmed droids to do the distribution, but she left them for the labor of hauling out the crates of rations. She wanted these people to see a living face smiling at them, living hands giving them something. *You aren't forgotten,* she thought as she held ration packs out to person after person after person. *The Empire won't let us save you, but we can still help.*

Such things couldn't be spoken aloud while she was surrounded by armed stormtroopers. Yet she felt the message came through.

After the rush of distribution, a few people stayed

behind to be seen by the ship's medical droid. The 2-1B could repair broken bones or stitch up wounds, and Leia was grateful for that much, but what these people truly needed was relief from desperation. She had only been able to provide the smallest measure of that, for what would be a very short time.

"Terrible scene, this." Captain Antilles stood next to her, his hands clasped behind his back. "It reminds you how fortunate we are on Alderaan."

"Yes, it does."

Leia had always imagined herself very aware of the wrongs in the galaxy. Her parents had been honest with her about the cruelty of Palpatine's rule. However, knowing about the suffering was very different from witnessing it. Coming here, she'd felt righteous; being here, she knew herself helpless.

How am I supposed to turn away from this? How am I supposed to fly away from Wobani knowing that these people are left behind?

It came to her in a flash: *I* won't *leave them behind.*

The Empire had given her permission to land. Next, they'd give her permission to load the *Tantive IV* with as many refugees as it could hold, and fly them away from this place for good.

CHAPTER 03

"Passengers?" Captain Antilles frowned as if trying to translate the word from an alien language. "Your Highness, with all due respect—I understand why you want to do this, but it's well outside the parameters of our landing clearance."

"Yes, but I'm going to talk with the Imperial official in charge of this zone. When I explain that we're actually helping to solve his problems, I'm sure he'll agree to it." Already Leia had cleaned her gown and rebraided her hair, in order to make the most regal impression she could. Really she ought to have brought a change of wardrobe along. She'd have to tell 2V that when she got back. It would make the droid's day.

Captain Antilles shook his head. "Imperial officers aren't known for flexibility."

Leia had never dealt with an officer on her own terms before, but surely they couldn't be more difficult than the palace majordomo. Besides, it wasn't as though she had to negotiate with a grand moff or anything. According to the records on file, the person in charge was a mere major.

She smiled to herself. *In any game of cards, a princess trumps a major every time.*

Although the captain still appeared wary, he nodded and pointed toward another officer standing around in the now-empty cargo bay. "Lieutenant Batten, you'll accompany the princess on her journey."

Lieutenant Ress Batten was a slender woman perhaps thirty years of age, with long black curly hair and golden skin. Arms folded across her chest, she said, "If they throw her in jail, do I have to go there too?"

"Yes," Captain Antilles snapped. "Assuming I don't throw you in the brig before the Empire gets the chance." Batten held up her hands in mock surrender before turning to ready one of the speeders. When Leia gave the captain a look, he sighed. "Lieutenant Batten has, shall we say, issues with her attitude. But she's a strong speeder driver and a better fighter. More than anything, she's got good instincts about people. If you're going into a dodgy situation and you're only taking one crewmember with you, Batten's the one you want."

He'd called the situation "dodgy." Leia liked the sound of that.

Batten readied the landspeeder swiftly, and almost before Leia knew it, the two of them were coasting through endless black fields of mud that had once been meadows. Other camps dotted the horizon, evidence of thousands more people trapped in unlivable circumstances, unable to go home and unable to leave the planet.

"Unbelievable," Batten said. "Did you notice not one person had their own vehicle along? Not a ship, not a speeder, not a sled. They must've been banned from bringing them." Leia hadn't noticed that, and was about to say so, when Batten pulled herself sharply upright. "My apologies for speaking informally, Your Highness. It's a bad habit of mine."

"That's all right. Military procedure is one thing, but sometimes royal protocol just gets in the way." That was what her father always said to keep people from feeling awkward about having broken the rules for conversing with the royals.

Those people usually smiled in relief and remained silent afterward. Batten, however, took it as permission to keep going. "The Emperor's plan didn't work, accidentally causing suffering. So how does he go about fixing it? He doesn't! He deliberately causes more suffering." She scowled. "People are getting tired of this. Worse than tired. They're getting angry."

"I don't blame them." Leia's gaze remained on the distant camps as she tried to guess how many people were trapped there.

•◆•

"Roughly one thousand families per camp," said the Imperial official in charge, a Major Tedam. His heavy-lidded eyes drooped as if he'd been interrupted mid-nap. "Give or take. One thousand shelters, at any rate."

"That must be a very great burden for you." Given that the Empire wasn't doing anything much for these people except holding blasters on them, Leia wasn't sure how much of a burden it could be. Still, this needed to sound like she wasn't asking for a favor, only trying to solve his problem. "I'm sure you'd rather have fewer mouths to feed. My ship stands ready to transport Wobani citizens off-planet, back to Alderaan—"

"Transport?" Briefly Tedam seemed alert, but the moment passed. "That's not allowed."

Leia nodded. "Not under my current clearance, no. We'd have to renegotiate terms, which could be done very quickly."

Tedam shook his head and repeated, "That's not allowed. Here, we stick to the rules." He blinked slowly, almost as if he expected her to be gone before he opened his eyes again.

Keep your temper, she reminded herself. "If you don't have the authority to renegotiate terms, can you let me know who does?"

"Nobody on this planet. Nobody in this sector."

"Then—then you *must* have some authority, if you're

this isolated." Would the Empire really drop so many troops and officials on one planet and leave them there without orders, so that they might starve and brutalize the citizens at will?

Yes. They would.

"I have authority to enforce the diplomatic permit as issued," Tedam said. "No more and no less. Your ship will leave this planet with no one on board except yourself and your crewmembers, as planned. I recommend you leave soon."

With that he went back to reviewing data. He didn't even glance up as Leia walked out.

The trapezoidal corridor of the local Imperial headquarters was, like most Imperial structures, dark, cold, and depressing. Metal beams seemed to be closing around her like the jaws of an old-fashioned trap, and the reddish hue of the floor reminded her of blood. She trembled, from anger and fear for others, and from sheer helplessness.

On Alderaan, they had no true poverty. All citizens were at least modestly provided for, and public facilities and services were both numerous and available to everyone. On Coruscant, Leia knew, people could be in difficult straits, but they were hard to pick out in the endless throngs of crowds that inhabited every lane and layer of that world. It was different to witness this kind of suffering with her own eyes. To end this day by flying away, having accomplished exactly no lasting good—

She couldn't stand it.

She *wouldn't.*

Batten gave her royal charge several sidelong looks on the way back to the *Tantive IV.* Leia noticed, but she was too deep in thought to worry about it. What could she do to set this right? Refuse to leave until the agreement was renegotiated? Tell them she'd be back every week—maybe every day!—until they let her take some settlers with her? There had to be a way, but she couldn't think of one.

On their arrival at the ship, Batten powered down the speeder to allow it to be reloaded by the hauler droids. As Leia stood outside, waiting for that to be done, she saw an elderly woman sitting in one corner of the small, roped-off area around a shelter. With shaking hands, she was mending some knitted garment—doing it herself, sewing with a needle like someone out of an old-fashioned storybook. Leia wondered whether the tremor in the woman's hands was from age or from cold. But she was using the one skill she had to protect herself and her family—

It was the word *skill* that did it.

Leia lit up and called out, "Captain Antilles! Lieutenant Batten! Come help me, will you?" As they headed toward her, confused expressions on their faces, she turned back to the old woman. "You seem to be handy with a needle and thread."

The woman seemed surprised to be spoken to, but she answered calmly, "Why, yes, Your Highness."

"You see, that's very interesting," Leia said. Antilles and Batten had reached her by then, and to them she said, "The Imperial officials say I can't take any passengers with me. Only crew."

"They don't budge on things like that." The captain managed to say it in a way that didn't mean *I told you so*, which Leia appreciated. But she wouldn't have cared what he said or how he said it, not now that the best idea she'd ever had was burning bright inside her.

She turned back to the old woman. "The thing is, sometimes our soldiers' uniforms rip or tear. We could use someone to help keep them in repair. So I'm hiring a new crewmember, an official ship's seamstress. If you take the job, you'll fly out of here with us immediately."

The woman's astonishment and delight would've warmed Leia in a snowstorm. "But—but my husband—" She pointed toward an elderly man napping on a nearby cot.

"What does he do?" Leia asked. Next to her, Antilles and Batten were exchanging incredulous glances.

"He's a mechanic, or he was back when we had a shop." The old woman smiled wider, anticipating the answer.

Triumphantly, Leia said, "So we're also hiring an official ship's mechanic. Done. That's two. Captain, how many extra people can we fit aboard for a short trip?"

It took a few moments for Captain Antilles to answer. "About one hundred."

One hundred individuals out of one thousand families? It wasn't enough, but it was a place to begin. "Then I'm about to hire ninety-eight more crewmembers. Help me register them in the ship's official log, will you?"

"You've got it, Your Highness," said Batten, who had a wide grin on her face. The captain still looked wary, but he nodded as Batten and Leia got to work.

Leia decided to find those who were youngest and oldest, sickest or pregnant, the ones who needed help most urgently. Two little children, neither of them even five years old: they could crawl into small spaces to retrieve lost things. A man with a racking cough: he knew how to fly a spaceship, so he could serve as an emergency backup pilot. A woman whose belly stretched large with a baby almost in this world: she'd owned a plant nursery, and it just so happened that the *Tantive IV* needed a ship's botanist. As Leia named every new hire, Batten instantly recorded it in the log, making their status as official as anyone else's on board.

Word spread through the camp quickly. People crowded around, all hoping to be chosen—yet they silently pushed forward those in greater need. Stormtroopers came close too; while they didn't dare interfere with a humanitarian mission, she could hear the buzz of comms in their helmets as they tried to get new orders that fit the unprecedented situation at hand. But the ones she was happiest to see were the hired, who grabbed their few possessions and headed up the ramp into the *Tantive IV*, into escape and freedom.

After a former percussionist was hired as ship's drummer, Batten quietly said, "That's one hundred."

"Already?" Leia felt simultaneously as though she'd been standing out here in the cold mud for hours—probably she had been—and as though she couldn't possibly be finished. Faces fell all around her as brief hopes flickered out. More loudly, she said, "You haven't been forgotten. We'll tell the galaxy what we've seen here today. Soon, I hope, other ships will follow ours, and then we can make a real difference."

They nodded. They believed her. None of that made it easier to walk away.

•◆•

The mood on the *Tantive IV* on the return trip couldn't have been more different from the way there. Their "new crewmembers" crowded every room and passageway, and while they were tremendously grateful and relieved, they were also hungry, exhausted, and often unwell. She could hear laughter, and tears too; so many of them had left people behind. The 2-1B began doing what it could for them as Leia returned to the bridge, just moments before they would go into hyperspace.

As she walked through the doors, she heard Captain Antilles saying, "—in accordance with our instructions."

"These were not *your instructions,"* insisted Tedam, from the viewscreen at the captain's station. He looked awake now. *"The limits of the landing permit are entirely clear that no extra persons can leave this planet with your ship!"*

Leia interjected, "Look at the permit again, Major. I think you'll find the rule is crystal clear. We can only leave with crewmembers? We *are* only leaving with crewmembers."

"You have Wobani citizens aboard—"

"Who have been hired as crew," she replied smoothly. "The permit doesn't forbid my hiring anyone. Like you said, let's stick to the rules. And the rules say we get to leave here whenever we choose." *As in now.*

Tedam looked like he'd rather swallow his own socks than accede to any of this, but like most Imperial officers, he knew when regulations worked against him. With a quick, irritable gesture, he shut off communications and the screen went black.

"Not bad, Your Highness," said Batten from near the door.

Captain Antilles remained sterner in every sense. "You realize we haven't made any provisions for these people on landing, Your Highness."

"Yes, of course." Their arrival at Aldera's main spaceport would be an enormous mess. But Leia had never minded making messes. "We'll get them settled quickly enough, I'm sure."

The captain nodded. "As you wish, Your Highness, but—if you don't mind—"

"Yes?"

"I've seen deadly combat before. Mass warfare. I'm not afraid to face it." A small smile appeared on Captain Antilles's face. "But *you* have to be the one who tells the queen about this."

She laughed loudly. "Deal."

Imperial restrictions around Wobani had made it impossible for them to jump to lightspeed and go directly to Alderaan; the *Tantive IV* would first have to stop at Calderos Station, a deep-space waypoint that served both bureaucratic and repair functions for Imperial ships around the sector and their rare invited guests. As one of those guests, Leia would send a simple signal requesting permission to leave for their home planet, which would receive approval within moments. So she watched the electric blue swirl of hyperspace with no foreboding, only impatience to get these people home—and to show her parents what she'd done—

The ship dropped out of lightspeed, and she gasped. Captain Antilles rose from his chair, and Batten said something considered indecent on most worlds, then, "Are you seeing this?"

"Yes, Lieutenant," Antilles said. "We see it."

Calderos Station—a large Imperial facility, important to this sector—had been damaged. No, *attacked*. Leia recognized laser-cannon fire all along the station's outer surface, and various search-and-track lights along the nearest side were out. With one side more or less whole and the other quiet, burned and black, it was easy to imagine the station having been torn in two.

A swarm of TIE fighters zoomed toward them as a message came through: *"Identify yourselves!"*

"*Tantive IV,* diplomatic vessel on a humanitarian mission from Alderaan," Captain Antilles said. "We've been on Wobani for the last many hours. Imperial records there will verify our whereabouts."

"Hold for confirmation."

Leia stared at the station, taking in the damage in full. Although it looked as though there would've been little to no loss of life, this attack had crippled Calderos Station—and as a result, made it easier for people to travel clandestinely to and from Wobani or any other restricted world in this area. That would be true for days, maybe many weeks.

It took serious firepower to damage an Imperial station like this. No one ship could do it except a Star Destroyer, and obviously that wasn't the case, so—

"Confirmed," said the voice on the speakers as the TIE fighters swerved away. *"You are to leave this sector and return to your home planet at once."*

As Captain Antilles moved to comply, Leia put the last pieces of the puzzle together.

Somebody—several somebodies—had put together the numbers and firepower necessary to attack and disable an Imperial station. That had taken money, planning, and time. People weren't just complaining about the Empire anymore.

They had begun fighting back.

CHAPTER 04

Alderaan was known to people throughout the galaxy for its beautiful scenery, its aesthetically pleasing architecture, and its commitment to preserving harmony and tranquility. Those people would have been very surprised by the scene at the Aldera spaceport, when the *Tantive IV* unexpectedly unloaded a hundred refugees from Wobani.

Some of the refugees had become hysterical with delight or disbelief; others slumped onto crates or helper droids, in obvious need of medical care or at least a place to rest. All of them were muddy, as was the entire crew and Leia herself.

"I let Central know we were coming!" Batten protested as they tried to assemble everyone into some kind of order. "I mean, I let them know when we hit the atmosphere, which wasn't that long ago, but that's as soon as we could've—"

"It's all right, Lieutenant." Captain Antilles seemed strangely distracted, Leia thought. "I should contact the viceroy immediately."

Why is he going to talk to my father? Leia watched, confused, as the captain strode away without looking back. *The viceroy takes charge of Alderaan's dealings with the galaxy at large. The governing of the planet itself is done by—*

"Her Majesty Breha Organa!" announced a droid from the far end of the bay, and Leia turned with all the others to see her mother walk in, a huge entourage behind her. As usual, she wore a long gown, this one of russet silk and blue velvet, and she had ribbons of each fabric braided into her elaborate hairstyle. No jewels, no crown: Breha didn't need them to command attention, to draw attention, or to appear every bit a queen.

Silence fell without being asked for. Leia watched her mother step up on a platform and begin to address them all, her rich voice carrying through the entire bay: "Good people of Wobani, you're very welcome to Alderaan. Forgive us for not being better prepared to receive you, but from this moment on, my team will see to your every need." She gestured to the entourage—medical personnel, social workers, and the like, who were already beginning to weave their way into the crowd. "No doubt you'll want a chance to rest, recover, and reflect on what you would like to do next. I pledge here and now that every single person arriving today will receive a stipend that will allow you either to travel to another world where you may have family or friends, or to begin a new life here on Alderaan. It is my welcome gift to all of you."

Someone yelled, "All hail Queen Breha!" which wasn't the way people cheered royalty on Alderaan. Leia was more accustomed to gentle applause. But the Wobani took up the chant with such enthusiasm that the crew joined in, and even Leia had to shout it once at the end.

As the queen stepped down from the platform and the refugees began getting the help they needed, Batten said, "Wow, your mom pulls her act together pretty quick."

"Her act is always together." Leia simultaneously admired this about her mother and envied it. "She was born with it together. I wish she'd teach me the trick."

"Well, if you ever learn, let me know, would you?" Batten gave a wink in Leia's direction before heading back into the *Tantive IV* to finish postflight systems checks.

Leia saw her mother coming through the crowd toward her; those nearby parted before her, clearing a path without Queen Breha having to hold out a hand or say a word. At last, Leia would be able to talk with her mother about what she'd accomplished, about the splendid rescue she'd just completed on a world most people were afraid to even mention, much less visit. Breha Organa would have to talk to her daughter as an equal.

The queen came to Leia and folded her in her arms. Their embrace was warm and true—but when Breha pulled back, her lips were pressed together in a thin line.

Leia knew what that look meant. "What? What did I do?"

"The palace," said Breha. "Now."

•◆•

"You should have run this by us first—"

"When would I ever have had the chance? You and Dad are always—"

"Your father and I have important business to conduct, and we should be able to trust you to understand—"

" 'Important business'? Like what? Planning another dinner party?"

"Leia!" Queen Breha rarely raised her voice, which gave it more impact when she did. Leia finally quieted herself and sat down on the long, low couch that curved around the east wall of the royal library.

The library, like everything else in the palace, had been the work of generations. Datacrons from countless worlds and eras shimmered in their cases, and one set of shelves bore precious, ancient paper books. Constellation globes of various systems stood in small nooks or hung from the high ceiling. A real fire burned in the center of the vast room in a spherical hearth made of copper and stone; that and the setting sun through the long, narrow windows provided most of the light.

There was, of course, another "Royal Library of

Alderaan," one open to all its citizens and with a collection even richer than this. But in this room, the royal family kept their own treasures and memories. It was more than a library. It was the place where they relaxed, where they laughed, where they spoke most openly as a family.

Which wasn't always a good thing.

Breha shook her head as she paced to and from the hearth. "Whatever possessed you to go to Wobani?"

"There were people in need," Leia insisted. She wasn't about to apologize. "If you'd been there and seen how desperate they were—"

"I know how desperate they are." The queen sighed. "I also know how dangerous the situation on Wobani is. It may be largely forgotten at the moment, but it's only one of many loose threads that could turn out to be a fuse."

What was that supposed to mean? Leia kept on. "It was a humanitarian mission. I put through for the proper approvals. You can see the records."

Breha gave her daughter a look. "Yes, you arranged things very well. But speak to me in truth. You knew that if you had come to us directly, we would've told you to choose another place for your first humanitarian mission. Didn't you?"

Shamefaced, Leia nodded. A lie of omission was still a lie.

"I've spent the past few hours on comms with angry

Imperial officials everywhere from Wobani to Coruscant. They don't like the idea of a young girl tricking one of their own—though as far as that goes, well, they can stuff it." Breha sighed, more casual now, less a queen and more herself. "What's more troubling is that they've asked some very pointed questions about our ship appearing at Calderos Station so soon after a . . . dissident action. We can't afford to be associated with that, Leia. The minute the Empire decides Alderaan has anything to do with rebellion—"

"Shouldn't we *want* to do something about the Empire?" Leia retorted.

"Don't change the subject. Do you see how dangerous that link is?"

"I do, but it's not as if I could've known that was going to happen," she pointed out.

Breha put one hand to her forehead, as if trying to ward off a headache. The steely gray streak in her black hair was painted gold by the firelight. "No. You couldn't have expected that. But you should've realized that you had no business going to Wobani."

"Why? Because it made some major out there angry? The Emperor doesn't like humanitarian aid going to *anybody*." Leia had noticed this for herself during debates in the Imperial Senate. "If I'm going to upset them no matter where I go, I figured I should go someplace where the help would really matter."

"And to take people away with you—through a *trick*, no less—"

Leia's temper flared fresh. "Yes! I brought people with me instead of leaving them there to starve! How can you be angry with me for that? What kind of person are you?"

Breha stared at her daughter, stricken. The words couldn't be unsaid, and Leia felt as though she'd crossed a much more dangerous boundary than she'd intended.

But her mother simply kneeled before her and took Leia's hands in hers. "My daughter. I thought you would've understood. Your father, Mon Mothma, and some of his other allies in the Senate have been negotiating for resettlement of the Wobani population for months now."

"What? It wasn't in any of the files I reviewed for his office."

"Your father doesn't show you everything, Leia. Some things require higher security clearances than interns have, even when those interns are daughters of one of the Elder Houses. Any deal regarding Wobani would have to be carefully negotiated, and kept secret, so that the governor in charge of that sector could agree to our terms and still save face." Breha's head drooped. "I'm still speaking as though that deal can happen. It can't any longer. Everyone with any authority over Wobani will be embarrassed, angry, and unwilling to bargain. Months of negotiation were effectively destroyed by what you did today."

The floor could've disintegrated beneath Leia, letting her tumble down through rock and soil all the way to lava, without her feeling more horrified than she did in that moment. "No. That can't be true. It *can't*."

"You're very nearly an adult, Leia. Past your Day of Demand, and so I'm trusting you with the truth about this, even though I know it's a hard truth for you to hear." One of Breha's hands stroked Leia's hair. "Take heart. In a few months, when this incident isn't as fresh, your father will take the cause up again. Maybe they'll make more headway this time."

Delaying the rescue of the people on Wobani wasn't much better than destroying that rescue. Leia had seen how desperate they were, and had unwittingly condemned them to so much more time trapped in that same hell.

Breha squeezed her daughter's hands, then rose to her feet again. "We'll speak no more of it. I know your motivations were good, Leia. You showed compassion and courage, and even ingenuity. But you have to choose your missions more carefully from now on. Recognize that you may not have all the information necessary to make the right decisions in a dangerous situation, because there are things your father and I cannot tell you."

"Yes, ma'am," Leia said. On the first day of the Apprentice Legislature, she'd check to see what kind of security clearance upgrades they received. "But—"

"Yes?"

"If you two had spoken with me about my humanitarian mission before I left, this wouldn't have happened. I *tried* to talk with you both. You didn't have time." The words came out small and quiet, unlike her. "I know that's not an excuse. But it *is* a reason."

Now her mother seemed as abashed as Leia felt. "You're right. We've been terribly busy lately, and I'm sorry about that."

"It's all right," Leia said, making herself believe it.

Breha put her hand on her daughter's shoulder, a signal that meant lectures were done and life would resume. "You should head back to the spaceport and help people get settled. It's back to the books for me."

"How many accounts can there be to balance?" Leia asked. Breha simply shrugged as she walked out of the library.

They'd parted well enough; still, there was no missing that, once again, her mother's attention was elsewhere.

Yet Leia couldn't be that angry with her mother when

she was so much angrier with herself. She'd been so proud of what she'd done on Wobani, so sure what she was doing was right.

It can't be all bad that I got those people out of there, she reminded herself, thinking of the ecstatic smiles on the faces of the people she'd "hired." *Some people who would've gone to bed cold, hungry, and afraid will instead be warm, well-fed, and happy. That's worth something. It's worth a lot.*

As she walked through the corridor, she passed her father's office. The gleam of a candledroid revealed he was working within. Their palace had many old-fashioned doors that opened and closed by hand, and this was one of them; it stood half-open, revealing a sliver of the scene inside. He sat at his great desk, speaking intently with the person opposite him—who appeared to be Captain Antilles.

Don't eavesdrop, she reminded herself, walking away quickly. But it scalded her pride to think that the captain of the *Tantive IV* had a chance to report everything she'd done on Wobani before her father even talked to her about it personally. There was nothing else the two men could've had to discuss.

CHAPTER 05

The next dawn saw Leia on a suborbital jumper, wearing all-weather gear and drinking caf from a travel mug as she leaned against her rucksack of gear. She sat in the back with a few members of the royal guard and the supplies they were taking to the Istabith range garrison. All of them frequently served the palace itself, so none of them were self-conscious around her; after the first several minutes, they chatted easily among themselves, as if she weren't even there.

(Well, she suspected they weren't swearing as much as usual.)

Leia preferred it this way. Instead of making stately small talk, she could remain on the jump seat and look out at the snowy hills and mountains beneath. With the plasma window keeping out the cold, she could enjoy the way the sky turned pale pink at the horizon, or how the deep snowdrifts softened the jagged peaks of the range.

In the far distance stood Appenza Peak. Although it wasn't the tallest mountain on Alderaan, it was perhaps the most iconic—a slim, needlelike sliver pointing far above the modest hills at its base. The flag of this region bore its silhouette; fairy tales often began with a spirit flying away from its home on Appenza Peak to choose an adventurer. Religious pilgrims claimed that at its height, one could commune with the Force, and the relatively easy climb meant that hundreds of people made the trek each year.

But *relatively easy* wasn't the same as *easy*. Even the fairy tales warned against trying Appenza Peak on a whim. Making the journey up the mountain required training, equipment, and will.

Equipment, check, Leia thought, feeling the backpack's reassuring heft against her shoulder. *Will, check. Training—coming right up.*

After Wobani, she craved a physical, material challenge. Exact parameters. On the mountain, success and failure would be as solid as the rock beneath her feet. The pathfinding class would prepare her for that.

The jumper landed at the designated coordinates only long enough for Leia to hop out. She waved over her shoulder at the guards as it took off again, sending swirls of snowflakes into the air, then turned to join the pathfinding students who had already gathered in the clearing next to the high, gabled chalet that served as their headquarters for the day.

"Wait—aren't you the princess?" said a slim, dark-skinned boy with aquiline features and an aristocratic accent. "How did you wind up flying here on that old barge?"

None of the royal family stood on ceremony except when diplomatic protocol demanded it. But proudly proclaiming you weren't too good to ride on a jumper was just the same as hinting that, really, you *were* too good for it and wanted a reward for pretending otherwise. She simply said, "They were headed this way. And yes, I'm Leia Organa."

"Chassellon Stevis of Coruscant." He gave her an overly elaborate bow, twirling his outstretched hand at the wrist to make her laugh. It worked. "My mother heads our diplomatic legation, as you probably know—and now you and I follow our parents into the family business."

When Breha Organa had arranged this class, she'd reached out to some of the other new members of the Apprentice Legislature to participate as well. The rationale had been for Leia to get to know a few people outside of Coruscant's sparkling but artificial social whirl. It felt more like her mother was hurriedly trying to find some friends for her daughter. *That way, she doesn't have to feel guilty about ignoring me—if she even feels guilty at all—*

"I'm looking forward to it," Leia said easily—or what she hoped was easily. Her parents' diplomatic polish still eluded her sometimes, and she envied the queen and viceroy their perfect, all-concealing masks. However, she knew the exact moment to stop favoring the aristocrat who'd greeted her and turn toward the others. Holding her hand out to a dark-haired girl, she began, "And you are—?"

She went from student to student, memorizing names and faces the way she'd been taught since childhood. Harp Allor of Chandrila, friendly and overprepared—Sssamm Ashsssen of Fillithar, an unusual student in a sport usually engaged in by bipeds—an Ithorian whose name she hadn't caught, would have to ask about that later—

But then she got to someone who stopped her cold.

This student was human, a tall, gangly girl with a narrow face and long nose. Her hair was acid green, which meant that either she was from Iloh or she really liked standing out. While the others mostly wore white gear with silver or orange reflective stripes, this girl wore a rainbow of bright colors that clashed so painfully Leia had to fight the urge to squint. Her goggles were already strapped on, and they were of antique make, with pink lenses that curved out from the frames to an almost ridiculous degree. Although she'd obviously noticed Leia, she didn't introduce herself. She just stood there, staring and smiling.

"Hi," Leia began. "I'm Leia Organa."

"Of Alderaan," the girl said in a curiously even tone, like someone groggy after a bacta treatment. Her thinness and gawkiness reminded Leia of a marsh crane.

"Um, yeah. And you are—"

"Amilyn Holdo of Gatalenta." The reply came in the exact same drawn-out monotone. "Thank your mom for inviting me to the class."

All right, good. She can make normal conversation. Maybe she just needs to . . . warm up first. "Are you looking forward to trying pathfinding?"

"Definitely." Amilyn's loopy grin widened. "I hope it's dangerous! I want to get more comfortable with the nearness and inevitability of death."

". . . okay." Leia froze her smile on her face by force of will while thinking, *There's no way she's handling my climbing ropes.*

(Her father sometimes said she made up her mind too quickly about people. Her mother told her to trust her instincts. Today, she'd follow her mother's advice.)

The final six students had all flown up with the instructor and were now tromping in from the nearby landing pad. Since Leia had already looked over the Apprentice Legislature directory, she recognized a few of them. One in particular stood out to her, a boy who wore what looked like cast-off military gear. He stood a head taller than her, which wasn't the same as being tall. Some observers would've called him odd-looking, with his deep-set eyes and sharply angular features, but others would've called him handsome. Leia wasn't sure which group she'd agree with. He was probably the one it was most important for her to know, so she trudged a few steps through the drift between them to hold out her hand. "You're Kier Domadi, aren't you?"

"Yes, Your Highness." Kier spoke with the deference she nearly always heard from citizens of Alderaan. His voice carried a surprising resonance for someone so young and wiry.

"I'm glad we'll be serving in the Apprentice Legislature together. Sharing the same pod, going over the same material—we'll have to cooperate almost every day." She felt her smile brightening, too much, really, for the occasion.

His expression was hard to read, but his focus on her had intensified. He wasn't greeting his princess any longer; he was evaluating her, the same way she was measuring him. "I look forward to it."

"Luckily it looks like we'll get along." *Did I just say that out loud? Am I* flirting? *Diplomats aren't supposed to flirt.* But she'd figured out that she was in the "handsome" camp.

"Luck didn't have anything to do with my being here." Kier straightened, and the intensity of his gaze became more uncomfortable. "I guess it didn't have anything to do with you being here either."

It felt like being slapped. Did he think she hadn't earned her own spot in the Apprentice Legislature? She'd interned for two years with her father, was as familiar with the Senate's workings as some senators (and more than others), and had passed every mandatory test with top marks. *I work as hard as anyone!* Leia wanted to protest. *Harder than most.*

Then she remembered Wobani, how proud she'd been of herself and her royal authority, so sure she knew what to do and how to do it. Instead she'd made a mistake that affected thousands of lives, maybe permanently. Never before had Leia doubted the wisdom of their hereditary monarchy, but now she thought, *I inherited power before I earned it. I misused that power, and people got hurt.*

Kier's expression clouded. "I didn't mean to—hurt your feelings, or—"

"I'm fine," she said shortly, turning away and pushing her doubts aside as best she could. This was something she'd have to consider, but she'd be damned if she'd let stiff-necked Kier Domadi think he had the power to make her upset.

"All right, everybody, gather around!" called the instructor, a dark, broad-shouldered woman with a wide grin who stood even taller than the Ithorian. "I'm Chief Pangie of the Chandrilan Pathfinding Corps. You'll address me as 'Chief' if you want to stay alive."

Leia observed a few worried glances around her, which clearly meant, *Is she joking?*

"Her Majesty Queen Breha was kind enough to set up this class, so assignment one is here on Alderaan. During the next few months, we'll visit different climates on different worlds. The goal here is for you all to know how to handle yourself anywhere, with nothing but your own two hands and some basic equipment." Chief Pangie paused to nod toward Sssamm from Fillithar. "If you don't have any hands, you're going to learn how to use your coils. Those of you with prehensile tails are in luck, because that's as good as an extra rope, out here."

"I *knew* I ought to have bioengineered a tail," Chassellon muttered.

Apparently tails were in vogue on Coruscant at the moment. Extra, bioengineered body parts never lasted more than a few months, and in Leia's opinion they never quite looked right. Maybe she'd feel differently about a tail once she tried to climb her first cliff.

Chief Pangie continued, "Pathfinding is also about orienting yourself with little equipment or none at all. Even celestial navigation won't help you if you're not on your home planet and you don't know the sky! So you have to notice every detail of your surroundings. Memorize every turn you take. If you don't, you're as good as dead."

Amilyn Holdo beamed. Leia wondered if heirs to the throne ever changed their Challenges of the Body after their Day of Demand.

Clapping her hands, the chief finished, "We're going to go over specific techniques later. Today, I just want to see who here has it in them to go the distance, and who's going to pay close enough attention to landmarks along the way. So get those packs on your backs and let's start moving. Has everyone got a field generator? Show me!"

Leia pointed toward the small box clipped to her belt. The generator would respond to sudden changes in velocity with a small personal force field that would shield the wearer and prevent any falls, rockslides, or collisions from being fatal—in theory, anyway. Everyone was duly equipped with one, even Amilyn Holdo, who'd decorated hers with some kind of glitter. Only after seeing every single anti-impact field generator did Chief Pangie nod and signal for them to get going.

As they began on a path leading into the forest, Leia glanced back at the faraway outline of Appenza Peak. Her courage returned at the sight of the challenge ahead.

It felt like she was taking her first steps up that mountain already.

•◆•

Five hours later, Leia had decided she never cared if she ever climbed a mountain again.

It felt like she had already climbed *eight thousand* mountains and still Chief Pangie wouldn't rest. Even lunch had been eaten on their feet while marching upward.

The slope of this hill wasn't that steep, and other than the thick snow, the terrain wasn't difficult either. For the first couple of hours it had been a pleasant walk. Now the backpack's straps seemed to be carving their way through Leia's shoulders, and her legs shook with exhaustion. As they made their way into a small clearing amid the tall firs, she couldn't help thinking what a great place this would be to take a short break.

Chief Pangie halted in her tracks, put her hands on her hips, and grinned. "Well, would you look at this?" A hoversled sat at the edge of the clearing in standby mode, just waiting for its fortunate owner. Leia wondered if taking the hoversled counted as stealing if she replaced it right away—or she could give the owner a better, newer one in return, the best the royal purse could buy—

As Chief Pangie went to inspect the hoversled, Chassellon leaned against a tree, and the Ithorian took a seat on the nearest boulder. Although Leia was tempted to set down her backpack, she knew putting it back on again afterward would feel so much worse. She took heart when she saw Kier rest one hand on a conifer's trunk; at least he knew by now she wasn't weaker than him. The only students not showing any signs of weariness were Sssamm of Fillithar, and somehow, Amilyn Holdo, whose smile remained as glazed as ever.

"This surely is a beautiful hoversled." Chief Pangie ran her hand along the streamlined steering console. "One gorgeous piece of machinery."

"I've got one nicer than that back on Coruscant," Chassellon sniffed.

This earned him a look from Chief Pangie. "Well, isn't that fun for you? But your fancy-pants hoversled is in a whole other star system where it can't do you a bit of good. Whereas mine is right here where I need it. I know which one I prefer."

With that, she hopped on, hitting the ignition switch to bring the hoversled back to full power. Leia and the other pathfinding students stared as realization sank in. It was Chassellon who said, "You're not—you're leaving us out here?"

"Check out the big-city brain on Coruscant boy!" The chief couldn't have been more delighted. "That's right, kids. I told you I wanted to see who'd pay attention to the landmarks along our way. We're about to find out who here can follow basic instructions."

Harp Allor had turned nearly as white as the snow. "But—but—you told us there would be special techniques we would learn!"

"And you will," Chief Pangie promised. "The thing is, none of those techniques will do you any good if you can't even bother to notice where you're going."

Sssamm hissed in dismay as Chassellon said, "Isn't this dangerous?"

Chief Pangie's good cheer only increased. "If you're

not careful? Yeah." Amilyn held both her hands to the sky as if thanking a sun god and mouthed the word *Yes.* The chief continued, "You're all tagged with trackers. So anybody who hasn't made it back to the chalet by nightfall—that's about four hours away—well, we'll be back up to collect you."

A sigh of relief escaped Leia, and she glanced sideways to see whether Kier had heard her. If so, he didn't seem to notice. Besides, she wasn't alone. Every one of the students had brightened at the prospect of a ride back.

Which was when Chief Pangie added, "Of course, anybody who hasn't got it together enough to make it back in that amount of time gets kicked out of the class. So you'd better hightail it down there, kids. Good luck!"

Cackling with laughter, she sped her hoversled down the mountain, quickly vanishing over a ridge.

Like everyone else in the class, Leia stared after the chief. She'd memorized a few landmarks. Maybe she could manage—

No. Not maybe. There's no way I'm going back to my parents and telling them I failed.

It didn't matter if every other student sat down in the snow and refused to budge. She was going to get down that mountain by sunset.

Somehow.

CHAPTER 06

Leia assumed Chief Pangie had stranded them to create a bonding experience for the whole group. Working together to overcome the odds was supposed to create camaraderie and make them all lasting friends.

If that was the plan, it was failing miserably.

"Could you guys at least try to move faster than a glacier?" snapped Harp Allor when she had to stop, yet again, for their slower classmates to catch up. "We have a lot of ground to cover before sundown, and you guys are dragging your hindquarters."

The Ithorian pointed at his cumbersome snowshoes, which were sturdy but slowed his pace. Sssamm of Fillithar hissed that maybe she could remember not everybody *had* hindquarters and to stop being so biped-centric.

Amilyn, who had clambered atop a stump, peered into the knothole of the nearest tree. "Nope," she said in her singsong voice, "no snow owls here either."

Kier had kept his temper so far, but this comment made him squint at Amilyn up on her perch. "Why are you looking for snow owls?"

"Why wouldn't I look for snow owls?"

Apparently Kier couldn't think of a good answer. After a long, silent moment, he nodded as though to say, *Fair point.*

Chassellon retied the expensive muunyak-wool scarf at his throat, making sure it had a rakish flair. Leia couldn't fathom caring about appearances at a time like this, and by this point they were all overheated from the work of the hike. He was willing to make himself sweat even more rather than wreck his look. 2V would love this guy. "Chief what's-her-name clearly resents us. Thinks she's too good for students instead of soldiers. Can you imagine what trouble she'll be in when this gets reported to Queen Breha? I can't *wait*."

"Can we all try to focus?" Leia held on to her temper, barely. "See that dead tree over there? The one that's split in two at the top?"

Kier nodded. "The one that was struck by lightning. I noticed it on the way up too. We need to turn west around here."

She was chagrined not to have realized the tree had been hit by lightning—but what did it matter? At least somebody else in this class could use his brain and his mouth at the same time. "All right. West we go."

Already Harp Allor had begun hurrying ahead,

bounding through the calf-deep snow. "The path's clearer here! We can make up some time!"

"Harp?" Kier called. "I think I remember—"

Suddenly Harp jerked to one side and toppled over into a drift. Her cry of pain echoed against the rock-strewn slopes.

"—some tricky ice around there," Kier finished.

Leia ran to where Harp lay in the snow, clutching one leg and wincing. "Are you all right?"

Shaking her head, Harp said, "I twisted my ankle."

"Oh, that's just sensational." Chassellon buried his hands in his wildly curly black hair. "Can't you walk it off?"

By now Kier had reached Harp as well, and the two of them tried to get her to her feet. Before Harp could try her weight on it, Leia saw the odd tilt of her boot and squeezed the girl's arm as a warning. "Don't! It's not twisted; it's broken."

Kier added, "It's nothing a few hours in a bacta tank won't fix, but there's no way you can get down the mountain without help."

Thanks for confirming the obvious, Leia thought but didn't say. She was getting better at figuring out exactly what she was mad about, when she was mad. Right now it wasn't Kier Domadi, just the mess they were in.

Tears had welled in Harp's eyes. "I screwed everything up for everybody."

"No, you didn't," Leia said, but Chassellon snorted. She glared at him. "What's *that* supposed to mean?"

He held up his hands in their expensive fambaa-leather gloves, a gesture of mock surrender. "I agree with you, Princess Leia. Allor didn't screw things up for everybody, just for herself. I for one intend to return to the chalet by sunfall with or without her. From the look of things, without."

When Leia got really, really angry, her temples would pulse, and sometimes she felt like the top of her skull would pop off to let out all the steam inside. Her head had already begun to throb. "You'd leave her out here on her own?"

Chassellon shrugged. "Apparently Chief Pangie thinks this stretch of wilderness is perfectly safe from all hazards except clumsiness. Therefore Ms. Allor here should be fine until we send a jumper to fetch her."

"That's unacceptable." Kier's tone remained even, but Leia could tell he was nearly as angry as she was.

"She would be lonely," Amilyn said, still swaying atop her perch on the stump, staring into the knothole as though the long-awaited owls might yet appear.

"Lonely. Oh, well, let's all get thrown out of the class to keep her from being *lonely* for a few hours." Chassellon folded his arms across his chest. "Or we could act like rational sentient beings and start moving."

"Go on ahead," Harp said, her head drooping. "I'll be fine."

"We're not leaving you," Leia insisted. She let go of Harp, trusting Kier to support her, and marched over to Chassellon. "Think about this, will you? If we all stay behind with Harp, Chief Pangie has to keep us in the class. She can't expel everybody."

"You might escape, Your Highness, but the rest of us have to look out for ourselves. Trust me, when someone like that wants to make life worse for the people who have power over her, she'll find a way. I don't intend to give her any extra ammunition." He reshouldered his backpack and put one hand on Leia's shoulder, his expression so genuinely sympathetic that for a moment she thought he'd come around. Instead, he said in a lower voice, "I realize you have to stay. Word can't get around that the princess of Alderaan abandoned someone on the slopes to save her own skin, can it? Appearances matter."

"*Appearances*?" Her temples pulsed again, and her cheeks flushed hot against the biting cold air.

Chassellon took no notice. Instead he called to the others: "All those for the chalet, follow me!"

To Leia's consternation, fully half the class started down the hill after him. Only the Ithorian even paused, inclining his head to say sorry. The others kept going without looking back.

And if I had to get stuck with only half the group, did it have to be this *half?* she thought. Kier stood there silently judging her while Harp sniffled against his shoulder. Sssamm seemed alert and calm but, as a serpentine life-form, couldn't be a whole lot of help carrying Harp, her gear, or anything else. And Amilyn was still looking for the blasted owls.

Every single one of them apparently expected Leia to be their leader. That made sense, given that this was her planet, but it would've helped if she had the slightest idea what to do.

But I do know. I do. Leia took a deep breath. Her father had always said she should take heart when she had others on her side. *Look deeply into them,* he'd say, *help them discover what they're capable of, and you'll always find you have the people you need.*

That was . . . not easy to believe right now. But there was nothing else to do but begin.

"We were turning west," she said. "Let's go."

•◆•

"I'm sorry you're hurting," Amilyn said earnestly to Harp as she took her turn dragging the makeshift travois Kier had put together. Her acid-green hair looked like a chemical burn against the surrounding snow. "But there's a bright side, too. Who would've guessed we'd encounter mortal peril so soon?"

Harp made a face. "I hope this isn't quite 'mortal' peril."

"It will be if we stumble into a crevasse!" Amilyn's glazed smile broadened while Harp looked around nervously.

They were reasonably safe from that danger, given that Sssamm was slithering ahead to scout the terrain; his scales hissed against the snow, in contrast to the crunch of the humanoids' footsteps. Leia wasn't scared any longer; among the five of them, they remembered enough of the way back to be sure they could reach the chalet. Maybe they'd make it before nightfall, maybe not, but the important thing was ensuring Harp remained safe and well.

Still, if I know my mother, she hired the toughest pathfinding instructor in the galaxy, Leia thought. Anyone who thought princesses were "pampered" had never spent time with the royal House of Organa. *Chief Pangie really might kick me out of the class if I don't get back before sundown. If she does that, I've automatically failed my Challenge of the Body. What happens then? Do I have to try again next year?* She'd never researched what happened to heirs apparent who didn't complete the challenges they'd named on the Day of Demand. The possibility of failure had never entered her mind.

"I'm so sorry, everyone," Harp said for about the eightieth time. But this time she kept going. "I've always done whatever it took to be at the top of my class, every single class. Stupid mistakes like this—" She breathed out sharply, like someone trying not to cry. "I guess I'm not used to failing this badly."

Kier kept looking forward, walking at the exact same pace, as he answered her. "Then this is the best class you've ever had. Nobody learns anything new without failing the first few times they try. You have to face that and figure out how to get back up again. That means learning how to fail is the most important lesson of all."

Although Leia said nothing, she felt the words as much as heard them, trying to process what he'd said. Her whole life had been like Harp's, constantly striving to learn more, do more, be more. Nobody had admitted failure was even a possibility, much less that it could actually be *good*.

Under other circumstances, she would've found their surroundings breathtaking in their beauty—the conifer-filled valleys stretching out beneath them, the endless stretches of pristine snow, the way the jagged mountain range cut the lowering sun's light into separate golden rays. Sssamm's iridescent green scales glittered with every bend of his tail, and even Amilyn's multicolored clothes were at least vibrant. Maybe if she could think of failure as a positive outcome, she could even enjoy part of this.

Someday, perhaps. As a memory. Today? She just had to keep marching.

Besides, failure wasn't always personal. When Leia had failed on Wobani, others suffered the consequences.

Kier fell into step beside her. "The others probably aren't that far ahead of us," he said. "We might make it by sundown."

"Maybe." Leia doubted they would, but it wasn't impossible. "Thanks for working on the travois."

He shrugged. "My historical anthropology teacher always insisted on making us try our hand at primitive skills, so we'd see just how much intelligence they really take. If you ever need somebody to knap a flint knife for you, let me know."

"Let's hope it won't come to that. Still, I just wanted to say, I appreciate it. You didn't have to stay and help."

Kier glanced sideways at her. "But you did."

"What?"

"Have to stay."

"What, because of appearances?" And here she'd been thinking they were at least jerk-free after Chassellon left. "That doesn't have anything to do with it. I'd always stay with someone who needed help."

"That's not what I—" Kier fell silent. She realized he was hunting for words, and then recognized something in the way he couldn't meet her eyes. This guy wasn't standoffish; he was *shy*. Finally he said, "I'm sorry. Sometimes I'm not good at saying what I really mean."

Now calmer, and curious, Leia took a deep breath. The air smelled of evergreens. "All right, try again."

Kier kept going for several paces, long enough that she'd started to think he'd given up, before he said, "I didn't mean you were staying because of appearances. I meant, your royal role means you have to stay."

She wasn't seeing the difference, but decided to hear him out. "You mean, people hold a princess to a higher standard."

"No. I mean, you hold yourself to a higher standard." Kier glanced at her. Their breaths were small puffs of white in the bitingly cold air. "We hear a lot about how the House of Organa dedicates everything to the good of the people—"

"We *do*," Leia insisted.

Holding up one hand, Kier continued, "Yeah. You really do. It's not just propaganda on Alderaan, the way it would be on almost any other planet in the galaxy. The queen, the viceroy—and you too, it seems like." Mollified, Leia nodded, and he took this as a cue to keep going. "So you don't really have a choice to stay or go. Just like you don't have a choice whether to be in the Apprentice Legislature or not."

"You think I got stuck with the Apprentice Legislature?" Well, it was better than his thinking she didn't deserve to be there. Now if only *she* felt she still deserved it, after Wobani. More forcefully—to convince them both—she added, "Trust me, I can't wait to get back to the Senate."

Kier's sidelong look felt like an appraisal. "Really? Or do you just think you should?"

"I understand my own motivations perfectly well, thank you very much." Leia meant for her words to sound angry. Meant to *be* angry. But really she wanted him to be quiet so she could mull over what he'd said. The idea of being able to choose her own future instead of inheriting the throne—it was so alien to her that she'd never consciously considered it, not even once. Only now did she realize that was actually very strange.

As if she'd sensed Leia thinking the word *strange*, Amilyn piped up, "Look at this!"

They had made it through another thick patch of woods into a wide clear space with stretches of slope completely free from trees; whiteness stretched out below them in nearly every direction. But those slopes were too steep to easily walk down, especially when one of them would have to pull the travois.

At least the path was easy to spot. "That's the way we

came up," Leia said, pointing toward a rockier line that traced its way downhill, maybe two hundred meters west. Sssamm hissed that he could just make out Chassellon's group farther down that path; with his sharp Fillithar vision, that meant the others could have been nearly two thousand meters ahead.

"When I was a little girl, I used to love tobogganing," Amilyn said.

Leia managed not to snap. "That's nice for you. Once we get back to the path, it's going to be too uneven for the travois. Kier—" She felt awkward about asking him this, which made no sense, so she kept on. "Do you think you can carry Harp?" He nodded, though he looked more wary than certain.

"What I loved best about the toboggan is how fast we could go." Shrugging off the straps of the travois, Amilyn began digging around in her pack.

When Sssamm hissed that he thought he might be able to balance Harp in one of his coils, Leia was going to object because the danger of them rolling out of control was too great. But the vision of them hurtling downhill made her realize what Amilyn had been saying—just as Amilyn pulled something bright yellow from her pack. She flung it down, at which point it popped obediently into its full shape, an emergency tent.

As Amilyn stepped on the corner of the tent, she bent

down to tether two of the flexible poles together. "See, if we can flatten it out—"

"—we'd have a toboggan big enough to carry all of us," Leia finished. "Why didn't you just say so from the start?"

Amilyn frowned. "I did. Didn't I?"

"It's too dangerous." Kier knelt by Amilyn's side, shaking his head. "We'd pick up speed quickly, and with that much weight on board, it would be hard to steer. If we crash, we could all wind up with broken ankles. The field generators protect us only so much."

That was when Sssamm slithered closer, hissing excitedly. He curled onto the tent-toboggan, expanded his coils to hold out the edges, and stuck his tail into the last unfastened flap. Then he lifted it to form a perfect sail, which he turned that way and this to prove how easy steering would be. Kier began to smile, and Amilyn clapped her hands.

For the first time, Harp looked hopeful instead of depressed. "Can we try it?"

They didn't need Leia's permission. Really she should've said so. Instead she began to laugh. "Let's do this."

The entire descent after that was a rapid blur of snowspray and distant trees. Sometimes they'd slalom from side to side so fast Leia thought they'd topple over, but Sssamm always managed to right their course in time.

Harp yelped a time or two when they hit a ridge—or when they'd briefly go airborne before touching down—but most of the time she was laughing, just like Leia.

It occurred to her that she hadn't had this much fun in a long time. And she hadn't had this much fun with people her own age since . . .

Since ever? I think ever.

•◆•

As the sun set that day, Chassellon Stevis and his group trudged up the steps of the chalet, each one of them clearly exhausted and miserable. That made it so much sweeter to watch them come into the great room, look at the enormous fireplace—and see Leia and her friends lounging by the hearth with oversized mugs of mocoa.

"Where have you guys been?" Harp called. She had an emergency bacta bag on her foot and foamy cream on the tip of her nose from her cup of mocoa. "We've been waiting for *ages*."

Chassellon sputtered, "You couldn't have—how could you—"

"They did it by showing some ingenuity, Stevis," said Chief Pangie, who had taken the second-comfiest chair by the fire, leaving the best for Harp. "And by showing some compassion, a quality *your* group could use a little more of."

"You're having a good laugh, are you?" Chassellon

held his chin high, looking as impressive as he could given his sodden clothes and damp hair—which wasn't very. "We'll see who's laughing when Queen Breha hears about you abandoning us!"

Leia shrugged. "I've been talking with the chief. Turns out this part of the challenge was my mother's idea in the first place."

"But—a queen—she would never—"

"Push us hard?" Leia could've laughed. "You've obviously never met my mom."

Chassellon deflated so pathetically that she almost felt sorry for him. From the corner of her eye she observed Kier lifting his chin as if in pride, maybe at the toughness of his monarch. He might give Leia a hard time occasionally, but she could tell a loyal Alderaanian when she saw one.

Chief Pangie lifted her mug toward the second group as if in a toast. "Since you failed to show any teamwork out there, I'm going to have to assign some extra duty for the group as a whole, next time. Say—carrying the others' packs for them? That sounds about right."

Thinking about the way Chassellon's face looked then amused Leia the rest of the evening, and the entire trip back to Aldera. As she walked back into the palace, worn-out and rumpled but exhilarated, she tried to find the right words to describe it. *Like one of those wilting vines from*

Harloff Minor. No, that wasn't it. *Like TooVee that time when I was a toddler and ran straight from my bath into the formal dining hall.* That last memory was one Leia had been told so often she wasn't sure if she remembered the event itself or the retellings, but it was easy enough to imagine 2V's horror at her tiny, wet, naked charge barreling into a diplomatic dinner.

"Good evening, Princess," said the guard standing duty in front of Bail Organa's stateroom, a kind of signal flag as to her father's location. The guard didn't immediately step aside to give her the door, but probably he assumed she'd want to wash up before presenting herself to her parents. Not this time, though. She couldn't wait to tell them everything. They'd be proud of her, maybe proud enough to erase the stain of her mistakes.

"Good evening." Leia's face almost hurt from grinning. "I'm here to see my parents. They're in, aren't they?"

"I'm sorry, Your Highness." The guard tried to say this gently, which only made it worse. "Your parents are in conference about their next banquet and gave strict instructions that they weren't to be disturbed by anyone."

It was a long moment before Leia decided to risk the question. "Not even me?"

"No, Your Highness. I'm sure they'll be eager to see you when they're finished."

When they're done planning their next dinner party.

"All right. Thank you." Her voice sounded calm, didn't it? Like a princess, and not a hurt little girl?

Maybe not. The guard looked so sad for her, almost pitying, and she couldn't even hate him for it.

•◆•

Days later, Leia remained moody. Even her long-awaited return to Coruscant for her first session of the Apprentice Legislature couldn't fully banish her gloom.

The adventure with her pathfinding class had brightened only one day. Afterward, she was left with her parents' continued absence, and her lingering remorse for what had happened on Wobani. She'd devoted herself to caring for the Wobani refugees in the immediate aftermath of their arrival on Alderaan; it was the only way she knew to make up for her errors in judgment there. But the refugees didn't know she'd messed up negotiations that might've saved the rest of their people, too—which meant their gratitude hurt more than it helped.

"We'll be moving along soon," one woman had confided as Leia helped them set up accounts for their stipend from the queen. "We've cousins on Itapi Prime—distant cousins, but we've done a little business together lately. I think we'll have a place there."

"I'm staying right here!" declared an old man nearby. "Alderaan's the most beautiful planet in the galaxy, if you ask me. I think of it as home already."

They were so *happy*. So satisfied with how things had turned out for them. Leia knew she ought to take pleasure in that instead of constantly reminding herself how much better their situation would've been, for them and for everyone on Wobani, if she had only . . .

Only what? Walked off and left them there to suffer? Leia could never have done that, not without knowing a compelling reason to do so. Her parents hadn't told her that reason because she still didn't have access to all classified information.

Well, then, that meant she had to be brilliant in the Apprentice Legislature. Here, at least, she knew what she was doing. It would be her first step toward real political power, and with power came knowledge.

On her initial visit to Coruscant two years prior, to serve as one of her father's interns, they had flown in together on the royal yacht, *Polestar*. Leia remembered her father pointing out various landmarks, legendary places becoming real to her at last. The bustle and brilliance of Coruscant overwhelmed nearly everyone who saw it for the first time, even girls who had grown up in palaces, and Bail Organa had laughed to see her wide eyes.

This time, he'd traveled here two days ahead of her, for yet more important business she apparently didn't get to hear about.

Leia took in the scene alone as the *Polestar* swooped

lower, taking its place among the intricate ribbons of traffic that covered the planet. In her opinion, Coruscant looked its best at night, when it sparkled with trillions of blazing lights, just like a galactic core. But it was daytime now, so she was buffeted by the frenetic energy of countless small craft, the bustle of individual traffic through transparent aerial passageways between blocks, and the ominous hulks of the tall buildings around them.

Only a place like this could make the Imperial Senate seem calm, she thought.

Since Leia was familiar with the Senatorial complex already and had her own place to stay in her father's apartments, she hadn't bothered to arrive early for the Apprentice Legislature opening. However, she hadn't meant to cut it as close as she did, hurrying through the winding corridors to find her pod in the chambers as the first fanfare played. As she slipped inside, Kier Domadi glanced over his shoulder. His simple gray clothes stood in stark contrast to the formal finery worn by most of those around them, and to her own high-collared violet dress.

He kept his voice low as he said, "I wondered if you weren't coming."

"Why wouldn't I be coming?" she whispered back. Speaking to him in such hushed tones meant leaning close to him, close enough to feel the warmth of his breath.

"Why wouldn't you be early?"

Again Leia felt stung. Kier had earned his place here and valued it more than she did. The Senate might be familiar to her, but for him, it was new. For both of them, it was important. "You're right. I should've been early."

"That's not what I—" he sighed. "I meant, you seem like the type to be early, most of the time."

She considered this. "I am, actually."

"We'll see." But he smiled as he said it.

Applause began as the guest speaker took the dais. It was a man Leia had never met before but one she had heard a great deal about . . . none of it good.

"Welcome to the Apprentice Legislature," said Grand Moff Wilhuff Tarkin. He stood thin, pale, and sharp, like a needle carved from bone. "Every one of you will now begin the process of representing your planet to the Senate, and indeed, before the Emperor himself. We all live to serve this great Empire, to increase its strength and work for its preservation. This is where your service begins."

To Leia that sounded less like service, more like servility, and that wasn't what the legislature was about. The Imperial Senate was one of the few checks on Palpatine's power, not that Tarkin would admit it.

"Some may say that you are only young people—still children, practically, and that you therefore have nothing to offer our Empire. Indeed, there were those in the Imperial Starfleet who were surprised to hear that

I volunteered to speak at your assembly today. Those people are far too shortsighted." Tarkin's hawklike gaze searched through the various pods; Leia wouldn't be surprised if he'd memorized all their faces by the end of his speech—if not before he even arrived. "When I was still a student, then-Senator Palpatine took an interest in me. He provided invaluable guidance, which shaped my path forward. His example taught me to look for the best when they are young, because the earlier we begin, the more influence our lessons will have. So know that you aren't merely practicing the form of government, deciding a few minor issues here and there. You're also proving what kinds of Imperial leaders you could someday be. Show us your potential, and we will show you the way."

Everyone applauded as Tarkin came down from the dais. Leia clapped along with the rest, but Kier did not. She pretended not to notice; it was safer for him that way.

•◆•

The reception afterward was relatively informal as such things went: food and drink set out on one of the high ledges overlooking a broad swath of the city. Sunset had painted the horizon rosy pink, and shafts of sunlight streamed between the craggy dark silhouettes of skyscrapers. A few Rodian musicians played a jaunty tune as everyone milled around and mingled. Of course the point was to meet people you hadn't talked to before, but still, the members of Leia's pathfinding class found each other.

Chassellon Stevis appeared to hold no grudges; he wore his hair in braids, a stylish silk suit, and a broad smile as he greeted her. "Good to be back in civilization, don't you think?"

"I like this better than being stuck halfway up a mountain, if that's what you mean," Leia said, smiling back. If Chassellon wasn't going to sulk, then she wouldn't hold his attitude during the first challenge against him . . . but she wouldn't forget it, either.

Harp Allor looked flushed and happy. "Isn't this exciting? Senator Lenz says he'll even introduce me to Grand Moff Tarkin personally, later on."

"Your senator came?" Leia was caught off guard. Her father hadn't mentioned the possibility.

"He said he wanted me to get off to a good start." Harp glanced around, then pointed to Winmey Lenz, senior senator of Chandrila. A lean, dark-skinned man with a nearly trimmed beard, he was familiar to Leia from the receptions that preceded her mother's dinner parties. He spoke with animation to a military official, one of the few in attendance. Lenz caught Harp's gesture and waved at her briefly before resuming his conversation. Now that Leia looked around, she realized not all the adults in attendance were staffers; there were a few other senators mingling in the crowd.

My father could've been here with me the whole time. He just didn't think it was important.

Kier interjected, "Senator Organa got our princess off to a good start years ago, I guess."

He was trying to make her feel better, which meant he'd realized she felt bad. His knowing about her embarrassment just made it worse. "He could've come here for *you*," she pointed out.

"I'm sure your father knows I'm in good hands," Kier said.

Interesting turn of phrase, Leia thought, but she'd consider that later.

"We meet again." Amilyn Holdo wafted along, the same slightly glazed expression on her face. Her hair had been dyed pale blue with orange tips, and she wore a flamboyant caftan in a dizzyingly bright pattern, trimmed with glittery tassels. Rather than stopping to chat, she headed straight for the snacks; at least she knew her priorities.

Leia leaned close to Kier and murmured, "I thought they valued simplicity on Gatalenta. Dressed plainly, except for those scarlet cloaks."

"I thought so too. Apparently Holdo goes her own way." Kier said it gently, which was a good reminder that it shouldn't matter to Leia what this girl wore, or what colors she dyed parts of herself, or that she always spoke in the same airy monotone. A member of an alien species she wasn't familiar with was currently hovering in midair near the punch bowl, its many striped tentacles gesturing in an elaborate and fluid sign language; if you took a galactic perspective, it was hard to call anything truly "weird."

Maybe to cover the awkward pause, Harp said, "So, how much do you think we'll get to do in the Apprentice Legislature? I know we have a few real tasks put before us, but how much do you think the Empire will listen to our recommendations?"

"Probably about as much as they listen to the Imperial Senate," Kier answered. "In other words, hardly at all."

"Excuse me?" Leia stepped back. "We work hard in the Senate. My father puts in ten-hour days, sometimes—"

"And so does Senator Lenz!" Harp protested.

Kier held up his hands. "Let's just say, I have a lot more faith in the viceroy's leadership on Alderaan than I do any leadership here on Coruscant."

"Don't go sounding like a *radical,*" Chassellon said, absently picking a bit of fluff off his jacket. "It's so gauche."

They needed a conversational segue, fast. Leia nodded toward Tarkin, who held court at the center point of the balcony. The setting sun silhouetted his stark profile.

Again she thought of hawks, and talons. "I suppose we have to work our way around to our guest speaker. Might as well get that over with."

"Seems like a bore, if you ask me." Chassellon shrugged with the indifference only wealth could provide. "I propose we ditch this and find ourselves some real fun. They know me at some clubs on the lower levels."

Since Chassellon was no older than Leia herself, she doubted this. But she said only, "No, I need to introduce myself to the Grand Moff. My father would expect me to." *Not that he's likely ever to hear about it one way or the other.*

Kier shook his head. "I doubt the Grand Moff cares much about meeting me, and the feeling's mutual. Besides, I need to get settled into my dormitory room."

Leia hadn't thought much about the fact that the other apprentices would be living in a dormitory. She'd stay in her usual room in her father's apartments. While the Organa family lived fairly simply on Coruscant—at least, for someone of his station—she felt sure her quarters were luxurious compared to the dorms. It was one more thing that set her apart from the others—apart from nearly anyone.

"I want to keep soaking up the atmosphere here," Amilyn said as she drifted over to them again. That came across as reasonable until she added, "If you don't let the gases in a new planet's air sink into your skin organically, it can cause disturbances in your dreams."

Chassellon rolled his eyes. Leia took that as a signal to head to the receiving line and get it over with.

So many of the apprentice legislators were nervous to meet a grand moff. She observed that feeling without sharing it in the slightest; she had been no more than six the first time she met a king. While the others trembled, stammered, and shifted awkwardly from foot to foot or tentacle to tentacle, Leia stood straight, glad she'd braided her hair in a coil atop her head to provide the illusion of extra height, and waited her turn. When at last she was face to face with Grand Moff Tarkin, she took his hand with assurance. "Princess Leia Organa of Alderaan."

"Your Highness," Tarkin said. His hand tightened around hers—only slightly more than would be customary, but enough that she felt he was holding her there. That lasted for only an instant, however, as did his brittle smile. "I look forward to discovering whether you'll be the same kind of senator as your father."

"I hope to be," Leia said. "I'll be visiting Eriadu for the first time soon, as part of a pathfinding class. They don't tell us which mountain ranges we might have to find our way through, but I thought you might have an idea." Diplomacy often meant flattering people. One way of flattering them was referencing their homeworlds; another was asking their opinion on a subject in which they would be well informed. She was proud of folding both into one question.

"The Rivoche Ranges," Tarkin said without hesitation. His eyes remained fixed on hers with an unnerving directness. "You've done your homework."

"I try to, sir."

"A good habit to cultivate." He paused, then added, "Unlike, for instance, looking for loopholes in Imperial regulations."

Outwardly, Leia didn't flinch. Inwardly, shock was followed by shame. Had word of her rescue on Wobani spread that far, that fast?

Probably it wasn't Wobani he was most interested in, though. More likely it bothered him that she'd witnessed what happened to Calderos Station. She'd been waiting for word of the attack to hit the HoloNet, eager to learn the different theories about who might be responsible. Instead, there had been total silence. That meant a cover-up.

That meant she was one of the few people who knew a secret the Empire very much wanted to keep. Leia understood enough to realize that was a risky position to be in.

Tarkin added, "You have a talent for finding weaknesses, Your Highness. And for exploiting them. That talent can work for you or against you. You'll have to decide which."

He moved on to the next young legislator, and Leia stood alone in the crowd, silent amid the noise, unsure of what surrounded her.

CHAPTER 07

Leia stayed up that night in hopes of seeing her father, but as the hours went on and she became more tired, she finally decided that he must've returned to Alderaan for a brief time. Or maybe he'd needed to go offworld on a fact-finding mission on short notice. Either possibility was plausible; she'd hopped back and forth between various worlds with him often enough. Since he knew she was now busy with the Apprentice Legislature, it made sense that he wouldn't have asked her to go along. Determinedly she convinced herself not to be upset about it, to go to bed and start fresh the next day.

When she emerged from her room the next morning, however, she found her father seated at the table, absently eating a slice of fruit loaf while his caf steamed in a nearby mug.

Bail Organa startled when he saw her. "Leia? You're here on Coruscant already?"

"Of course. The Apprentice Legislature came into session."

His gaze turned inward. "I thought that was . . ." Then he grimaced. "Yesterday."

"Yeah." But she felt a little better already. It wasn't okay for her father to have missed everything, but at least he felt bad about it.

"I can't claim I'm sorry to have missed the speeches, but I'm sorry I wasn't there with you." He gestured to the nearest chair as he began cutting her a few slices of fruit bread. She grabbed her own cup of caf before sitting beside him. Her father raised an eyebrow. "They say caf stunts your growth."

"My growth is stunted already. If I'm stuck being short, I might as well have the caf."

Bail laughed out loud, and Leia had to smile.

Many senators dressed in ornate, luxurious robes trimmed with fur, or plated their hides with precious metals. Bail Organa wore simpler clothes with nothing finer than an everyday cape. With his height, broad shoulders, and striking dark eyes, he didn't need shallow grandeur to command attention or respect. Until recently, Leia had thought her father didn't even age the way other humans did. However, in the past few months, time and stress had begun to weave gray into the hair at his temples, to etch new lines on his forehead and around his eyes.

"Now, tell me about the other apprentices," Bail said.

"We don't have much time, but there must be a few who stand out."

"Kier Domadi—"

"The other representative from Alderaan? His mother's a professor who teaches at Archipelago University. What about him?"

Leia realized she wasn't sure what she wanted to say, even though Kier was the person she'd thought of first. "I thought he was standoffish at first, but that's not it. He's shy. Smart, interesting." It occurred to her that she was spending too much time on just one apprentice legislator. Swiftly she added, "Then there's Chassellon Stevis, from Coruscant, who's totally full of himself."

"Shocking," Bail deadpanned. The two of them shared the same opinion of most natives of Coruscant.

Warming to her subject, Leia said, "Then there's this girl from Gatalenta named Amilyn Holdo who is . . . let's say, a little odd."

Her father shook his head in affectionate disbelief. "I trust your judgment, Leia, but don't be too quick to write people off. Sometimes they can surprise you." With that he rose to his feet and downed the last of his caf.

Unable to hide her disappointment, she said, "You're leaving already?"

"I have a meeting with Mon Mothma first thing this morning." Bail said it in the tone of voice that meant his mind had moved ahead; already he was more there than here. "Then the session, and afterwards I'm taking the *Tantive IV* on a fact-finding mission for a week, perhaps two."

"That's a long time." Leia had stayed in their Coruscant apartments on her own before, but rarely longer than a night or two, and even then 2V had been with her.

"You'll be just fine here." Her father's hand rested on her shoulder. "No wild parties while I'm gone."

That made her laugh, but his attention had already drifted elsewhere. He kissed her forehead absentmindedly before walking out without looking back.

Their apartments on Coruscant—a penthouse suite independent from the rest of its building, known as Cantham House—would be considered relatively modest by either senatorial or royal standards: a few bedrooms, a great room, and a crescent-shaped balcony that looked out on a wide swath of the cityscape. To Leia, who had been raised in a palace, the apartments had always seemed small.

They felt too big when she was alone.

•◆•

The first real session of the Apprentice Legislature began with introductions. Leia had never been more grateful that only forty worlds sent representatives these days.

If she'd been involved a generation ago, she wasn't sure she could've endured thousands of people naming their homeworlds and a hobby. She paid careful attention the entire time—you never knew what detail might offer common ground or an interesting insight—but concentrating on this kind of minutiae for so long made her head hurt.

Chassellon Stevis talked about restoring antique landspeeders to luxury standards. "Takes a while to hunt down the right parts, I can tell you, but the end result is worth it." *Note: More patient and methodical than I would've guessed.*

Amilyn Holdo had woven feathers into her braided blue hair, which gave her the look of a fledgling chick. "I like comparing different planets' traditional astrological charts to see if they agree on the influences exercised by various stars. The parallels are uncanny!" No need for an extra note there—Leia had understood this girl from day one.

When they reached the Alderaan pod, she gestured for Kier to go first. His interest surprised her more than anyone else's had. "I plan to be a historian, specializing in the Clone Wars era, so I take part in Clone War reenactments whenever I can. I usually play a clone SCUBA trooper, whenever aquatic battles come up."

She'd known from his dossier that he studied history, but she'd imagined him as someone who spent all of his spare time quietly bent over books. Apparently not. *Note: Comes across as shy and silent, but he has a fighting spirit.*

The lights fell on her as the amplifier droids hovered close. Leia stood, glad for her experience in public speaking. Some of the others had stammered or hesitated, but she addressed the chamber smoothly. "I'm Leia Organa, princess of the ruling house of Alderaan, heir to the crown, and now a member of the Apprentice Legislature. Since I expect to be involved with the Imperial Senate throughout my life, I'm glad to be able to make a start here, and I'm looking forward to getting to know you all." There. She'd mentioned the royal status without overemphasizing it, and hopefully nobody would dwell on it. . . .

Kier whispered, "Say something personal." When Leia glanced at him, he raised his eyebrows. "Everyone else did."

He was right. They were supposed to mention a hobby or personal interest of some kind, and she needed to follow the format. She collected herself to say . . . what?

I've studied Alderaan's history going back to the first human settlement. That was part of her royal education. *I've been an intern in my father's senatorial office for two years.* That wasn't personal. *I'm in a pathfinding class with a few other apprentice legislators.* But that, too, was her Challenge of the Body, an official step on her way to being monarch. She'd never before realized that she didn't really have a lot of personal interests; her duty and her future consumed nearly every moment, so completely that she hadn't even been able to see it.

"I like storms," she said. "Thunderstorms, I mean. I like to watch them." With that she sat down, hands clasped in her lap. As the members from Glee Anselm began their introductions, she caught Kier watching her. No doubt he was wondering how a princess—no, how *anyone* could be so devoid of a personal life. "Mine was the dumbest one," she murmured.

"It's not dumb. It's honest. Everybody else puffed themselves up, me included. You spoke from the heart. That takes courage."

Either Kier Domadi was a deeply nice guy beneath all the awkwardness, or he had a big future in diplomacy. Leia gave him a broad smile before turning her attention to the other students, learning what she could about them from the few clues they gave.

What would someone be able to tell about her, from the fact that she liked thunderstorms?

She became more comfortable when they finally moved on to their first real order of business. The lights went down as a holographic image coalesced in the center of the senatorial chamber: four different star systems, from disparate parts of the galaxy. An automated voice spoke: "The issue: the Emperor will soon build a new academy of aeronautical engineering and design, but has not yet chosen a host planet. The Apprentice Legislature shall weigh the worlds according to the criteria provided in your session notes, and make your recommendation for the site of the new school."

This was the kind of work the Apprentice Legislature undertook—no security issues, relatively low importance, but with real-world consequences. Leia cheered up at the prospect of flexing her senatorial muscles, because she'd learned a thing or two while working for her father.

One of the things she'd learned: even the simplest debate could turn into a total disaster.

"You can't be serious!" demanded one of the apprentices from Malastare. "Iloh is the only choice!"

"How can you say that?" Harp's cheeks flushed from the emotion of the debate. "Iloh is a waterworld. There's hardly even space for a landing field! Harloff Minor is more suitable in every way."

"Except for the high levels of air traffic," Kier pointed out. He was one of the few still speaking in a normal tone of voice. "At least with Iloh, the skies are free for test flights and experimental designs, including the ones that could be unstable."

Chassellon gestured toward the hovering hologram planet nearest him. "Not one person is going to think of Lonera?"

“It’s practically in the Expansion Region,” scoffed someone in the Arkanis pod.

Sssamm hissed that this would be a problem if nobody had ever figured out how to fly past lightspeed. Since they had, what was the issue?

More squabbling broke out, until the moderator droid began to blink yellow. The warning quieted people, but made them sullen too. *Everybody wants to win the first debate,* she thought. *The point of a negotiation is to make each party feel as though they’ve won.*

“If I might,” she began, speaking for the first time since very early on. “We’re spending almost all of our time talking about three of the four worlds. Nobody’s argued on behalf of Arreyel.”

After a few seconds of silence, Chassellon said, “For good reason.” A few murmured assent.

Arreyel was a small Inner Rim world, a former Separatist planet that had never recovered from choosing the wrong side in those disastrous wars. It had fallen into disfavor with the Emperor early in his reign for reasons that were now murky, almost forgotten, but the stain lingered. Arreyel’s economy was depressed, and with no unique materials or talents to offer, the planet had little chance of improving its fortunes soon—

—unless something important were to be built there. For instance, a major new Imperial academy.

"I admit, Arreyel isn't the first planet that comes to mind." Leia gestured toward the hologram in a way that expanded Arreyel's system to fill more of the space. The blue-and-white planet rotated before her. "But it was included in this group of four. That means the Emperor's open to doing something there again. The world has a chance to start over."

"That's not really the question," Kier said. Somehow he managed to speak in a tone of voice that made it clear he wasn't arguing with her, only expanding the discussion. "We're supposed to choose the planet best for the school, not the world that would benefit the most."

Leia held out her arms, encompassing the entire apprentice chamber. "After the past two hours, I think we all know—none of these worlds is clearly better than the rest. They all have pros and cons, but they're evenly matched. Any of these planets would make a good home for the academy. So that frees us to consider which one would benefit the most. That's clearly Arreyel."

People remained quiet for a few moments, until Chassellon shrugged and said, "Might as well spread the wealth."

Not everyone agreed—but they got the votes needed to push it through. With Arreyel chosen, everyone applauded, and Leia couldn't help feeling proud. She'd found a way to do a good deed from the very heart of

Palpatine's government; that was how you could sometimes make the system work.

"Good job," Kier said.

Like she needed this guy to tell her how to operate in the Senate. "I know."

He gave her a sidelong look then, and she wasn't sure whether he was amused or offended. She hoped she was equally mysterious to him.

But mostly she was thinking about telling her parents of her accomplishment . . . whenever she next got to speak with them.

•◆•

On her first night, Leia worked late. Her "office" was a tiny cubby just off the Apprentice Legislature rotunda, hardly bigger than a closet; she knew most apprentices used the rooms more as lockers than as places to do work. But Leia had a place for her things here on Coruscant, and she liked work. So she'd wedged in a tiny chair and desk and now sat scrolling through various screens of data.

She wanted to get a head start on things, and besides—she wasn't in a hurry to return to the emptiness of Cantham House.

Having completed the dossier on Arreyel, she scanned through a few other documents to see what was worth considering. A word caught her attention and made her scroll back; once she'd read it, she sat up straight.

Calderos Station.

Still, she'd heard nothing about the attack. The Empire clearly wanted to hush it up. So how was this in her files?

A quick review turned up the answer: Calderos Station was referenced in an older file, one that hadn't been updated to reflect the events of the past few weeks . . . or deleted to erase those events, either. The data before her summed up shipping in that area, as part of the background for a tariff debate they'd take up later in the session.

But whoever had attacked that station must have arrived disguised as any old cargo convoy—

Leia began searching through the data for the most common vectors of space traffic through Calderos Station in its final months. Most of the worlds were larger ones like Bilbringi and Arkanis—no surprise there—and a few shipments still went to Wobani, however infrequently.

But a couple of unlikely planets kept coming up over and over. First there was Crait, which she'd never heard of; when she pulled it up from memory banks, she saw why. It was a salt-covered rock in the middle of nowhere. How did that planet have *any* trade, much less enough to have repeatedly gone to Wobani? And Itapi Prime was a world very near Coruscant, prosperous in its own right and wholly loyal to the Emperor. What it *wasn't* was a major exporter of goods to distant planets like this one.

Didn't I hear someone mention Itapi Prime recently? Leia frowned. She'd figure out when and where later.

For now she only knew that the traffic patterns through Calderos Station in the past few months had been abnormal—not so much that they'd draw immediate attention, but noticeable after the fact. Was it possible that those patterns were linked to the attack?

If so, these were traces of people who were rising up against the Empire, but in the most terrifying way possible.

Leia knew she should bring this to her father. Or maybe even to her mother. Or she could bury the files deep in databanks, hiding them so well nobody would ever know she'd reviewed them.

Instead she pulled up star charts that revealed travel lanes to Itapi Prime, and to Crait.

CHAPTER 08

Alderaan never seemed so beautiful to Leia as when she had returned from Coruscant. After that world's metropolitan crush, she always welcomed the feeling of freedom that swept over her when she saw her world's snowcapped mountains, shimmering glacier lakes, and broad blue sky.

Usually she celebrated her homecoming by taking a long walk outdoors, or even going for a dip in one of the lakes. This time, much more important tasks demanded her attention.

First Leia found one of the Wobani families she'd spoken to several days prior; she caught them on the eve of their departure, already preparing for their trip to Itapi Prime. "Why, yes, Your Highness," said the father of the house. "My cousins have done a fair bit of trade through Calderos Station. I haven't heard of that planet you mentioned—"

"Crait," Leia repeated, hoping it would stir a memory.

He shook his head. "No, I don't know that one at all. But Wobani and Itapi Prime, yes, very active through that station."

"I don't suppose you know exactly what trade they were active in?" She raised an eyebrow.

"Not at all, though I suppose I'll find out soon. Going into the family business." He smiled broadly; if he was lying to her, he was doing a good job of it.

As she'd anticipated, Breha was too wrapped up in plans for the next big party to welcome her daughter back home. The knowledge stung, but less than it usually did. Nothing comforted Leia as much as having work to do, or a puzzle to solve.

That night in the library, sitting beneath one of the star-globes, she reviewed the Calderos Station findings she'd been able to salvage. And *salvage* was the right word. When she'd gone into the senatorial databanks in search of more recent data, she found everything had been deleted, going back months before the attack on Calderos. Leia was used to information suddenly "disappearing"; Palpatine's government was blatant in its erasure of history. This time, however, she thought the Empire might not be the ones to blame.

If some people are actually organizing to take action against the Empire, she reasoned, *they'll cover their tracks as well as they can. If those people were using Calderos as a vector for trading ships and armaments, they'd try to erase any data that could lead back to them—and they might even choose the base as a target. Cripple Imperial traffic in the area and conceal themselves, all at the same time: it's a smart move.*

Leia caught herself. She hated the Empire, of course, but that didn't mean she should just pick up a blaster and start shooting at the first thing that made her mad. Her father had always stressed the importance of their work in the Senate, the need to fight for change through the law. Could she condone these people resorting to violence? Casualties at Calderos Station had been limited to a few injuries, but that kind of large-scale action would ultimately lead to loss of life.

How many people die because of Palpatine's rule every year? Is it deadlier to fight against that kind of tyranny or to let it flourish? When is it time to give up on peace and take up arms?

She didn't have answers to those questions. Probably she wouldn't even if she had a degree in philosophy. Leia knew only one thing for certain: she wanted to know more.

•◆•

There could be no question of taking the *Tantive IV* on a secret mission. Instead, Leia commandeered the *Polestar* and asked for a crew of only one.

"Crait?" Ress Batten frowned at the star charts. "I've never even heard of that system."

"With good reason," Leia said. She wore a pale coverall and had already stowed hiking gear on board the yacht. Finding activity on a planet as desolate as Crait might take a while. "There's nothing there—or there shouldn't be. I'm on a fact-finding mission for the Apprentice Legislature." Since she was an apprentice, and the one in search of facts, she figured that didn't count as a lie.

Batten wasn't convinced. "I didn't know you guys had fact-finding missions."

Okay, add a little more detail. "I'm tracking a couple of shipments that headed out that way."

"Who's shipping anything out to the back of beyond?" Batten folded her arms, warier than before.

"That's what we're going to discover." Leia smiled with as much confidence as she could muster.

This won her a raised eyebrow. "These people are going to try to shoot us, aren't they?"

"No!" Leia protested, then caught herself. "I mean, I doubt it. We'll let them know we're friends."

"What if they shoot us before we get to make friends?" Batten shrugged in answer to her own question and began inputting their course. "Guess we'll have to send some party invites out ahead. Takeoff in ten, Your Highness. The trip shouldn't take more than a few hours."

Briefly Leia considered leaving a message for her mother. Of course she couldn't explain where she was going, much less why, but she could at least tell Breha that she was headed offworld. *I could say I was going to pathfinding practice on Gatalenta or Chandrila. Or maybe that I'd be hanging out with some of the other apprentices on Coruscant.*

Those were perfectly plausible cover stories Leia didn't need. In her heart she knew her mother would never even realize she was gone.

•◆•

Running through the palace corridors, giggling as she went, her mother's footsteps fast behind her. Looking back to see the queen of Alderaan with her hair down and her dressing gown flowing behind her as she called, "I'm coming to get you!"

"Can't catch me!" Laughing as she ran even faster, trusting her mother to be no more than a few steps behind.

"Look." Her father's voice low in her ear as he cradled her in his lap, pointing at the distant mountain. "That's Appenza Peak. Your mother climbed that mountain to prove she was ready to become crown princess of Alderaan."

"All by herself?" Leia not yet able to get into her high bed without 2V's help, unable to imagine anything so bold as climbing a mountain.

"All by herself." Bail Organa hugging her tightly, making her feel snug and safe against the world.

•◆•

Leia forced herself to stop reliving old memories once she realized there was a lump in her throat. Batten was already suspicious of this trip; she'd definitely know something was up if Leia broke down in tears.

Why didn't it stop hurting? Her parents had shut her out months ago—nearly a year—and that was enough time for her to understand how things were. Still she couldn't accept it. Her heart refused to acknowledge that anything had changed; it just kept aching for people who no longer answered when she called. The pain never lessened. Even worse, whenever she was hurting, her first instinct was to turn to her mother and father. The wound stayed fresh. Maybe it always would.

"Your Highness?" Ress Batten spoke from the cockpit, so gently that Leia wondered if her sadness had shown on her face. "We're about to come out of hyperspace."

"Ready." Leia ran her hair over her braids and tucked in one escaped lock of hair. She wanted to be prepared for anything, whether that meant looking her best or . . .

After a few long seconds, she took a blaster from the locker and holstered it to her hip.

Batten glanced over her shoulder. "So you're not putting my confidence in those party invitations."

"We'll be fine," Leia promised, in hopes she wasn't lying. "I'm just—cautious."

"Sorry, Your Highness, but cautious is one thing

you're not." Batten had a smile on her oval face. "Brace yourself in three, two, one."

The electric-blue waves of hyperspace vanished, replaced by an unfamiliar starfield and the white expanse of Crait. A small planet, it was as desolate as its out-of-the-way location implied. A thick crust of salt covered nearly the entire surface, though here and there Leia could spot the planet's vivid red soil showing through, and narrow carved lines amid the white that hinted at canyons and deeply sunken waterways.

"I'm not picking up any space traffic signals," Batten said, frowning as she stared at the controls. "No orbital stations, no spaceports—wait, there it is." She pointed at a small variance in one signal hinting at a tracking signal, so faint that Leia was certain she'd never have spotted it on her own. "We're being monitored."

The blaster felt heavier against Leia's thigh. "Are they sending anyone this way?"

Batten shook her head. "Nobody's coming after us. I'm not picking up weapons signatures. The tracking signal could be automatic."

Leia took the jump seat in the cockpit. "Are there any life signs?"

"Some movement in the canyons, possibly aquatic creatures, but on the surface—" Batten's voice trailed off as she zeroed in on the signal. "We've got one tiny scratch of a settlement up here on the northern continent."

"Then that's where we're headed," Leia said with more confidence than she felt.

As Ress Batten brought the ship down toward the surface, Leia donned her hiking gear—simple white clothes that would blend with the salty landscape, a full utility belt, and a visored cap to protect her from either bright sun or easy visual identification. The holster with her weapon fit just right, though the sensation of having a blaster at her side was one she didn't want to get used to.

From the outside, she now looked like a woman of action. Inside, her nerves were beginning to get the better of her. It was one thing to want to investigate this potential rebellion against Palpatine's rule, another to actually walk up to the people responsible and trust them. Even scarier would be asking them to trust her. Anyone taking action against the Empire would be on guard, wouldn't they?

They haven't shot us down so far. Besides, you're here to help.

How, exactly? She couldn't promise troops or safe harbor on Alderaan. She'd need her parents' cooperation for that and she no longer had any faith in her ability to persuade them. Whatever a rebel group needed, it probably wasn't a stray sixteen-year-old girl.

Yet she was a sixteen-year-old girl with access to her

share of the royal purse. That money was meant to serve humanitarian purposes, and what could be more humanitarian than pushing back against Palpatine's rule?

Or maybe they're not freedom fighters. Maybe they're just terrorists in training and you're walking right into their trap—

Leia double-checked her blaster, then tucked it into her long jacket, out of sight. Although she'd never played sabacc, she'd seen enough of it in holovids to know good players kept their best card a secret until the very end.

From the bridge, she heard Ress Batten repeating, "*Polestar* of Alderaan to any vessel within range, requesting landing clearance on Crait. This is the *Polestar* of Alderaan, over. *Polestar* of Alderaan to any ve—*stang*!"

Leia didn't ask what the problem was. She just grabbed the nearest safety harness, only an instant before the ship tilted sharply to one side and began to shudder.

"Tractor beam!" Batten shouted. "Weak one, though—for towing cargo, not to capture ships—hang on."

Larger Imperial ships and stations had tractor beams. Maybe this wasn't resistance to the Empire after all. Maybe they'd flown straight into a trap.

The prospect didn't scare her too much. As long as the *Polestar* wasn't shot down, she'd be fine. Once Imperial officers learned who she was, her release would be only a matter of time. *But I'll always be watched. Under suspicion. My parents will find out what I've been up to. And what about Batten? Will they release her too?* Fear for her pilot eclipsed any worries Leia had for herself. *Please don't let me have hurt someone else. Not again—*

The *Polestar* pulled free of its tether with a jerk that nearly sent Leia crashing to the floor. She couldn't be relieved while the ship was still headed toward the ground at considerable speed. "Batten? Are we all right?"

"We will be! Gonna be kind of a rough landing, but we'll make it. Just don't tell the other pilots about this."

"We're never telling *anyone* about this!"

With a lurch and a thud, the *Polestar* made contact with the ground, skidding across the salt flats for what felt like a long time. Finally, they came to a stop. Leia pulled up a visual on the nearest screen and saw blank whiteness surrounding them in all directions—except for the one slash of red that marked their path along the surface and pointed to them like an enormous arrow. The first thing that told her was the most important: *If anyone's looking for us, we won't be hard to find.*

By the time Ress Batten joined her shortly afterward, Leia was already half suited up. Batten shook her head. "We're just running out there? Not checking around first?"

"We've found as much as we're going to find with ship's sensors." And if she waited very long, fear would get the better of her. Nobody liked to admit this, but courage had a short half-life. You had to act while you had it.

When the two of them set out from the *Polestar,* the opening of the hatch allowed gusts of wind to blow through the yacht; pinpricks of salt stung Leia's nose and cheeks. At least the harsh wind meant the red trace they'd left on the ground would soon be erased—but that was the only good thing she could say about it. She pulled her safety goggles up to protect her eyes and walked out.

Crait was as featureless a world as Leia had ever seen or imagined. At least in this vicinity, nothing marked the landscape but salt drifts sloping toward a mountain range ahead of them and an indistinct horizon behind. Everything was white on white, with only the faintest pink patches visible on the ground where the *Polestar* had skidded on the surface. She felt a moment's gratitude that they'd landed at sunset. At midday, the shine of sunlight on salt would be blinding.

"Not exactly the hottest holiday spot in the galaxy, is it?" Batten said, her voice crackling through the speaker on her breath mask. "Though I guess if you really want to get away from it all, this is the place."

Snow might be difficult to hike through, but Leia quickly learned it had nothing on heavy, slippery sodium. She trudged through salt several centimeters thick to get to a slightly higher spot on the ground, then took out her macrobinoculars. If their early scans were correct, the structures they'd seen would be approximately half a kilometer ahead, nearer the base of the mountains. No signs of activity in the distance, which suggested that they'd managed to land without being detected.

That, or they were being watched.

"Let's keep moving." Leia nodded toward Batten. "Repeat our earlier message on comms as often as you can. I want them to know we're not trying to sneak up on them. This is a . . . friendly visit."

"We're all great pals. Check." Batten began walking toward the horizon, clicking *resend* every few steps.

Another sharp gust of wind sliced through the air, sending up flumes of white salt around deep red gashes of soil. Leia was reminded of blood oozing through makeshift bandages—not the most reassuring image. The red never remained bright for long, though; salt settled back into the grooves almost instantly with a low, constant hiss. It sounded enough like a whisper to send chills along her skin. Impossible to stay calm when it felt like the planet itself was trying to warn her, drowning out the recorded call echoing from Batten's comm.

Taller salt drifts marked the terrain as they moved forward. The wind picked up too, making the salt swirl low on the ground like smoke. Although Leia had always found Coruscant claustrophobic, its skyscrapers were reassuring compared to this stark, featureless land. Its din would've been a comfort after Crait's eerie near-silence.

From Batten's belt Leia could hear fragments of their message: "Polestar *of Alderaan to base—please respond—*"

A deeper rumble behind one of the salt drifts made the hair along her arms prickle. The enormous salt mound nearest them trembled with the vibration, grains skittering along its surface. She shouted, "Is it an avalanche?" Or whatever you called it, when what was falling was salt instead of snow.

"I don't think so," Batten said. "Sounds more like—like a vehicle. Or like machinery—"

The salt drifts exploded, or seemed to. Waves of salt sprayed out in every direction, lashing Leia's thighs and midsection and knocking her backward. The grainy stuff made for a hard landing, one that scraped her hands and cheek. She coughed, tasting sodium in her mouth and feeling scratches in her throat.

"Hands up," came an unfamiliar voice. Amid the whirling salt, figures took shape—five soldiers, each of them armed with blaster rifles. Batten twitched, clearly considering going for her weapon, but had the good sense to remain on her knees. The soldier said, "Identify yourselves."

Leia got to her feet, lifted her chin, and spoke in the same bold voice she had used on her Day of Demand. "I am Princess Leia of the royal House of Organa, future queen of Alderaan, and I demand to speak to your leader, *now.*"

The soldiers exchanged glances. Apparently they weren't used to people giving orders while being taken prisoner, but they'd just have to get used to it. She was a princess, dammit, and there was incredible power in knowing that.

Finally the lead soldier motioned toward Batten. "You, there, return to your ship. The princess comes with us."

"No way." Batten stepped sideways, trying to come between the blaster rifles and Leia. "I'm her guard. I stay with her."

The lead soldier shook his head. "Either the princess comes with us, or both of you get on that ship and fly away now."

Brightening up, Batten replied, "I say we go with that. Righto, nice meeting you, we'll just be going."

Leia put out her hand. If they flew away, they might be shot down. These people had to be convinced she was a friend, not only for her own safety but to protect her pilot, too. She didn't intend to get anybody hurt ever again. "I'll go with them."

Batten shook her head once more. "Your mother will skin me alive. I mean this in a literal sense. My hide will be tanned and turned into some kind of belt or purse or other accessory."

"Don't exaggerate," Leia said firmly. "You'd just spend some time in the brig."

"Oh, that's where we are," Batten muttered. "Spending time in the brig counts as the bright side."

The lead soldier said, "She'll be safe." Leia wanted to believe him.

Either way, she'd go where he led.

•◆•

The shelters weren't that far away—but trudging through the shifting salt made the hike feel as though it went on forever. Or maybe that was the distinct knowledge of the guns in the soldiers' hands. Either way, by the time they reached a low-roofed, gray structure jutting from the salt drifts near the mountains, Leia's breaths came fast and she was sweating. The soldiers led her through the door and down a few steps; echoing sounds in the distance revealed most of this base or station was located underground. However, Leia was steered through a narrow, featureless corridor that revealed nothing of this place's layout or capacities.

By that point, it was fine with her. She wanted to simply drop to the floor in gratitude for a place to rest, but she couldn't betray any weakness. These people needed to understand she'd come to them as an equal and a potential ally.

If they didn't believe her . . .

Is this the most danger I've ever been in? Probably. Almost certainly.

"Stay here," the lead soldier said as they ushered her into a small room half-filled with pale equipment crates. The activity within came from a tiny MSE-series droid, rolling through to scan content codes. As Leia took the one chair, the soldier continued, "We'll bring our leader to you soon, or we'll let you go." He didn't say which option was more likely, or what would make the difference. When he shut the door behind him, it locked with a solid metal *chunk*, which sounded very final.

"Why tell me to stay here if you're going to lock me in?" Leia grumbled. But she didn't think much about it. She was too busy unfastening her jacket to provide easier access to her blaster. They hadn't even thought to check her for weapons. There were advantages to being a teenage girl in the middle of a situation like this; her opponents underestimated her, which made so many things possible.

Leia took the blaster in hand. She wasn't a practiced shot, but in a room this small, surely it would be hard to miss.

Could she really fire at a person? Maim or kill them, even to save her own life?

Hopefully it wouldn't come to that . . . but Leia knew it could.

All right, I sit in this chair right in front of the door. I point the blaster at the leader right away—no, that might look like an attack, and they'll fire immediately—but if I don't have it in my hands, they might search me after the fact and find it, which will leave me both a prisoner and unarmed—I can't do that.

She didn't make the decision with her conscious mind. When the door clicked again and swung open, Leia obeyed her instincts and swung the blaster up into position, ready to fire.

Then she saw the man stepping forward into the light, pulling back the hood of his jacket to reveal the shock on his face—a face she knew by heart.

Leia whispered, "Daddy?"

CHAPTER 09

Bail Organa took another step forward and stared at Leia as though he'd never seen her before. The shock weakened every muscle in her body, and she let her arm drop to her side, the blaster now dangling from slack fingers.

"They told me you were here," her father said, "but I didn't believe it. How did you find us?"

"I traced some strange traffic through Calderos Station." But why were they even talking about that? "Dad, what's going on?"

"You don't need to know."

"Well, I *do* know." Shaking off her stupor, Leia reholstered her blaster at her side. "Are you really going to try to keep hiding this from me? Here and now?"

Bail put one hand to his forehead like a man with a headache. Probably she'd given him one. "Tell me what you've learned, Leia. And tell me how you learned it."

Shock was quickly morphing into anger. "I find you in the middle of some kind of . . . insurgent camp, and *I'm* the one who has to answer questions?"

"It matters," he said, a note of urgency in his voice she'd never heard before. "If you could find us, so could the Empire. We thought we'd erased all data about Calderos Station, but if we missed something—lives are at stake."

A jolt of fear straightened her spine. Her vivid imagination showed her visions of Star Destroyers overhead, TIE fighters swooping down like rye-crows to destroy them all. "The data about shipping traffic between here and Calderos was stored in some older records I'd put together for the Apprentice Legislature. And some of the hostages I rescued from Wobani mentioned Itapi Prime, that they had cousins there who did a lot of business through the station. Something about that link seemed odd, so I followed the trail. It brought me here."

"I'll need you to destroy that data as soon as you return to Coruscant," Bail said. His stance relaxed slightly as he nodded, answering a question within his own mind. "Thank the Force it came from your private records."

"All right, I'll destroy it," Leia promised. "But what is this? Whatever it is—you attacked Calderos Station, right? You attacked the Empire!"

Her father held up one hand to forestall any more questions, but at least he'd accepted he couldn't get out of this without telling her something. "Not personally. But our . . . one of our groups was responsible, yes.

We're carrying out a few tactical strikes meant to weaken Imperial control."

"You always said we had to exercise influence through the Senate, to change the system from within."

"I still believe there's valuable work to be done there. But Palpatine's rule only grows more despotic as time goes on. A few of us have come to accept that operating within the law won't be enough." He sighed heavily as he sat on the edge of one of the crates, the tiny MSE droid whirring near his feet. "I realize this must be upsetting for you. That you're disappointed in me. I don't blame you for feeling that way, Leia. I only ask that you try to understand."

"Disappointed? Dad—this is *amazing*." Her doubts about violent action had faded the instant she realized her father played a part in all this, that he even seemed to be the one in charge. Despite the recent distance between them, her trust in his goodness remained absolute. For Leia, it was this simple: if Bail Organa led this movement of rebels, then they were doing the right thing.

And she wanted to be a part of it.

"Does Mom know?" she asked.

Bail gave her a look. "As if I could hide anything from your mother. The truth is, she had the idea even before I did. She remains on Alderaan, but she has a role to play. Let's leave it at that."

Not likely. "What about me? What can I do?"

"Leia, no. You're not to have any part in this."

"I already do," she pointed out. "I let you know how people might find this base!"

"That doesn't count," he said, in her opinion unfairly. "How did you get here?"

"Commandeered the *Polestar*—"

"With what crewmembers?" Her father's voice sharpened, and his gaze intensified. This was the stage that came immediately before *You're In Serious Trouble, Young Lady.*

"Just one," she said quickly. "Lieutenant Ress Batten. She stayed with the *Polestar.*"

Relief gentled Bail's expression. "I know Batten. She can be trusted. I'll still need to talk to her in person when we're back on Alderaan."

"When will that be? How long do we stay here? What is there to do?" Questions bubbled up inside Leia, dozens and dozens of them, but mostly she wanted to be put to work. Constructing shelters? Cleaning up? Any task, no matter how mundane, seemed like an exciting chance to help her father stand against the Empire.

"You? You can go home," Bail said. "You don't mention this to anyone, ever, do you understand?"

"But—Mom—"

"Yes, obviously we'll talk about this with your mother.

But that's *it.* After that conversation, you pretend your trip here never happened. Do you understand?"

"No! That doesn't make any sense!" Leia stamped one foot on the floor. "Not the part where I don't tell anyone—obviously I'm not going to tell—but how am I supposed to pretend I don't know what's happening?"

Bail held out his hands in a gesture of helplessness, or exasperation, maybe both. "If you want to be a part of a rebellion, you have to learn how to lie."

Brightening, she said. "So when I know how to lie, I can be a part of this."

"I didn't mean—that was only a general—" Breathing out in frustration, he paused before he continued, "Do you realize the risk you took, coming here? If we hadn't identified your ship as civilian in time, we might've shot you out of the sky. Batten's a good pilot, but we have even better gunners. I would have been the one to give the order. I could've *killed* you, Leia." His voice shook. That idea scared him even more than it did her. "What if you'd been followed by an Imperial scout? Every single person on Crait could've been killed. Everyone. That includes my soldiers, your crewmembers, me and you. All those lives could've been lost, only because you couldn't leave well enough alone."

The memory of Wobani made her waver, but she couldn't back down, not now. Instead she crossed her arms in front of her chest. "I wouldn't have to investigate things on my own if you'd just tell me the truth!"

"That's it," Bail said. "I'm taking you home."

•◆•

Leia flew home on the *Polestar,* with her father's ship, the *Tantive III,* off their wing and flying as close as any military convoy sent out for an arrest. Ress Batten did her job without so much as a sideways glance; obviously she understood the value of discretion.

Still, as they finally reentered the Alderaan system, Batten ventured, "Are we in trouble or aren't we?"

"You're not in trouble," Leia replied. *Me, on the other hand . . .*

"So we never went to Crait, never even heard of any such planet as Crait, and so definitely didn't find your father there, because how would we find the viceroy on a planet he never visited and we're not even sure exists?" Batten shrugged and raised her eyebrows. "It's a mystery."

"We went on a . . . survey run," Leia tried. "Turned up absolutely nothing."

Batten nodded firmly. " 'Nothing' would include planets that probably don't exist. Got it!"

If only all Leia's questions could be resolved so easily. It felt as if nothing made sense anymore, and maybe it never would, unless her mother could explain.

After landing in the middle of Aldera's night, she hurried from the spaceport without waiting for her father's ship to land. Bail Organa would no doubt have sent word ahead to the palace, so Leia harbored no illusions about getting to tell her mother her version of events first. She only wanted a few moments to speak freely, one on one.

As she'd anticipated, as soon as she walked into the inner chambers of the palace, she saw Breha standing in the great hall, waiting. No doubt she'd been awakened by the message, because her hair hung long and free down her back, and she wore a simple velvet robe instead of the usual royal finery. Faint golden light glowed at the neckline of the robe, hinting at the pulmonodes underneath. None of that mattered as much as the haunting, unfamiliar expression on Breha's face. It took Leia a moment to recognize what she saw there as uncertainty—an emotion she'd never believed her mother felt.

"Leia." Breha held out a hand to her. "My child, you should never have had to know this."

"I wanted to know," Leia insisted. Her mother's hand was strangely cold, as though she were ill or in shock. "Why didn't you tell me?"

"Because the knowledge is dangerous—to you, to me, to your father, and to every single being who has allied with us in this fight." Shaking her head sadly, Breha added,

"You have to go on as though you had never learned of this."

"How am I supposed to do that? Mom, you've raised me to know how evil the Empire is, to want to do something about it—"

"This is different," Breha said. "Don't ask me how, thinking you can score a point. You know how."

Leia did.

The wide doors to the hall swung open again, this time admitting her father. Bail Organa had changed from his gray-and-white Crait gear into the long coat of the viceroy, although he didn't need that to look intimidating. "You couldn't wait at the spaceport?" he said to Leia.

"I wanted to talk to Mom," Leia insisted. She caught herself pushing out her lower lip and stopped it; she was too old to pout. If she wanted to make a point, she'd have to argue it. "Who started this? Where did it begin?"

Her parents turned to each other, silently weighing between them what could and couldn't be said. They had a way of speaking to each other without words, such a perfect understanding that sometimes Leia thought they didn't need to talk at all. It had taken her a long time to realize not all spouses were like this, that not everyone found the kind of love that was like sharing souls.

At last Breha answered, "No one person started it.

Many of us around the galaxy have seen the need for greater action, and began taking the first steps on our own. We found each other. We're still learning to trust each other. The work ahead requires extraordinary trust."

"The work ahead," Leia whispered. "What does that mean?"

"We don't know yet." Bail took his wife's other hand and held it to his chest. "We have to be ready for anything."

They were determined. They were steadfast. And they were afraid. Seeing their fear made Leia believe more firmly in their courage than anything else could've done. If they could be this brave, she could as well. "I can be ready too. Let me help."

"Absolutely not." Breha snapped back into mother mode, the version of it closest to queen mode. "The danger we're facing is too great."

"Do you think not telling me anything is going to protect me?" Her parents might be courageous, but to Leia, they seemed shortsighted, too. "If the two of you are found out, do you really think the Empire won't come for me?"

Her mother made a low, anguished sound in the back of her throat, not quite a moan. Bail gripped his wife's hand more tightly for a few long, silent moments before he said, "They would. We *know* that. We carry the burden of that knowledge every day. And if they do come for you,

you have to be completely innocent. Do you understand, Leia? If they question you—if they torture you—" His voice cracked, and he couldn't go on.

Breha picked up where he left off. "If you truly know nothing, eventually they'll realize that. There's a chance—a good chance, I think—that they'd let you go. Probably they'd feel the need to leave someone from the royal house of Alderaan alive, and if you're blameless, they could install you as queen to try to make it seem like a normal transfer of power. It's the only shield we have for you, Leia. Don't ask us to destroy it. Otherwise we couldn't endure another day of this fight, and we must endure it. The fate of the entire galaxy is at stake. I don't think we could risk you for anything less." Tears welled in her mother's dark eyes, and Leia felt powerless to comfort her. Instead she watched as Bail brought Breha into his embrace and brushed his lips against her black hair.

"I thought—" The words trembled more than Leia had thought they would. "I thought you two had forgotten about me. I thought you were ignoring me for no reason."

Her parents instantly turned back to her, eyes wide with dismay. Bail shook his head as he said, "Sweetheart, no. We would never do that. Never."

Breha pulled Leia into the embrace, turning it into a family hug. "Nothing less important than this work could ever take us from you," she whispered as she stroked Leia's braided hair. "Not even this changes how much we love you. It's your future we fight for. Do you understand?"

Leia couldn't answer out loud. She just nodded, burrowing deep into her parents' arms, wishing they never had to be farther apart than this.

•◆•

By the time she reached her bedroom, it was very nearly dawn. Her window faced away from the sunrise, so the only proof she saw was the graying of the night sky. Dully she wondered whether the household staff would remember to override 2V's standing orders to wake Leia up early in the morning. Probably not.

If she fell asleep this instant, she might get two hours of rest. That was laughable. Leia felt as if she would never be able to sleep again. Her mind raced wildly in a dozen directions at once, full of new knowledge and countless new questions her parents would refuse to answer.

However, she had realized something even the formidable Bail and Breha Organa didn't know: They were fooling themselves about shielding her.

If her parents were revealed to be in rebellion against Emperor Palpatine, the entire House of Organa would be destroyed. Leia would die alongside her parents. Maybe the stormtroopers would even burn the palace to the ground. No mercy would be shown, and no innocence could protect her from the fate that would follow.

Really, her parents were too intelligent to believe otherwise. Only the desperation of their love had convinced them that part of their plan had any chance of success. Leia knew better. She hadn't had enough time to deceive herself.

The danger terrified her, but it excited her, too. Instead of grappling with mystery and uncertainty, she saw a fight on the horizon, one with a clear enemy. Leia was sick of living in confusion or fear. She wanted to take action.

But how could she do that? Bail and Breha wouldn't easily surrender their illusion of her safety. They would never willingly bring her into the fold of whatever organization this was they were forging. (She still didn't understand exactly what that was, which was maddening, but her parents hadn't betrayed one whisper of information beyond what Leia had already discovered for herself.) More than that, her mother and father were deceiving themselves about her safety because it was the only way for them to go on. She didn't want to hurt them or make them more frightened than they already were. What if they pulled out of the fight entirely just to keep her from it?

But if the battle ahead was one for her future, then it was Leia's battle too—whether her parents knew it or not.

CHAPTER 10

I could be a courier, maybe. If I'm offworld where nobody knows I'm a princess, nobody pays any attention to me because they think I'm too young to be doing anything important. That means I could deliver critical secret messages without anybody noticing—

"Watch it!" Kier called, just as Leia slipped on her foothold. She was able to compensate in time, but hearing the rocks rattle down the mountainside beneath her was sobering. Newly alert, she took stock of her position on the ridge. Her entire pathfinding class was working on rock-climbing skills today, on the fog-shrouded planet Eriadu. Their trail led them along the outskirts of a richly forested gorge, one shadowed in moss and mists; even though Eriadu City could be seen in the far distance, they were beyond the town noise. She could hear nothing but the scrabbling of her classmates on the mountain trail, and the occasional rustling of tree branches beneath when one of the world's large flying reptiles swooped through them, visible only as shadow.

A couple of meters away, Amilyn Holdo dangled from a climbing rope. She swung sideways toward Leia, purple hair peeking out from under her climbing helmet. "I understand the urge to explore extreme terror," she said in her odd monotone, "but maybe this isn't the time."

"I got distracted." That was as much of the truth as Leia could share. Amilyn smiled airily and swung back to her original place.

"Pull it together over there," shouted Chief Pangie, who was taking up the rear. "We need to get back from this trip with the same number of princesses we started with!"

Leia called out, "Sorry! It won't happen again."

Under his breath, Kier said something she probably wasn't meant to hear: "Yeah, it will."

She turned toward him. "Excuse me?"

His face remained impassive, his dark eyes more curious than defensive. "It's true. Your head's been somewhere else all day. I don't know what's more important to you than not falling down this mountain, but whatever it is—"

"You don't know what you're talking about," Leia insisted. "And I don't see how it's any of your business how I climb."

"We're roped together," he pointed out, not unreasonably. She recognized as she hadn't before the tension in his wiry, muscular arms, and the sweat that shone on his brow. "If you fall, I probably fall too."

That snapped her out of it better than anything else could've done. Of course they had portable force fields projected only a few meters beneath their climbing position; a tumble wouldn't be fatal, only embarrassing. But Leia had gained a sharper appreciation for not putting other people at risk. Newly focused, she dedicated herself to getting up the ridge, paying attention to nothing farther away than the stone against her gloves and boots.

Within another half hour, they'd reached the high plateau that marked their goal for the day. Sssamm, who could secrete an adhesive substance from between his scales to aid in climbing, made it up so long before the others that they found him stretched out, basking in the sun.

"We're taking a hopper down from here, aren't we?" Chassellon's long face was shiny with sweat, and his usually well-tended curls frizzed in every direction. "Right? There's got to be a hopper."

"Weak, Stevis." Chief Pangie had taken a seat by Sssamm and was already digging into her packed lunch. "Can't act weak if you want to be strong."

He folded his arms. "I'm rich. I don't have to be strong."

"You never know when you're going to lose all your money," Amilyn pointed out as she removed her helmet, then shook her purple hair free. Chassellon's eyes got larger, as though she'd just described the greatest disaster that could ever unfold.

Leia took a seat at the far edge of the plateau, her booted feet just shy of the edge. Thanks to sweat and dust, she was filthy—a line of grime marked the length of her sleeve—but she liked the sense of exhilaration that came after exertion. *See?* she said to the parents in her head, who were much more pliant and easily surprised than the real ones. *I'm not afraid of taking risks. I'm ready for hard work. Let me try.*

Then she remembered her father's voice breaking when he talked about the possibility of her being captured. How could she ever push them when they were already so afraid for her?

But how could she not stand against the Empire?

Leia unscrewed the canister of soup she'd brought for lunch and set out a bandana as a sort of placemat. Only then did she realize Kier was settling in not far away. When he noticed her looking at him, he said, "This is okay, right?"

"I don't own the mountain."

"That's right. We're not on Alderaan anymore."

She breathed out, a little huff of exasperation. "I don't own the mountains on Alderaan either."

He didn't look up from unwrapping his sandwich as he said, "No, they own you."

"What are you getting at, Kier?"

"On Alderaan, you're stuck being a princess all the time. On Coruscant, you're a senator in training. But here, when we're climbing—I think that's when you get to be yourself."

She'd never thought of it that way before. "Why are

you so worried about whether or not I'm happy being a princess?"

That wasn't exactly what he'd said, but he glided past it. "You're the future ruler of my planet. So I'm kind of curious about what you're really like."

". . . I guess that makes sense," Leia admitted.

"That's not your only reason," sang Amilyn Holdo, who turned out to be sitting on a boulder that loomed over their ridge. She gave Kier a loopy smile. "But it's a good excuse. Maybe go with that."

Kier ducked his head, more amused than abashed. "Can't 'go with' it if you're blowing my cover." With a shrug, Amilyn turned back to her lunch, which seemed to be some sort of multicolored pasta.

It wasn't like Leia hadn't considered the possibility before. Kier was difficult to get to know—but he was smart and insightful. Interested in the larger galaxy around them. Willing to pitch in and help. Unawed by her royal status, even if sometimes he pushed too hard to prove that.

And good-looking. Can't forget good-looking. Not that Leia was in much danger of forgetting it. She'd gotten to like his whipcord thinness, his heavy brows, and his deep-set dark eyes . . .

Still, looks weren't everything. She had to figure Kier Domadi out a little more before she could know what she wanted from him.

Gazing toward the horizon, she again took in the buzz of air traffic around Eriadu City—as much as could be seen around Aldera, even though Alderaan was a Core World heavily connected by trade to many planets in the galaxy, while Eriadu had been a little-remarked-upon way station in the Outer Rim until a generation or two ago. Nodding in that direction, she said, "I guess Grand Moff Tarkin looks after his own."

"Obviously. It's not like anybody would have a reason to refuel here, unless they were officially diverted." Whatever embarrassment Kier might have felt earlier had already faded; his attention was on the distant metropolis. "Tarkin's not the only Imperial higher-up who channeled money back home. That's how the Empire operates—favoritism and graft."

Leia agreed with every word but had never heard anyone speak so openly about it, not even her parents outside the privacy of the palace. "You should be careful," she said in a low voice. "Not everyone appreciates honesty." Her eyes flickered over to Chassellon Stevis, but he lay sprawled on the ground, exhausted to the point of semiconsciousness.

Kier only shrugged. "I don't lie to people."

Leia remembered how thoroughly her parents had lied to her, and how she was now lying to Kier, and to the entire galaxy, through her silence about their plans. Honesty and deception were more complex than they first appeared.

She only smiled and said, "If you don't like lying, then what are you doing in politics?"

That made him laugh out loud, the first time she'd ever heard him laugh. The rarity of it made it feel more worth winning. "I'm moving on as quickly as possible. Hopefully someday I'll teach at a university like my mom. She teaches political science, but I want to become a historian. The Apprentice Legislature seemed like a good place to synthesize the two. To build on what she taught me while I move in my own direction." He leaned forward, resting his forearms on his knees. "We don't all get tutors, you know."

Kier wasn't needling her, she finally realized. He was studying her with the avid curiosity he brought to every subject, every moment. "Sometimes tutors aren't especially helpful." She pointed her thumb back at Chief Pangie, who was no doubt grinning in glee at the thought of sending them back down the mountain again. "Especially when you have a dozen."

"A dozen? Really?" He shook his head like someone surfacing from underwater, readjusting expectations. "Royalty don't use educational droids?"

"Sure, for standard academic subjects. But I've also had tutors in pathfinding, diplomacy, piloting, navigation—you name it. I've even studied hand-to-hand combat, though I'm still advancing there."

"I never realized the House of Organa got into so many fistfights." The joke was implicit; everyone throughout the galaxy was familiar with her parents' reputation for peacemaking. *If only the worlds knew the truth.*

Hurriedly Leia said, "Honestly, I think my parents just want me to blow off some steam. I wish the lessons could start tomorrow."

Kier took another bite of his sandwich, chewing thoughtfully before finally saying, "I've never studied hand-to-hand combat, but I'm pretty good at sharpshooting."

"What, like with blasters?"

He nodded. "If you're game for a thirteenth tutor—and not afraid of a challenge—we could try that sometime. If you'd like."

Leia could get a sharpshooting tutor from anywhere, any time she wished. Probably that would've been covered by her combat instructor anyway. And she knew full well that Kier wasn't offering to teach her because he thought she needed to know. He was making an excuse to spend time with her.

She said, "Yeah. I'd like that."

•◆•

Two days later, on Coruscant, Leia and Kier walked into a target practice arena—a skinny, pyramid-shaped space that at its highest point reached ten meters over their heads.

The faint metallic shimmer of its pale walls hinted at the holographic projectors and electronic scorers embedded within. Beneath her booted feet, the darker floor had some springiness to it, not unlike a gymnastics mat.

As she bounced on her heels, Kier noticed. "You can request the softer surface, so you get used to judging your terrain without relying on a flat, solid floor every time."

"Makes sense." Like her, Kier wore a formfitting white coverall lined with silver reflective piping. The pale clothing emphasized the golden tan of his skin. She blinked hard, refocusing her attention. "Let's get started."

"Show me your firing stance," he said, and she went into the position she'd seen her guards in several times. After a second, Kier nodded and raised his eyebrows, impressed. "Okay. You've got that part down."

She'd thought he might put his arms around her to correct her position, and wondered whether she should've fudged the stance just a little bit. . . .

No. Leia wanted anyone who was interested in her to know who she really was, what she could really do. If Kier Domadi wanted to put his arms around her—well, he'd find a way.

Or she would.

Focus, she told herself as the lights lowered to one-quarter their usual brightness. But she'd spent so little time with anyone her own age, much less anybody she was attracted to. Being close to Kier energized her in a way she hadn't experienced before, and she liked it.

"Run target practice simulation one," Kier called out as he took his position, his back almost against Leia's. "On my mark—go."

A small golden polyhedron appeared in the air overhead, on Kier's side of the arena. Instantly he fired one of the bluish test-pistol blasts, which "shattered" the holographic image. A transparent scoreboard hovering above showed ten points.

"Points? We're scoring this?" Leia adjusted her grip.

At the edge of her peripheral vision, she saw him turning his head toward her. "You're not scared of a challenge, are you?"

She answered him by pointing her weapon at the next floating polyhedron and firing. The bolt only clipped the hologram, but that was enough to hold it in place for a few moments, more than long enough for her to fire again and finish it. "*Five points*," said the scoreboard.

"All right, then," Kier said, and somehow she could hear the smile in his voice.

Most of the next hour passed in a happily violent blur. Leia kept winging her targets instead of hitting them straight on until she realized she was regularly leading left. Once she'd figured out how to adjust for that, her scores started rising dramatically. When the lights finally came up, she was thirty points behind Kier—but she'd been more than a hundred and fifty points behind at the halfway mark. "Another few minutes," she panted, surprised at how tired she was, "and I would've caught you."

Leia expected him to argue, but he nodded. "You would have. I think you have a talent for this."

"We'll have to practice again and see, won't we?" She raised one eyebrow.

Luckily, Leia wasn't the only one who enjoyed a challenge. A slow grin spread across Kier's face. "Yeah. We will."

•◆•

That night she took the *Polestar* back to Alderaan, her mind filled with thoughts about the day's target practice, and when she could go again. For the first time in months, she came in without wondering where her parents were, or whether they'd even notice she had returned. So, naturally, this was the time they were waiting for her.

"We were hoping you'd be here for dinner," her father said as he walked into the library, where Leia had planned on a long daydreaming session. "It's been too long since we ate as a family. And you look hungry."

Was that what she looked like? Leia sat up straighter, trying not to look like anything at all.

She failed. "To me she looks happy." Breha came in

only a couple of paces behind him, carrying a frosty glass of mintea, Leia's favorite. "What did you do today?"

"Sharpshooting. Kier and I practiced together. He goes a lot, and I thought it sounded like"—*Good practice for combat* probably wasn't the answer her parents wanted to hear—"lots of fun."

Bail and Breha exchanged glances. "Kier?" Bail said. "That's Kier Domadi from the Apprentice Legislature, right?"

"And from the pathfinding class," Breha added.

At least the shadows in the library would hide any hint of a blush. She didn't want her parents prying. How was she supposed to explain what was going on with Kier before she knew herself? Time to switch to a distracting new subject. "Yeah, that's him," she said as airily as she could manage. "He won this time, but I nearly caught him. I think I might be good at this."

"We might have a target shooting champion on our hands," Breha said to Bail, her smile widening. "Do you think she could compete incognito?"

"Until she wins her first major match." He put his arm around Breha, pulling her close. "Then we have to announce our daughter's latest brilliant talent."

Her parents' approval had always warmed Leia, and after so long without it, she felt as if she wanted to drink it all in. She even had news that would increase it, she hoped. "By the way, I'm leaving for my next humanitarian mission tomorrow."

Breha folded her arms across her chest, deliberately theatrical. "Nowhere dangerous, in any sense?"

"Onoam," she answered. "It's a moon, actually. Mining conditions there are rough, so I'm taking them new safety equipment. That's *all*."

"That should be fine," Breha said in obvious relief.

Bail frowned slightly. "Onoam. I think I've heard of it—years ago, maybe—"

"Viceroy? Your Majesty?" Captain Antilles appeared in one of the doorways. He had the tense, distracted look that Leia was beginning to recognize. "We should speak in your office."

Her parents instantly walked out, without another word to Leia. She wasn't offended. Obviously they were discussing their actions against the Empire—whatever those were—and those were conversations Leia still had to earn her way into. The trip to Onoam would be a critical step toward that goal. At least this target was a safe one. What place could be farther from anti-Imperial activity than Palpatine's home planet?

They'd be nothing but happy to learn of her trip to the Naboo system.

CHAPTER 11

As the *Polestar* slid through the electric blue of hyperspace, Leia ventured, "Seems like it's been longer than a couple of weeks since we traveled together last."

"Has it been?" Ress Batten said. She seemed very interested in the controls in front of her, too much to even look up. "Maybe I'm getting it mixed up with another flight. The trips all start to run together in my head after a while."

Disconcerted, Leia turned back to her datapad, but the information on the screen meant nothing. Her thoughts ran in other directions.

It made no sense for Batten to declare, *Yes, I remember traveling to that illegal military outpost and running into your father there!* Acknowledging what they'd seen would be hazardous for both of them, and for Bail Organa too. Still, Leia found their shared silence uncomfortable. *Maybe I only want someone to talk to about this,* she thought. *Someone besides my parents.*

But Ress Batten couldn't be her confidant. If she admitted what she knew, it could only put them at risk; her father had always said you shouldn't put anyone in royal service in jeopardy without their free consent. Besides, Batten was sworn to serve as a pilot and an officer, not as a would-be conspirator, much less as a friend.

The divide between princess and pilot was one her mother had warned her about. *The palace can be an isolated place, Leia,* Breha had said to her little girl many times, beginning when she was too small to understand how their happy home could ever be lonely. *We have so many privileges, but we have to make sacrifices, too. We have to bear our burdens on our own.*

That still didn't make total sense to Leia. Her parents supported each other, and they could have her support too if they'd just make her a part of their plans to push back against the Emperor.

But this painful silence—this awkwardness between her and the other person on this ship, where neither of them would admit what they'd seen—that was one of those burdens Breha had spoken of.

She'd have to get used to carrying the weight.

•◆•

Leia's plans didn't call for traveling to Naboo itself. She hadn't been in any hurry to set foot on Palpatine's homeworld, but as the *Polestar* settled into Onoam orbit and Naboo hung large in the starfield, she felt an unexpected pang. It was a beautiful planet—green and blue, laced with faint misty clouds—and surely it could be forgiven for one of its citizens turning out so badly.

Then she reminded herself of Wobani, and Arreyel, and countless other worlds that had once been this beautiful before they were poisoned by Palpatine's Empire. She couldn't enjoy Naboo's beauty knowing the cost of so much of its prosperity.

Anyway, their destination had its own charms. Unlike most moons and smaller planets with mines, Onoam remained a lovely place to be—at least, on the surface. Gentle winds stirred tall grasses that spread across vast rolling planes, beneath a pinkish sky. Many wealthier citizens of Naboo had second homes there, including the provincial governor of this sector, and only a few kilometers from the spaceport stood a secondary royal palace.

As chance would have it, the royal personage in question happened to be visiting Onoam. Leia knew enough protocol to know that even their mercy mission had to wait for an hour or two, because it was the duty of a princess to call on a queen.

"You are welcome to our system, Princess," said Queen Dalné in the lower, more formal voice traditional for the ruler of her world. She sat on a high golden throne, dressed in the sumptuous regalia of a ruler of Naboo; her long robes were a shade of violet so dark it was nearly black, shot through with ornate silver embroidery. Her dark hair had been woven through the lattices of a silver headdress that spread out like a fan, and white makeup on her face made the red on her lips look stark. "If we had been given more notice of your visit, we could have prepared a banquet in your honor."

"I hadn't expected to find you here," Leia said, which was as close to an apology as necessary. "I had thought surely the many concerns of your world would keep you on Naboo." Uh-oh. Did that sound like she was criticizing the queen? *Great. Your second diplomatic incident in two trips. At this rate you'll start a war before the month is out.*

Yet Queen Dalné smiled, a touch sadly. "Once the queens of Naboo truly were rulers of this world. But since our Senator Palpatine has become emperor, his governors have taken Naboo's concerns in hand. Really there is very little for me to do beyond the ceremonial."

Breha's words came to mind again: *The palace can be an isolated place.* Dalné was a girl no older than Leia herself, with no ruler parents to support her and no meaningful duties to perform. She led a life of gilded luxury that some would envy, but Leia understood the bars of the cage around her.

Still, royalty didn't have to mean total solitude. "Your Majesty, if you have both the time and the will, you could join me today. We'll be distributing safety equipment to the miners." She half expected Dalné to refuse immediately. No doubt there were political pitfalls to this that Leia, as an outsider, couldn't understand.

Instead, the queen of Naboo smiled. Her heavy makeup could no longer conceal her true face. "I have the will, Princess Leia, and so I shall make the time."

According to the files Leia had studied, the relationship between Naboo and its mining colony on Onoam had always been fractious. A generation before, the miners had repeatedly gone on strike for larger shares of the profits, and some splinter groups had even committed minor political violence—breaking windows and security shields, even burning a vacant warehouse on Naboo itself.

No doubt the present miners would have given much to work in the conditions their predecessors had found so objectionable. Before, the miners of Onoam had wanted to be treated more fairly; now, they wanted to be acknowledged as human beings. As the cargo lift with the first load of equipment sank lower into the shaft, light became a rarer resource; the scanty illumination down here was hardly enough to work by, and no more than that. Heavy dust seemed to hang in the air. Leia coughed more than once, and Dalné's snowy makeup had already begun to look dingy. This couldn't be a safe environment for them or for anyone.

But only sentients were allowed to mine for medicinal

spice. Droids could be too easily hacked or hijacked to smuggle out amounts sufficient for cooking into new, more potent substances—in other words, illegal ones. Humans could cheat too, but they were rarely as skilled at it, and other motivations could keep them honest. Leia would have thought the best of these motivations would be a fair wage, good working conditions, and a sense of community and camaraderie.

Palpatine preferred to "motivate" through cruelty and terror.

When at last they'd sunk to the deepest level of the mine for the equipment, a small group of miners waited for their royal visitors. They might have been any other committee come to greet a visiting dignitary if it weren't for the handful of stormtroopers milling around in the background, one for every exit.

Dalné's protocol droid announced them, then gestured at one tall, skinny man and said, "Brel Ti Vorne, designated representative of the miners."

"My queen," Ti Vorne said, bowing to his queen first, as was proper. But he turned his attention to Leia immediately after. "Princess Leia of Alderaan, we receive you with gratitude."

"You'll receive something more useful than a princess." She gestured to the crates coming in by hoverdroid. "We've brought supplies for five hundred miners: safety belts, atmosphere masks, portable force fields that can purify the air, and a few other things I thought you might need."

She expected smiles, or at least nods of acknowledgement. Instead, Ti Vorne's face fell, and the miners behind him shuffled from foot to foot and murmured among themselves.

Queen Dalné said, "These gifts trouble you. May we ask why?"

"If you need other things more urgently," Leia hastily added, "I'll try to get those too. Just tell me what they are."

Ti Vorne shook his head. "These items would make our labors much easier, Your Highness."

Would. Not will. She cast a surreptitious glance toward the nearest stormtroopers; they didn't appear to be paying any particular attention, but behind those helmets, who could tell? So Leia stepped closer to Ti Vorne and pitched her voice lower. "They can't hear us. Tell me the truth."

He hesitated a moment longer, so uncertain she nearly took back what she'd said, but finally Ti Vorne sighed. "You may give the equipment to us, Your Highness. We may even be allowed to use some of it, at least for a shift or two. But eventually everything will be taken away—as a punishment, or because the equipment's supposedly 'defective,' or we'll be told it was lost. Something like that. We'd managed to save up for a few things of our own, every now and then, until we realized they'd all meet the same fate. The Imperial major in charge of the mine sells them off and pockets the profit."

Leia could hardly speak for her indignation. "What—they—that's criminal!"

Ti Vorne shrugged. "Not if the one in charge does it."

"No, because then it's even worse. Then it's—it's just—total *poodoo*."

That made Ti Vorne's eyes go wide, and Queen Dalné choked back a laugh. So much for diplomatic language.

"Forgive me," Leia said with as much grace as she could retrieve. "Your plight upsets me, and moves me to action."

"Then you're already better than most, Your Highness." Ti Vorne had a curious expression on his face—as if he were even more afraid of his next words. But all he said after that was, "We've reached out to others recently. Including some we thought might take action for us. Nothing yet."

Leia clasped her hands in front of her. "Then let me do what I can for you. Please accept these gifts on behalf of all the miners. I intend to find a way to ensure that this time you keep them."

"We both shall," Queen Dalné added, with a force in her voice Leia hadn't heard from her before.

Ti Vorne's smile was sad. He didn't blame them, but

he didn't believe them, either. "Your goodwill is a gift in itself."

Shortly afterward, when Leia and Dalné were rising from the catastrophic bloom of the mines on the cargo lift, Leia muttered, "They can't eat goodwill. Can't breathe it, either."

"We all know of Imperial corruption." Dalné sounded miserable. In the brief time they'd spent underground, her facial makeup had been rendered almost entirely gray by the disgusting dust. "It reaches everywhere. But not even I realized it dug so far underground."

"Is there anything you can do? Any—old rule, or ceremonial duty, that lets you step in?"

Dalné thought for so long that Leia assumed she was mostly coming up with a tactful way to say nothing could be done. Then she snapped her fingers. "I can demand an audience with higher officials. The provincial governor himself has a chalet here on Onoam; I think he might even be visiting now."

"That's—Moff Quarsh Panaka, yes?"

"Yes. He's a native of Naboo, so it's not like going to an offworlder. And for all he turns a blind eye, he's not corrupt himself." Dalné hesitated. "He *is* personally loyal to Palpatine."

That loyalty made him dangerous, but—"We should

give him a chance. Honest Imperial officials are pretty rare. It would be a shame to waste one."

Having something important to do had clearly invigorated Dalné. Much too cheerfully, given the risks, she said, "Shall I request an immediate audience, then?"

Leia nodded. "I think it's time I met Panaka."

CHAPTER 12

Moff Panaka's office granted the queen of Naboo and her guest an audience—though the only window they offered was that same day, very soon. Leia wondered whether the moff's underlings hoped to avoid the queen's request by simply ensuring she arrived late.

To complicate matters, Leia needed to change clothing. Her simple white gown suited most occasions, or it had, before she'd worn it down in the belly of a mine. Although she tried to convince herself that walking into the audience grimy and gray would make a strong point about mining conditions, she couldn't do it. Apparently 2V's constant admonitions about looking her best had sunk in. So they found the time to fly to Dalné's home on Onoam, where sumptuous royal finery was available in abundance.

I'm never going to tell TooVee about this, Leia decided as she slipped into one of the queen's gowns. *She'd gloat for days.*

She had borrowed the simplest dress on offer, another one in white, but the simplest dress of a ruler of Naboo remained ornate in the extreme. Pale pink and yellow veils fell in layers from the cape, and a white net stretched behind her head like a ruff. The effect was beautiful, but to Leia's eyes, extravagant.

"This is traditional dress," Dalné insisted as she fluffed the veils cascading over Leia's shoulders. "Queens and other high officials wear this at times of rejoicing. It's appropriate to wear when first meeting a dignitary; that way, you're signaling that you expect negotiations to be successful."

"It's just—a lot."

Dalné nodded in resignation. "After I was elected queen, it took me months to get used to the weight of the headdresses. The one I'm wearing now is one of the lightest. Though the one that goes with the jubilation dress is really very easy to—"

"No, no." Leia held up one hand. "I don't want to come across like I'm pretending to be queen myself."

This amused Dalné. "You're overqualified to be a handmaiden!"

As Batten sped the *Polestar* over the tall swaying grasses of Onoam, Leia listened to Dalné talk about all the many roles Naboo handmaidens had played in the past, serving as everything from personal counselors to intelligence operatives. The tradition had faded as the queen became more of a figurehead than a ruler, but handmaidens still had to qualify through a series of mental and physical tests that would've challenged even Imperial Academy cadets.

What must it have been like, to be a true queen of Naboo? *The weight of it would be heavy,* Leia thought, *in every way—from the responsibility for a whole planet to the ceremonial head-dresses.* Even some of the gowns in Dalné's closet must have weighed five or six kilos. Thank goodness Alderaan's royal traditions called for nothing more than the monarch wearing braids.

Batten would stay with the *Polestar,* which set down a respectable distance from the chalet. Imperial security regulations didn't bend, not even for princesses or queens. It was a civilian worker who registered the landing, however, an odd tall fellow who wore a breathing mask. How strange it must be for him, surrounded by such natural beauty and fresh air he couldn't safely inhale.

The veils of her cape rippled around Leia's feet as she and Dalné climbed the steps leading to the moff's chalet, an imposing structure built of thick beams of richly patterned red wood. But she was able to walk smoothly and with assurance, and with no fear of tripping. She hadn't been a princess her whole life without learning how to deal with a gown that had a train.

A squat little LEP droid showed them into a high-ceilinged room with broad windows that revealed the beautiful vista spreading out to the horizon in three directions. But that, Leia noted, was the space's one true luxury. Most higher Imperial officials liked to surround themselves with the overripe glamour of ill-gotten gains: statues looted from museums, ostentatiously expensive furnishings, and the like. Moff Panaka preferred the simple and practical, while still showing good taste.

Despite her many years of experience with Imperial authorities, Leia began to feel hopeful. Dalné had told her Panaka was a decent man. This room confirmed at least that he wasn't like most of the Empire's higher-ups. Maybe negotiating would actually get them somewhere.

"Your Majesty." The deep masculine voice rang through the room. Leia half-turned to see a tall, handsome, dark-skinned man walking toward the queen, a cup in hand. He was about her father's age, though not quite as tall, and flecks of gray marked the hair at his temples. Another LEP droid waddled behind him with a steaming pot and more cups for the guests. Moff Panaka continued, "You caught me having my afternoon tea. I hope you and your guest will—"

Panaka's gaze finally turned to Leia. He stopped short, eyes wide with shock. Although he managed to hold on to his cup, some of his tea splashed onto the floor.

"Moff Panaka, are you well?" Dalné hurried forward

as the little droid reached out an extender to mop up the spill.

"Of course. Forgive me. Your guest—reminded me of someone else." Recovering his dignity, Panaka straightened and walked toward Leia, seemingly at ease again. Yet she could see the intense curiosity in his eyes. "You are Princess Leia Organa of Alderaan?"

"Yes, Moff Panaka. It's a pleasure to meet you." Leia felt more disconcerted by Panaka's odd behavior than she should've. Instead of engaging in the usual pleasantries, she got directly to the point. "We need to discuss the situation of the miners here on Onoam."

He took a deep breath, still visibly steadying himself. "By all means. Let's discuss this over tea, assuming there's any left in the pot instead of on the floor."

She smiled. It wasn't much of a joke, but it was more than many Imperials would offer. Surely it had to be a good sign, especially after such an awkward beginning.

They sat with Panaka on his terrace overlooking a narrow river that gleamed like silver in the sunlight. Leia laid out what they had seen in the mines, and described the problems Ti Vorne had told them of, though she knew not to mention the miner's name. Panaka pressed his lips together, perhaps in anger, as she spoke, and she could tell the anger was for Imperial grifters.

"Of course Emperor Palpatine encourages a certain degree of"—Panaka sought a word that would be tactful enough—"initiative among its officers. They're meant to handle disobedience through economic means when possible, rather than resort to violence."

Is that *what you're calling it? People should be grateful they're being robbed instead of being shot?* Leia simply nodded and gave him a noncommittal "Mmm-hmm."

Panaka shook his head. "The problem arises when less experienced officers begin to believe they can act this way against all citizens, instead of only lawbreakers. We need to be vigilant against such behavior, or else discipline among the troops will disintegrate."

Virtually every other planet in the Empire saw "such behavior" constantly. However, maybe Moff Quarsh Panaka was willing to make sure Naboo wasn't one of them. Leia ventured, "If you could establish some oversight in the mines—beginning now, with the new equipment I've brought—that could begin to make a real difference."

"Then let it be done," Panaka said.

She turned to Dalné, smiling in victory. Although Dalné smiled back, the elaborate makeup on her face couldn't disguise that she was as confused as happy. Apparently Panaka wasn't always as obliging. Why was he making an exception in Leia's case?

He settled back in his wroshyr-wood chair, teacup still

in hand, though he hadn't drunk from it in so long that the tea had to be cold. "It truly is a pleasure to meet you, Your Highness. I met your father a few times during the Clone Wars."

Leia brightened. Ever since the earliest days of her childhood, she'd thrilled to her father's stories of adventure during the wars. When she'd been tiny, he'd kept the stories simple—tales of narrow escapes, or dashingly heroic Jedi Knights. As she grew older, he'd talked to her more about the diplomacy, the complexity, and the tragedy of the battles. Still, she couldn't resist thinking of the Clone Wars as exciting. "Did you serve together with him and General Kenobi?"

As soon as the name left her mouth, she wanted to bite her tongue. Not everyone in the galaxy wanted to remember the Jedi. Palpatine certainly didn't, and Panaka was loyal to his emperor.

But Panaka nodded. "I knew Kenobi as well, though that was before the Clone Wars began. Before he was a full Jedi Knight, even."

"Really?" There might be dozens of other stories about the great Obi-Wan Kenobi, ones even her father had never known.

Before Leia could ask, however, Panaka shifted slightly in his chair to look at her straight on. "Forgive me if this is a personal question, but—I believe I remember hearing that the viceroy and his queen adopted their child. Is that true?"

"Yes, of course. It's not a personal question at all. My adoption was celebrated publicly on Alderaan." It was a *weird* question, though. What did that have to do with anything?

Panaka nodded, as if considering her words very carefully. "How many years ago was that, now?"

"I turned sixteen a few months ago. My parents took me immediately after my birth."

"Sixteen years almost exactly." Panaka's eyes had regained the intensity of the moment he'd first seen Leia. "And your biological parents were—"

That *was* a personal question, but one Leia didn't mind answering. The little information she had was known by many on Alderaan and elsewhere. "I've been told my biological father died in one of the last battles of the Clone Wars. My birth mother was badly injured and lived only long enough to deliver me."

"Do you know their names?"

"No," Leia said. "I've never asked."

"Why not?" That question came from Dalné, who valiantly tried to soften the conversation, to move it from the specific to the general. "Aren't you curious? Most adoptees are."

Leia shrugged. "If either of my birth parents had

survived, I'd want to know them. But they were lost before I was even one day old. My adoptive parents are the only family I've ever had and the only ones I'd ever want. Not every adoptee feels that way about it, but for me—my family is complete, just as it is."

"The disintegration of the Republic was a dangerous, chaotic time," Panaka said. His eyes had never left Leia. "So many were lost, and it was difficult to know what had become of them. One heard so many rumors, and could never be certain which to believe."

"I'm sure." Leia wasn't quite sure how to take this digression, but at least he wasn't digging into her biological parentage anymore. Was he adopted as well, or had he adopted a child himself? Either explanation made sense, but neither entirely satisfied her.

Their strange tea party ended shortly afterward. Moff Panaka walked them to the front door himself, making pleasant chitchat, though he continued to watch Leia carefully the entire time. In irritation she wondered if he thought she was going to steal a teacup.

"Thank you again for your audience and your kind attention, Moff Panaka," Dalné said.

Panaka's smile for her looked entirely genuine. "For many years, I served queens of Naboo. It is a privilege to serve you as well."

"Today you've also served a princess of Alderaan."

Leia held out her hands, and Panaka took them. His grip felt uncomfortably tight, but her facial expression never betrayed her discomfort. "I'm reassured to know that someone in authority is looking out for the miners' interests." *Finally,* she added, but only in her head.

"Meeting you has been a . . . unique experience." Panaka cocked his head, still studying her with that laser gaze. "I shall speak to Palpatine himself about this."

"About the miners?" That was much more than Leia had dared hope for.

Panaka shook his head. "About you, Your Highness. I think he should know that the Organas adopted a daughter of such distinction."

Whatever *that* meant, and now he was focused on adoption again. Leia managed to politely extract her hands from Panaka's grasp. "If you'd mention the miners too, I'd appreciate it."

He seemed to catch himself. "Of course. I meant what I said, Princess Leia. The miners' supervisors won't be getting away with such petty thievery ever again."

With those words, the whole peculiar afternoon was made worthwhile.

After he turned to reenter the chalet, Leia and Dalné descended the steps toward the *Polestar.* The winds that rippled the grass around them tugged at their robes and capes, and hopefully muffled their words as Leia muttered, "What was all *that* about?"

"I can't imagine. Do you think that perhaps"—Dalné hesitated—"that your father and Moff Panaka were once friends, and had some kind of falling out? He might be angry about any good fortune for an enemy, even the adoption of a child."

That seemed like a stretch to Leia. Still . . . "My father's an open critic of Palpatine's. If Panaka's extremely loyal to the Emperor, probably he resents—"

A wall of heat slammed into Leia and knocked her off her feet as the world turned brilliant white. Roaring sound swallowed every other noise until Leia's ears rang too much to hear anything else. Dalné was a blur next to her, tumbling down the steps beside Leia, and the only other sight she could make out in the glare was that of plumes of flame stretching high into the pale pink sky.

Explosion, she thought. That was the only coherent word she could come up with.

Leia hit the ground hard, flat on her belly, and couldn't inhale for what felt like far too long. Dalné crawled to her side, long locks of her black hair dangling free of her silver headdress and tears dissolving her white makeup. She said nothing, only gripped Leia's hand.

Something exploded, Leia thought in a daze. *The moff's chalet.*

But that doesn't make any sense. It was a house built of wood, not a ship or station—

Which meant the house had been destroyed by a bomb.

Sitting upright, Leia looked around to see mayhem. Smoldering droid parts lay scattered across the lawn beside burning chips of wood and debris. The chalet itself, or what remained of it, couldn't be seen through the thick black smoke billowing into the sky. Stormtroopers were running toward the fire, no doubt in an attempt to save Quarsh Panaka, although it seemed impossible anyone could've been closer to the blast and lived. Ress Batten, too, ran toward them, only steps behind.

In the distance, one man was running away.

It's the civilian worker, the one with the breathing mask! Leia tried to rise to her feet but couldn't. She lifted her hand to at least point toward the escaping figure—

—until she realized this was an attack on an Imperial official. An attack on the Empire.

That meant this could possibly be linked to her parents' shadowy activities on Crait.

Leia couldn't identify the bomber as long as there was any chance this was connected to her family. Never had her loyalty to Bail and Breha Organa wounded her, but it did as she sat there, forced to let a murderer get away.

Had her parents become murderers too?

CHAPTER 13

The chaos after the explosion left Leia badly off balance for the better part of an hour. One moment she was staring at the burning chalet, thinking, *I was just drinking tea inside there, with a man who's dead now.* The next, a medical droid was hovering around her, scanning for injuries; by the time the droid was done, she had synthplast over the few bad cuts she'd received and a binding field around her ankle, which throbbed menacingly. Then she remembered the masked man who had run away—wondered if he was tied to whatever shadowy group her parents were a part of, whether they'd known this would happen to Quarsh Panaka and anyone who stood near him—and thought of the shamefaced way the miners' leader had spoken of reaching out for "help"—

"You, there." The stormtrooper's metallic voice jolted Leia back into the here and now. He stood over her, smudges of soot marring his white armor. The way the sunlight hit his mask, she could almost see the human eyes within. He gestured with his blaster rifle toward an area where a few shell-shocked, grimy people were being cordoned off by his fellow troopers. "Assemble with the other suspects."

"Suspects?" Her temper returned to fiery life, but before she could speak, Queen Dalné of Naboo stepped in, already dusted off to a semblance of her former grandeur.

"This is not a suspect," Dalné said in the deeper, flatter voice that meant she spoke not as an individual, but as monarch. "This is Leia, princess of Alderaan, daughter of their queen and their representative in the Imperial Senate. It would be absurd to accuse her of terrorist activities."

With a jolt, Leia realized she was closer to the true cause than anyone else nearby.

But Dalné's explanation worked for the stormtrooper. The strict hierarchies of Imperial service meant the average soldier of the line was quick to defer to authority. "Excuse me, Your Majesty, Your Highness. I wasn't informed."

"It's quite all right," Leia said as smoothly as she could manage. "I think we're all shaken up."

The stormtrooper was clearly torn between wanting to seize that excuse and not wanting to admit he was "shaken up" in front of two teenage girls. Finally he simply waved toward the *Polestar*, where Ress Batten had been forced to wait.

Leia got to her feet, wincing as she put her weight on

her ankle. Upon seeing her discomfort, Dalné quickly took her arm. As they walked toward the royal yacht together, Dalné murmured, "If we hadn't been who we are, we'd be carted off to detention with the others."

"What if none of them are guilty?" Leia hadn't seen the masked man again; he'd timed his getaway well.

Dalné's scowl creased her thick makeup. "One of them will be, before the local legal officer is through. They'll want blood for this, and they won't dare report to their superiors that they couldn't solve the terrorist murder of a provincial governor. A moff." She shook her head as if in wonder. "Someone must have known Naboo and Onoam well, to have thought this out so well. There are few other places where a moff would be so unguarded."

Another pang of fear wrenched Leia's heart. Her father had mentioned visiting Naboo several times; apparently he'd had friends here in the days of the Clone Wars. Although he'd never gone into any detail about his time on Naboo, he could feasibly have traveled to Onoam. He might know this area well.

Bail Organa could have been in league with whoever planned this attack.

He didn't set it up for sure—he knew I was coming here—but he didn't remember what planet Onoam orbited. Maybe he only knew the attack would be on one of Naboo's moons—

Dalné, apparently unaware of Leia's disquiet, kept

talking. "Soon they'll put this entire system on lockdown. Your royal status will protect you from arrest, but they could still hold you here."

"We'll leave immediately," Leia promised. The winds had calmed, and the high grasses around them seemed like impenetrable walls of green, the pathway through a maze she hadn't known they were in. "But you—"

"Yes?"

"If—if they're going to lock the planet down for a while—that means no other Imperial authority will be able to seize control very soon. For a few days, or even weeks, maybe the queen of Naboo can be a true queen again. You might have the power to help the miners after all."

Almost as soon as Leia had spoken the words, she realized how risky that direction would be for Dalné. Even a temporary assertion of power by an individual planet might be seen as insurrection. The smoldering building on the horizon had shown her how dangerous, even vicious, a revolution against the Emperor would be, but she needed no such example to demonstrate how cruel the Empire was. She knew that as well as every other citizen of the galaxy.

Dalné had to know it too. Yet instead of refusing or pretending not to hear, she lifted her chin. "Maybe there's a chance," she said to Leia. "It's worth trying, at least for the miners' sake."

Leia took her new friend's hand. "You'll always have an ally on Alderaan."

"And you'll always have one here."

•◆•

The return home was tense. For the first time in her life, she dreaded a reunion with her parents. She had to ask them more hard questions, harder than ever before, and this time, she wouldn't be put off by talk about how she needed to be wiser or more responsible or a corpse halfway in the grave before she'd earned the right to hear the truth. If Leia had nearly lost her life because of her parents' work—if they had murdered Moff Quarsh Panaka—then she needed to know that.

What if they did? whispered a traitorous voice in her mind. *What are you going to do?*

She could never report her parents. Never. That was impossible.

But she couldn't go on as she had before, either. Not if they were guilty.

"Thank the Force you're alive," Ress Batten said as they disembarked in the Aldera spaceport. "If I'd had to come back and report to your mother that you'd been killed on our watch, I'd have been reprimanded for sure." Then she caught herself. "What I mean is that I would've been distraught with grief."

"It's all fine," Leia said absently. The buzz of the busy spaceport around her might as well have been mere holograms, flickering and insubstantial, visions of someplace much farther away. "Thanks for everything."

Batten frowned. "Your Highness, are you sure you're all right? I could take you to a hospital, or find the nearest medical droid—"

"No, really, it's nothing. I just need some rest." With effort, she smiled for the pilot. Batten didn't look convinced, but contented herself with dropping her off at the palace.

When Leia walked into the private area of the palace, the only one waiting for her was WA-2V, who flung her metal arms open wide. "Your Highness! It's amazing!"

"I was amazed, I guess, though that's not how I'd word it. . . ."

"Yes, it's dirty, but this is by far the most beautiful gown you've ever worn!" 2V wheeled up to her, reaching out skinny metallic fingers to touch one of the pale pink veils on the cape. "Of course anyone who knows anything about fashion knows that Naboo is *the* place for formalwear, but I hardly thought you'd pick up so much so quickly!"

Her grooming droid's single-minded dedication to hairstyles and clothing usually amused Leia. Today, it took all her self-control not to snap at 2V. *It's her programming.*

She didn't get to choose her programming. "Sorry, TooVee. I borrowed this from Queen Dalné. We need to have the gown cleaned and returned to her."

2V's joints went slack in disappointment. "Oh. Oh well. At least we have a wonderful example to draw from, don't you think?"

"Sure, fine. Where are my parents?"

"The queen and her viceroy are in the library, but really you should let me tidy you up before you present yourself to them. Though maybe it's worth letting them see the dress! Then they might approve a shopping expedition back to Naboo."

"Let's not ask them about that yet." By which she meant, *not ever.* Leia felt as though she'd prefer never to be near the Naboo system again.

She managed to send her droid off to lay out comfortable nightclothes and fold down the coverlets, though she felt certain she wouldn't be going to bed for hours yet. Evening had fallen, and exhaustion made every muscle of Leia's body ache—but it was impossible for her to rest until she had talked with her parents.

Leia approached the library more slowly as she saw that one of the tall bronze doors remained open, and heard her parents talking to each other in pitched tones that betrayed their terror, or anger, or both.

"—a stand, immediately," said her father, who paced

back and forth along the wooden floor. "Otherwise, soon there will be no controlling the partisans, and no telling how far they might go."

Her mother spoke in the tone that Leia recognized as the one for delivering harsh news. "Saw's judgment is faulty, but it's time to ask ourselves how far—Leia!"

They both wheeled around to see her as she stepped through the door. Firelight flickered through the great hall of the library, very nearly the only light in the room, but Leia could tell how stricken her mother looked. Her father, however, looked . . . angry.

Furious.

Her mother spoke first. "Are you all right?"

"I'm not injured much," Leia answered. That wasn't the same as *yes*, and both her parents would know it.

Breha came toward her daughter, hand outstretched, the hem of her deep red robe whispering as it brushed along the floor. Yet she stopped a few paces short of Leia, her expression unreadable. When she spoke again, her words were low and even, the way they'd been when Leia had fallen as a child and scraped her knee. "Sweetheart, is there a particular reason you chose to go to the Naboo system? Were you interested in that world because of something you haven't wanted to share? You can tell us."

After everything that had happened, how was *that* her mother's first question? "You two said I couldn't go to a planet that would be politically sensitive. I figured the Emperor's homeworld was about as far from that as I could get, especially since I was only on one of the moons. It's not like I knew someone was going to assassinate a moff." When her mother flinched, Leia feared she had her answer. "Did you?"

"What?" Bail snapped.

Leia squared her shoulders. "Did you know what was going to happen to Moff Panaka?"

Breha's hand covered her mouth, and for once the queen of Alderaan had no words. It was Bail—the more even-tempered of the two, usually—who retorted, "You think we'd stoop to assassination? Leia, what's gotten into you?"

"How am I supposed to know differently? You won't tell me what you're up to, which means I have to guess."

For one of the only times Leia could remember, Bail raised his voice to her. "So you guessed we'd become *murderers*?"

"You're planning on attacking the Empire!" she shouted back. "Sooner or later, that means killing people!"

"Exactly." Breha said it calmly, looking only at her husband. Jolted, Leia took a step backward; if her mother noticed, she showed no sign.

Bail shook his head. "I can't talk about this any longer right now. I have to—to rest, to think."

"That would be best." Breha brushed her hand along his shoulder, and it was as if she'd infused him with a new source of calm.

Still, he walked toward the door, pausing by Leia's side only long enough to say, "We're relieved to know you weren't hurt. We love you."

"I love you too." It came out in a small voice. Leia felt as though there were another presence in the room with them—the unknown, or maybe the future. Something bigger and darker than any of them.

Once her father had left, Leia turned back to her mother, who said, "Let's walk in the gardens."

"We have to talk about this."

"The gardens are as good a place to talk as any. Besides, I want to give your father some privacy."

The palace offered more than enough privacy for a hundred people, but Leia understood what her mother meant. Her parents needed to feel the separation between each other for a short while.

The palace gardens, like the palace itself, had been the work of centuries. Richly designed beds of flowers and ferns painted patterns through the large central courtyard. Sculptures in pure white marble or shining metal nestled within arrangements of ivy meant to serve as frames. Leia found the gardens most beautiful in wintertime, when snowfall made the intricate designs look like a blanket of lace. Yet late spring could be lovely too, as it was now; the night-blooming candlewick flowers had opened to reveal their luminescent petals in pale orange and gold.

When she was a small child, Leia had believed that the soft glow within her mother's chest was a bouquet of candlewicks in her heart. By now she understood the working of her mother's pulmonodes and had met many other people with mechanized organ replacements—but the affection she felt for candlewick flowers had never faded. To her, they would always suggest magic, and love.

Breha took a seat on one of the polished stone benches. Although Leia knew she could sit too, she didn't. She wanted to remain on her feet a while longer. Her mother began, "The report we received from Lieutenant Batten indicated that you met personally with Governor Panaka. Is that true?"

"Yes. I'm probably the last person he ever spoke to."

"Tell me what passed between you."

Leia's frustration threatened to burst forth again. "I don't think what I said to the governor matters as much as the fact that someone murdered him, and—"

"No, Leia." It was not a gentle mother who spoke now; it was the queen, whose word was law. "I know we've tested your faith in us, but you must trust me tonight. It's vitally important that you tell me precisely what you and Panaka discussed. Leave out no details. I have to understand what happened before we can proceed."

It made no sense . . . and yet still Leia trusted her. So she told her mother about the miners, about Queen Dalné, about their decision to visit the chalet, even about the process of picking out a dress to wear. When Leia mentioned Panaka's strange surprise upon seeing her, Breha tensed, but said nothing. By the end of the story, her mother was trembling so much that Leia had to force herself to look at the candlewick blooms instead. Otherwise she wasn't sure she could've kept talking.

"He said he would let Palpatine know that my parents had adopted an—outstanding daughter, or distinguished—something complimentary, I don't remember what. We said goodbye, Dalné and I started down the steps, and that's when the explosion happened."

"How much time elapsed from the time you parted to the time he died?"

"Not long at all. If we'd said another two or three sentences to each other, I would still have been in the chalet when it blew up." Leia finally turned back to her mother. Breha Organa looked as though she had aged years in a minute. One hand was pressed to her chest, where her pulmonodes faintly glowed between her fingers, and the other clutched a fistful of silk from the skirt of her robe.

Her skin, normally golden, had gone ashen. Alarmed, Leia came closer. "Are you going to faint?"

"I don't think so." Her mother shut her eyes and took a deep breath. "We came so close to utter destruction."

"I came closer than you did." Leia folded her arms across her chest. Her dress still smelled like smoke.

"Oh, sweetheart, I didn't mean it that way. You were the one in the greatest danger, more than you could've known." Rising to her feet, Breha swept her daughter into her arms. "But if anything were ever to happen to you—I can't even say it. Your father and I would gladly have taken that risk in your stead. You know that, don't you?"

Although Leia was moved, she resisted the urge to hug her mother back. "You haven't answered my question. Did you two have anything to do with this?"

The pause that followed lasted long enough that she thought at first their conversation was over, that she would simply be put off again. But finally Breha said, "We didn't know this would happen, no. We wouldn't have condoned it if we had known. Quarsh Panaka was by far the highest-ranking Imperial official we had any hopes of contacting someday, perhaps even working with. It would have been a risk—maybe one we'd never have taken. Panaka's loyalty to Palpatine was great. Still, he was as good a man as anyone in the Emperor's inner circle could ever be, and much better than most. Panaka was . . . an option I wish had been left open to us."

"I saw that in him too. But if you wanted to talk to Panaka, then why—"

"That was the work of an associate," Breha began, then shook her head as she gestured for Leia to sit beside her this time. "No. You deserve some measure of the truth. The bombing was the work of a group that calls themselves the partisans, led by a man named Saw Gerrera. He's a brave man, an intelligent fighter . . . but his methods are becoming more violent, more extreme. Saw's alienating some of the people your father and I most need on our side. I don't know how we're ever going to resolve it. You can be sure I intend to tell him how close he came to killing our daughter. If that won't shock him into reconsidering his ways, nothing will."

Leia was being treated as an adult and wanted to reply like one. She weighed her next words carefully. "You say you don't approve of his methods. But when I asked about violence before, you said 'exactly.' What did you mean?"

It was her mother's turn to think over her answer. "I'm a daughter of Alderaan. My mother raised me to cherish peace, as I am trying to raise you. I'm no warmonger. Yet I am also no fool, and only a fool would believe that Palpatine's rule could be ended without violence. When he learns of an organized rebellion—as someday he must, if we're ever to accomplish more than whispering in back rooms—he'll demand our blood. If we aren't ready to fight back, we'll be doomed."

Leia felt as though she ought to argue with this, or as though she ought to *want* to argue. Yet as intimidating as her mother's words were, she knew the fundamental point was true. "Why was Dad so upset when you mentioned it?"

"He hasn't yet fully accepted that any successful rebellion will have to be on such a large scale. After what he lived through in the Clone Wars, that's understandable. Those battles scarred the galaxy for a generation, and no doubt that's why so many people are reluctant to take on such a fight again. But others have begun to see that truth."

"Like you."

"Like me, and a few of our friends, and no, I'm not telling you who. Even revealing Saw's identity was more information than I should've given you." Her mother brushed a loose strand of Leia's hair back from her forehead. "Let's just say that we have a great deal of negotiation ahead, with many parties, representing many points of view."

Leia would've thought any movement against Palpatine would be united by the pure goodness of its purpose. Instead, through her mother's words, she glimpsed a larger, more complicated alliance, one in which the parties shared a goal but agreed on very little else. "Aren't they all on the same side?"

"In the most important sense, yes. But there's no one path. When it comes to the morality of what we may have to do . . . we have to find our way through many shadows."

"Together," Leia said, meaning to complete her mother's sentence.

Breha's smile was crooked. "We have to hope so."

CHAPTER 14

When Leia went to bed that night, exhausted and scrubbed clean, she felt as if everything had been put right between her and her mother—maybe even better than before, since Breha had finally begun to reveal some details of her parents' shadowy alliance against Palpatine. They could trust each other again. Her father hadn't reached out to her after storming from the library, but she felt sure they'd speak again in the morning, when he'd have calmed down. Yet as she lay under the silk coverlets, despite all her weariness, she couldn't go to sleep. She wanted answers for the moral questions her mother had raised, but they were hard to find.

Quarsh Panaka was a decent man who served the Empire out of personal loyalty rather than ambition. Murdering him and others in his household—how can that have been the right thing to do?

Mom's right, though. Palpatine won't surrender power unless he's forced out. If the Imperial Senate hasn't been able to hold the Empire in check by now, they never will.

That last thought shocked her; it was a truth she hadn't realized she knew. Her father and his allies in the

Senate worked tirelessly to ameliorate the greatest evils of Imperial rule. He and his closest political ally, Mon Mothma of Chandrila, had managed to moderate punishments levied on individuals or even entire star systems. With the help of the other Chandrilan senator, Winmey Lenz, and Senator Pamlo of Taris, they had turned down motions to punish Imperial crimes through slavery. Leia herself had helped him draft legislation that had outlawed conscription of stormtroopers, in response to rumors that some of the admirals were campaigning for such a move.

They had done so much, but it wasn't enough.

She told herself, *You can't be afraid to get your hands dirty.*

But this wasn't dirt. This was blood.

•◆•

The sunlight streaming through her window the next morning told her breakfast would be served on the south terrace. Simple a pleasure as that was, she needed a reason to be cheerful, at least for an hour.

Their south terrace looked out over the River Wuitho, and the smaller villages on the outskirts of Aldera. More candlewick flower vines had wrapped themselves around the terrace's carved rails, although by morning they'd closed up into tight little buds. A flock of thranta swooped through the sky, their gray wings flapping distantly overhead. Leia brightened when she saw the table spread out with cheeses, rolls, and sweet green juice—and when she saw that her father had lingered with his breakfast. Usually he and her mother were working by the time she rose, but maybe he'd waited just to talk to her.

"Good morning." She smiled brightly at him, but stiffened as he looked up at her, stone-faced. "I, ah, I guess you don't have a busy day today?"

"All my days are busy, now." His tone was solemn, not angry, but somehow that made her more uneasy. "You and I should talk about your future humanitarian missions."

"I should probably discuss them with both you and Mom in advance."

Bail raised an eyebrow. "You're only now coming to this conclusion?"

Putting her hands on her hips, Leia retorted, "It's not like you two are easy to catch up with. You never have time for me anymore."

She'd expected him to be shamed by this, sure he would feel guilty when confronted, but instead her father said, "No, we usually don't. Now that you understand the true reasons why, I'd expect you to be more forgiving of that."

"I am! It's just—I've become used to doing more things on my own."

His tone gentled somewhat. "That's only natural. But the potential cost of another mistake is too high. We have to eliminate even the slightest chance that you'll be in harm's way. I've put together a list of approved worlds from which you can choose your future missions. All of them have pressing needs that make them worthy recipients of whatever aid you can give."

Leia told herself it should make no difference whether or not she chose her own missions of mercy, as long as the world in question needed help. Yet she felt crushed. Her Challenge of the Heart was meant to be a step toward adulthood. Instead, it was being laid out for her like she was still a child. "What if I choose my own missions, but I absolutely make sure to run it by you and Mom in advance, every time?"

Bail's expression again became forbidding as he set a datacube in front of her, tapping the screen to display the planets he'd selected, her newly limited cosmology. To her he seemed so distant he might as well have been on one of those faraway worlds. "The list is final, Leia. We won't discuss this again."

With that he set down his cup and walked off the terrace, leaving her to begin her day alone.

•◆•

Her mood remained dark even days later, as the *Tantive IV* swooped into the soupy green atmosphere of Chal Hudda for her to begin her first paternally sanctioned mission of mercy. This planet might need her help as much as any other, but it would be easier for her to *act* charitably than to *feel* that way.

Chal Hudda was an Outer Rim world of interest to virtually no one. Its marshy surface made landings difficult for all but the lightest spacecraft, and its natural resources held use for almost no life-forms except the ones who had evolved there. It was a stubbornly independent, self-sustaining society—or it had been until recently, when a fearful disease had begun to affect the Chalhuddans' young. The sickness incapacitated adults for a short time, but the children often died. Reports indicated that the disease had reached epidemic proportions, and Chal Hudda's relative poverty meant they could import very little medical treatment.

The vaccines Leia had brought would inoculate nearly half a million Chalhuddan young, and yet fit into a set of cases that wouldn't even have filled her bedroom at home. She'd had to bring the *Tantive IV* instead of the yacht, however, because only a ship that large could carry the landing craft.

She walked into the launching bay in her pale blue all-clime suit, fastening the high neck as she headed toward Captain Antilles. It took her a moment to recognize him in his own all-clime, formfitting and slightly shiny, instead of his usual uniform. "Are we ready, Captain?"

"Ready to launch on your word, Your Highness. If

you'll join me?" He gestured to one of the bubble-shaped landing craft, and she hopped in. They took with them only two other crewmembers and a protocol droid. As Captain Antilles took his seat next to her, the transparent plasma door shimmered back into being. Ress Batten's voice came over the speakers: *"Ready to launch on five, four, three—"*

The landing bay doors slid open, allowing milky green fog to swirl inside.

"Two, one."

Antilles hit the controls, sending the bubble forward through the doors—and then plummeting downward. Leia sucked in an involuntary breath as she saw the water beneath rushing toward them, until they plunged below the surface. As the last sunlight from above faded into the gloom, the captain hit the searchlights and sent them forward.

"How does anyone live in this?" she muttered. An ocean world was one thing—but this muck was too opaque to even be called a swamp.

"Different worlds for different lives," Antilles said cheerfully. It was an old aphorism, one she'd rarely found so difficult to believe.

Their craft slipped into a grotto, then surfaced into one of the underground pockets of air in which the

Chalhuddans lived. Leia had seen members of this species before—they did travel and trade, however sparingly—but was still caught off by the sheer size of them. Chalhuddans stood nearly as tall as a dewback, with shimmery olive-toned skin, two tall hornlike protrusions on either side of their heads, and black manes that were neither tentacles nor fur but somehow in between the two.

The protocol droid, designated C-3PO, piped up, "In case you were unaware, Your Highness, Chalhuddans have five different genders and shift through them throughout their lives. Their native pronoun cases are rather complex—indicating not only current gender but two or three previous ones, and occasionally the gender they feel most likely to be next, but as our language has no equivalent words, 'you' or 'they' can be used in all cases."

Leia didn't think she'd be needing that many pronouns, but protocol droids never knew when to stop—this one in particular. "Thank you, See-Threepio."

This mission promised to be brief, very nearly rote. She would drop off the vaccines, accept the Chalhuddans' thanks, and leave. The next session of the Apprentice Legislature would begin soon, and she was eager to return to Coruscant. Partly this was because it would be good to get back to work, but she was also looking forward to seeing her friends again—Kier most of all.

This won't even take five minutes, she thought as they drifted to the disembarkation point. *If my father has to pick out my missions, at least he chose quick and easy ones.*

Or so she thought, until five minutes later, when she stood in front of the Chalhuddan leader and repeated, "You *refuse* to accept the vaccines?"

"We refuse your pity. We refuse your condescension." Their leader, Occo Quentto, puffed out the air sac under their lower lip, rendering them even more intimidating. "Always, we have supported ourselves, and we always shall."

"This—this isn't some kind of threat to your independence." Leia had never imagined such a response, and struggled to even come up with words. "It's not intended as condescension—"

"Of course not!" bellowed Occo Quentto. "You dry ones think yourselves so high above us that you never ask what *we* would think of *you*. You speak falsely, with elaborate words that mean nothing, instead of dealing with us as honest beings. We do not trust you, we do not like you, we do not want you. Go away."

Occo Quentto began to waddle off their high dais to approving croaks from the other Chalhuddans, leaving Leia standing there with her mouth agape. She looked over to Captain Antilles, who shrugged.

Think of something! She called, "Occo Quentto! Please, hear me out."

They kept waddling. "I have heard you. You think we have no strength. You think we have no pride."

That did it. Leia shouted, "To hell with pride!"

The Chalhuddans fell silent as one. Occo Quentto shuffled around to face Leia again, protruding eyes staring at her in what was probably indignation.

Leia was past caring. She was too angry for diplomacy, so angry she shook. "This disease is killing your children! If that were happening on my planet, and the only way to save them was to swallow my pride, I'd do it. I'd go down on my knees in the dirt. I would beg or plead or do *anything* to preserve the lives of my people. If you wouldn't do the same, you don't deserve to be a leader."

Her last words echoed in the grotto for what seemed like a very long time. The Chalhuddans stared at her; so did Captain Antilles. In a low voice, C-3PO said, "Oh, dear, this isn't going well at all."

Leia wondered if she ought to regret what she'd said, but she didn't. She was *right.*

Then Occo Quentto nodded. "At last one of them speaks their mind." A few other Chalhuddans croaked their assent. "You are still arrogant, but at least you are honest. So few dry ones are."

Leia decided to let the epithet *dry one* go. "Does that mean you'll take the vaccines?"

Occo Quentto stood still and silent for so long that Leia went past worrying they would say no to wondering if they'd gone into some kind of trance. Finally, however, Occo Quentto said, "On one condition."

"Name it."

"You must ask a favor of us in return. You cannot come to us as a wealthy savior. You must come to us as an equal. That means you must owe us a debt equal to the one we will owe to you."

What am I supposed to ask for? Swamp water? But Leia thought fast. "I, ah, wouldn't want to call on you for a favor undeserving of your generosity, Occo Quentto. May I claim this favor at some point in the future? When I have a worthy task, I'll ask you." She folded her arms and looked as stern as she could manage. "And when I do? I'll expect you to come through."

Occo Quentto blew a huge bubble, which floated in the air. C-3PO leaned forward. "Your Highness, that is the way in which Chalhuddans laugh."

She began to be able to read the expressions on Occo Quentto's face, and this one was very close to a smile. "We are willing to be in your debt, as long as it is not for too long."

"Is that a yes?" Leia said. And this time, she knew the smile for sure.

•◆•

A few days later, as she hurried along one of the skyways of Coruscant, Leia was still rehearsing the story in her mind. Which detail would be most likely to make Kier laugh?

Nearby, a shimmering electronic screen showed the Emperor's face as various patriotic slogans slithered along the bottom. The image of Sheev Palpatine had to be decades old. She'd never been in the Emperor's presence personally, but she'd heard the whispers about his ghastly appearance and bleached-white skin. The man seen on the screens, however, looked like any other middle-aged man, smiling pleasantly. She thought it might be the same images they'd used for the past two decades, but with occasional digital editing to update his clothing to more current styles. Everyone had to know the images were fake—humans showed the marks of greater age within twenty years—but nobody ever said so out loud

We live so many lies, Leia thought. *Maybe Occo Quentto had a point about "dry ones" never telling the truth.*

When she entered the antechamber of the Apprentice Legislature, she brightened to see Kier already chatting with a few of their peers, especially when he caught sight of her and immediately excused himself to walk in her direction. Leia would've started toward him, too, if Amilyn Holdo hadn't appeared in front of her, wearing green hair, glittery metallic pompons on her many ponytails, and a tragic expression on her face.

"It's a time of great mourning," Amilyn said, taking Leia's hands. "I know you grieve even as I do."

"Did someone die?" Leia hurriedly glanced around the room. Nobody seemed to be missing.

"Leia." Kier's voice was pitched just above a whisper. "I tried to reach you earlier today. I wanted to tell you the news personally, when we weren't in public."

A knot had formed in Leia's stomach. "Tell me what?"

Amilyn said, "The Apprentice Legislature received a special commendation for recommending Arreyel for the new academy."

Leia frowned. How was that bad news?

Kier put one hand on her elbow. "The first engineers who scouted the site found a radiation source well beneath the surface—shielded by rock, but that rock's about to be blasted away so Arreyel can power massive new factories for the Empire. As in, planet-wide factories."

"They're giving the populace six weeks to evacuate," Amilyn added. She no longer looked ridiculous. "No compensation."

Kier's dark eyes narrowed in anger. "Apparently Grand Moff Tarkin informed them that they were lucky not to be fined for concealing this from the Empire all along."

The horror Leia felt didn't cloud her thinking. If anything, she saw more clearly. "It was a trap," she whispered. "They suspected the power source. They knew we'd wind up picking Arreyel for the school. Then they'd be able to use that excuse to run the intensive scans they needed to confirm what was under the surface."

"Probably," Kier said. "Leia, don't be upset. It's not your fault."

"It's so not your fault, nobody else would *ever* blame you," Amilyn added. "But you will, because that's how you are."

"I'm not upset," Leia said, and it was true. Instead she was furious. She'd been tricked into doing the Empire's dirty work for them.

Silently she swore, *Never again.*

CHAPTER 15

By all official metrics, Leia's first session of the Apprentice Legislature achieved all of its goals. They were commended for their successes . . . including the identification of Arreyel as a planet of "extraordinary interest."

But to her, the days slipped by in a kind of haze. She reviewed their informational packets over and over again, yet remained indecisive, desperately looking for more loopholes and traps that might not even exist. The others went on some of Chassellon's nightlife excursions, even coming to the Organas' apartments to try to drag Leia along with them, but she always turned the invitations down. It felt wrong to go out and celebrate when she was responsible for the undoing of an entire world.

When she stayed in, Kier Domadi often stayed with her. The first time he lingered behind after everyone else left, she had wanted to be alone so badly that she'd nearly thrown him out. She tried the tactful approach first. "I'm not doing anything but watching a holovid."

"Sounds good."

"You don't even know which holovid."

He gave her a look. "It's going to be something that lets you turn your brain off for a while, right?"

". . . yes."

"Sounds perfect."

Kier had the rare quality of knowing when someone wanted to be quiet, and the even rarer one of accepting that silence. Leia soon felt comfortable with him—and soon after that, truly relaxed. They slipped into the habit of spending time together not as any sort of special occasion, but more as though they'd always belonged in each other's daily lives. Some sons of various Elder Houses had tried to charm her in the past, thinking of a princess only as a prize to claim, the ultimate conquest to brag about; Kier took her measure as an individual and asked for nothing more but to know her.

So far. Leia was vividly aware of the weight of unspoken words between them, of the way they silently negotiated sitting closer to each other. But Kier never pushed. Although she'd told him nothing of her fears for her parents, her uncertainty about their plans, he seemed to sense that she was working through something confusing and difficult, something she had to figure out on her own.

But he did try to help when he saw she was in pain.

"It's not your fault," Kier told her more than once, usually under his breath as they sat together in their legislatorial pod. "They set us all up to support Arreyel. One of us would've taken the bait. It could've been anybody."

"It could've been. But it was me," she would whisper back.

Leia went out only once, for Harp Allor's seventeenth birthday party. Harp's senator, Winmey Lenz, had personally reserved the venue as a gift—which was how they all wound up in a water park entirely enclosed in an energy-field bubble a hundred meters above the tallest Coruscant skyscrapers. Only a few short months before, Leia would've reveled in the chance to slalom through an invisible spiral in the sky, splashing water on her friends, but the entire day, she felt as though she was going through every action, every sentence as mechanically as a droid.

Even Kier's company only helped so much. Bail Organa's travels remained mysterious—in particulars if not in purpose—and so when Kier was back on Alderaan, Leia was usually left alone. But she never felt as lonely as when her father was in their Coruscant apartment. Apparently he had yet to forgive her for her trip to Onoam, because for reasons he'd never explain, going to the Naboo system seemed to be the worst, most heinous thing anybody had ever done.

Leia sometimes stopped herself there. She wasn't too grown-up to sulk, but she'd matured enough to realize when she was doing it. Probably she was overreacting to her father's moods. Still, the bigger overreaction was his, and she knew it.

Her sour temper returned to Alderaan with her. On her first night back, she couldn't hide herself away in the library or travel to the Istabith Falls to refresh her soul; no, she had to submit to WA-2V's ministrations to make her a glamorous princess again, so she could be shown off.

"Another dinner party," she groused as 2V slid a soft blue wrap around the shoulders of her white gown. "How many has my mom thrown this year? A dozen? Twenty?"

"Fourteen. Now, hold still. These are the old-fashioned pins that can still stick you." 2V adroitly fastened the wrap in place with two jeweled brooches, one at each shoulder. They sparkled prettily, but Leia couldn't have cared less. "I think two side buns tonight. Do you agree, Your Highness?"

"Whatever."

2V tilted her torso forward to study her charge, perhaps thinking such insensitivity to fashion was evidence of an imminent collapse. Leia simply sat down at the vanity to let the droid do her work. As she stared at her reflection in the mirror, she remembered how, as a little girl, she used to look for proof that she resembled her parents in some way. Although Leia had always known herself to be adopted, had realized any shared traits would be only a coincidence, she had still hoped to see a little of her mother's wisdom and beauty, or some of the kindness she had once found so easily in her father's eyes.

Now it's like I hardly know them, she thought as 2V began refashioning her messy topknot into an actual hairstyle. *They're braver than I thought, but maybe more dangerous than I thought, and somehow they still want to throw their idiot banquets—*

Wait.

I'm the one being an idiot.

Leia didn't attend the banquets themselves, since she wasn't yet invested as heir, but she always put in an appearance at the receptions beforehand. That meant she knew who the guests usually were: Mon Mothma and Winmey Lenz of Chandrila. Pamlo of Taris. Vaspar of the Taldot sector . . .

Every single one of them was a senator or planetary leader known to oppose Palpatine's harshest policies.

Leia's dark eyes widened. These weren't banquets. They were *strategy sessions.*

"I don't believe it," she whispered.

"I know," 2V said, leaning back to admire her work. "You're almost beautiful!"

We have got *to disconnect that droid's honesty routine,* Leia thought.

Invigorated and curious, she hurried down to the reception. While official functions demanded larger, grander rooms, these more informal gatherings usually began on the western terrace. Leia walked through the wide doors to see a handful of guests already chatting to one another with glasses of teal-blue Toniray in their hands. Kitonak musicians in the corner played a soft melody, and in the distance, the city lights of Aldera glittered brightly against the first darkening of sunset. Her mother was deep in conversation with Senator Pamlo and Cinderon Malpe of Derella; her father had yet to appear, which was odd. Or maybe he was having a private conversation in the library with another guest, about Crait or Saw Gerrera or any of the other things Leia wasn't supposed to know about. Maybe she'd have the chance to soak up a little information tonight.

"Princess Leia." Mon Mothma, the senior senator from Chandrila, came up to her, smiling pleasantly. She wore the usual white robes of her planet, complete with her silver chain of office. "It's good to see you again."

"You too, Senator Mothma."

"Please. Call me Mon. You're very nearly a grown woman, now." When most adults said things like that, they came across as skin-crawlingly superior. From Mon Mothma, the sentiment sounded sincere. "Soon to be invested as heir to the throne."

"If I fulfill my challenges." Leia carefully used no term of address at all. As much as she liked being asked to call this powerful woman by her first name, she couldn't bring herself to do it yet. "I'm not sure how well that's going."

"Which one has turned out to be most difficult?" Mon Mothma asked.

"The challenge of the mind, I guess." Pathfinding was tough, but she'd managed well enough so far; her mercy missions had proved to be overly complicated, but for reasons Leia didn't think were her fault. "After interning for my father in the Imperial Senate, I thought the Apprentice Legislature would be easy. Instead it's turned out to be . . . let's say, slippery."

Mon Mothma frowned and nodded, the same way she would if discussing topics with adult senators. "Go on?"

Leia hadn't shared this with her parents yet. After the last few blow-ups they'd had, she hadn't wanted to show them another of her mistakes. She wasn't used to not confiding in them. So it was a relief to tell the story of what had happened with Arreyel.

Even better was the way Mon Mothma responded. "Try not to be discouraged," she told Leia. "Officials with decades of experience have fallen into similar traps. Palpatine knows how to bait his hooks."

The fact that this was being said so openly was proof that Leia's theory about the banquets was right; only in a group of assured allies would anyone be so openly critical of the Emperor. "You think Palpatine himself was behind it?"

"Probably not. But he's taught his moffs and admirals to follow his example. I've been tripped up by his machinations before. It's been a while since the last time he caught me, but I never let down my guard. That's the most any of us can do."

Leia felt a surge of hope. Mon Mothma, at least, could speak to her as an adult, and trusted her with her real opinions about the Imperial hierarchy. If one of their allies came to believe Leia could play a meaningful role in their efforts against the Emperor, maybe that would convince her parents.

"Forgive me, everyone," said Bail Organa as he strode out onto the terrace. Instantly the musicians played more softly to allow the viceroy to greet his guests. "Am I the last to arrive?"

"I think that's me," said Kier.

Leia blinked in surprise. Kier Domadi—who so far as she knew had never met her mother and only encountered her father at the apartments a couple of times, and briefly—had just walked through the wide doors. Although he must've felt out of place in the palace, he didn't look it; not only did he wear a fashionable pale-gray jacket and dark trousers, but he held himself well and spoke with assurance.

"Mr. Domadi." Breha swept to Kier's side, holding out her arm in a way that made it clear he was to offer his. When he did, she led him toward Leia. "Thank you so much for accepting our invitation, particularly on such short notice."

"It's an honor to be asked, Your Majesty." The only sign that Kier wasn't totally at ease was the way his dark eyes kept glancing down at his queen's hand on his forearm.

"Hi, Kier." Leia would've felt like her smile gave away too much, if it weren't for the fact that his presence made it obvious her parents already knew as much as she did. "Mom, what's this about?"

Breha shrugged, then readjusted the folds of her silvery shawl. "I know it's lonely for you sometimes while we're having our banquets. Tonight, I thought you might enjoy some company. We've ordered a wonderful supper for you both; the droids will set up a table for you right here."

Leia was torn. On the one hand, dining all alone with Kier, in front of this spectacular view—she'd had daydreams very close to this. But she'd begun forming other plans for the night, ones that felt even more urgent.

Behind her, she heard her father greeting Mon Mothma. "Was Senator Lenz not able to make it?"

"Winmey sends his regrets," Mon Mothma said. "But of course I'll meet with him upon my return."

To talk to him about a dinner party? I doubt it.

It occurred to Leia that her mother might not have invited Kier only as a kindness to her daughter. She might've intended to distract Leia from what was really going on.

If so, this was the first time Leia had gotten one step ahead of the queen.

•◆•

When the banquet began, and the other guests departed along with the musicians, Leia and Kier were left all alone except for the servitor droids who swiftly brought their dinner. Although Leia took her seat and ate and drank at the appropriate moments, her mind raced toward the banquet room and what might be happening there.

It was a measure of her curiosity that even Kier Domadi couldn't hold her attention completely.

"So you never get to attend the banquets?" he said, carefully sipping the nectar in his dark red glass. "Even though you're a princess?"

"Princesses don't get everything, you know."

Leia intended it only as a joke, and was surprised when he ducked his head as if in apology. "I know that. I realize—when we met, I might've come across—"

"Kier. It's okay. I *am* ridiculously privileged. But my family and I try to use our privileges to benefit others even more than ourselves." That was a rote answer, the kind of diplomatic response her father might give. Never before had that reply seemed inadequate to her. It was such a thin sliver of the truth.

Her parents were doing more for the galaxy than anyone else could dream. More, even, than they should?

"I believe in the royal house of Alderaan," Kier said sincerely. His eyes met hers with his usual uncanny intensity, as if catching the light of the candledroids floating overhead. "We've been served well by our monarchy for a hundred generations. That's more than most planets can say, and a hell of a lot more than the galaxy at large could ever claim."

That was the second time today she'd heard someone freely criticize Palpatine without looking around to make sure nobody was listening. Kier's courage struck her even more powerfully than Mon Mothma's had. Leia lifted her chin. "You don't believe in the Empire."

"Who does, besides his brainwashed cannon fodder? Palpatine's rule is a—a mockery of what government should be. Corruption is everywhere, and they don't even bother hiding it. His cruelty is known to everybody, but the only ones who admit it are the ones loathsome enough to praise him for it. I know the Republic had its problems, but compared to this, they were nothing." Kier leaned back in his chair, turning his gaze toward the russet-red horizon. The first stars had become visible in the darkening sky above. "Every day I thank the Force I was born on

Alderaan. At least I can be loyal to my planet and its rulers. At least I know our happiness and safety isn't bought with other people's misery. We're free here in a way almost no one else in the Empire will ever be."

A shadowy idea in Leia's mind began to take form. Even minutes ago, she'd thought this move would be too daring for tonight—that it was something she could consider later on, weeks or even months in the future. But now . . .

I trust him. He's a good person who cares about our planet and believes in my mother's rule. Maybe he cares about me, too. And Kier would always want to do the right thing.

Maybe he can help me figure out just what the right thing would be.

She took up her own goblet of nectar, mostly to have something to do with her hands. "You know," she said as casually as she could manage, "the most ancient parts of this palace are more than a thousand years old?"

Kier nodded. "I've studied the palace—even wrote a paper on it once. It's the whole history of Alderaanian architecture in one massive building." His smile turned shy. "What are my chances of a tour?"

Stay focused, Leia told herself. "The banquet hall is one of the oldest rooms of all. Back then, everything was lit with lamps and candles, and servants were all living beings instead of droids—"

"Only living servants? Sounds . . . primitive," he said, straight-faced.

In the same dry tone, Leia replied, "Somehow we endured. *Anyway*, back then, if you wanted to listen to what was being said—without being seen—you couldn't plant listening devices. They had other methods."

Kier sat up straighter, a hint of a smile playing on his face. "Your Highness, are you considering eavesdropping?"

He was eager to play a game. For one instant, she wished that was all she was inviting him to do.

The invitation she had to offer was far more precious, and far more dangerous.

Leia sat up straight and leaned across the table, willing him to understand at least part of how serious this was. "You have to make me a promise. No matter what you hear tonight, it goes no further than this palace. You never mention it to anyone but me, ever. I don't want to reveal my parents' secrets. I just want to—to share them." *So someone else will know what I know. So I don't have to carry this information alone.* "You have to *promise me* on whatever it is you hold most sacred."

Kier's entire demeanor changed. Maybe he couldn't guess what he was about to discover, but he knew this was far more than a game. Slowly he nodded. "I promise you on Alderaan itself."

"All right then." A shiver swept through Leia, and she wasn't sure if it was fear or anticipation. "Follow me."

CHAPTER 16

Several hundred years before, Alderaan's people had favored a style of architecture featuring ornately carved screens of pale stone. Sometimes these screens would be inlaid with precious gems by the rich and powerful, while the common citizen enjoyed intricate patterns carved straight through the rock. Truly fine artisans would cut spots in the stone so thin that light could shine through it, though the surface remained unbroken.

For the most part, it was this last, most finely wrought stone that lined the banquet hall of the palace. The royal family back then had conducted espionage the old-fashioned way, by eavesdropping. Their artisans had skillfully crafted the walls so that natural indentations or shadows in the stone hid tiny openings, each of which was angled to amplify sound from the room into the small passageways between these carved screens and the inner walls.

Very small passageways.

"Were humans smaller back then?" Kier whispered as they crawled along the floor. Shadows and dim light played in patterns along their bodies as they went.

"Probably." The passage wasn't as uncomfortable for Leia, but even she found it a squeeze. Then again, maybe the royals of old wanted espionage to be difficult.

They reached one of the tiny chambers large enough for someone to sit down. It was barely big enough to fit both her and Kier, and they could only manage by sitting side by side, shoulders and legs touching, their faces very close.

Leia didn't mind.

"The soup is delicious," said Cinderon Malpe. "Really, Breha, your chefs have outdone themselves."

"Why, thank you." Leia's mother spoke in her most queenly voice. "I shall be sure to share your compliments."

Kier raised an eyebrow. "Scandalous."

"Just wait, all right?" Doubt nagged at Leia for an instant. What if she was wrong about the purpose of these dinner parties? What if it was really all rich food and conversation?

No. I'm right about this. But that doesn't mean they aren't already done talking about their plans for the night.

"Do you hide down here all the time?" Kier murmured. The light filtering unevenly through the thin-carved stone painted half his face in shadow. "Storing up secrets?"

"I used to sneak around in here when I was little. Not so much anymore." The last time she'd ventured behind these screens had been about seven years prior, when her parents were dining alone a week before her Name Day. Leia had been young and self-centered enough to assume they'd probably talk about her presents. Instead, she'd heard them laughing softly and flirting . . . and she'd wound up scurrying out, red-faced, just in time to avoid a very unwelcome lesson about exactly what spouses did together in their private hours. That had been enough to keep her from ever venturing back here until this night.

"Was it lonely, growing up in the palace?"

Kier's question caught her off guard. "I don't know," she admitted. "It's not like I have much to compare it to. Sometimes I wished I had more playmates, but—it's not like I didn't have fun."

He looked up and around, clearly indicating their secret chamber. Obviously he was about to speak—but then one of the servitor droids rolled closer and they both fell silent.

"—and so I said, if that's the shortest route you can find, never mind." Senator Pamlo sighed, a touch melodramatically. "It's not like traveling around the various restrictions isn't hard enough already."

A thump on the table, and then Vaspar said, "And the situation's only gotten worse after that fiasco on the moon of Naboo."

Leia sucked in a sharp breath. She hadn't told Kier

about her trip to Onoam; she'd known her parents wouldn't want her to. But from the way he looked at her now, she knew he'd heard the news about Moff Panaka's death—and at the least understood that the situation was even more complex than the murder of a provincial governor.

"Saw Gerrera has gone too far," Senator Malpe said, his reedy voice growing louder by the word. "This isn't the way we intended to operate!"

"We have to put a stop to it," agreed Pamlo.

Breha spoke next. "Gerrera's partisans were horribly out of line. They murdered innocent people, and perhaps the closest thing to an ally we'd ever have found in the higher echelons of the Empire. But—I would ask you to consider—we cannot expect our struggle to remain bloodless forever."

"That's a slippery slope," came a voice Leia didn't recognize. "You're dangerously close to condoning an *assassination*, Your Majesty. Where do we go from here?"

"To war," said Breha.

A silence fell. Leia stole a glance at Kier, whose lips were parted in astonishment, but he was listening too raptly to notice her observation.

After a few long moments, Cinderon Malpe said, "May that day be far in the future."

"I agree wholeheartedly," Bail replied, "but we must

begin to steel ourselves. Darker days are coming, whether we act or not. If we do act, however, we can hope for a better dawn." He showed no hint of the doubts that plagued him, the arguments he'd had with his wife. Either he'd finally been convinced, or he understood the importance of presenting a united front.

"Those are considerations for the future." It was Mon Mothma who spoke next, as calm and steady as any queen. "For now, we must find a way to get Saw Gerrera's partisans in line. His use of violence is indiscriminate and premature, and therefore just as dangerous to us as it is to the servants of the Empire."

"If not more," Bail said.

"Do you hear yourselves?" It was the man whose voice Leia didn't know. "We hate the Empire's cruelty and violence. How can we claim to be morally superior when we stoop to violence ourselves?"

Mon Mothma answered him. "There comes a time when refusing to stop violence can no longer be called nonviolence. We cease to be objectors and become bystanders. At some point, morality must be wedded to action, or else it's no more than mere . . . vanity."

"If you mean—" Senator Pamlo's voice trailed off as the great doors to the banquet hall swung open.

"Esteemed gentlebeings!" announced one of the protocol droids. "We will now present a musical interlude for your enjoyment." The soft shuffle on the floor was the sound of Kitonak footsteps.

Just great, Leia thought, and knew her parents felt the same way. They'd hired living musicians for the night instead of droids. Living musicians were harder to dismiss without suspicion, which meant any rebellious talk was over for the time being, if not for the entire evening.

She and Kier shared another wordless look. Instantly understanding her, he began to crawl backward out of the passageway, and Leia followed.

They didn't speak until they were back on the terrace. The servitor droids had already cleared away the table, though one instantly rolled out with two more goblets of nectar. Leia accepted hers without even looking at it. Studying Kier's reaction was more important.

Finally he said, "How long have you known about this?"

"Not very long." Leia had chosen to trust him, but she already knew that giving him specifics would endanger him just as much as her parents and their allies. "I want to support them, but after what happened in the Naboo system . . . I don't know what to think."

"Someone has to take action against the Empire." Kier breathed out sharply and said something she hadn't anticipated: "But I wish they'd have this conversation on any other planet in the galaxy."

She frowned. "What difference would that make?"

He turned back to her and briefly touched her hand, maybe trying to soften the impact of his words. "You have to realize that your parents being involved in this puts our entire world at risk. If Emperor Palpatine ever learns about this, we could be bankrupted. Put under blockade. Younger people could be conscripted, or we could even be put in work camps. Who knows what else?"

Leia's worst fears for her parents flickered feverishly in her mind. Would they be executed publicly, graphically, as an example to other rulers? The thought made her feel seasick and weak. Almost as bad was the thought of Alderaan reduced to the devastation and desperation she'd seen on Wobani.

Yet she summoned the nerve to say, "Alderaan is a key Core World, which means we have power, money, and influence. We shouldn't hide behind those things. We should use them for the common good."

Kier considered that for a while before answering. She liked the way he thought through things carefully before he spoke. "It's not just your family 'hiding' behind Alderaan's status. It's not just people like me, either. It's millions of children, and elderly people, including countless settlers and refugees from hundreds of troubled planets. Alderaan may be the one truly safe place in the entire Empire. Protecting that place isn't cowardice, Leia. It may be the greatest gift we could ever give the galaxy."

"I have to think about that," she said. "But you do agree . . . something has to be done?"

After another pause, he nodded. "Your parents are brave, and they're strong. We'll need a lot of people like that if the Empire's ever going to fall. But the bickering around that table—I can't tell whether that's a political movement or a disaster waiting to happen."

As much as she would've liked to argue with that, she couldn't. The lack of unity among the potential rebels against the Empire was even worse than Kier could know only from what he'd overheard in the dining hall.

He continued, "What if they're being led astray? Deceived, even entrapped?"

"My father fought in the Clone Wars, Kier. He knows how to tell friend from foe. If he couldn't, he would never have survived."

Kier inclined his head, acknowledging her point. "They've got to cover their tracks. Make it possible to deny their involvement if the Empire ever learns about this. Your parents are clever enough for that, surely."

"They're clever enough."

They were. However, Leia knew that her parents were at the core of this movement; any revelation of the rebellion's existence would necessarily condemn them. Even if her parents could think of a way to conceal their involvement and protect themselves, they would scorn to do so if it meant it left their allies in jeopardy.

But telling Kier that would only worry him. Better to let him believe that some kind of safety could still exist. At least he was on their side.

Leia stepped closer to him. "You already promised never to say a word. But I need you to promise again."

"I swear on Alderaan itself," he repeated. His eyes met hers with that intensity she was coming to know so well. "Our secrets stay between us. *Always*."

She wanted to hug him in thanks—or maybe she just wanted to hug him—but then the terrace doors swung open, revealing her parents and their guests. A few paces behind them rolled more servitor droids with glasses of Toniray. If Leia hadn't felt so tense, it might have amused her, watching all of them pretending to have nothing more substantial on their minds than the beauty of the night and the sweetness of the wine.

•◆•

Leia sent 2V to get recharged so she could ready herself for bed in silence. As she sat in front of the window, absently brushing her hair, she thought about what Kier had said. Were her parents being irresponsible to risk their world? Or would it be more irresponsible not to use the power and wealth of Alderaan in the service of good?

A rap on her door made her turn. "Yes?"

Her mother stepped in, her black hair hanging loose around her shoulders with the one lock of silver tracing the side of her face. What struck Leia the most was the mischief in her mother's smile. "Well," she said. "I thought I should mention—your father and I liked Kier Domadi very much."

Someday, Leia hoped, she would be too old to blush. She wished that day would hurry up and arrive. "Oh. Um. He's—" At the last minute, she decided to try a different tack. "Thank you for asking him."

"We thought you should have some company for a change." Breha spoke so sincerely that Leia felt bad for having suspected her mother of ulterior motives. "He's intelligent, he carries himself with poise, he obviously thinks the world of you."

How do you know that exactly? Leia wanted to ask, but kept her mouth shut.

Breha concluded, "And he's very handsome, which a young man should be if at all possible. You've chosen well."

Leia wasn't sure she'd made any choices for sure yet, but something about her mother's tone distracted her. "So what's the problem?"

With a deliberately melodramatic sigh, Breha put one

hand to the front of her scarlet silk wrapper. "I suppose a tiny bit of me hoped that my daughter's first romance wouldn't be so . . . suitable. Sometimes it does a girl good to fall for a bit of a scoundrel, now and then."

An utterly novel idea occurred to Leia. "Mom—when you were young—you never—you *wouldn't*—"

"Good night, dear." Breha turned back toward the door.

"Mom?"

Her mother simply waved airily as she went out.

The question of exactly who her mom had fallen for before meeting her dad was equal parts disquieting and intriguing. Not even that could distract Leia for long. What she'd overheard tonight was far too incendiary for her to lie in bed thinking of anything else.

Mon Mothma's right. It's our responsibility to do something, *even if we still have to figure out the best steps to take. And she talked to me like I was an adult, not a little kid. If she sees that I can be trusted, maybe my parents will see that too.*

As Leia balled her pillow beneath her head, she began to shift her plans.

Forget winning over Mom and Dad.

If anyone's going to bring me into this struggle against the Empire, it's Mon Mothma.

CHAPTER 17

The next day, Leia spent hours holed up in the library, eating fruit and bread from a tray and drinking countless cups of tea. Neither of her parents appeared, but if they had, she was completely prepared to show them what she was working on: a thorough review of every single planet on the list of "approved" mercy missions her father had put together. Going over those worlds' cultures and needs was worthy and responsible, exactly the kind of behavior they would approve of.

They didn't need to know that Leia was figuring out how to turn a voyage to one of these planets into action against the Empire.

Not action the way this Saw Gerrera person defined it. Not even the kind of action her father was preparing for on Crait. She understood the limits of what she could accomplish as a sixteen-year-old girl with a ship at her disposal and very little else. The most she could offer in the struggle against Emperor Palpatine was *evidence.*

The Empire presented a polished, impervious façade

that supposedly represented the strict rule of law. While they maintained many of the trappings of the Republic—modifying armor and uniform designs only slightly—those external signs of power had been made sharper, crisper, and more imposing. So much of Palpatine's authority rested on the illusion that he alone had been able to provide order after the chaos of the Clone Wars. But what he called order was merely control, and that control was exercised solely for the benefit of the most powerful among his sycophants.

Planets that had their own wealth and influence remained sheltered from the worst of the Empire's excesses. Leia had learned the truth first from her parents, then through her work in the Senate. Surely very few people were still completely deceived. But the galactic populace at large couldn't possibly understand just how huge the gap was between Palpatine's promises and the tyrannical reality.

They don't see the worst of what he does, she thought, frowning as she crossed Dinwa Prime off the list of potential candidates. *I can document some of that and get that documentation to the people who'll know how to use it. That doesn't put anyone at risk but me.*

Not that her parents would want her to put herself at risk—but Leia didn't think the danger would be too great. She had diplomatic immunity thanks to her work with the Senate and her status as a princess of Alderaan. Any number of plausible explanations would cover the kind of recordkeeping she intended to do.

But where to begin? She had to work from her father's list, or else her parents would catch on before she'd had a chance to accomplish anything.

Ruoss Minor remained shattered after Palpatine's last crackdown, but the harm had been done long ago, which meant proving the cause and effect might be difficult with her limited resources. Anelsana suffered in the aftermath of a trade embargo, but most of the proof of that would be found in their main cities, while her father had specifically limited her travel to the more rural northern continent. . . .

The famine on Chasmeene.

Leia sat up straight, re-angling her screen to avoid the glare of the afternoon sun now filtering through the tall windows. The famine on Chasmeene had raged for years now, but it had begun when retaliatory strikes by the Empire irradiated vast swaths of farmland. The "crime" for which that planet was being punished: failing to meet an Imperial quota. It was a punishment that might devastate Chasmeene for generations to come. She could take readings to prove the source and extremity of the damage done; the signs of it might even be visible in regular holo images.

A smile stole across her face as she thought, *Thanks for the suggestion, Dad.*

•◆•

Famine relief required considerable stores of food, seeds, and agricultural equipment, which meant it was necessary for Leia to commandeer the *Tantive IV.* She'd have been tempted to take that ship in any case; it was easier to avoid being noticed in the middle of a larger bustle of activity.

As the crew hurried around, preparing shipment bundles for each area they'd help, she began looking for a little help of her own. *I'll need to be involved virtually every moment; it's not like I don't want to help these people too. But these images have to be carefully shot, not chosen at random. . . .*

"You, there," she said to one of Captain Antilles's droids, a blue-and-silver astromech. "Can you help me?"

It whistled in the affirmative, immediately wheeling over to her side of the cargo bay. Leia leaned down closer to it—the instinctive movement of someone who wanted to keep a secret, even if the droid was capable of "hearing" instructions whispered from much farther away. "I have special instructions for you."

The little droid's semispherical head seemed to look up at her as it tilted back on its arms. She found herself smiling; it was always nice when a droid had personality—though what she needed most now was discretion.

"I need you to keep these instructions secret," she ordered. "That means you reveal them to no one, not even Captain Antilles. I promise they don't break any regulations."

The droid hesitated for a moment, a startlingly lifelike act, but then beeped in affirmation.

Leia lowered her voice even more. "I need you to take holos and scans of the surface of Chasmeene, most particularly the areas targeted by the retaliatory strikes from a few years ago. They're mapped out here." With that, she slid a datacard into the reader slot just beneath the droid's semispherical head. "Get as much information as you can, all right? I want everything."

The droid whistled cheerfully and then rolled off, directly toward the central area for ship's sensors. *Clever little thing,* she thought.

And that gave her another idea.

"One more thing?" The droid stopped rolling and turned its head around to face her as she hurried after it. "If you have the chance—maybe you could tap into the local databanks to back some of this up? I know that gets closer to violating regulations, but if you put it through as 'cross-referencing ship sensors' as a kind of maintenance check, I bet you won't be blocked."

Apparently the droid agreed, because with a few clicks and whistles, it went back to its task.

The only hint of trouble came at the very end of their stay, when Captain Antilles began easing the *Tantive IV* out of orbit, only to have a holographic image of a commander in the Imperial Navy shimmer into unwelcome life on the bridge.

"I'm afraid a review of our long-term databanks reveals we've picked up some highly irregular scans," the commander said, her thin face pointed in nose, chin, and glare. "Someone on your ship may well be responsible. We'll want to run a search."

Keeping Captain Antilles out of the loop had been a good idea, Leia realized, because even a professional actor couldn't have been as believably indignant. "This is a diplomatic vessel with clearance! We were here on a mission of mercy, as your own records should show. This is harassment of a member of the Imperial Senate, Commander, and it *will* be reported."

An apprentice legislator as a "member of the Imperial Senate"—that was stretching the truth a little bit. Leia's best move now was to stretch it more, until it broke. She came up to the hologram, wide-eyed, making sure to appear slightly nervous. That always made her look younger. "Is something wrong, Captain Antilles? I didn't mean to—" Turning to the Imperial commander, Leia clasped her hands together as if beseeching her. "I'm only a member of the Apprentice Legislature. I promise, I didn't mean any harm."

Captain Antilles gave her a sideways glance suggesting he didn't relish being publicly undercut in this way. Then again, he didn't know Leia was guilty. So he couldn't fully appreciate the relief that flooded through her as the Imperial commander's expression shifted from doubt, to contempt, all the way to amusement.

Nobody looked at a young girl and saw a threat. That was an advantage her parents didn't understand yet, one Leia intended to use to the fullest.

"I stand corrected," the commander said, a thin-lipped smirk on her face. With a hand gesture, she signaled to someone outside of the holographic imager, and various flashing red signals on the *Tantive IV* bridge controls turned green again. "Far be it from me to importune such a critical member of the government."

As the ship swooped out of orbit, one of the bridge officers muttered, "They get more paranoid all the time." Captain Antilles didn't respond out loud, but the expression on his face revealed a moment of satisfaction; Leia could imagine him thinking, *Good. They* should *be afraid.*

She made her way over to a small dataport alcove where the blue-and-silver astromech had tucked itself. Bending low in front of the droid, she murmured, "We cut it a little close there."

In response, the droid brought up one of the screens, which began to flash with data. A lot of data. Leia's breath caught as she realized that the droid hadn't only gathered information about the current state of Chasmeene, but had also collected information going back years—decades?—which proved beyond any doubt the Empire's direct responsibility for the devastation. Few humans would've shown such initiative, and even fewer droids.

"This is perfect," she said. The astromech whistled in a self-satisfied way, as though saying, *I know.*

Exhilarated, Leia input the commands to prepare multiple datacards. She'd rarely felt as powerful as she did in this moment, when she held the proof of Palpatine's wrongdoing in her hands.

•◆•

Her euphoria lasted for two days, until she returned to Coruscant and brought her evidence to the person she thought most likely to take action.

"Your Highness," Mon Mothma said, perhaps using the title to soften her words, "I'm afraid we can't do much with this."

"What do you mean?" Leia protested. "It's proof of

what the Empire's done to a world that only failed to meet a quota! People are going to be furious when they see this."

Mon Mothma folded her arms atop her desk. Behind her, small ships darted through the Coruscant sky. "Here in the Senate, where we see so much of the 'official' versions of events, we sometimes forget that the average person on the average planet is subjected to less propaganda than we are. They listen to conversations and rumors far more than the official infocasts. We have to engage with the artificial narratives of politics because that's how things get done in the Senate. But those narratives don't have much currency outside of Coruscant and a few other Core Worlds—yours and mine included."

Either Leia wasn't understanding this, or Mon Mothma wasn't. "But—this is *proof*—"

"No one needs any more proof. The people of the galaxy *know* Palpatine is corrupt and cruel. They've known that for a generation." Mon Mothma leaned back, as if the weight of that knowledge had wearied her. "It isn't ignorance that keeps worlds in the Empire. It's tyranny, and fear."

Leia slumped in her chair. She'd been so sure she'd accomplished something meaningful—that it had been worth the minor risk to the crew of the *Tantive IV*—that this would help her parents see what she could do. Instead it was the exact opposite: proof she didn't understand what she was dealing with, that she was in over her head before she was actually in at all.

"Don't be discouraged, Leia." Mon Mothma managed a faint smile. "If you think about this, you'll realize it's one of the most powerful weapons we have. Palpatine can dictate history here, in his academies, and in the Imperial Starfleet—but that tricks him into believing he dictates it everywhere. He doesn't. Trillions of people understand what he truly is, and with every day that passes, more of them become willing to do whatever it takes to see the Empire fall. Right now they only lack a flag to rally around. Soon, I hope, we'll be able to give them that."

Even through her gloom, Leia was struck by how utterly calm Mon Mothma was. Her parents were courageous, but their dread of what was to come was both palpable and understandable. Only this woman looked completely ready to accept whatever came. She wasn't afraid, and it was difficult to feel afraid when with her.

Maybe it's not a flag we'll rally around, Leia thought as she watched Mon Mothma rise from her desk. *Maybe it's a person.*

The senator paced the length of her office, seemingly searching for the right words. The atmosphere suggested serenity and peace, with its pale colors, cushioned seating, and view overlooking the clouds. Even the cup of Chandrilan tea steaming on the desk promised calm. But the office, like its occupant, had concealed complexities.

Finally Mon Mothma said, "The day will come when evidence like this matters. When Palpatine has finally fallen, we'll need to rewrite their false history to reflect the truth. Documentation like this, gathered by honest people—that's going to give us a place to begin."

Leia hadn't been angling to become a historian. Someday, when she could tell Kier about this, he'd appreciate the irony of her being the one to make the textbooks. "I'm glad it's useful." The words came out evenly. At least she could be proud of her self-control.

Mon Mothma seemed to be proud too, because she came to Leia's side and put one hand on her shoulder. "More than anything else, I'm honored that you trusted me with this. The Empire's worked so hard to destroy our faith in one another, throughout the galaxy. Only by daring to reach out will we ever make the allies we need."

"Maybe someday I'll be one of those allies," Leia said.

"You already are."

The kind words helped, as did Mon Mothma's smile. But Leia walked out of the office that day with a new sense of her own powerlessness.

How could they fight an entire government? A way of thinking, a skewed lens for viewing the world?

Maybe Mon Mothma and her parents would find a way. If they did, Leia doubted she'd get to play any part in it.

CHAPTER 18

If only the next day's session of the Apprentice Legislature had been about something else. Anything else.

"The issue before you today is to advise on sanctions against the planet Lolet," intoned the RA-7 droid. "Their planetary government stands in violation of Regulation Sixteen-ME, regarding supplying fuel as necessary to Imperial pilots."

Leia sat in Alderaan's senatorial pod, sad almost to the point of numbness, as holos played out the Empire's version of events. In the official telling, Lolet had selfishly failed to assist a stranded TIE convoy. However, it was easy to glimpse the half-hidden truth.

That TIE convoy would only have been left in the Lolet system for one reason: to intimidate the local populace. The planet had resisted refueling the ships sent to terrorize them; now every person who lived there would have to suffer.

And the Emperor had done the Apprentice Legislature the *honor* of deciding just what form that suffering would take.

She glanced over at Kier to find that he was already watching her. If she'd been any less miserable, that might have flustered her, or delighted her. Instead, she could only shrug helplessly. He frowned in concern, but before he could say anything to her, the debates had begun in earnest.

"I don't see any need to elaborate on the usual penalties," Harp Allor said, her black hair shining in the brilliant light at the center of the chamber. "It's not as if this was an especially egregious offense—"

"*Any* offense against the Imperial fleet is egregious!" protested one of the representatives from Arkanis. "And such offenses are growing more common. We need to take a hard line, now, before planets begin to believe they can get away with such blatant disrespect."

Chassellon Stevis's drawl was so casual as to be cutting. "Oh, spare us the patriotic drivel. The standard procedure will be acceptable. If it weren't, do you think we'd have been sent this issue to deal with in the first place? The Senate doesn't delegate work to the Apprentice Legislature in the hopes we'll do something novel and creative. They delegate work to us when they already know what the outcome will be."

Leia's heart sank further. It wasn't as if she hadn't figured this out for herself after the fiasco with Arreyel. But admitting that the Apprentice Legislature had little power and less autonomy meant acknowledging that here, too, she was entirely helpless.

The standard punishment for violations of Regulation 16-ME was an increase in tribute paid to the Empire, with the specific amount at the discretion of the provincial governor in question. If the planet was valuable enough, that amount could triple—creating a staggering debt no world could possibly pay. The only way out of debt like that was to surrender what little autonomy the planet still had and become fully, firmly under Imperial rule.

Lolet would be far from the first planet to suffer such a fate. It would follow the dark pattern set by Umbara, Raxus, Castell. . . .

It's a puppet show for children, she thought bitterly. *We're both the audience and the props.*

The Gatalentan pod swooped down, bringing Amilyn Holdo into the limelight. Holdo's hair had been dyed the same green as her cloak, though at least only the cloak had little bells sewn all over it. "If I may have this assembly's attention—surprises are yet in store!" Then she caught herself. "I mean, I have some more information that might shed light on this subject."

From the Glee Anselm pod, Leia heard someone mutter, "Is this where she tells us how her dreams prophesy future fashion trends or something?" She would've glared at them for ridiculing a fellow apprentice, if that prediction hadn't sounded exactly like something Amilyn would say.

Amilyn's long face was tinted blue by the lights of the three-dimensional charts she brought up on the holos. "If you'll look at this, you'll see that it represents Lolet's fuel reserves at the period in question. Those levels are much lower than usual, to the point most planets would consider themselves in a state of crisis. My research indicates that the Lolet had taxed their reserves almost to the breaking point while evacuating one of their moons after major geological instability earlier in the year. They didn't give the Empire the requested fuel because they *didn't have it*."

It seemed to Leia as though she hadn't known she was asleep until Amilyn's words had woken her up. While she'd been searching for proof of Imperial wrongdoing in the farthest reaches of the galaxy, it was Amilyn Holdo who'd turned up another crime right under their noses. Never again would she let her mood make her so careless.

"They had it!" protested the kid from Arkanis. "The chart clearly shows they could've filled the quota."

"Only by completely depleting their reserves," Amilyn answered, pointing one of her skinny arms toward the holographic chart; she was so long-limbed it looked as though she might push her finger through the blue columns of data. "Lolet would have had nothing left to deal with any future emergencies in their system. Imagine their—" She visibly caught herself; at least she was trying to come across like a normal person, even if she wasn't quite managing it. "No regulations require a planet to put itself at risk in that way."

The Arkanis kid was unbowed. "No regulations say a planet can hold fuel back for that reason, either. If the Imperial Starfleet reported Lolet, and we've been assigned to levy sanctions, then that means planets *are* supposed to hand over that fuel when the Empire needs it."

"Besides," one of the Glee Anselm apprentices chimed in, "why does Lolet have to worry about some hypothetical emergency that might never happen? If something did come up, they could call on the Empire for help."

Amilyn shook her head. "The Empire doesn't always respond to those calls!"

It felt like a punch to Leia's gut. Saying such things even in private, among friends, felt like a risk. Only someone as guileless as Amilyn Holdo would ever speak a truth that explosive in public.

"Excuse me?" The Arkanis apprentice seized the opportunity. "The Emperor has made it clear that his concern extends to all his peoples, and denying that is very nearly an act of treason!"

Or sedition, Leia thought automatically.

Kier leaned so close to her that she could feel his breath against her ear as he whispered, "We have to come up with a distraction, or else this is going to end with stormtroopers dragging Holdo off to jail."

She nodded—he was right—but what kind of distraction could they possibly come up with? For one crazy moment, Leia imagined pretending their pod was broken and driving it wildly through the air like this was kiddie bump-speeders instead of a legislative assembly.

Amilyn either hadn't caught on to the danger yet or didn't care. "It's a big galaxy! Entire planets sometimes escape our notice! That's just—natural."

"Maybe it's natural for *you*," sniped the Glee Anselm apprentice. "With your head filled with feathers—that's why they're always poking from your hair, I bet."

Leia decided rage was distracting. She got to her feet and raised her voice. "That's enough! If you're shallow enough to care about what anybody's wearing, then maybe you need to go back to playing with the other children and leave governing to people who've grown up a little."

The Glee Anselm apprentice had the grace to look embarrassed, but that only seemed to goad the one from Arkanis. "So you think it's appropriate to criticize the Emperor in public?"

As baited hooks went, that one was pretty clumsy. Leia only raised an eyebrow. "I think criticizing other apprentices' *clothing choices* in public demeans this entire assembly."

Amilyn didn't appear to know a lifeline when she saw one. "I just don't think it's right to penalize a planet for—for—" She struggled for words that wouldn't doom her, and came up short.

But that was when Kier cut in, "For a lack of clarity in the law. As you've said, no regulations clearly state what a planet is supposed to do in this situation."

Leia seized on this. "Exactly. What we need to do is recommend new language for the legal code, so no other world will make a mistake out of confusion, like Lolet did."

The idea of recommending new legal code was novel for most of the apprentice legislators, and exciting—a hint at real authority. Immediately people began discussing who might draft the language and how they'd present it. Even the ones who wanted to make an example of Lolet were eager to establish a new regulation that would turn their severity into law.

It occurred to Leia that Lolet would almost certainly be punished anyway. Whatever new law they proposed would have to be draconian in its harshness, requiring every planet to deplete its own emergency stores at the whim of any Imperial commander who came by, regardless of genuine need. But they'd bought Lolet a little time, a chance to maybe come up with sources of funding to deal with the eventual penalty. Not much help—but something.

"That is, Amilyn Holdo bought them that time," she said to Kier later as the two of them walked along one of the broad skyways that led away from the senatorial complex. "There was a weakness in the Imperial case, but I didn't even see it."

"It was tricky." Kier wasn't the kind of guy who felt the need to point out that he'd spotted the critical flaw for himself. He was more interested in what she was driving at.

Leia considered her words carefully as they went along, a flickering hologram for some advertisement or other throwing prisms of multicolored light through the skyway. It felt like walking through a kaleidoscope. Beneath them, thick ribbons of hover traffic levitated almost at a standstill, a true Coruscant traffic jam in three dimensions.

"I've been feeling discouraged lately," she admitted. "Knowing . . . what we know reminds me of how much there is to be done. When I let myself get discouraged, though, I don't see the opportunities to actually accomplish something good."

He weighed her words for several paces more. She liked the comfortableness of the silences between them. "You're always asking what you can do for the greater good."

Nonplussed, Leia nodded.

"You know, every once in a while, it's okay to just live for yourself." Kier held up a hand, forestalling her objection. "I'm not telling you to be, I don't know, selfish or trivial. You'd never want that; that's not who you are. But it's all right to just, you know, *be a person*. Every once in a while, you can let go and live in the moment. I think you have to. Because if you're carrying the weight of the worlds every single day, you get tired. You don't have your strength when you need it most, because you already burned yourself out."

That sounded . . . much too familiar.

He continued, "It's okay to want some things just for yourself. To go out and have fun once in a while. To be glad your world is secure, and the people you care about are safe."

"Sometimes it feels like we don't have a right to be happy when so many others are suffering."

"We don't have a right *not* to be happy, if we can be." When she stared at him, Kier nodded. "I mean it. If we all live in fear and misery all the time, his victory is complete."

She knew whom he was referring to. On a public walkway on Coruscant, it would be suicide to use Palpatine's name openly like this. Besides, they were learning to understand each other without words.

Quoting an Alderaanian philosopher, Leia said, "Strength through joy."

Kier grinned. "Exactly."

"Got any suggestions?"

"Let's see." He pretended to consider the situation

seriously for a long moment. By now they were walking very slowly. "We could . . . go to the Glarus Lagoons together, the next time we're home."

The Glarus Lagoons were known for their spectacular scenery and sea life. Located in one of the thin ribbons of Alderaan's climate that was warm enough to be called balmy, the lagoons drew many travelers who longed for heat, sunshine, chances to swim or dive—or the famously romantic atmosphere.

She tilted her head. "You and me."

Once again she glimpsed the shyness she'd seen in him at first, back when she didn't even understand it was shyness at all. "If you'd like."

Leia didn't answer right away. There was something about his face when he looked at her like this, that mixture of uncertainty and hope and something else she couldn't name but recognized within her own heart. This silence wasn't comfortable at all, and somehow that made it even better.

"I would," she said. "I'd like that a lot."

The smile returned to his face. "Yeah?"

"Yeah."

Maybe she didn't have to fight the entire Empire every single day. Maybe it was all right to find out who she was besides a senator-in-training or a princess. To find out what it meant to just be Leia.

CHAPTER 19

Step one in being a totally normal person with totally normal concerns was to spend more time hanging out with friends, doing nothing. Leia had become comfortable with the people she'd gotten to know in her pathfinding class, but they still mostly spent time together on expeditions or in quasi-official gatherings tied to the Apprentice Legislature. Time to try doing something purely social, for no purpose besides wasting time, having fun.

But she hadn't expected to be "hanging out" quite so literally. . . .

"Imagine you're carved of wood!" Amilyn Holdo held herself firmly in the splits, despite the fact that she wasn't on the floor but suspended in midair, held aloft by brilliantly colored scarves she'd acrobatically twisted around each leg. "Unbending! Unyielding!"

"Unbelievable," muttered Leia, who had only just managed to wrangle herself into a seated position without feeling like she'd topple four meters to the floor at any second.

Apparently this was a Gatalentan calisthenics practice

called skyfaring, which was said to make their entire world stronger. The supposed reason for this was that advanced practitioners could meditate in place, "unmoored to the ground," and so enhance their spiritual well-being and that of those around them. Leia thought the real reason was that the weak hung themselves in these damned scarves, and only the strong survived.

She also wasn't sure she was going to make it into the "strong" category. As far as she could tell, skyfaring mostly involved pale blue leotards and a disregard for human life.

"All right," Leia muttered to herself. "One leg out. You can do this."

As she awkwardly reached out with one foot, trying to snag the nearest scarlet scarf, Amilyn easily unwound herself from the splits. She kept one leg tethered as she let her body fall back until she was suspended upside down. For someone so awkward and ungainly on the ground, Amilyn possessed considerable grace midair.

"Remember," she said in her odd, singsong voice, "you're made of wood. Strong but organic! Life force–made material!"

I'm carved of wood. I'm carved of wood. Leia bent her knee and made a circle with her leg, capturing the scarf just right. For one instant, she felt a flicker of understanding of what "carved from wood" might actually mean. Encouraged, she eased herself into one of the lunging stances. Her sides ached, but she could keep her balance.

"That's it!" Amilyn clapped her hands together. Her long hair (currently magenta) streamed down from her head like another of the bright scarves. "You're getting there!"

In a rush of confidence, Leia extended her arms to complete the pose—

—and then spun out like a cyclone for a long second before she tumbled onto the floor. Fortunately the surface was so springy she bounced once before making a soft landing. Still, she groaned as she flopped down with her limbs splayed wide.

Amilyn rotated down to her, slowly spinning along the length of a pink streamer with such elegance that if Amilyn were anybody else, Leia would've assumed she was showing off. She simply flowed into her position at Leia's side. "You didn't hurt yourself?"

"No, just drank deeply from the cup of humiliation."

"Don't be humiliated." Amilyn had a funny, crooked grin. "You did very well for your first time, especially as an offworlder. Even natives don't get the swing of it until they're five or six, sometimes."

Leia made a mental note to look up the child mortality rate on Gatalenta.

This skyfaring room was part of the Gatalentan

senatorial complex, something they considered important enough to maintain along with their offices. Many planets had such unique "essentials," such as the Mon Calamari saline tanks and the Toydarian wind tunnel for wing exercise. Maybe a meditative-gymnastics complex seemed odd to Leia, but each planet set its own priorities.

Amilyn said, "Why don't we do some basic floor stretches? That would get you more used to the muscle combinations involved."

Leia had the distinct sense she was being coddled. After her last tumble from the streamers, however, some coddling didn't seem like a bad idea. "Let's try that."

Even on the floor exercises, she had to work to keep up. Although her dancing and exercise classes kept Leia lithe and flexible, Amilyn could twist and turn her limbs in combinations seemingly impossible for a species with a skeletal structure. But she was good at suggesting modifications Leia could use, and helping her find the right mental state. "Any imbalance we carry within us, we carry into the sky. You have to be firmly grounded before you can try anything in the air. Would some more incense help?"

Incense smoke already drifted so thickly through the air that they could've been in one of the fog-forests of Eriadu. "I think we've got that covered."

"Then maybe you should talk through the imbalance."

Amilyn struck a pose on one foot that looked easy to accomplish. "If you don't want to reveal too much in front of me, speak in metaphors. Many people find that enlightening."

Leia hit the same pose and discovered it was easy—at first. Holding it required significant muscle control. "I can't come up with metaphors and do this at the same time. But—I guess I can talk about a few things." Bottling it all up inside definitely wasn't helping. And as peculiar as Amilyn Holdo was, she genuinely tried to help people around her. That had to count for something.

"All confidences during skyfaring remain in the room to dissipate with the smoke," Amilyn promised.

"Uh, great." Leia steadied her balance as she lifted her arms higher. "Well, for one, I've always been close to my parents, but it seems like we don't understand each other anymore." The specific reasons why had to remain unspoken; only Kier could be trusted with that truth. "Every once in a while, we'll connect, but most of the time—I feel like they're so far away from me, even when we're in the same room."

"That's the evolutionary principle at work."

"Come again?"

Still on one foot, Amilyn lowered herself gracefully to the floor. "If the young of the species don't have motivation to leave the care of their parents, they'll never lead an independent existence, which means they'll never reproduce. The species would soon die out. Ergo, the last stage of life before adulthood always involves conflict between parent and offspring."

Maybe the incense smoke was getting to Leia, because that seemed to make a kind of sense, even if it certainly didn't explain everything between her and her parents. "I'm also frustrated by how little we can accomplish in the Apprentice Legislature. The Senate has more power, but even they're subject to the Emperor. My whole life, I've expected to go into politics, to try to make the galaxy a better place. Now I wonder if that's even possible."

She flinched from the memory of the explosion on Onoam, the terrible smell of smoldering rubble and death. Her mother and father hadn't wanted that—but was that where plans like theirs inevitably led?

"The Force gains strength from our intentions as well as our actions," Amilyn said brightly. "We must try to stand and succeed, but we must never fail to stand."

"No." The word came out harsher than she'd meant, and for the first time that day, Amilyn's smile faltered. Leia managed to be calmer when she added, "Good intentions aren't enough. They're not meaningless, but—that's where we have to start. Not where we end."

"That's—that's a good point, actually." A wrinkle appeared between Amilyn's eyebrows as she considered this. "On Gatalenta we try to lead the life of the mind, and in our culture intentions can have great influence—we discuss them, judge by them—but in the galaxy at large, things are—well—less pleasant."

Leia nodded. "Unfortunately, yes."

"This will be the focus of my next meditative trance." Amilyn shifted into a spine-defying backbend. "You've already given vent to your frustrations. Now speak to the joy in your life. What makes you happy, here and now?"

Leia's heart provided the answer instantly—so much so that she was startled. Something in her quailed from that knowledge, but something else, far more powerful, kept taking her back to the shooting arena, or the hidden passageways of the palace, or the snowy lodge where Kier had brought her that first mug of mocoa.

She didn't say his name out loud. As she made her own attempt at the backbend, she asked, "Can it be morally right to feel happy when there's so much injustice all around us?"

"Of course. Happiness is our moral imperative."

"That sounds"—Leia actually got into the backbend, but felt like her abdominal muscles were pressing the breath from her—"like—like hedonism."

"Not at all." Lifting herself upright again with damnable ease, Amilyn said, "Great evil can only be fought by the strong. People need spiritual fuel as much as they need food, water, and air. Happiness, love, joy, hope—these are the emotions that give us the strength to do what we need to do."

That wasn't just the incense; that was genuine and true. Leia flopped back down on the bouncy floor, really relaxing in Amilyn's company for the first time. "I guess all that meditation pays off for you guys."

"Yes. Well, that, and it's pretty obvious you like Kier. You might as well use that energy, you know?"

Leia opened her mouth to protest, but what was the point? "It's like—like everything else is this raging storm, and he's . . . the only safe place. The only one who lets me just be myself."

"Beware words like 'only,'" Amilyn said, wagging one long finger, but she was smiling. "Don't let your head be turned by the most dangerous substance known to exist."

"Which is?"

"A pair of pretty dark eyes." Then Amilyn thought about that for a moment. "Or more than a pair, if you're into Grans. Or Aqualish, or Talz. Or even—"

"That's all right!" Leia said through laughter. "It's just humanoid males for me."

"Really? That feels so *limiting.*"

"Thank goodness it's a big galaxy."

And she'd already found someone extraordinary in it.

•◆•

Later that afternoon, Leia walked through the senatorial complex in a good mood. Whether it was the incense, the conversation with Amilyn, or the promise of another pathfinding trip with Kier in the near future, her gloom had been banished for the first time in too long. Apparently this "being normal" thing really worked.

But her steps slowed as she saw staffers ducking into offices, hurrying along corridors, gesturing to each other to hurry into their planet's suite.

Luckily the Alderaanian suite wasn't far away. She reached it within minutes and rushed inside to find absolutely no one in the outer room; a crowd had gathered in her father's office. Leia poked her head through the doorway to see everyone clustered around the HoloNet viewer.

"—no loss of life, only through the courage of our Imperial stormtroopers. However, the attack on the convoy represents a profound danger to outposts in the Mid-Rim region, and to the interconnectedness of our Empire."

Only someone who knew Bail Organa as well as his daughter would've caught the slight exhalation of relief on the words "no loss of life." That was the only emotion he displayed, not disquiet or even surprise.

This isn't like what happened in the Naboo system, Leia concluded. *This is something my parents knew about.*

Something they planned.

Something they helped to do.

"False reports circulating through various informal channels claim that a medical frigate was captured," the infocast reader continued. "Although many members of the frigate's crew were found to harbor treasonous beliefs and attempted to aid in the attack, the ship remains in the control of the proper authorities."

Most informed members of the Senate knew how to read through the lines of official HoloNet reports. If the medical frigate in question were still under control, its name would've been given. If crewmembers had been captured, at least one or two would've been named; Palpatine never hesitated to identify his enemies. The real message was that someone higher up on a medical frigate had wanted to remove it from the Imperial Starfleet, and with the assistance of starfighters—starfighters provided by her parents or their allies—had escaped with the sophisticated ship, its supplies and its equipment intact.

No loss of life, Leia reminded herself. Her parents had supported a swift, smart, nonviolent operation, the kind of action she felt she could condone.

But they'd taken a medical frigate. Those frigates were designed to handle casualties on a massive scale, like after a planetary catastrophe, or—

—or a large-scale military conflict.

She only knew that from history lessons about the

Clone Wars. In her lifetime, no such battles had taken place. Leia had always hoped none ever would.

Apparently her parents had other plans.

After the HoloNet had reported the exact same information three different ways, the huddle of viewers began to break up. From the outer corridors of the Senate chambers, Leia could hear numerous people talking among themselves; this would be the only subject most people on Coruscant discussed for the rest of the day.

In Bail Organa's office, however, the staffers remained quiet. They went back to their tasks without a word. How much did they know? Were they working with her father—or, if not his co-conspirators, were they at least willing to remain silent rather than confront the truth?

She waited until she was the last person in her father's office, then pressed the panel to shut the door behind her. "Dad—"

"This isn't a conversation we're going to have." Bail met her eyes for only an instant before pulling up his work on a datapad.

"How can you say that? I know what this means. If I know, that means the Empire knows too."

His hands on his datapad stilled, but he didn't look up. "Undoubtedly. Which means discretion has become even more important."

"But, Dad, how can the two of you—"

"Leia, stop." At last Bail lifted his head again, considering his daughter from what seemed to be far away. "The less you know, the safer you are. The less is said in this office, the safer the others here will be. Do you understand?"

She already knew her safety was forfeit, but she hadn't considered his staffers. He'd found the one point that could make her let go. Nodding, Leia walked out of her father's office with a placid expression on her face, as though she were completely unbothered.

Inside, however, her emotions were in a tumult, and she couldn't tell what was worse: the separation between her and her parents that seemed to widen all the time, or her fear of the nameless conflict taking shape on the horizon.

CHAPTER 20

Fifty years ago, Felucia had been a remote jungle world on the outer edges of the Outer Rim, of interest to almost no one who didn't already live there. Twenty years ago, it had become critical to controlling the Perlemian Trade Route, which made it a key battleground in the Clone Wars. Ten years ago, it had been a shadow of its former self, cities devastated by conflict. By the time Leia went there, Felucia was fulfilling the Empire's goal for it, which meant serving as a source of the healing plant nysillim but nothing else.

Yet the planet still claimed thick, near-impenetrable jungles and rainforests over much of its surface, which made it a good place for pathfinding practice.

"I suppose I should be glad we're not climbing as much today." Chassellon led the way as the humanoid members of the class slogged through mud up to their knees. (Sssamm swam along merrily, feeling entirely at home.) "But even snow's easier to march through than this muck."

Chief Pangie called from behind, "Our first cliffs are coming right up!"

"*Kriff,*" Chassellon muttered. Leia wanted to laugh at him, but she was dangerously close to agreeing. They could see little in the distance but mist and the shadows of enormous trees. Surrounding them on all sides were tall, two-branched ferns that rose in striped arcs like a Togruta's montrals, oversized vines and roots that jutted up from the soil, and orange flowers that looked pretty but had stems with sharp thorns. Short as Leia was, the mud came up higher on her and was making the hike tough going.

Kier walked alongside her. Never once did he try to take her arm and help her along; he obviously understood how much she would hate that. But he matched his pace to hers to keep her company. Originally Amilyn had done the same, but after a raised eyebrow at Leia and Kier, she'd gone ahead, making her way easily through the mud on her long, stilt-like legs.

At one point when Chief Pangie was busy shaking off a slimesnipe, Leia dared to whisper to Kier, "You heard about the frigate, right?"

He opened his eyes wider, clearly in warning. "Of course. But we shouldn't—"

"No! I didn't mean to—" Leia glanced around. A few dangling strands of hair were plastered to her forehead and neck by sweat and sheer humidity. "I just meant, that's more of the idea—more the right way to go about things." *Something I don't have to forgive my parents for. Something I could support them in. Unless it leads to a more dangerous path—*

"I'm not so sure," Kier replied.

They'd have to discuss that further. But Leia was distracted as their group stumbled from a thick patch of fog to a clearing that revealed the cliffs they'd climb that day. They weren't nearly as tall or as steep as the rock faces they'd dealt with so far, but every stone shone wetly with condensation or algae.

"Does it look slippery?" said Chief Pangie, with her usual fierce glee. "That's because it is! Fillithar boy, you've had it easy up until now, but you've got one hell of a slog ahead of you."

Sssamm's tongue flickered out nervously, but he didn't protest, only nodded.

The chief continued, "That's another thing you should be learning through pathfinding. Every single one of you has unique skills and weaknesses. Each of you is going to run across tasks you can do better than anybody else, and you're also going to run into a few at which you are, let's just say it, pathetic."

Leia looked down toward the mud plastering her pale gray climbing suit all the way to mid-thigh. *Well, if I had to be pathetic at one thing, at least it's this and not something dangerous.*

"I'm splitting you up into teams of two," Chief Pangie

continued, "and taking you around to different bases from which to climb. You won't be that far apart, but good luck catching a glimpse of anybody else. Coordinates for our meeting place have been auto-downloaded into your equipment. You have to figure out how to meet in the middle. Oh, and be sure to activate those anti-impact fields! If you don't have those on, your first slip on those cliffs will be the last of your lifetime."

"As though we needed reminding about *that*," Chassellon said. He was already surrounded by the faint, telltale shimmer of his field.

Amilyn peered at him down her long nose. "For someone who grew up in a skyscraper, you're awfully scared of heights." Leia stifled a giggle as Chassellon sullenly folded his arms across his chest.

To Leia's satisfaction, she and Kier were paired for the climb. It seemed like a good time for them to talk on their own, but she hadn't counted on what difference a little slipperiness would make. Although the grade of their ascent was low enough that they could've walked on other terrain, the slick surface required them to go up on all fours, and it was hard going. Talking about anything other than the essentials of climbing proved impossible.

"All right," she panted. "Looks like there's a kind of ravine or something coming up. Not very wide, but we'll want to use ropes."

From his place below her, Kier said, "Don't be afraid. We've got this."

She hadn't been especially worried until he said that, because it meant he had to be worried too.

As they moved along the diagonal ascent that brought them closer to the ravine, Leia got a better look at what they'd have to deal with. It was a solid three meters to the other side; they'd have to use ropes and swing across. Challenging, and more than a bit scary, but fun.

"I always like this part," she confessed as they anchored their tethers to the stone.

"Really? I hate it. Usually I have to close my eyes."

"Come on. The anti-impact field protects you."

Kier shook his head. "Doesn't make that fall any less terrifying."

"Then don't think about it." After a couple of hours skyfaring with Amilyn, Leia had gained more experience in tumbling down. "Just think about your first handholds on the other side."

She spotted her own potential holds, double-checked her rope, and pushed off as hard as she could. For one second she could have been flying—swinging sideways through midair, hardly even able to feel the tether's pull at her harness. But that momentary exhilaration had to give way as the other side came close. Leia hit it with her arms and legs braced properly to give a bit, and instantly found purchase. She shoved a new bolt anchor into a crack in the stone until she felt secure enough to tether herself to that.

Breathing heavily and smiling, she called to Kier. "Come on! Try it!"

The way he smiled at her then made her feel as if she'd just performed a magic trick and offered to teach him how. He shoved off—

—in the same moment Leia saw grains of rock dust falling from his anchor. Before she could even shout in alarm, it gave way, and he dropped from her sight.

"Kier? *Kier?*" Twisting around as best she could, she saw to her relief that he'd managed to make the other side, barely. He clung to the inner lip of the gorge, his handholds precarious. The useless anchor and rope dangled from his belt.

"I'm all right," Kier said. "Sort of."

"What do you mean, 'sort of'?"

"I hit the other side hard. I think—I'm pretty sure it took out my field generator."

Leia went from mere fright to near-paralyzing horror. If Kier's generator was broken and he fell, he would be killed. He was completely untethered to the rock face, and in a poor position to climb. It was too easy to imagine him tumbling down, broken against the stones long before he ever hit the ground.

Yet after that first rush of terror, her mind cleared.

Resolve focused her better than anything else. "I'm coming down for you."

"Don't. Your rope might not support two."

"It could," she protested, though she knew their weights together would be near the limit of the hold she'd prepared.

But she hadn't yet unclipped herself from the rope on the other side. Quickly she spooled out more length on her newer tether, hopefully enough to reach her and Kier.

He still didn't want her to risk herself; she knew that because she could see him trying to angle himself for a better foothold. There wasn't one to be found, and he was only endangering himself in the process. "Will you just hold still?" she shouted. "Hang on!"

Leia pushed off yet again, swinging back to the other side of the gorge—a far longer and steeper arc this time, which gave her the full effect of falling. She didn't love that part. Yet again, she made a solid landing, and instantly she shoved off again, this time going straight toward Kier.

He flattened himself against the rock as she made impact just next to him. Grabbing the edge of the gorge was harder than she'd thought it would be; Kier had done well not to fall immediately. Still, she had it.

Up close, she could see how pale Kier was, but somehow he managed to smile. "My hero."

"Not yet." She craned her neck around and realized

just how tough it would be to get out of the gorge, with its many sharp, jutting stones. Any outcropping could easily slice their ropes, or Leia and Kier themselves. In fact, swinging back over to the other side—her original plan—looked extremely likely to do just that. *Okay, we need a new plan.* "We're going to have to—somersault, throw ourselves, however you want to put it—around the lip of this gorge. That's the only way we're going to get over."

"We shouldn't try a maneuver like that blind. The chief told us a hundred times."

"Chief's not here, and this is our best option." Nothing was more sobering than realizing the "best option" was still bad.

She used a locking carabiner to clip her belt to Kier's. This close she could make out the muscles in his arms, and how they were shaking from the sheer strain of holding himself on such a tenuous perch. His eyes met hers at the sound of the metal clip, and he said, "I should try this on my own."

"There's no place to put in a bolt anchor."

"You shouldn't have to put yourself at risk for me."

"Hey, my field generator's still working, remember? You're the one on the line here." She grinned at him, hoping he wouldn't think about the fact that in a fall as precarious as the one below them, there was a chance her generator would also be damaged before the emergency activation.

Either he had thought about it, or he'd picked up on her nervousness. But he didn't argue, only steadied himself as best he could as she slung one arm around him. They pressed together tightly, enough that she could feel his heartbeat hard and fast against her own chest. He said only, "Out and over?"

"On three. Count it off for us."

As soon as she said that, Leia felt . . . centered, in a way she hadn't before. Her nervousness fell away, and she took a deep breath. It wasn't just an inhalation; it felt as though she were taking in the scents, the moisture, becoming part of the planet itself.

Kier asked, "Are you sure?"

"Yeah." Leia was surprised at how much she meant it. "I have a good feeling about this."

"Okay. One."

She shut her eyes, breathed in again. It seemed to her she could feel the shape and dimension of the rock around them, that she knew the location of every spar and outcropping as automatically as if they were a part of her.

"Two."

Instinct told her to connect to what she was feeling, to make herself a part of it—no, to *know* that she was a part of it, because of course she'd been a part of this planet all along—

"*Three.*"

Leia leapt at the exact moment Kier did, her limbs flooded with strength beyond what she'd thought she possessed. They swung around the outcropping and easily reached the other side. The instant Kier made contact, he shoved in a bolt anchor and clipped himself to it, independently supporting himself so Leia's rope wouldn't have to bear all the weight. For a few seconds afterward, they hung there, panting hard, steadying themselves.

"That was one hell of a jump," he finally said. "How did you do that?"

"I don't know." Already that odd spell that had fallen over her was broken. The strange vital energy that had so briefly sung to her had gone quiet again.

Together they clambered up to a small plateau where they stopped to rest and regroup. Leia had thought Kier would check his field generator first, but instead he turned to her. "Why did you do that?"

"What? Save your life?"

That didn't faze him. "Yes. And risk your own."

"I couldn't let you fall."

"You could, and you should, rather than endanger yourself."

His words made no sense. "Even if you weren't my . . . my friend, I would try to save you just like any other citizen of Alderaan. No, like any other being, from anywhere." Except maybe Palpatine. He was welcome to break his head wide open.

"Will you listen to yourself?" Kier's hand closed around her arm. "It's like you think your own life doesn't belong to you."

She started to protest, but stopped herself, because the first words that came to mind were, *It doesn't.*

Kier leaned closer, speaking with an intensity that sent chills through her body. "Of course you want to do the right thing. Of course you want to serve the people of Alderaan. And yeah, of course you hate the Empire. But you don't always have to be selfless. You don't always have to be the one making the sacrifice."

"You were hanging on by your fingernails! Nobody else is around—"

"And if you'd fallen? What then? Think about what it would've done to the people of Alderaan. To your parents."

Leia had never considered that. Even as she inwardly quailed at the idea of her mother and father in that much pain, she didn't think that changed anything. If they'd seen her there, the only individual able to save someone in peril, they would've told her to do everything she could regardless of the risk. They were the ones who'd taught her about duty and selflessness in the first place.

Kier took her hand. His skin was as scraped and raw as her own; the touch had to sting for him like it did for her. She wouldn't have let go for anything.

"You keep trying to take the whole galaxy onto your shoulders." His words were almost a whisper, and she bent toward him to hear. "If you're like that when you're just a princess, what happens when you're queen?"

"I serve my people." The response was automatic.

"You deserve to have your own life. You deserve to have someone who puts you first."

"Maybe." They were so close now Leia could feel his breath against her cheek. "Do I have somebody like that already?"

Kier tilted his head, studying her expression. At least, she thought he was. At the moment it was hard to look anywhere but his lips. "Yeah. You do."

His other hand cupped the side of her face, but Leia was the one who leaned in for a kiss.

It wasn't like she had tons of experience, but the kiss seemed like a good one to her. Great, even. Possibly even spectacular. Then Kier kissed her again, and she realized it could get even better, more than she'd ever dreamed.

They were the last team to the rendezvous point,

which earned them a scolding from Chief Pangie before they told her what had happened. One look at Kier's damaged field generator changed her attitude so completely that she was soon promising to find them an easier hike next time. This earned them a huge grin from Chassellon as they rode back to their ship, plus a friendly tail rattle from Sssamm. But Leia couldn't pay much attention to any of them, not even to Amilyn's knowing glance, as she and Kier sat side by side, shoulders and knees touching, his smile matching her own.

CHAPTER 21

Leia had wanted to learn so much during her challenges, but new lessons kept presenting themselves—unexpected ones, on things she'd never guessed she'd need to know.

For instance, she was now learning that the impatience you felt before kissing someone you liked wasn't nearly as bad as the impatience you felt afterward.

"Concentrate," Kier murmured as they stood in the center of the target dome. He sounded very severe, which was ironic given that he was the one who kept brushing his hand along her back.

"I'll watch my targets, hotshot. You watch yours." A glittering at the edge of Leia's peripheral vision made her spin sideways, her fingers tightening on the trigger the very moment she'd taken aim. The holographic target "shattered" into dizzying swirls of light before vanishing. She gave Kier a glance over her shoulder, as if she were being smug.

He obviously understood what she really felt, because he breathed in sharply, his targets forgotten. When she smiled, he leaned closer to her, the way he had back on Felucia . . .

. . . which gave her the chance to reach past him and blast one of *his* targets to bits.

"Stang," he muttered, which made her laugh. "You're distracting me on purpose, aren't you?"

"A girl's gotta win somehow."

"You usually win by just outshooting me."

Leia shrugged. "If I don't change it up, how can I keep you on your toes?"

Abandoning all pretense of paying attention to the game, Kier slung one arm around her and pulled her close for a quick, tantalizing kiss. Too quick, in Leia's opinion. She drew him back to her, and for a few long minutes the shimmering holographic targets spun and swirled around them in the darkness, safe from harm.

So this was what it felt like to live only in the moment—to forget responsibilities and rules—to find a secret part of yourself within another person, where somehow it had been hidden all along. The ominous future no longer loomed constantly over her; it had been banished to the distant place where it belonged. (It was only a possibility, not even a real thing yet, a prediction that might not come to pass.) She could hardly sleep for thinking about Kier at night, but woke up smiling every morning. After months of loneliness, she was again cherished. Even that wasn't as sweet as the feeling of cherishing someone back—caring about someone else so much that it felt as if she had two lives to lead, two perspectives on the galaxy, instead of just one. How had she ever managed with just one?

The end chime sounded, startling them from their embrace. Leia laughed when she saw their abysmal scores projected into the arena, and Kier groaned. "Okay," he said, "next time we have to concentrate, or else our skill levels are going to reset back to beginner."

"Think about it." Leia ran her hand along his wiry black hair, idly wishing he'd grow it long enough for her to weave her fingers through. "If our levels reset to beginner, we'll have to work our way back up again. That means hours and hours of practicing together, all alone in here, just you and me."

Exaggerating his thoughtful expression, he nodded. "You know, we could use lots more practice like today."

"So much more."

"Infinite amounts."

Before Leia could respond again, a red light shone down from the ceiling of the arena—a familiar signal in the senatorial complex, one that indicated a special announcement. Lettering appeared on the highest screen as a droid voice intoned, "There will be a formal address in the main chamber at sixteen hundred hours. All senators currently on Coruscant are required to attend."

Such mandatory addresses were rare, and they never meant anything good. A queasy uncertainty punctured Leia's giddiness; one look at Kier's face made it clear he felt the same way. He said only, "I don't think the requirement applies to apprentice legislators—but I think we ought to attend."

"No, it doesn't apply to us, and yes, we absolutely have to go."

Instantly Leia hurried toward the changing rooms. At least being so distracted with each other meant that she and Kier hadn't worked up a sweat in the arena. If they only changed, with no need to shower, they could make the session easily. She hadn't realized she could snap back into official mode with such speed. Probably that was a good thing.

However, there *was* a moment when Kier came out of his changing room still tying his wraparound jacket shut, revealing a glimpse of his bare chest—

"Let's go," she said to him, adding inside her head, *Snap out of it.*

•◆•

Leia had been allowed to sit in her father's senatorial pod a few times as a little girl, and she'd accompanied him to most of his sessions while she'd been working as his intern. To her it felt very familiar, or it should have.

Yet as she took her place in the pod that afternoon, she became sharply aware that the mood in the Imperial Senate had shifted in the past few months. Normally senators spoke to each other via comms almost constantly in the minutes before an address began, mostly bureaucratic chitchat, the verbal equivalent of the majority of the work they did. While the Imperial Senate was too heavily yoked by Palpatine's rule, they maintained a sense of busyness and endeavor—an eagerness to accomplish whatever they could.

Today the chamber was very nearly silent. Senators filed in, took their seats, and said almost nothing, not even to the staffers sitting with them in their pods. Most of the sounds Leia heard were the thumps of footsteps and the rustles of robes, along with a few odd coughs and chirps. The stillness unnerved her.

Come to think of it, the Senate sessions had been quieting for a while. The boisterous beginnings she remembered as a tiny child had become more subdued later on, the stillness falling so gradually that Leia had missed it until now. Had the senators forgotten that they still held some authority? That they were one of the few forces standing between Palpatine and absolute power? They couldn't afford to become passive in the face of resistance; that was when they needed to bear down and work harder. . . .

Then she remembered Arreyel, and sagged in her seat.

"Are you all right?" Kier murmured next to her. Despite his concern, he didn't seem to recognize the depth of her disquiet—but of course he wouldn't. He didn't know her reasons.

Instead of answering his question, she said, "This is your first time in the Senate chamber, isn't it?"

"Except for one introductory tour." His grin pierced her through. He was excited about this, thrilled to see it, because he had no better days to compare it to. *He still believes. I have to believe too. We* can *accomplish something in this chamber, even if it's harder than it used to be.*

The entry to the pod slid open, and Bail Organa walked through. His expression seemed as distant as usual, until he saw Leia and Kier sitting side by side, closer than she'd realized they were until now. He raised one eyebrow in what ought to have been a gentle joke. Instead it sparked Leia's temper. How could he shut her out for so long and yell at her when she was only trying to help, then act like nothing was wrong?

At least she was grown-up enough not to say any of that out loud. She simply half-turned her head, refusing to meet her father's eyes.

Kier, however, was already getting to his feet. "Good afternoon, Viceroy. I hope it's not inappropriate for us to attend."

"Of course not, Mr. Domadi. It's good you're both here." Bail took his seat, drawing his long coat closer around him. The Senate chamber was kept relatively cool—a concession to the many senators whose planets' elaborate court dress could be suffocating. But Leia knew her father well enough to recognize that gesture and know it had nothing to do with cold. It was a sign he was worried.

Bail Organa was a calm, even-tempered man. He didn't worry without reason.

The hushed room fell completely silent as the speaker's pod rose to the center of the room, all lights swiveling to refocus on that spot. Grand Moff Tarkin stood there in his olive-green uniform, a figure as narrow and sharp as the blade of the Rhindon Sword. His image on the pod's console screen revealed a thin smile on his face—the most ominous sign of all.

"Esteemed senators." His thin voice rang throughout the chamber, and Leia didn't think that was just the amplification droids at work. This man knew how to project his authority without seeming even to move. "You will remember the terrible incident but a few weeks ago, when insurgents attempted to compromise an Imperial medical frigate. As paltry an effort as it was, it nonetheless represents an egregious disrespect for the law of the Empire, and for Emperor Palpatine himself."

Paltry? Taking a whole medical frigate? Leia tried to call to mind the sheer size of the enormous Imperial Starfleet; its ships were so numerous, so titanic, so populated with millions upon millions of officers that it was hard for a human mind to truly comprehend it. Maybe losing one frigate didn't matter so much.

No. It mattered. Otherwise Tarkin wouldn't be so determinedly pretending it didn't.

Tarkin had a prim smile, one that looked as though it knew it didn't belong on his face. "A thorough investigation revealed that the instigators of this action came from within the government of the planet Christophsis, which has received untold riches from this Empire in order to rebuild from its devastation in the Clone Wars. These leaders chose to reward our generosity with rank ingratitude."

Bail Organa's hands closed into fists in his lap. Following her father's gaze, Leia saw that the Christophsis senatorial pod remained empty.

"Therefore, we have made an example of these leaders—I should say, former leaders. While the ex-senators and territorial supervisors have been jailed for terms of four years or more, the prime minister has been tried, convicted, and executed for treason. Furthermore, his home city of

Tophen—found to be the center of this activity—has already been pacified." That meant hundreds of thousands dead, if not millions. The shock numbed Leia to her fingertips. Tarkin raised an eyebrow, as if he could hear the cries of protest silent within every person in that assembly. "It is hoped that this action, drastic though it is, has served to quell the radical elements at work on Christophsis, to restore the planet to order, and to deliver a message to all those who would threaten the peace our Emperor has given us: we stand here now, always, and forevermore. No matter what else may come, the Empire will endure."

A few senators from Coruscant and Glee Anselm began to applaud wholeheartedly. Others joined in almost immediately, Bail Organa among them. Although Kier stared at his viceroy clapping for an eternal Empire, Leia understood and put her hands together too.

The recorders would be focusing on every pod, every person. Anyone who failed to show the appropriate enthusiasm for Palpatine's latest outrage would become a likely target in the future.

Tyranny turns us into liars, she thought, hating herself even as she applauded. Leia looked sideways to see her father smiling sadly at her. He felt exactly the same, she knew, and she couldn't be angry with him any longer. Although he continued clapping, Bail turned back to Tarkin with his chin held high, his gaze unblinking, in a silent show of defiance.

Her attention shifted over to Kier, who wasn't clapping. No doubt he didn't yet understand the full political ramifications of this moment. Maybe he saw her and her father as hypocrites.

Worrying about what he'd make of her didn't trouble Leia as much as the way he stared at her father. Kier didn't appear admiring, intimidated, or confused.

He appeared . . . angry.

When he'd first learned of the plans against the Empire, he'd said her parents were endangering their world through their involvement. This news proved his point. What happened on Christophsis could happen on Alderaan, any day, any moment.

CHAPTER 22

"We should return to Alderaan for a few days," Bail Organa said after the session, as all around them other senators walked back to their offices in various states of ill-concealed anger and shock. "I have business to conduct there, and besides—I've missed your mother very much." *Translation: I have to talk to your mother about what happened on Christophsis.*

Leia wanted to be home as well, safe within the palace walls, hopefully discussing this openly with her parents. She was also aware of an urge to burrow deep into her own bed, beneath the covers, which was embarrassingly childish but would feel so good. "When will we leave?"

"As soon as the *Polestar* can be readied." Bail turned to Kier, who was walking silently slightly to the side of father and daughter. "You're very welcome to return with us, Mr. Domadi. There's more than enough room aboard."

"It's an honor to be invited, sir. I accept."

Leia's heart leapt at the thought of spending still more time with Kier, at least until she realized that they'd have her father as a chaperone. Even worse, her dad's presence would keep her from discussing Christophsis openly with Kier—and Kier's presence would keep her from discussing it openly with her dad. Bail's generous offer to his daughter's friend had bought all three of them several hours of strained conversation about absolutely any subject other than the one they all had foremost on their minds.

She sighed. Conspiracies were harder than they looked.

•◆•

The Organa family didn't speak of Christophsis until dinnertime, when they dined alone on the terrace. As soon as the last human attendant left, leaving behind only a few servitor droids, Breha uttered a swear word Leia had never heard from her mother's lips before, then added, "How could they do it?"

"You know how." Bail shut his eyes briefly, and his fingers closed around the handle of his dinner knife as if he might soon have to use it as a weapon. "Palpatine's maintained his stranglehold on this galaxy for nearly two decades. An entire generation has grown up with no memory of the Republic and no idea of what true freedom would look like. Perhaps he thinks he doesn't need to respect even the last vestiges of self-rule our worlds have."

Leia would've protested that she knew what true freedom would look like, as did Kier and probably most of her other friends. That was something you could recognize even when you'd never seen it before. But she wanted her parents to get used to talking about this with her in their presence before she jumped in.

Rising from her chair, Breha paced the length of the terrace. The dark red caftan she wore was cut just low enough in front to reveal the soft glow of her pulmonodes, which had replaced her heart and lungs after the long-ago accident that had so nearly killed her. Most people who'd received pulmonodes kept them visible only temporarily, until they went through the bacta sessions necessary to encase them in new flesh and skin. However, Leia's mother wore hers proudly. *It reminds me that I lived,* she'd told Leia once. *That I cannot be so easily stopped.*

"Do you think this will finally make the others see what I've seen?" Breha continued gazing out toward Aldera on the horizon, hugging her arms against her chest. "Do you think they'll finally accept that the Empire will only be defeated through direct action? Are they ready to take up arms?" When her husband didn't answer right away, she added, "You still see it, don't you?"

Bail nodded as he leaned back in his chair, and a squat little droid took the opportunity to refresh his Chandrilan tea with hot water. "I meant what I said a few months ago. While I still don't think such conflict is inevitable—I accept now that it's likely. Even advisable. Mon

Mothma believes so, and she works even harder on me than you do."

Breha smiled ruefully. "Good for her."

"You must see that what happened on Christophsis makes things harder for us," he said. "Getting everyone on board after something like this will be difficult."

Leia could remain silent no more. "Standing up to the Empire means taking a risk. A big risk. Everybody has to have known that already."

Her mother returned to the table, though her attention was for her daughter rather than the meal. "Of course they knew before now. But there's a great difference between knowledge in the abstract and the concrete reality of dead bodies and destroyed cities. We have to live with the absolute certainty that our freedom from the Empire can't be bought only with information, resources, and money. In the end, the price will be blood."

Hardly able to believe she dared, Leia said, "What if that means the blood of the people of Alderaan?"

Sharing a stricken look, her parents gazed at each other for a few long seconds before Bail said, "If we're to be true to Alderaan's ideals of justice, dignity, and peace for all peoples, then we must share equally in the necessary risks."

His words resonated inside Leia, ringing true to everything she believed. Yet she couldn't forget what Kier had said, either. "We've created justice, dignity, and peace here. One place in the galaxy where people can live the way they should live, not kneeling at Palpatine's feet. We have to protect that, don't we?"

Bail rose to his feet, a move so sudden that it rattled the table and made both mother and daughter jump. "I thought we raised you better than this, Leia. You're not a selfish girl, and you're not a cowardly one. So stop acting the part." With that he turned and stalked off the terrace without looking back.

Leia stared down at her plate. Her mostly uneaten meal blurred with tears she refused to shed, and she bit down on her lower lip, hoping one pain would erase another.

"Sweetheart. It's all right. He shouldn't have said that." Breha came to her daughter's side and took one of Leia's hands in her own. "You're not the one he's angry with."

"That's not what it sounds like." Leia blinked back the tears just in time.

Her mother shook her head. "What you're saying now isn't so different from what he was saying last year. After the Clone Wars, your father hoped never again to see a larger galactic conflict. He accepted this only with great difficulty, and I think hearing you make those same arguments—it forces him to confront just how serious circumstances are, that this is what we have to contemplate."

Larger galactic conflict. That could mean a number

of things, none of them good. "What exactly are we contemplating?"

Breha pulled back; Leia had finally found the new boundary of what her parents were willing to reveal. "Let us be the ones to worry about that." She ran one hand over her daughter's braids. "I'm sorry we've burdened you as much as we have already."

"The truth isn't a burden."

"Oh, sweetheart." Breha's smile was sad. "If only that were so."

•◆•

That night, Leia was distracted for a brief time by a video Kier had sent her, a time-lapse image of the candlewick flowers in his family's garden opening to the night; he'd chosen beautiful music to go with it, and she felt almost as though he'd given her a bouquet.

Even that thrill faded quickly when she thought back on everything that had happened that day. Her father's harsh words felt like lash strokes that would take a long time to heal; even that wasn't as bad as remembering the fate of Christophsis. Grand Moff Tarkin's chilly satisfaction in the deaths of so many people—

So much for sleep, Leia decided, throwing off her coverlet. By this time the palace would be silent and still. Her parents and the human staff were probably asleep, and the majority of the droids would, like 2V, stand dormant in their charging stations.

In other words, it was the perfect time to sneak around.

•◆•

Slipping on her blue robe, Leia tied her long hair back in one tail before tiptoeing into the hallway. Although the ancient stone walls could muffle any number of sounds, she trusted the silence that surrounded her. No light shone beyond a few candledroids hovering every few meters. Her heart thumped as she hurried along, checking each new room as she went. It felt almost absurd to be so worried about moving around her own home, particularly since no one but her parents would dream of stopping her, and she'd never been forbidden to go into the queen's private stateroom when her mother wasn't present.

But the fact was, she intended to snoop.

Breha had said, *Our freedom from the Empire can't be bought only with information, resources, and money.* That suggested their allies were already pooling funds. All those hours her mother now spent huddled over the ledgers and accounts—Leia suspected that wasn't just the usual work of handling the crown's purse. The extra time could well be attention the queen was giving to the monies for whatever great effort her parents had in mind.

Breha's private stateroom was a smaller space, bordered

on one side by the vast chamber of the public stateroom and on the other by the library. One of the oldest areas of the palace still in common use, the room had stone walls, exposed wooden rafters, and a fireplace so enormous it stretched nearly the entire length of the room and was deep enough to walk into. The thick hand-woven rugs kept the chill of the stone floor at bay. So cozy was the ambiance of the space that her mother occasionally abandoned the queen's offices to work in here, in the light and heat of a real fire.

Which meant the info portal in that room was cleared for access to the royal accounts.

Leia placed her palm over the silver circle of the sentry, then smiled when the portal lit up. Every member of the royal family could delve into the accounts, though she'd never done so except during her ill-fated attempt to learn bookkeeping. While her parents might have sealed off strategic information about their efforts, she was wagering that they wouldn't have thought to hide the funds.

The wager paid off. Her brief acquaintance with the royal accounting told her which expenses were normal, and which were more unusual. Immense amounts of credits were coming in and out under the suspiciously generic-yet-unfamiliar label *Spaceport Development.* Leia knew full well Alderaan wasn't currently building or even planning a major new spaceport. That meant she also knew where to start digging.

She hadn't been examining the funds under that label very long before she first ran into Itapi Prime. Chandrila. Ocahont. Paucris Major. Crait. Unzel. Mon Cala.

What she already knew about the senators and places involved told her that probably all of these worlds were in some way connected to her parents' efforts against the Empire. Paucris Major in particular seemed especially active in the past few months; the amount of credits directed there was staggering—far beyond the capacity of even the royal purse of Alderaan. Furthermore, like Crait, Paucris Major sent no money in, only received it.

They must be building a base there, she thought, just like Crait. But that explanation didn't satisfy her. Paucris Major had received more than fifty times the credits given to Crait; whatever was going on there operated on an entirely different scale.

Leia had no intentions of dropping into yet another military outpost with a blaster on her hip. Her father's words about shooting down possible intruders had stayed with her.

But that didn't mean she couldn't take a look. Evaluate.

Once she'd memorized the information that seemed most pertinent, she eased out of the private stateroom and headed down the hallway. As she walked past the library, though, she heard her father's voice: "Leia?"

Her first thought: *busted*. She caught herself, though. The act of walking around her own home wasn't inherently sneaky. Guilt just made it feel that way.

She went through the library door to find her father sitting in one of the large leather chairs by the far windows. Outside the dark blue night was spangled with stars in the sky and candlewick blooms on the ground. He wore a deep green robe—once almost as impressive as his viceroy's coat, now worn almost shabby. One of the old paper books lay across his lap.

"What are you doing with that?" she said as she came close.

Bail gestured idly at the book. "Looking for wisdom in the past. Though of course they had no more then than we do now." His warm brown eyes regarded her more tenderly than they had in a long time. "I'm sorry I've been so short with you of late."

Leia's first impulse was to say "It's okay," but she resisted. Better to tell the truth. "It feels like I can't do anything right where you're concerned."

He shook his head in disbelief. "You've done almost everything right your entire life! We've always been so proud of you, so fortunate in you. Sometimes I still can't believe that of all the children in the galaxy, fate brought you to us."

They'd always said such things to her, but it had been a while since Leia had last heard those words, and they affected her more than before. A lump in her throat, she said, "I got pretty lucky too."

Bail held out one hand. She took it, sinking down onto the padded bench at his feet. As he squeezed her fingers, he said, "What your mother and I are trying to accomplish . . . it's the most ambitious, dangerous, terrifying thing we've ever done. We're risking everything, even you. The weight of that knowledge bears down on me every day. If I've taken my frustrations out on you, I apologize."

Her voice wavered as she replied, "I can't imagine how hard that must be."

"I hope you never have to know."

As long as they were being honest, Leia figured she might as well acknowledge the hardest truth of all: "You know keeping me in the dark won't save me, if the Empire discovers what you're doing."

Her father closed his eyes, as if in pain. "Maybe not. But if there's any chance, any at all, we have to give you that."

"I still think I could help."

"You can, in the Senate." She rolled her eyes, but

Bail leaned closer to her and continued, "Making allies, forming allegiances that exist independent of Palpatine's control—that's the most important work in the Imperial Senate, these days. If I hadn't worked together with Mon Mothma for so long in the Senate, do you think we could be allies in this?"

Leia had never considered this angle before. "So it's not just about the official work. It's about the unofficial connections."

"Precisely. Nowhere else can so many planetary leaders come together without danger or secrecy. The Imperial Senate is only a shadow of what it was in the days of the Republic, but someday, I hope, it will be remembered as the cradle of an alliance that brought freedom back to the galaxy." He smiled gently at his daughter. "Learn to play your part in the politics *behind* the politics, Leia. There truly is valuable work to be done."

"I never thought of it that way before." Brightening, she added, "And the people in the Apprentice Legislature are the ones who might be senators in their own right in a few years."

"Exactly. These are the people who will be important in your future." Her father's dark eyes took on the mischievous twinkle she knew so well. "Like, say, this Kier Domadi—"

"*Stop.*" Leia mock-shoved her father away, which made him laugh. She'd missed the sound of his laughter more than she'd known.

"You can't stop us from asking questions forever, you know." Bail's curiosity appeared very real, but she knew him well enough to understand he wouldn't pry if she didn't want, and she didn't. What she had with Kier was too new, too fragile to fully reveal yet. It would be like prying open the petals of a candlewick blossom in the daytime, only to have the sunbeams scorch the bud within and permanently extinguish the light.

"I'll tell you about it when there's more to tell," she finally said. "Okay?"

Her father nodded once, sharply, like a man making a deal he was happy with. "Okay."

When she left the library that night, she felt aglow with happiness and relief. Being at odds with her father had haunted her; at least now they were friends again, and she understood him better. More than that, she saw a way for her work in the Apprentice Legislature to be truly useful.

But that didn't mean she'd forgotten about Paucris Major.

CHAPTER 23

Looking for allies in the Apprentice Legislature also meant looking for them in her pathfinding class. It made sense to start with Harp Allor, since Chandrila was already so strongly allied with Alderaan; Mon Mothma appeared to be even more central to the work against Palpatine than Leia's parents were, and the other Chandrilan senator, Winmey Lenz, had attended several of the banquets-that-weren't-really-banquets. Together, Leia figured, she and Harp could assess everyone else.

So she managed to get on to Harp's team for the next pathfinding trek, through the marshlands of Chandrila itself, hoping they'd have a chance to talk.

They didn't.

"This is disgusting." Chassellon waded through the hip-deep mud, wiping his sweaty forehead with the back of his hand. "I thought Felucia was bad. And I thought Chandrila was supposed to be a *civilized* planet."

"It is! We are! But the marshes are—well, they're like this," Harp finished, deflated.

One of the few wildernesses remaining on Chandrila, the marshlands were swampy and hot, wreathed in opaque mists exuding from the twisty, blue-leafed trees that formed at least ninety percent of the landmarks. Chief Pangie had told them that finding their way through the marshes would test their ability to observe and remember small details. Leia decided she should've known from the chief's grin that the trip would also involve extra misery.

"We're running behind, I just know it," Harp whined. "We'll be the last ones to the rendezvous point."

Leia managed to smile for her. "Doesn't matter as long as we get there."

"Aren't marshes supposed to be flat?" Chassellon griped as they trudged on, their way illuminated by sunlight filtered greenish by the mists. "Because we've been going upward at a small incline for the past three hours, and I'm bloody well sick of it."

"We'll get to the mud flats in a few klicks," Leia promised. At least, they would if she was correctly remembering the oddly splinted-together roots of one particular tree.

Chassellon looked toward the skies for mercy that wouldn't arrive. "Mud flats? *Mud flats* represent our big opportunity for everything to get better?"

"You said you wanted to stop climbing!" Harp retorted. "Well, this is your chance!"

Would I fail my Challenge of the Body if I abandoned two of my pathfinding partners in the wilderness? Leia gritted her teeth and pushed onward.

Sure enough, once they reached the mud flats, she was glad to see them. The flats rose up from the swamps in a series of plateaus, none of them appealing but at least more solid than liquid, unlike the gunk they'd been soldiering through. If they could just work their way up the flats, they'd have a clear view to the shorelands beyond, which would lead them to the rendezvous point and home. Leia glanced down at her skintight trek suit and sarong—both thickly coated with mud—and wondered what Kier must look like. She couldn't wait to tease him about it, or to be teased in return—

"Finally," Chassellon said. "All right, Harp, boost me up and I'll pull the two of you after me."

Harp put her hands on her hips. "Why should I be the one to boost you up? Why shouldn't you boost me? You're taller than me; you'd be better at it."

He doubled down. "Well, I'm also stronger than you, so I'd be better at pulling you up, too."

"You don't know that you're stronger."

"Oh, please, Harp! You hardly come up to my elbows."

"That doesn't make me weak!"

Force give me the strength not to actually murder them, Leia thought. But their endless bickering, combined with her exhaustion and the general grossness of the day, had worked on her temper until it was near the breaking point. Once again her temples throbbed, and the only thing she could think of to be glad about was the fact that she was a few paces behind them and still—for the time being—out of the argument.

"You're just angry that you can't buy your way to the top of the class, like you do with everything else!" Harp shouted. "Some of us actually care about doing the right thing!"

Chassellon yelled back, "Some of us just want to get out of the mud already!"

The anger within Leia boiled hotter, until it felt like the only strength left in her body. Surely, at any moment, she would snap—

That was when she heard the distant rush, and felt the faint rumble beneath her feet.

Leia lifted her head, looking up the flats. Through the greenish mists, did she see . . . movement?

The sound loudened until it caught Chassellon's attention. "What's that?"

"Oh, kriff," breathed Harp, her eyes widening. "*Mudslide.*"

It was as if the name made the image snap into focus. Horrified, Leia realized half the hillside was now sluicing down toward them. Those on the bank could run for it, but anybody still in the mud when the slide hit would be swept away.

"Chassellon, you go first!" Leia cried. He was right about being stronger. She cupped her hands together, and he instantly stepped into them, hurling himself onto the bank. Over the roar of the mudslide—louder every second—she said, "Come on, Harp! Now!"

Harp took the step after that, reaching for Chassellon's outstretched hands as he pulled her onto the bank. Then he lunged forward, desperately reaching for Leia—

The wave hit her as hard as anything solid, as hard as a tree or a wall. The breath left her lungs; the light left her eyes. Her body tumbled over and over, surrounded and suffocated by heavy mud rushing along at incredible speed. She felt as if death itself had swallowed her whole.

Pathfinder training kicked in. Squeezing her eyes shut, Leia forced her hand down to her belt, where she hit the field generator. She heard a horrible slurping, liquid sound all around her—then startled as the mud popped out to the edge of the field, leaving her bobbing in an energy bubble. By the dim light at her belt, Leia could make out the swirls and ooze of the mud rushing by.

Although panic tugged at the edges of her consciousness, she managed to keep her body still; the bubble was strong but not impermeable, and thrashing around could compromise the field's integrity. She had to trust it. *Air is lighter than mud. Lightness rises and heaviness falls. Wait it out.*

But there's only so much air in this bubble—

Light slowly began to filter in, then burst upon her in a rush as the bubble surfaced. Bobbing within it, Leia rolled sideways toward the nearest dry land, or what passed for it on Chandrila's marshes. Once she saw wet, flattened grass beneath her, she turned off the field generator and flopped onto the ground like a caught fish. Her breaths came too quickly in her chest, and mud covered nearly every millimeter of her body. It didn't matter. All she wanted was to lie here, not moving, preferably forever.

From a distance she heard her name being called. After another few moments, she regained enough energy to care, and to recognize the voices.

"Leia?" Harp was very nearly screaming. "Leia?"

"Your Highness!" Chassellon had pitched his voice to carry, a surprisingly deep, booming shout. "We're looking for you! If you can hear us, let us know where you are!"

After a couple of tries, Leia was able to take a deep enough breath to cry back, "Here!"

They ran up to her moments later, each of them so obviously terrified that Leia almost wanted to laugh. "Field generator," she said, coughing once. "Remember?"

Harp collapsed by Leia's side. "I forgot all about it."

"You won't next time," Leia pointed out, then had to

cough again. Maybe she'd swallowed a little mud at the beginning.

Chassellon pulled himself together almost instantly, and held out his hand to Leia, courtly and formal. "Will you rise, my lady?" Usually she found his emphasis on her royal status irritating, but today it felt comforting, like being wrapped in a familiar blanket. Leia let him pull her to her feet. Although the world tilted oddly at first, she soon regained her balance. Wet mud slithered down her body, and Chassellon put his free hand to his chest. "Your royal robes are stunning, Your Highness. Designer?"

She laughed again. "One of a kind."

•◆•

They belatedly made it to the rendezvous point, so late that Chief Pangie and the others had begun assembling a search party. Kier went to Leia immediately, gathering her in his arms. *So much for being discreet,* she thought, although at the moment she couldn't care.

Chassellon's temper had returned, and this time it was directed squarely at the chief. "This is ridiculous! Harp gets injured on Alderaan, Leia and Kier nearly fall to their deaths on Felucia, and now this? Pathfinding's supposed to be a learning experience, not survival of the fittest!"

Chief Pangie just shook her head. "Field generators, Stevis. You're supposed to use the field generators so that nobody gets hurt. You have to remember that."

"Or else what?" Chassellon retorted. "We die?"

"Exactly." The chief let the word hang in the shocked silence that followed, until she continued in a quieter, more serious tone than Leia had ever heard from her. "Pathfinding can be dangerous. Every single one of you knew that before you began. Every single one of you thought that danger somehow didn't apply to you, because you're young and stupid about that kind of thing. You have to learn better, and I'd rather you learned it out here with your field generators to save you, than somewhere else in the galaxy where you get no safety net, no teammates, and no second chances. Pathfinding isn't just about learning how to find your way around. It's about learning how to think on your feet. How to deal with real risks. Even how to face the fear of death."

Did my parents realize this? Leia wondered, before deciding that of course they had.

In the circle of her classmates, everyone remained hushed and subdued—Harp pale and shaky, Sssamm with his head hanging low, Chassellon unexpectedly solemn—except for pink-haired Amilyn Holdo, who grinned and said, "I *knew* it!"

•◆•

Originally Leia had planned on returning to Coruscant with the others, but after her tumble through the mudslide, she felt the need to go back home at least for a night or two.

"I could come with you, if you want." Kier held one of her hands in both of his as they stood at the spaceport. The class's transport sat a few meters away, their friends already climbing aboard. "Look after you on the way back. Then we could return to Coruscant together."

"It's all right. Honestly, I'm exhausted. I just want to sleep." Which was true—if not the whole truth. Leia wasn't so shaken by her experience that she'd failed to see an opportunity, one she wasn't yet ready to share with anybody else, even Kier.

"If you're sure," Kier said. When she nodded, he kissed her forehead once, brushed his thumb along her cheek, and headed off to the transport.

Leia didn't have to wait on her own very long. The *Polestar* arrived promptly, with Ress Batten alone at the helm. Batten hurried out to greet her, then frowned. "You look fine. I was told you'd been in mortal peril, and this is, what, slightly mussed hair?"

"You should've seen me before I washed up." Even though she'd changed back into her dark blue traveling gown and now looked almost as polished as 2V could wish for, Leia's skin still itched from the mere memory of mud. "Come on, let's go."

They took off from the surface of Chandrila without more than half a dozen extra words exchanged between them. Never had Batten mentioned their voyage to Crait, but Leia could sense the knowledge between them at times, a silence more energizing than intimidating. Although she wasn't certain how to read Batten's reaction, it certainly wasn't disapproval, or fear.

Hopefully it was curiosity.

"So," Leia began, a few minutes before they would make the jump to hyperspace, "would you say that we've—taken some interesting trips together?"

Batten shook her head. "They've been pretty dull, really. Average. Everyday. Humdrum."

"Humdrum. Like that run to Crait."

"*So* boring."

Leia made sure to look down at the console, not at Batten's face, as she said, "On the way home—I was thinking—if it wouldn't take too long, maybe we could take another boring trip. Something completely average."

"Oh, yeah?" The note of pure anticipation in Ress Batten's voice made Leia look up to see the older woman's grin. "Turns out I could use a little more humdrum in my life."

She wants this, Leia thought. *She knows this is action against the*

Empire, and she wants in. How many others must be ready, willing, even eager to join us as soon as we speak the word?

To Batten she said only, "The Paucris Major system. No landings this time—distance observation only. And let's leave it off the logs."

"Your Highness, I like the way you think."

As the *Polestar* hurtled through the blue shimmer of hyperspace, Leia lay back on one of the long couches. Adrenaline battled with exhaustion and won—barely—as she counted through the possibilities. *Batten's probably a good candidate to join us someday. Chassellon Stevis? Maybe not as bad as he seems at first, but still, he'd report us in a heartbeat. Amilyn Holdo . . .* Leia frowned. By now she genuinely liked Amilyn and believed her to have noble ideals, but that didn't change the fact that the girl seemed highly unlikely to be useful in a crisis situation.

Thinking of Kier made her smile. Of course Kier would want to play a role. She hadn't forgotten his concerns about protecting Alderaan, but lots of planets were joining forces now. He loathed the Emperor and was braver about speaking out than most. When they took action, he'd be by their side.

"Coming out of hyperspace in a moment, Your Highness," Batten called back to Leia.

When she stood up, Leia felt another wave of tiredness hit her. She reminded herself of the bed waiting for her back on Alderaan. It wouldn't be long now. They were only here to take a few scans of the system. To her it seemed no more than feeling out the dimensions of what her parents were planning, getting an idea of scope and scale that would let her know what to prepare for. Would they be going after targets like Calderos Station? Trying to persuade more ships to defect?

The small shudder that went through the *Polestar* meant they were back in realspace. Leia joined Ress Batten in the cockpit and found her already running scans. "You sure are interested in this boring planet," she said.

But Batten had lost interest in the joke. "Oh, kriff," she said as data scrolled by her. "Kriffing kriff."

"What? There aren't—is the Empire—"

"No, that's not it." Batten brought up a visual on the screen. "Look at this."

The scans hadn't even touched the planet's surface; instead, they focused on what floated in orbit. Dozens of larger ships, from midsized transports to enormous planetary battleships, were tethered to spindly deep-space repair stations, no doubt by tractor beams. Some of the ships were newer, but most looked old—though Leia could tell they were being repaired. *No. Refurbished.* Kier had shown her enough of his Clone Wars historical materials for her to recognize that some of the planetary ships dated from that era, but they now sported newer, top-of-the-line engines.

"They're fixing them up," Batten said, more to herself than to Leia. "Getting them ready."

Up until this moment, Leia had believed her parents would support strike attacks. Controlled, directed military action, nothing like the terrorist acts of Saw Gerrera. Resistance to Palpatine's forces, maybe defense for those most directly endangered. Pressure that would force the Emperor to listen, to moderate, maybe even to abdicate.

She'd been fooling herself.

Looking out at the sheer scope of the armada in front of her, Leia finally understood that her parents were preparing to go to war.

CHAPTER 24

"The Clone Wars." The docent of the Emperor's Museum addressed the Apprentice Legislature tour with the clasped hands and carefully monotone voice of a funeral guest. Behind him, a flat screen showed images of thousands of clone troopers marching in lockstep across rugged terrain. "A tragedy such as has rarely been seen before, and thankfully never will again."

Leia flinched, then glanced around her, hoping no one had noticed. Nobody had. Most of her classmates were visibly, profoundly bored; Kier, who stood by her side, was of course completely engrossed in the images playing before them, real footage of the Clone Wars he'd studied so much.

Real footage. False history.

"Count Dooku of Serenno led the Separatist faction away from the faltering Republic," the docent continued. "Although he acted out of craven ambition, with disregard for the billions of lives that would be lost. Dooku was correct about one thing. The Republic had indeed become rotten at its core, no longer governed by law, order, and discipline. Had the Senate chosen a different chancellor after the deposition of the weak, ineffectual Valorum, galactic order itself might have fallen apart. But the times we live through create the heroes we need."

The inaugural portrait of Palpatine filled the screen until it seemed as if the Emperor himself was smiling down at them with kindly eyes. Leia wondered how much digital manipulation had been necessary to create that illusion of kindness. Or maybe he was only acting. Either way, she couldn't see the point of projecting a benevolent image while doing everything necessary to prove himself a cruel man and a warmonger.

Palpatine started the past war. Was her father starting the next one?

As the docent led them into the display about Palpatine's childhood (titled "From Humble Beginnings," like Naboo was poverty-stricken), Leia trailed behind. Kier murmured, "Are you all right? You've been quiet all day."

"I guess. It's all just so—" She made a hand gesture instead of outright saying the word *fake.*

Kier considered that carefully. "When I go looking for deeper background information, it's . . . hard to find primary sources."

"You should talk to my dad sometime. He could tell you stories you wouldn't believe. Like the time bounty hunters took him and several other senators hostage in the heart of the Senate itself." It was safe to mention that incident publicly. Most of the stories Bail Organa had to tell about the Clone Wars were far more politically sensitive.

"Would he tell me about it? Really?" Kier had the fascinated gleam in his eye that most guys his age only had for new speeders.

Leia managed a smile. "Yeah. My parents adore you, by the way."

"Hope they're not the only ones."

She nudged his side, he nudged back, and they took each other's hands. A few steps away she saw Chassellon pretending to vomit; the joke was probably meant to be more friendly than not, but Leia had no patience for it. In truth she found it hard to concentrate even on Kier's presence, or the museum of lies around them.

Her mind kept going back to the fleet around Paucris Major, preparing for a conflict with the potential to make the Clone Wars look like a dinner party.

•◆•

"Another dinner party?" Leia said in dismay as she stood in the great hall of the palace, watching the servitor droids whir about in a bustle of activity.

"Yes, our queen is holding yet another banquet." 2V practically gleamed with satisfaction as she rolled alongside her royal charge, weaving through droids carrying wine-glasses and bundles of flowers. "I must say, it's so good to see a return to proper courtly standards of hospitality and conviviality. Now, spit-spot, off to your room. We've got to make you presentable, and the Maker knows we hardly have the time!" There was nothing for Leia to do but follow.

She'd decided to come clean with her parents about snooping around the Paucris system as soon as she returned to Alderaan. Probably their explanation would be terrifying in its own right—as would the inevitable lecture she'd receive—but she'd decided she could endure any concrete truth better than the suspense of not knowing.

Instead, she'd have to bear at least one more day of it, plus the knowledge that her parents were hard at work planning this right here in the palace, around a dinner table with their co-conspirators.

Listen to me—"co-conspirators," Leia thought as she absently shimmied into the pale yellow gown 2V had laid out for her. Her brain had already run ahead to one potential future, where this had all gone horribly wrong, where her parents were jailed or executed for treason, and where she was either left utterly alone or made to die by their side. It was as though she could hear the judicial officer speaking the charges already.

"Shall I put on the cuffs?" 2V said.

Leia stared at her until she realized the droid was talking about the broad silver cuff bracelets set out atop a cabinet. With a sigh, she held out her hands.

By the time she emerged onto the terrace, the guests had already assembled. This appeared to be a smaller banquet than most; no doubt the people gathered around formed the core of the anti-Palpatine movement. Bail Organa was deep in discussion with Winmey Lenz, while Breha spoke with Senator Pamlo. In the distance, Aldera sparkled on the twilight horizon. It was Mon Mothma who first welcomed Leia, walking closer with a smile on her face. "Princess. How very good to see you again."

"It's good to see you too," Leia said, but it wasn't. How was she supposed to get through the usual small talk with what she'd seen at Paucris weighing so heavily on her? Then it hit her—she could just ask Mon Mothma herself. Nobody else at this gathering would tell Leia the truth, maybe not even her parents, but Mon Mothma probably would. Leia began, "My class took a trip to Chandrila recently—"

"I heard you fell prey to the mud flats." Mon Mothma put one hand on Leia's arm, a brief touch of apology. "If you come back sometime and let me know, I can make sure you spend your time somewhere more agreeable."

As in, anywhere else ever. But Leia didn't get sidetracked. "On the way back, I took a short side—"

She broke off as the doors to the terrace swung open wide, revealing the palace majordomo, Tarrik, who looked on edge and discombobulated. Leia understood why the moment she recognized the figure behind him.

"Your Majesty, Viceroy," Tarrik announced in his booming voice, his eyes darting from side to side. "Presenting Grand Moff Wilhuff Tarkin."

Silence instantly fell. Everyone went utterly still, except for Tarkin, who strolled onto the terrace as though it were his own. He wore full military uniform and a thin-lipped smile. "Your Majesty," he said, half-bowing to Breha, his behavior as polished and polite as though he had actually been invited. "Forgive my intrusion."

"Governor Tarkin." Breha responded so easily, smiled so gently, that any outsider would've thought nothing was wrong. "To what do we owe this unexpected pleasure?"

"I was traveling in my personal vessel, the *Carrion Spike*, when it suffered a systems malfunction." Tarkin sighed. "Nothing too major, I hope, but we needed to put in for repair, and Alderaan was the closest world. Naturally I knew I must pay my respects to the queen and her viceroy as soon as possible."

"You're very welcome here," Bail said. Even after working with her father for two years in politics, Leia had never before seen him lie so smoothly.

Tarkin took the measure of the terrace. His mind was

even sharper than his gaze, which meant he no doubt recognized all of them instantly. "I appear to have interrupted something."

The knowledge froze Leia faster than carbonite: *He knows.*

Her mother had to realize it too, but her smile never wavered. "A simple dinner party, Governor. You are of course invited to join us."

Of course she'd invited Tarkin—what else could she do?—but Leia still felt herself newly wrenched by horror when Tarkin said, "How very gracious of you, Queen Breha. I accept."

Everyone else on the terrace was beginning to adjust, mustering smiles and nods, but Leia felt sure they all wanted to faint and/or scream, just as badly as she did.

But one new realization gave her the strength to hang on: Tarkin *didn't* know. He suspected, which was bad enough, but if he'd been absolutely sure what her parents were up to, he would've arrived flanked by stormtroopers, and a Star Destroyer would be hanging over the city of Aldera. Tonight he intended to take the measure of the gathering, to evaluate whether his suspicions were correct. If her mother and father and their friends betrayed even one hint of fear, Grand Moff Tarkin would pounce on it. The banquet had become a piece of grand theater in which the lives of every other guest were on the line.

Breha spotted Leia and brightened. “It’s bad luck to seat an odd number for dinner. Our daughter will join us.”

“Your first official banquet,” Bail said to her, and gave his daughter a look in which only she would see the apology.

“The first ever?” Tarkin seemed pleased. “Well, well. What an honor to be present.”

“Usually the heir doesn’t get to attend banquets until after her investiture,” Leia said as she walked closer and offered her hand. His fingers were cold. “So I owe the honor to you, Governor.”

Apparently she could lie just as well as her parents.

•◆•

Even before the recent wave of “banquets,” Queen Breha of Alderaan had been famed as a hostess. Leia had never understood exactly what went into that besides throwing many parties, serving food and drink on a lavish scale, and gracefully greeting everyone who attended. On the night of her first banquet, however, Leia understood her mother’s true skill, very nearly an art.

Breha steered the conversation to Eriadu, to the redesign of military uniforms, and other topics with which Tarkin was known to be especially familiar. Naturally he dominated the conversation, which both flattered him and cut down on the amount of playacting for the other guests. She had arranged the seating so Tarkin was on her right hand, honoring him above all other guests and also keeping him close, so she could personally manage him. And she kept everyone talking, which was critical, because every silence that fell was charged, nearly excruciating.

The queen's most brilliant move, however, came when the wine was served. Tarkin and a handful of the other guests received true Toniray, but all of the Organas, Mon Mothma, and most others had wine one shade too pale. The difference in color was too slight for any offworlder to notice, but Leia recognized it instantly. This was a sibling wine to Toniray, one far less strong, more juice than intoxicant. She'd been served this until her Day of Demand, after which she'd finally graduated to the real thing.

So the Organas stayed sharp, while Tarkin's edges were slightly dulled.

Not much. Leia noted how little of the wine he drank; he was far too cautious a man to become inebriated among potential enemies. But on a night like this, her family needed every advantage they could claim.

"We're so fortunate, here on Alderaan," Breha said as the servitor droids cleared away plates to prepare for dessert. "Our realm is clearly defined. It must be much more difficult, balancing the needs of so many worlds, and sectors, even military divisions."

"It's not work for the faint of heart." Tarkin offered no details. Although he'd relaxed slightly through the course of the dinner, his hawklike gaze remained focused. "Though of course many planets have similarly complex concerns. Wouldn't you agree, Senator Malpe?"

Cinderon Malpe paused, napkin in his hands. It was all Leia could do not to wince. "Of—of course we have our own challenges in our system, and in the Senate." The stammer made Leia want to cringe. Was he about to ruin everything, this moment?

Tarkin leaned forward. "What would you say you find most difficult?"

"We—" Malpe had to swallow hard. Leia imagined she could hear the stormtroopers' boots on the floors already. "We have to divide our time between two places, of course, needing to spend time on Coruscant—"

"I'll say," Breha muttered.

Bail set his glass down too heavily on the table, with a thump audible throughout the room. "Don't do this here."

"Do what?" Breha took another drink of her wine—a little too swiftly, a little too much. If the beverage had in fact been alcoholic, it would've been the gesture of someone who hoped to get drunk.

"Start in on this." Bail's glance around the room revealed more embarrassment than Leia had ever seen from him before, or at least it was meant to.

Her mother shrugged, exaggerating the gesture like an intoxicated person might. "Oh, I'm the one who started it. Me, here at home, while my husband finds every excuse he can to run off to Coruscant or—" She put one hand to her throat, as if physically holding in the words.

"Out with it," Mon Mothma interjected. She flung her napkin down on the table, glaring at Breha with anger Leia had never seen in her before. "I've had it with your suspicions and your insinuations. Go on, Breha. Grow a spine. Say the words."

Breha put both hands on the table and spoke with exaggerated sweetness: "My husband enjoys running off to Chandrila. And I'm sure you could tell us why."

It felt like a slap. Even though Leia knew this was an act—at least, figured it was almost certainly an act—she'd never once imagined either of her parents being unfaithful to the other. The idea of her father and Mon Mothma made her want to cry. But she understood why someone might believe it.

"This is what I live with." Bail gestured toward his wife. "Endless paranoia, a grasping, insecure wife who imagines betrayals every time I fail to send a message within a few hours. It's like living on a leash."

"Imagines? *Imagines?*" Breha rose from her chair, eyes blazing. "Did I imagine the girl from Corellia last year?" Bail winced, and Pamlo turned her head, raising one hand as if to block herself from witnessing any more of the scene. Leia struggled for composure until she wondered why she was doing such a thing.

For once, the best move was the most honest move. She released the terrible tension inside by bursting into sobs.

"This is inappropriate," Tarkin said, his voice sharp enough to puncture steel. "Look at what you've done to the child."

Leia kept weeping, head down and hot tears streaming down her face, even as she realized that her breakdown had convinced Tarkin this whole terrible scenario was real—or, at least, that the fight between her parents was real. He probably hadn't been persuaded that everyone in the room was innocent; Leia doubted they'd get that lucky. But he no longer believed himself to have infiltrated a meeting of conspirators, only a drunken dinner party that had just turned disastrous.

"Forgive us, Governor Tarkin." Her father rose from his chair and bowed his head, even as her mother slumped back down again and lowered her head and arms upon the table. "An excess of wine—"

"Is something you should avoid in future." Tarkin rose to his feet, drawing himself in like a great cat pulling back its claws. "This disgraceful display would not be tolerated were this an official visit. As I invited myself here, I suppose I have only myself to blame for expecting anything better from members of the Elder Houses. I bid you good day." With that he stalked out.

No one said a word until the old-fashioned doors slammed shut, and for an instant after that, during which the room seemed to have no air. Then everyone simultaneously deflated. Her father collapsed into his chair as the others slumped backward or rested their heads in their hands.

Breha reached across the table to grasp Leia's wrist. "Sweetheart, none of that was real."

"I *know* that," Leia said, wiping at her face. Sobbing was easier to turn on than off.

"That was acting?" Cinderon Malpe began to laugh, an almost broken sound. "You're better at it than I am."

Mon Mothma's face relaxed into a smile. "Good work, Leia. You convinced Tarkin when none of us could."

She had done something for their rebellion at last, something important and useful, and instead of feeling triumphant, she only wanted to be sick.

"Wait." Senator Pamlo's face was drawn as she turned from Breha to Bail and back again. "You told your *daughter* about all of this? Your teenaged daughter?"

"They didn't tell me," Leia insisted. "I figured it out on my own."

A few groans from around the room told her she'd just

made the situation worse. Bail cut in, "We did explain the truth behind some of what Leia was seeing. She's surrounded by this, living in the heart of it. Her discovering some portion of the truth was inevitable."

"But you've brought her into our work!" protested Vaspar. "A mere child!"

It was Mon Mothma who said, "Leia Organa is not a child." Her voice carried through the room, commanding the kind of attention that would halt a more crowded gathering than this one. She slowly stood. "Leia has had her Day of Demand. She's growing into an adult—a representative of the next generation. And make no mistake, they're the generation who will bear the brunt of what's to come. They're the ones who'll do most of the fighting and most of the dying. They're the ones who will do most of the rebuilding afterward, if we are so fortunate as to see an 'after.' We need the young with us. Without them, this war is lost before it's begun."

Leia's heart stirred at the thought of Mon Mothma's faith in her, with her need to rise to that challenge. Yet she couldn't entirely banish the dread of what was to come.

CHAPTER 25

Pamarthe had a reputation as a fierce, dangerous world, but so far as Leia could tell, that had more to do with the people than the terrain. The island chains could be difficult to travel between on water, and even on land for those who were afraid of heights. But Leia wasn't, and fortunately, neither was her teammate—someone who was very comfortable floating around in midair, in more than one sense.

"The stars are so clear here," Amilyn said as they crossed one of the long rope bridges that connected the islands of Pamarthe. "No light pollution! Hardly any clouds!"

"At least not tonight." Leia had heard tales of the storms on Pamarthe.

Once the pathfinding class had caught on to the real moral of the class, Chief Pangie had lessened the difficulty levels considerably. It turned out that learning to find your way around wasn't that hard when you weren't fighting desperately to stay alive. She'd pulled Amilyn as a teammate for this round; after she'd gotten over her disappointment at again not being matched with Kier, she'd realized this was for the best. Amilyn Holdo might be bizarre, but she was also interested in the astrology of various systems, which made her uncannily skilled at navigating by starlight.

"Let me see." Amilyn stopped and held her hands up to the sky, touching her fingers together in an odd pattern that made her squint her eyes, consider, and nod. The tiny glowing pins in her multicolored hair blended in with the night sky above. "All right. Two more islands to the left, and I think we're nearly there."

"More rope bridges." Leia sighed, and they kept going.

Their current bridge swayed and bounced beneath their feet as they went. Far beneath, she could hear the roar of the ocean, waves breaking against the rocks that jutted up from the wide oceanic spaces between islands.

Maybe it would be worth getting wet, to feel the strength of one of those storms, Leia thought. She imagined dark clouds rolling in across churning gray water. Maybe someday she could come back here with a friend—Kier, even—

She caught herself. The future had become a tenuous thing for her. Never before had she understood how often she reveled in the simplest expectations for the rest of her life—serving in the Senate, spending more time with the people she cared about, eventually becoming queen, even maybe having a child at some point many years away. None of that could be guaranteed any longer.

Best not to plan ahead.

The next Pamarthens island they reached was one of the larger ones, which meant it served as a busy spaceport. Pamarthe had a reputation for producing fine pilots, and its trade thrived as a result. People would detour systems out of their way to pick up crew or a hauler there. It was almost bizarre to suddenly walk into a bustle of people and activity on a pathfinding trip, to hear them shouting out passengers and destinations, but it was the fastest way to reach the next wilderness.

"The chief said at least eighty bridges anchor on this island." Try as she might, Leia couldn't remember the precise layout; she was getting better at memorizing visual information quickly, but not *that* good. "If we take the wrong one, we're going to wind up on the wrong island, which might or might not connect to our goal point, so—hey. Still with me?"

Amilyn stared off to the side in what Leia first assumed was one of her usual trips into mental hyperspace. When she followed Amilyn's gaze, though, she realized what had drawn her friend's attention: a group of Gamorreans, grunting and shoving, herding shivering humans onto a transport, with the humans packed together so tightly it was difficult to see the binders on their wrists.

Slavers. The thought alone could turn Leia's stomach.

Watching it happen was harder. But what did her discomfort matter compared to what the poor slaves were enduring, and had yet to endure?

She forced herself to watch the entire time. *Bear witness,* she thought. *That's all you can do for them now, so do it.* Mon Mothma's words about the histories to come sustained her, but barely. A lump had formed in her throat long before the boarding ramp was pulled up and the ship lumbered into the air. Only when it had vanished from sight did she turn back to her companion. Amilyn's cheeks shone with tears.

"Like they're in a duraplast bubble," she said, which made no sense to Leia until Amilyn continued. "We can see through like there's nothing between us. We can even push against the surface until it bends in. But we can never push through. We never touch them."

Leia nodded. "Yeah. Just like that."

"We never had slavery on Gatalenta." Amilyn began walking in the vague direction of their goal, and Leia fell in beside her, but they were both in a kind of nauseated daze. The pathfinding games didn't matter much any longer. "Not ever, and our Council of Mothers doesn't allow slaves to be brought to our planet at all. If they are brought there, and their master is caught, the slave is declared free."

"That's a good rule." Although Alderaan also banned

slavery, Leia didn't know whether they had a law that would free slaves brought to their world. How could she not know that? She'd bring it up with her parents as soon as she got back. If she could do nothing else for the suffering people she'd just seen, she could at least free others in their name.

They trudged on in uneasy silence for a few paces, hearing the shouts and cries around them—"Ores from Mahranee to Riosa! Need a hauler!" "Passengers for Pantora!"—without ever taking them in. Then one of the announcements caught her attention: "Senatorial charter to Chandrila!"

Amilyn perked up too. "Do you think that's Harp?"

"Why would she charter a flight to Chandrila in the middle of a pathfinding trip?"

"She could've been injured. Or maybe there was a family emergency."

"I guess so." It seemed more likely that either Chief Pangie or the local medics would handle any injury. However, a family emergency was plausible—more so than finding either Winmey Lenz or Mon Mothma on this random island on a random planet. "We should check on her, just in case."

Together they moved toward the voice they'd heard announcing the charter, weaving their way through the passengers, pilots, and cargo droids that crowded the spaceport. Although they were surrounded on all sides by ships and tarmac, Leia could still hear the rush and roar of the ocean nearby, reminding her how small this little sliver of civilization was.

They reached the clearing, and she saw the passengers for the charter ship. Instantly she stopped walking and put her hand out to grab Amilyn's arm and tug her around the side of a cargo container large enough to conceal both of them.

"Isn't that Winmey Lenz?" Amilyn tilted her head that way and this, like a marsh crane spotting food. "That's Harp's sponsor. Would he have come to pick her up?"

Leia shook her head. It wasn't Lenz's presence that unnerved her. As unlikely as his presence here might be, any number of reasons could explain it. But Winmey Lenz was talking with an Imperial official—one in a white uniform jacket.

Not many senior Imperials wore white jackets. Those were reserved for ISB officers, a handful of more obscure ranks that held similar levels of authority and power, and even grand admirals. White jackets were said to inspire respect; really they instilled fear. Leia's heart thumped faster at the sight of this man, whoever he was. Far worse than the white jacket was the fact that the unknown Imperial officer was talking easily with Winmey Lenz, as though they were friends.

That doesn't mean anything. Mom and Dad made nice with Grand Moff Tarkin not so long ago. Still, Leia couldn't shake her uneasiness.

"Stay out of sight," she told Amilyn. "I want to find out if I can overhear what they're saying."

Only after she'd said it did she realize she had absolutely no good explanation for what she was doing. Luckily her companion was the person least likely to require one.

"What about over there?" Amilyn pointed to a fuel crawler parked close to the charter ship, definitely close enough for Leia to eavesdrop. Swiftly she fell into step behind a group of Pau'ans, whose tall stature and long, flowing robes provided good cover. Once she'd reached the fuel crawler she ducked behind it—then realized Amilyn was right behind her.

"I told you not to come with me!" she whispered.

Amilyn frowned. "No, you didn't."

Choose your words more carefully next time, Leia reminded herself. But Winmey Lenz was speaking again, and she focused entirely on him.

"—pleasure is entirely mine, Director." Lenz smiled at this mysterious director as easily as he'd smiled for everyone at the last banquet. "Petty regulations mustn't be allowed to stand in the way of necessary construction."

"You're a sensible man, Lenz. Are you sure you're from Chandrila?" The director's smile didn't reach his eyes. "What luck, you having so much quadanium at hand."

Lenz's gaze no longer met the director's. "Sometimes the fates align us with what we need most."

As their conversation shifted into farewell pleasantries, Amilyn straightened and took on an unfamiliarly serious expression. "Why would the Empire be buying cut-rate quadanium from a senator? Why wouldn't they just take it from a planet that's on penalty?"

Leia put that together fast. "It could be a few reasons. Most likely, some project is experiencing budget overages that the director doesn't want to take to his superiors." Especially since the superiors of officers in white jackets were exclusively those at the topmost levels of the Empire—not the kind of people you wanted to disappoint.

"Is this illegal?" Amilyn clasped her hands together as though in delight. "Did we find crime?"

"I don't know. Some sales like that are illegal, but some aren't. Maybe the director asked Lenz to keep the deal secret for his own reasons."

Regardless, Leia realized, Winmey Lenz's behavior was troubling. At the very least, the man had a strong relationship with a senior Imperial official, one he was actively assisting in some major building project. He'd specifically denied having any substantive Imperial contacts in the past; that was a lie. And if he was lying to her parents and Mon Mothma about this, what else might he be lying about?

Worse: what might he be telling the truth about?

Panic seized Leia as it hit her that Lenz might already have informed on her parents. *No, he can't have—if he had, we'd already be in prison, or dead. But he knows everything about my parents' plans, everything Mon Mothma is trying to put together. He has their trust, but he's lying to them. That means he could turn at any minute.*

"Cloud-colored," Amilyn said.

"What?" Leia sounded snappish and didn't care. This wasn't the time for any of Amilyn's wandering metaphors.

"You've gone so pale you're cloud-colored." Amilyn clasped Leia's upper arm, as though she thought Leia would faint at any moment. Cargo shipments and travelers kept hurrying past them, reminding Leia of the mudslide on Chandrila, tumbling over and over in the muck without any way to right herself. "What's wrong? Why is it so bad that Lenz is selling the materials?"

Telling her the entire truth was impossible. Leia managed, "He's being deceptive. Chandrila always stands up to Palpatine in the Senate, but privately? Lenz is good buddies with a high-ranking Imperial official."

"It's like the cream side of the muffin."

Leia refused to ask. She just stared at Amilyn, wondering when the tide of weirdness would ever run dry.

"They say that when you drop the muffin, it always lands cream side down," Amilyn said, repeating the old saying like it was some profound discovery. "So I always wondered, what if you covered the muffin with cream completely, and then dropped it? There wouldn't be a side left to point upward, so the muffin would never fall. It would remain in the air, skyfaring without scarves."

Enough of the ridiculous—Leia opened her mouth to utter the angry thoughts in her head, before understanding came rushing in. "Wait. You mean Lenz is playing both sides. He wants to curry favor with the Empire and the ones who oppose it, so that if Palpatine does ever fall from power, he could still benefit."

"Senator Lenz is the muffin in the analogy," Amilyn said. "Just to be clear."

"I got that part." Leia's mind was racing, considering all the possibilities. Winmey Lenz wouldn't expose her parents, Mon Mothma, and their allies for no reason. He wasn't a risk . . . yet. But the first time they faced real danger, the immediate threat of exposure, Lenz might well turn informant to save his own skin. It would be the smartest move.

An assistant was speaking with Lenz now, talking over the quadanium shipments. Probably they should seize the opportunity presented by his distraction to get away. It was difficult to remember that they were still on a pathfinding trip. Before she'd turned, though, she heard the assistant say something that pricked at her ears and made the noise of the spaceport seem very far away.

"Did he say Ocahont?" Leia asked.

Amilyn shrugged. "I wasn't listening. I was envisioning a levitating muffin."

"I think he said Ocahont." That name had figured heavily in her mother's so-called spaceport development accounts. It had to be linked to the rebellion plans. Was it possible Lenz had already betrayed them after all? The shipment to Ocahont could be bait—something for the Empire to follow and then "discover" whatever outpost awaited there.

"You're cloud-colored again," Amilyn said.

"I have to find out what's going on with that shipment to Ocahont." Leia gestured to what seemed to be the cargo vessel in question. Frantically she tried to think of ways to investigate that she could somehow implement in the next few minutes. Maybe she could access the manifest. Her royal rank didn't give her the authority to pull a random ship's manifest, but it was possible a Pamarthen local wouldn't know that.

In her reverie she stared at the ground, or really at nothing, so it took her a moment to realize Amilyn was gone. Leia jerked her head upright, looking around wildly, then gaped as she saw Amilyn sneaking on to the vessel headed for Ocahont. She tiptoed up the boarding ramp, paused at the door, smiled back at Leia, and waved her forward.

"No no no no no," Leia whispered. Stowing away wasn't the answer. Stowaways could be put off on remote planets, jailed, sometimes even indentured as servants—

Come on. Even if any of that happened, you'd only have to get word to your parents. That's assuming they didn't find you first, because you know they'd search for you the instant you went missing.

She tried to push the reckless thoughts away. If this shipment was intended as a kind of sting operation by the Empire, with the help of Winmey Lenz, then it would be at the heart of military action. In that case, she and Amilyn wouldn't be risking their freedom but their lives.

But when Leia tried to wave Amilyn back, she only got more cheerful beckoning before her friend disappeared into the cargo hold, no doubt looking for a better place to hide. Amilyn, who had no idea of the real danger ahead, was apparently determined to see this through.

Leia couldn't let her go alone.

Looking from side to side, she chose a moment both Ishi Tib and Aqualish groups were hurrying by, chattering loudly among themselves. She wove through the crowd, made sure no one was watching, and ran for the gangway. Amilyn had recklessly dragged them into the mess; it was Leia's responsibility to get them out.

So she told herself. It helped her pretend that, down deep, she wasn't a little bit excited.

CHAPTER 26

Chief Pangie sounded incredulous, which under the circumstances was fair. *"A family emergency?"*

"Exactly," Leia said into her comlink, bracing herself against the wall of the storage bay as the cargo vessel's engines hummed to life. As the ship lifted off, she said, "I apologize for the sudden departure. Amilyn Holdo's coming with me so I won't have to travel alone."

"Well—" The chief clearly wanted to object, but a royal family emergency probably sounded important. "You check in once you reach Alderaan, got it?"

"Got it!" Leia promised. *Assuming I return home ever again.*

Chief Pangie signed off just in time, because the vibration that rippled through the ship meant acceleration. No doubt they were now soaring upward at a velocity that would take them out of communications range within seconds.

Amilyn, meanwhile, had made herself comfortable, laying her waterproof mat on the floor and wrapping herself in a warming blanket. The blanket was designed to fend off harsh weather conditions but would work on the chill of a cargo bay just as well. "Come on," she said, patting the floor next to her. "You should make your nest. It's six hours to Ocahont, so we might as well get some sleep."

"There's no way I'm going to be able to sleep." Leia sat by Amilyn anyway. There wasn't any point in pacing the whole time.

"Why not?" Amilyn asked.

"Because I'm nervous and upset, and I don't know what's waiting for us when we get there."

"Neither do I," Amilyn said quietly. "I'm not afraid, because I'm never afraid of the things that scare other people, not even the unknown. But if I *should* be scared—well, you might as well tell me."

Regardless of how this played out, Amilyn would learn some of the truth. It would be better for her to hear most of it from Leia, as clearly and honestly as possible. Her parents' refusal to inform Leia had led to dangerous complications; if she refused to inform Amilyn in turn, what else could go wrong? Though it would be hard for even Amilyn Holdo to come up with something more ill-advised than stowing away on a traitor's ship headed toward an illegal military outpost. . . .

"It's like this," Leia said, forcing herself to focus. "Some individuals have decided that—that the worlds of this galaxy need a defense other than the Empire—a defense against the Empire—"

"An *uprising*." Amilyn pronounced the word with relish. "About time!"

"Don't be so happy about it. Do you realize what that would mean? For us, for the whole galaxy?"

The smile fell from Amilyn's face, replaced by a solemnness Leia had never seen in her before. "Yes, I do. It's still time."

Once again Leia's mind filled with images from Paucris Major, the ships all being refitted for battles to come. For bloodshed, for death.

Amilyn continued, "A few weeks ago, you made me realize that intention alone isn't sufficient. Goodness is proved through action rather than ideas. Since then I've been thinking about what that means in the greatest sense, and—and I knew that meant standing against the Emperor." Her solemn expression shifted into a smile. "I'm just really relieved I don't have to do it on my own."

"I bet." Leia rubbed her temples with her fingers. "Can you keep a secret?"

"You'd better hope so," Amilyn replied with unnerving honesty.

Not even Kier knew as much as Amilyn Holdo would have discovered by the end of this trip. Leia steeled herself to reveal all, then froze as the doors to the cargo bay slid open. She and Amilyn scooted hurriedly into a corner, hiding themselves as best they could behind some crates.

"Someone will catch us," said a giggling Quarren, who was allowing another to pull them deep into the hold.

"No one's going to see." The other Quarren stroked the first one's facial tentacles lasciviously. *Is that one of their mating rituals?* Leia thought, trying to look anywhere but at the groping couple arranging themselves atop one of the nearby containers. *Or is that just, I don't know, this one's fetish?* She had a disturbing feeling she was about to find out.

"I suppose we may as well seize the moment," the first Quarren murmured. A hand with suction-tipped fingers went to the other's collar, and Leia heard snaps being pulled free. "Who knows when we'll get another chance to—*aaaghhh!*"

Leia winced as the Quarrens scrambled backward, staring at the two huddled stowaways they'd just glimpsed in the corner. She could only gape at them, even more horrified to have been discovered than they must be.

Amilyn folded her hands over her heart. "I'm so happy you two have found each other!"

•◆•

Less happy to have been found was the person in charge at Ocahont, who on that particular day turned out to be Mon Mothma.

As she and Amilyn were hustled into the outpost's headquarters, Leia caught sight of the familiar red hair and white robe and breathed a sigh of relief. "Senator. I'm so glad to see you."

"The feeling isn't mutual." Mon Mothma raised one eyebrow. "You brought a friend?"

"I stowed away," Amilyn said cheerfully. "Technically we both did, but it was my idea. So don't blame Leia."

Mon Mothma raised her hands as if to say, *I need time to find the words.* With a glance she dismissed the two Quarrens, who'd considered Leia and Amilyn their prisoners and didn't look too thrilled about having them treated as guests instead. Leia figured they'd get over it as soon as they got another chance to be alone.

The outpost on Ocahont had apparently been built longer ago than the makeshift shelters on Crait. Although the crew of the cargo vessel had made sure she couldn't get a good look at the total layout of the place, the differences revealed themselves. Substantial data centers ringed the room in which Mon Mothma stood, including a circular map display at the very center. The sheer length of the hallways she and Amilyn had been hustled through suggested a large compound. And anyplace that needed an enormous cargo shipment of quadanium . . . well, however big this outpost was, it would soon be even bigger.

Mon Mothma leaned against the map display for a few long seconds before saying, "Princess, you know that I've supported your playing a larger role in . . . our endeavors, but this is going too far."

"This was an accident, and a lucky one," Leia insisted. "What do you know about Winmey Lenz's dealings with the Empire?"

There was every chance that Mon Mothma would say she knew all about it. It had occurred to Leia that Lenz might be setting up some sort of elaborate operation to sabotage Imperial works, maybe. When she saw the frown lines appear between the older woman's eyebrows, though, she knew better. "What do you mean, Leia? Of course Lenz arranged for us to receive this quadanium—"

"He traded even more to the Empire," Leia said. "We saw him conclude the deal with our own eyes. I didn't recognize the official, but he certainly had a high rank, and Lenz called him 'director.' "

Amilyn chimed in then: "The guy wore a white jacket. That's how bad."

Mon Mothma took a step backward. From most people it would've been a very small reaction, but from the calm, collected Mon Mothma, it might as well have been a scream. "Force around us. How did you discover this?"

"Our paths crossed on Pamarthe. Maybe it was a lucky accident—maybe it was the Force at work." Although Leia believed in the Force, she rarely thought it directly guided actions. On this day, though, she was willing to consider the possibility. "Regardless, Lenz has connections high up in the Empire he hasn't revealed to the rest of you, and that can't be good news."

"No, it can't." Mon Mothma's long fingers tapped against the edge of the map display, as if she were working out a code. "We can't let him know we're on to him. We simply have to . . . phase him out. Make him believe we're fighting among ourselves, less certain of our plans. If he believes the coalition is falling apart, getting nowhere, he'll let it lie. Reporting us at that point would only expose himself."

"*Can* you make him believe that?" Leia had thought politics involved more lying than any other activity. Apparently rebellions put politics to shame.

"He's never been at the center of our plans. There are limits to what he knows. So yes, I think he can be persuaded." Mon Mothma shook her head as though to clear it. "Besides, we don't have to lie about the infighting. Only about our lack of resolve to overcome it."

That sounded ominous, but also like something Leia should take up with her parents instead, at some other time, preferably far in the future. "So," Leia began, "since this intel is highly confidential, you'll keep this whole trip a secret from my parents, right?"

With a gentle smile, Mon Mothma stepped toward Leia, put her hands on her shoulders, and said, "Not a chance."

Leia winced. From her chair, Amilyn murmured, "Ouch."

"We're still working out exactly who's in charge of this great endeavor," Mon Mothma continued. "Maybe it will be me, but maybe not. All I know for certain is that your parents are in charge of their own household, of which you are still a member. That means you'll have to take this up with them."

•◆•

Before they'd parted ways for their separate transports home, Amilyn had tried to be encouraging. "You brought valuable intel!" she insisted. "That's got to count for something."

"Let's hope so."

It counted for *nothing.*

"We can't keep having this conversation, Leia." Bail Organa paced the length of the library, his hands clasped behind his back. "How many times do we have to beg you to let us handle this? To go enjoy your youth instead of rushing headlong into this?"

"I told you, I wasn't investigating Winmey Lenz. I just

happened to find out what he was up to. After that I had to do something, didn't I?"

"Something, yes," her father said. "Stowing away on a cargo vessel? No."

"I was going after Amilyn!" Leia insisted. "And don't give me that whole, if all of your friends were jumping out windows on Coruscant, would you do it, because this is different."

"She's right." Breha spoke with unexpected calmness; her sorrowful dark eyes met her husband's. "Leia responded to the situation she was confronted with as best she could. We can't ask for more than that."

"We can ask for her to stay out of harm's way, and if she won't, we can *keep* her out of it." Bail stopped pacing and pointed downward, at the seldom-used lower areas of the palace. "There used to be dungeons down there, you know."

This time her mother's voice was sharp. "Bail!"

He held up one hand. "You know I wasn't serious."

"Don't even joke about that." Breha rose from her seat, the wide skirts of her green dress rustling around her. The constellation globes overhead caught the last rays of sunset light, which turned their stars red and gold. "There's no hiding from what's coming. Not for anyone in this galaxy. We were fools to think we could ever hide our daughter from it and keep her safe. Safety was the first sacrifice we made, when we decided to oppose Palpatine. It won't be the last."

"You can't mean this." Bail took a step back from his wife. Leia had rarely seen them argue in earnest; the melodrama performed for Tarkin's benefit was the ugliest confrontation she'd ever witnessed between the two. The sick feeling in her stomach told her that might be about to change. "Our daughter is only sixteen! We've told her too much already—failed to discourage her—"

"What would discouraging her accomplish?"

"It would protect her a while longer." Bail winced with a pain that must have been nearly physical. "I would do almost anything to keep her safe for even one more day. Why won't you?"

"Secrecy isn't keeping her safe!"

Leia tried to jump in. "I've brought good information to you already. Isn't that worth something? Don't you trust me?"

Her father turned to her with such pain in his eyes that she wished the words unsaid. "I trust you *with my life*. But I don't trust the Empire with yours."

Breha persisted, as she always did when her mind was finally made up. "We could begin slowly, Bail. In secure conditions. When you lead the supply convoy to where we refurbish our ships in a few weeks—take her with you. We have more defenses there than anywhere else. She can look at what we've accomplished and start to understand."

Leia had already seen the nascent fleet at Paucris Major, but this wasn't the time to bring that up, if in fact that time existed. She bit her lower lip and tried to look innocent.

Her father wasn't even paying attention. "I won't have this. I won't treat our daughter as a—a skifter in a sabacc deck. If you would, I'm not sure I've ever even known you." Breha closed her eyes, and Bail breathed out sharply, as though he were the one who had been spoken to so hurtfully. Then he stalked out of the library, leaving mother and daughter alone.

By now, Leia felt so wretched she could hardly look at her mother's pain-stricken face. She whispered, "I'm so sorry I caused trouble."

"You didn't. You had a lucky break that may well have saved lives. Eventually your father will see that." Breha opened her eyes, which were red-rimmed, but her voice remained clear. "Your father isn't himself right now. It's a hard thing, allowing your child to go to war."

Leia nodded, trying to remember the warmth and happiness between them not so long ago in this very room. The memory felt far away. "The rebellion has its own three challenges, I guess."

"What do you mean?"

Her mother sounded more eager for distraction than interested, but that was reason enough to go on. "Before it becomes what it's going to be, it has to be strong in mind, body, and heart. The Challenge of the Mind is getting everyone to agree. The Challenge of the Body is what you're doing on Crait and Ocahont. Making the idea of rising up something real."

"And the Challenge of the Heart is moving forward without becoming what we have beheld." Breha sighed. "Well seen, my daughter."

Mother and daughter sat together on one of the low couches, and Leia hugged her mom tightly, unsure whether she was taking comfort or giving it. When her mother rested her head atop Leia's, she decided maybe it could be both.

"You have a role to play in the struggle to come, Leia. We'll figure out what that role should be over the next months and years. Your father will fight us for a while yet, and we have to respect his feelings enough to let him fight." Breha's tone betrayed how difficult that would be for her, but her words to her daughter remained calm and steady. "I ask only one thing. From now on, whenever you undertake something like this—even if you fall into it by happenstance—you come to me or to Mon Mothma about it immediately. The very first moment you can tell us, whether in person or via holo, you do so. That way we can make sure what you're doing is both as safe and as helpful as it can be."

"You didn't say to tell Dad."

"Not yet," Breha admitted.

Never before had Leia's mother asked her to keep a secret from her father. She'd always thought that might be fun, but it wasn't.

CHAPTER 27

What do you do when you're a sixteen-year-old girl who knows her world is about to end?

Leia felt as though she walked through the next several days in a trance. The palace, as familiar to her as any place ever could be, suddenly seemed too large, too dark, its layout complicated and knotty as the braids 2V insisted on weaving into her charge's hair every single morning. Her father had left for Coruscant late on the night of that last, terrible family argument; he'd made that trip regularly throughout her entire life, but this time his departure carried an ominous sense of division. Her mother—always so strong, graceful, and poised—wore her wrapper and nightgown in the private areas of the palace until very nearly lunchtime, and once when 2V tried to cluck about it, Breha even snapped at the droid. Of course she apologized in the next breath, but Leia remained shocked all the same.

The trouble hasn't even started yet, she reminded herself one night at dinner, while she and Breha ate silently on the terrace, looking at Aldera instead of each other. *If everything's so screwed up and strange already, what will it be like when things really get bad?*

Her mother's voice broke into her reverie. "Aren't you supposed to return to Coruscant soon?"

"The Apprentice Legislature's next session isn't for a week yet."

Frowning, Breha said, "I thought I remembered something about you scheduling a transport several days back."

"There's a party tomorrow night," Leia admitted. "One of the formal balls they invite the Royal Academy grads to every year. The apprentice legislators usually attend too."

The first smile in days appeared on Breha's face. "Weren't you planning on going with Kier Domadi?"

Leia shrugged. "I thought I might ask him if he wouldn't rather come here instead. I could invite him to the palace, couldn't I?" She badly wanted to talk with him about some of what she'd learned. Maybe he couldn't yet know the truth about Paucris Major, but they could discuss the particulars about Winmey Lenz and his double-dealing—and, more importantly, about whatever role people their age ought to play in the coming fight. That conversation was one they should have on their own planet, beneath their shared sky.

"You can always invite your friends to our home," Breha said. "Which is why you should go to the ball tomorrow night on Coruscant. That will only ever happen once, while your home will always be here."

"It feels wrong," Leia finally admitted, as a servitor droid rolled up with the after-dinner caf. "Going out to celebrate, while out there—" She gestured at the darkening sky, through which a few brighter stars had begun to twinkle.

" 'Out there' is exactly why you should go to the ball." Leaning across the table, Breha took her daughter's hand in hers. "We won't always be free to travel wherever we will. We won't always be able to take the time to attend elaborate parties. We won't always have the chance to dance with the ones we love." The quaver in her voice made Leia's chest ache as she finished, "So dance now."

Leia hadn't realized she could love her mother even more than she already did. She squeezed her mother's fingers tightly, and for a few long seconds they simply smiled at each other in the most perfect understanding they would ever share.

It was Breha who broke the silence: "And TooVee will be so happy to pick out your gown."

"Overjoyed."

•◆•

The next night, Leia walked into the Imperial Palace on Kier's arm, wearing a white-and-silver gown that had fulfilled all 2V's wildest dreams. Her hair had been braided into a tall coil atop her head, and jewelry sparked at her throat. Kier wore a dark blue suit of Alderaanian make, slightly out of step with the uniformed and stylish men around them yet, to her, far more handsome. When she heard the music, she longed to sweep Kier onto the dance floor—

No. She longed to long for that, to fulfill her mother's command to dance while she could. Instead, the tumult inside her seemed to have intensified. Every time she looked at one of her friends, or at Kier, or at the happy throng celebrating with no idea of what was to come, a pang pierced her heart. The emotion that ached within her wasn't fear. Instead she felt the intense sadness that came from recognizing the beauty of her reality while newly, sharply aware of how fragile it was. How quickly it would all vanish.

Will everyone be so carefree ten years from now? Five years? Five months? Leia couldn't yet tell how fast it was slipping away, but the stability of the existence she'd known was already beginning to give. As dedicated as she was to fighting Palpatine—as willing as she was to pay whatever price that fight would demand—she still found it hard to accept the fragility of everything and everyone she loved.

"Are you all right?" Kier squeezed her hand, pressure that sent a small thrill through her, despite everything. "You seem—far from here."

She blinked hard, forcing herself back into the moment. "I guess I am. Could you get me a glass of the glowwine? That should help." Glowwine wasn't intoxicating, exactly, but it sparked a rush of endorphins that could turn the dull into the delightful. Younger people on Coruscant and many other worlds drank it regularly; even some adults preferred it to true wine.

Kier's lips brushed her cheek. "As you command, Your Highness."

The way he said it—low and soft—did as much to distract her as the glowwine ever could. She let go of his arm with some reluctance, already missing his warmth by her side.

Someone else found her almost immediately. "Were you in awful trouble?" Amilyn Holdo asked in the monotone Leia no longer thought of as being so odd. "At least you could tell your parents what you were really doing. I had to pretend I honestly thought stowing away on a cargo vessel would be fun."

"Did they believe you?"

Beaming, Amilyn nodded. "They know how I get about my enthusiasms."

Leia imagined what toddler Amilyn must have been like and couldn't suppress a smile. "No doubt."

"Your dress is beautiful." Holding out her arms in a pose, Amilyn said. "What do you think?"

It took most of Leia's royal training to keep that smile on her face. Amilyn wore possibly the most *Amilyn* thing ever: a flowing caftan of a dress in a swirling, multicolored pattern that reminded Leia of the storms on gas giants. Tiny bells jingled at the ends of the wide bell sleeves, and metallic, sparkly fringe trimmed the hem and the high neck. Amilyn had even managed to dye her hair the same combination of colors as the dress, which made her look like a psychedelic blur broken only by her smiling face. Leia ventured, "It's very bright. Very original and daring."

"Leia." Amilyn's face took on an unaccustomed seriousness. "On Gatalenta, we honor kindness and courtesy, but we also honor honesty."

True courtesy meant treating people the way they wished to be treated. "Well, then, I think the dress is too busy. I can see why you like it, but for this gathering, it's a bit much."

"I knew it." When Amilyn slumped, she appeared even ganglier than usual—like a marionette when the puppeteer let go of the strings. "On Gatalenta, you get tired of everyone wearing the same scarlet cloaks, and everybody's clothing is pale gray or white, and it's supposed to be soothing and tranquil—I guess it is—but that's just not who I am."

"You're expressing your individuality," Leia said, and

as she spoke she found that, somehow, she'd gotten to like most of Amilyn's bizarre clothing. Maybe it was garish and strange, but the brilliant colors and constant variety reflected something of the person within.

"Exactly." Amilyn picked forlornly at the fringed trim of her sleeve. "I want to be the precise opposite of Gatalenta."

Leia shook her head. "Don't do that. If you're only trying to be the opposite of a thing, you're still letting that thing define you."

"I never thought of it that way."

The insight was new to Leia, too, but she recognized the truth in it. "Dress how you really want to dress. Be who you want to be. Not whatever they are on Gatalenta, or whatever they aren't."

She brightened as Kier wove his way through the crowd back to them. He must've seen Amilyn standing by Leia's side, because he returned with three glasses of glowwine and, somewhat clumsily, managed to give Amilyn the first one. "Good to see you."

"You too, Kier." Amilyn promptly gulped the glowwine down with abandon; maybe this was what happened when someone from Gatalenta let loose.

Now he could present Leia with her glass properly and clink his rim against hers, but then he took as deep a draught as Amilyn had. When Leia raised her eyebrows questioningly, he grinned. "The sooner we finish this, the sooner we can dance."

"When you put it that way—" She lifted the glowwine to her lips and went for it.

Within minutes, her worries had vanished—as if the tension within her had been a balloon swelling tighter until it popped with a spray of glitter. Leia's courtly training meant she could swirl around the dance floor without even thinking, her feet and arms naturally finding the steps. The other dancers moved around them with fluid grace, everyone finding the patterns as if they were shards of color in a kaleidoscope being turned on the beat.

Kier danced with nearly as much ease as she did. Twirling beneath his arm, she said, "You're good at this."

"I am *now*." His hands found her waist at that exact moment, and she helped him lift and spin her, a dizzying whirl that exhilarated her. "After I spent most of the past month practicing with a Beedee droid."

Leia laughed so loudly that a few heads turned around them. "You didn't."

"It was awful," Kier confessed. "Nothing like this."

The song drew to a close, and they finished the dance perfectly, with him pulling her to his side, arm around her waist. They'd been this close before—many times—but tonight everything felt sharper, realer, more urgent.

Dance now.

Probably this wasn't exactly what her mother had meant, but—

"Let's get out of here," Leia said.

A slow smile spread across Kier's face, even as he said, "Aren't we supposed to stay?"

They were. They ought to be dancing with the other apprentice legislators and with the graduating academy cadets.

But to hell with "ought to."

Leia pulled Kier closer and whispered, "I don't care."

•◆•

They ran out of the gathering together, second glasses of glowwine in their hands, into the dazzling lights of Coruscant at night. At first they dashed across the suspended walkways, happy to dodge the passers-by around them, to feel as if they were racing on thin air. Even the holoprojections of the Imperial symbol on huge screens all around couldn't dull Leia's giddiness.

When they found a hoversled rental place, Kier steered them directly to it. Once he'd given the Rodian proprietor some credits, and taken the scan that proved they'd imbibed nothing stronger than glowwine, they were off—zooming through the air, wind rushing around them. Leia kept their course simple, partly to be safe but also because it let her attention wander to the warmth of Kier's arms wrapped around her as he embraced her from behind.

"Hey," he called, pointing toward the senatorial complex. "Let's head up there."

Atop the complex, an elaborate garden had been planted for the enjoyment of senior members of the government; on Coruscant, the rich greenness of leaves was the ultimate luxury. On most nights, a number of people could be found there relaxing with family and friends. Tonight, however, the Senate was in late session and the other apprentice legislators remained at the ball, so Leia was able to land in the very center, and they had the garden to themselves.

Kier took her hand as he drew her away from the hoversled to walk on the soft ground. The belomi-palm fronds swayed in the breezes, surrounding them so fully it was almost possible to believe they were on a planet's surface instead of high above it.

"No place is as beautiful as Alderaan," Kier said, "but this comes close."

She thought of his fierce wish to protect Alderaan against the coming conflict, the danger again intruding on her happiness.

"Hey." He brought his fingers up beneath her chin, tilting her face toward his. "Are you sure you're all right?"

"I am, really."

Kier knew her better than that. "Are you worried about your mother?"

He'd been so concerned about the so-called family emergency that took her away from the challenge on Pamarthe. She'd been forced to concoct a lie, which she hated—but this lie was intended to protect both Kier and her parents, so she stuck to it. "Everything's okay. Her pulmonodes really only needed a small repair. It scared us, that's all."

The light filtering through the palms highlighted the sharp angles of his face, the depth of his dark eyes. "Then what is it? Are you nervous about your challenges, after what happened on Pamarthe?" His smile warmed her through. "You'll make that ascent of Appenza. I'd be honored to climb it with you, if you'd like."

The would-be heir could take a companion on the climb, and she could imagine nothing better than standing atop that mountain, declaring herself the next queen, with Kier by her side. "Yes. I'd like that."

"But it's not what you're worried about."

Surely he deserved some small measure of the truth. How much could she parcel out and declare safe? Leia finally said, "Recently I traveled somewhere that made me—made me realize that what my parents are planning—that it's inevitable."

His expression clouded. "Are they about to do something dangerous?"

"No, no, not yet." She shook her head vehemently. All of this was dangerous, but Kier was asking whether action was imminent. That, at least, Leia felt sure she could deny. "I don't know how long it's going to be, though. I just know it's going to happen. Everything about our lives is about to change."

He embraced her tightly. She rested her head against his chest, at the exact place where she could best hear his heartbeat. They were so breakable, so mortal. The fight to come would overtake them, and there was nothing she could do to protect either of them.

"I know it has to change," Kier whispered. "The Empire can't stand. People can't live like this, and that means an uprising is inevitable. We have to prepare for it; we *need* it. But what's about to happen—"

"Don't." She placed two of her fingers over his lips. "I shouldn't have said anything. I want to forget about it completely, just for tonight."

Leia sank down onto the soft ground, relishing the coolness of grass beneath her palms. After a moment, Kier knelt beside her. When he hesitated still longer, she started to ask him what he was thinking—but then he reached out, fingers trembling, and removed one long pin from her hair. He held it between them, a silent question as to whether he should continue.

Alderaan had any number of traditions about braids, about who wore them, and when, and why. The customs varied from continent to continent, age to age. But always, one of the most profoundly intimate acts was to allow someone else to take the braids down.

After one deep, shaky breath, Leia turned, offering him the back of her head.

Kier went slowly at first, figuring out how to proceed, but he gained confidence as he went. Each pin was carefully placed in a pile off to the side so that they could keep only the slightest sliver of space between them. Every time their eyes met, the troubling world around them fell further away.

2V knew her work. Leia's hair didn't begin to tumble free until the very last braids were loosed. When at last it fell heavy and dark around her shoulders, Kier buried his hands in it, and she didn't have to think or worry anymore, just close her eyes, kiss him, and let go.

CHAPTER 28

Apprentice legislators rarely contented themselves with the experience itself. Kier's academic interest was the exception; most apprentices hoped for political or Imperial careers, and their time with the Senate served as a mere starting point. Therefore, attracting the attention of a senior official usually meant good news.

A princess of Alderaan didn't need that kind of attention—and even if she had, Leia would've been horrified to receive the summons to meet with Grand Moff Tarkin.

"What can he want?" Kier shook his head in consternation when she showed him the screen. They sat together in her family's apartments, watching one of the famously melodramatic holovids from Shili. "It's not like we've seen him anywhere near the Apprentice Legislature since day one."

"He's been to Alderaan, though." Leia remembered that terrible dinner party, the suspense that had hung over them all like a canopy of black. "Recently. I think he was trying to rattle my parents."

"You think he suspects something?" Kier sat upright, almost as if he would leap to his feet in alarm. She remembered the sharpness of that initial fear. "Why didn't you tell me?"

"It would only move you into the bull's-eye along with us." She curled into a ball on the sofa, hugging her knees to her chest. Their family apartments hadn't felt as empty since she began spending more time here with Kier, but Tarkin's message had made her father's absence freshly vivid. "I wish I could ask my dad about how to handle this."

"Could you call him?"

Not where he's gone. Leia pulled herself together. "Not in time. The summons says this morning."

When she rose from the sofa, smoothing the simple tunic she wore, Kier got to his feet beside her. "Do you want me to come with you?"

"Tarkin's not going to allow that."

"I didn't mean into his office. Just to walk there with you, if it would help you stay calm."

His sweetness eased some of the tension within her—not all of it, not even close, but enough for her to collect herself. Leia put her hands on either side of his face. "What would help me is knowing you'll be here when I get back."

"Then I'm staying right here."

Kier kissed her goodbye so thoroughly that the warmth of it buoyed her up during the entire journey through the labyrinthine set of lifts, skyways, and corridors that brought her to Tarkin's Coruscant offices. When she got there, however, and saw the imposing Imperial seal on the doors, the chill began to creep back in. But royal training could carry her through far more than ceremonial rituals of the court. *Commanding and confident? No. That's not what the Grand Moff wants to see. Demure and innocent—that's better.* Leia clasped her hands in front of her, lowered her chin slightly, and walked inside.

Before the protocol droid had even finished introducing her, Tarkin had risen from his desk. Not even his polite smile could gentle his cadaverous face. "Your Highness. How good of you to come."

It took every minute of every year of her training for her not to flinch when taking his outstretched hand. His fingers could've been fleshless bones. "Thank you, Governor. I appreciate the honor, but I admit, I was surprised to hear from you." *Lower your eyes, tighten the throat as though you were sad.* "After how I behaved—"

"Now, now, none of that. You were hardly responsible for that disgraceful scene." His "kindly" pat on her shoulder didn't fool her; he was trying to discombobulate her under the guise of comforting her. "In fact, since that night, I've been concerned about you. I felt I should take some kind of action, were such required."

"You, sir?" Leia couldn't keep the incredulity out of her voice, but that was all right. He'd expected to catch her off guard and would be pleased to have done so.

He gestured toward the chair in front of his desk and politely didn't sit until she had. "Yes. Forgive my interference, but it occurred to me that if the daughter of a queen and a viceroy had difficulties, there would be very few people to whom she could turn."

"That's an extremely kind gesture." From another sort of person altogether, it might have been. "Really, though, what happened that night—it's between my parents. I have to let them work it out in their own time."

Tarkin nodded, and though he studied her avidly, she detected no suspicion . . . at least, not yet. "That's a very mature attitude, allowing your elders to act as they see best."

Eyes downcast, she said, "I know this is the right way to handle it, but I admit, it's hard sometimes." Did he hope to reduce her to tears again? If that was what it took to end this interview, Leia was prepared to sob until he had medical droids wheel her out for observation.

"Undoubtedly." To her dismay, Tarkin gestured for a servitor droid to bring them tea as he settled into his chair like a man prepared to talk at length. "But it's that kind of self-control that will make you a fine senator and an excellent queen. Your parents have quite a reputation, Your Highness, but I dare say you'll eclipse them when the time comes."

Why is he talking about this?

She kept a tiny, uncertain smile on her face as she accepted her cup of tea. Tarkin kept on while the droid poured next to him. "Although the centralized governance of the Empire is what provides our stability and our strength, planetary leaders nonetheless play a critical role. The Emperor needs to know that monarchs, presidents, prime ministers, chieftains, and senators will support his rule, and monitor activities more closely than we can hope to from Coruscant."

Cooperate with us. Do as we say, and you keep your throne. He wouldn't be having this conversation with her unless he thought she'd inherit that throne soon.

Since her parents were still hardly even middle-aged, there was only one reason for Tarkin to think that.

Her entire body tightened—her throat strangling her voice, her ears trying to shut out sound so she couldn't hear any more of this. Leia's heart beat wildly in her chest, and the impulse to dash out of the room was almost overwhelming. She simply sipped her tea before saying, so steadily it shocked her, "I realize how important that is to Emperor Palpatine."

"I believe you do. You're a good girl." Tarkin smiled,

obviously thinking her young and naïve enough to be flattered by such condescension. "While I commend your attitude toward allowing your parents some, ah, distance, I want you to know that in the future, should you feel uncertain and require guidance, I shall be glad to give it." *Be our puppet ruler, and I'll hold the strings.*

"Thank you, Governor. I appreciate that." *On more levels than you can ever realize.*

Maybe some hint of emotion slipped out. Maybe he was simply too calculating a man not to apply one final test. She knew only that Tarkin cocked his head, studying her like a predator about to pounce, before he said—with courtly flourish—"I see such attentions as an investment in our Empire's future. Someday, I hope, we will achieve perfect rule and perfect peace, from here on Coruscant to the farthest systems of Lothal, Paucris, Rattatak—or whatever worlds we may yet find."

Paucris. It sliced through her like a sword's blade. Tarkin certainly hadn't named that system by chance. He hoped to shake up a young girl who—so far as he knew—he'd already seen easily reduced to tears. His eyes locked with hers as he searched for the telltale slip that would betray her, and doom them all.

Leia didn't flinch. With the full force of her imagination, she pictured Kier sitting in front of her, imagined it was him she was smiling at, and heard the warmth in her voice as she answered, "May we someday see that perfect peace."

For one seemingly eternal instant, nothing changed—and then Tarkin ever so slightly relaxed. "Hear, hear."

She had to make chitchat through that entire cup of tea. Had to allow him to escort her out of the office, her arm through his, and tell him goodbye. She even made sure to walk at a normal speed for the first while after she left, until she'd taken three lifts and one skyway back to the senatorial complex. But as soon as she'd entered the inner corridors, Leia broke into a run.

She burst into her father's office, startling the staff. "Please tell me Dad is here."

"I'm afraid not, Your Highness," said the protocol droid, with a distinct undertone of *and you should know that.* "Senator Organa's return is still scheduled six days hence—"

"I need to use his private office. Excuse me." Leia rushed straight in, knowing nobody on her father's staff had the rank to prevent her, even if they'd wanted to. She pulled up the HoloNet and put in a call to the palace, directly to her mother; as the connection was made, she brought up Mon Mothma on audio only.

Mon Mothma answered first. *"Princess Leia?"*

"Yes—hold on, I'm getting my mom—" Queen Breha shimmered into holographic form in the office, wearing the exercise gear no one but her family would ever see her in. Before her mother could even ask what was happening, Leia blurted out, "The Empire knows about Paucris Major."

Her mother blanched so visibly it was clear even via holo. Mon Mothma's voice was sharp. "How do you know this?"

"I didn't go snooping, I swear—"

"It doesn't matter if you did!" Breha said. "How do you know?"

"Tarkin called me to his office. Acted like it was this friendly mentoring thing, but he was sounding me out. Saying things that suggested I'd inherit the throne soon." Her mother's hand went to her own throat, a sight that seared Leia almost past endurance. "Then he was naming far-off systems like it was random, but he named Paucris. He was looking directly at me. I'm positive he did it to rattle me. There's no way that's a coincidence."

"I'm sure you're right." Mon Mothma sounded as though she'd aged years in mere seconds. "We have to send a messenger to warn them—we can't trust droid probes with this, and we hardly know who to trust until we've patched Winmey's leaks—"

"I can't leave Alderaan," Breha said. "We're holding a medals ceremony in only a few hours."

"Nobody cares about the medal ceremony," Leia began before her mother cut her off with a gesture.

"Of course nobody cares about that, sweetheart, but if I suddenly cancel a public event, word will travel back to the Empire. For all we know, they're already prepared to strike. We can't run the risk of tipping them off, or else they'll pounce before we can evacuate."

"I have a meeting with one of the grand admirals this evening," Mon Mothma said. "Princess, you must go, immediately."

As much as she'd hoped to do for this movement, as often as she'd begged to help, Leia hadn't expected to be called on for anything as urgent and serious as this. Yet she understood instantly. A senator or a queen would be missed; an apprentice legislator would not. Leia already had all the information necessary to complete her task. And their trust in her was absolute.

"I'll leave right away," Leia promised. "Is the *Polestar* on Coruscant?"

"It's here on Alderaan." Her mother swore, which under other circumstances would've been shocking. "You'll have to hire a ship. An independent freighter, the type not to ask too many questions."

That sounded intimidating, but Leia nodded.

Mon Mothma added, "As tight as time may be, you

should stop somewhere along the way and change ships. We don't want anyone to be able to track your movements directly."

"Got it," Leia promised. "I'll need credits." The funds necessary to hire at least two freighters went beyond even the generous stipend she had on Coruscant.

"I'll personally bring you an untraceable credit solid," Mon Mothma said. "Where are you?"

"Dad's office."

The only goodbye that followed was the click of a voice link deactivating. Leia refocused on her mother, who had sunk into a chair, her hands woven through her loose hair. Breha said only, "I'm not even going to ask how you know about Paucris."

"That's probably a good idea," Leia admitted.

"You realize that the Empire could be moving in on our base there even now?" Her mother was shaking so much that it was visible even through the blur of the holo. "You realize the danger you're in? I can't let you go unless I know you understand, completely."

"I understand." Yet she wasn't as afraid as she'd been in Tarkin's office. She'd come to realize that she would never be overwhelmed by fear as long as she had something to do. Leia's mind raced ahead to the journey, the message, to all the details that would carry her onward and keep her from imagining her arrest by the Empire and the horrors that would surely follow. "I'm all right, Mom. I'm ready."

"Yes, I think you are." Breha blinked fast. It hit Leia that her mother knew both her husband and her daughter were in imminent danger, and yet there was nothing she could do but perform her duty, wear her crown, and smile. It seemed unbearable. Yet she lifted her hand as though she could touch Leia's face and said, "I love you."

"I love you too."

Instantly the holo went dark. Leia understood why. Extending the conversation would only have tormented her mother. It was better to focus on what had to be done. The Apprentice Legislature didn't have another session for a few days—she'd turned in her proposals early, as usual, so that deadline didn't matter—Harp had invited her over to watch some holovids tomorrow, by which time Leia would either be back or in prison—

"*Kier*," she whispered. He would still be waiting for her in their family's apartments, in suspense. When she snapped open a new holo-channel, he appeared in front of her almost instantly; he must've been waiting directly in front of the camera. "I'm all right," she began. "But I think Tarkin's on to my parents. I have to go to the Paucris system, right away."

"Wait, what?" Kier put his hands out as if he could dam the flood of information. "You have to go where?"

"It doesn't matter." Really she shouldn't have burdened him with that information in the first place, but everything was happening so fast. Leia continued, "Just cover for me if anyone asks, okay? Tell them I had to go home on short notice."

"Leia, this sounds bad."

She nodded. "It could be. But maybe—maybe I'll be in time." Holding her hand out, much as her mother had, she said, "I'll talk with you soon." *Please, let that be true.*

Kier looked like he wanted to argue, but he also knew when arguing with her would prove useless. "Soon," he repeated. "Promise?"

"Promise." With that, she shut off the holo, leaving herself alone in unnatural stillness for a few breaths. It was almost long enough for fear to creep in—but then Mon Mothma rushed through the doors, white robe fluttering, more flustered than Leia had ever seen her before.

"Credit solid," Mon Mothma said, breathless. "Linked to banks so obscure even Palpatine doesn't have their information, and adequate to cover the cost of ten ships if you need them."

Leia took the gold-striped solid and slipped it into one of the secure pouches at her belt. "If two ships won't do it, eight more won't help." It was gallows humor, but it helped her smile.

Mon Mothma paused, still winded, obviously searching for wisdom or at least helpful advice. Then she shook her head, put her hands on Leia's shoulders and spoke the only words that mattered. "May the Force be with you."

CHAPTER 29

Leia had never had to hire her own ship before, but she figured it couldn't be that difficult. What she didn't realize was that she'd never tried to do much of anything without presenting herself as the crown princess of Alderaan, and just how much easier it was for a princess to get things done.

"A freighter?" barked a Loneran pilot. "A little scrap of a thing like you? What are you hauling?"

Leia wondered wildly whether she ought to come up with some kind of cargo to bring along, but how could she do that in time? "Ah, just me."

The Loneran's fur raised in consternation. "To Pamarthe, you said?"

"Right." It was the first heavily trafficked but remote layover she'd been able to think of.

But she'd chosen poorly, because the Loneran said, "So take a passenger ship and save yourself the credits."

"I need to get there as soon as possible—"

"Passenger ship won't take you half a day longer." The Loneran patted her on the head. "Now, hurry along, pup."

How old does he think I am? Eight? As the Loneran loped away, Leia glanced around the busy spaceport in search of another freighter that looked small enough to be of use to her. Hiring one sounded so easy, but in practice, getting a ship to take off within a brief time span, without questions, could be a challenge. Three pilots had turned her down so far; she'd also hurried after one YT-model ship that had looked promisingly run-down and probably in need of money for repairs, but it took off before she could even reach it.

Spotting another ungainly, patched-together ship across the hangar, Leia headed toward it. As she pushed through the crowd, ducking around a group of Arconas and an enormous, scowling Crolute, she tried to come up with a better cover story. *I'm eloping, and my parents are after me!* No, because someone would sensibly ask why she was eloping all alone. *My grandmother on Pamarthe is incredibly sick, and I need to get to her right away!* That might do.

Leia ran up to the ship, then stopped short when she saw not one but two people she knew standing in front of it, arguing.

"Excuse me," Chassellon Stevis said, "but if I don't get to the auction on Arkanis in time, someone's going to snap that speeder up. Do you know how rarely this model comes available?"

"Rarity is an illusion, because every person and object

in the galaxy is in some way unique." Amilyn Holdo—her hair still brilliantly colored, but her clothing a simple traveling coverall—smiled benevolently at him. "Anyway, I'm signed up for the meditation retreat at home, and it's starting tomorrow."

Chassellon's hands stiffened, as if he wanted to physically shake sense into Amilyn. "You could take a passenger ship!"

For her part, Amilyn folded her long arms across her chest and dug in. "I could, if I hadn't already hired the *Moa*, which I have. Oh, hi, Leia!"

Leia blurted out, "I need this ship."

"Oh, come *on*." Chassellon stared skyward, perhaps asking for help from gods who didn't answer. "You're a bloody princess! You can get whatever ship you want!"

But Amilyn had seen something in Leia that she recognized, maybe from their journey to Ocahont. She brought her hands together, closed her eyes, and said, "All right."

Chassellon's eyes widened with anger—Leia didn't entirely blame him—but then he, too, seemed to glimpse the genuine fear and need she felt. He took a deep breath, adjusted the collar of his violet jacket, and spoke with better grace than she'd known he had. "Fine, then. Take the ship."

Leia was taking a risk saying even this much, but she had to: "Chassellon, please, don't tell anyone you saw me."

Although he clearly didn't understand why she was asking, he must've known it was important. His voice was solemn as he said, "Not a word. Not a soul." With that he walked off, never glancing back.

"Sometimes people surprise you," Amilyn said. "By the way, this trip that has to happen in such a hurry—are we talking about things we don't talk about?"

It took Leia a second to parse that. "Yeah. We are. And I have to go."

"You mean *we* have to go." When Leia stared at her, Amilyn shrugged. "I did hire the ship. Plus I already know all the stuff I can't know."

I'm definitely getting better at translating Holdo-speak, because that made complete sense to me. Leia wanted to protest that Amilyn *didn't* know everything, and for her own good shouldn't—but in truth, what Amilyn had already learned was undoubtedly more than enough to destroy her if the Empire found them out. The best way to keep the Empire from finding them out was to leave immediately, without any further arguing.

There were other advantages too. "It might be better if the ship were hired in your name," Leia admitted.

"So let's go." Amilyn pulled Leia up the gangway. "Where are we going, by the way?"

"Pamarthe again."

Amilyn smiled as easily as if they were on a pleasure

cruise and called, "Brill? Slight change of destination! As in, we're headed to a completely different planet!"

•◆•

Leia had wished to see one of the famous storms of Pamarthe. Of all her wishes, the Force picked that one to come true, and at the worst possible time.

The *Moa* set them down in the middle of storms both terrestrial and celestial: while the sea around their port island churned black beneath a darkening sky, the auroras flared pink and green overhead, testifying to solar storms that would disrupt many ships' sensors.

Why did it have to be Pamarthe? Leia asked herself as she and Amilyn disembarked from their freighter, its Ithorian crewmember waving goodbye as the *Moa* drew its ramp up again. *I could've chosen any planet in the galaxy, and I had to pick the one that's about to shut down all space traffic.*

Even Amilyn's daffy good spirits wilted at the sight of it. "Normally being marooned here would be frightening in a very good way, but right now it's frightening in a bad way, isn't it?"

"The worst." Leia kept imagining her father's face, which shifted in her mind from moment to moment. First she'd see him warm and loving, as he'd been when they spoke in the library—but then she'd recall his fury at their last meeting. Would that be her final memory of her father? *Please, not that. Let me have one more chance to make things right with him.* "They say the Pamarthe pilots aren't scared of anything. Let's hope that's true."

Unfortunately it turned out that Pamarthens were afraid of exactly one thing: losing their beloved ships. After the first three refusals, Leia wanted to hurl herself down and have a tantrum on the ground like a child. She took a few deep breaths, trying to channel her anger in better directions, and then heard Amilyn say, "What about those . . . giant hairy-frog guys?"

Turning in the direction of Amilyn's pointing finger, she saw a squat group of creatures waddling onto their low, flat ship, and gasped with new hope. "The Chalhuddans!"

"Who?"

"I'll explain later. For now, let me do the talking."

Leia dashed toward the Chalhuddan vessel, a wide smile on her face—but when they noticed her approach, it was obvious these Chalhuddans had no idea who she was, because they scowled, shuffled, and averted their gazes. No doubt she didn't look that impressive, a wild-eyed teenage girl in nondescript clothing. 2V's admonishments rung in her memory: *A princess is known in part through the grandeur of her attire!*

"Points to TooVee," Leia muttered.

As she and Amilyn came up to them, the largest of

the Chalhuddans pointedly turned his back. "We need no drylander assistance," they mumbled, "and we give none."

Amilyn piped up: "It's paying work. *Well*-paying work! She's a princess—" Her face fell as she took in Leia's disheveled appearance, and feebly she added, "Really."

This wasn't the way to impress the Chalhuddans, who only harrumphed and turned aside. Leia stepped into the center of their group, lifted her chin, and demanded, "You'll put me in contact with Occo Quentto, immediately."

They stared at her. One of them scoffed, a gruff and discouraging sound, but the others exchanged uncertain glances. The mere fact that she knew their leader's name had probably startled them into paying attention.

"You heard me," Leia continued, with all the regal chill she could muster, which was a lot. "Now."

Within a few minutes, she sat within the humid Chalhuddan ship, wiping sweat from her brow, as the sepia-tinted holo flickered to life. "You are the princess," Occo said, which was their version of a pleasant hello.

"Yes, I am." She kept her face impassive and her tone demanding. "You owe me a favor, Occo Quentto, and you will repay it today."

The large air sac beneath Occo's chin puffed up,

then deflated again. "This favor is owed. What do you demand?"

"Immediate passage to Paucris Major for myself and one companion."

Occo nodded. "Then it shall be so."

Without any further order or persuasion, the Chalhuddans began waddling off to make ready for the journey. As badly as Leia needed this, however, she knew it would be unfair not to say more. "Honored leader, you must hear more of the truth behind the journey."

Occo's enormous, wide-lipped mouth pursed in a frown. "The favor was asked. The favor will be given."

"Your favor will be far greater than mine," Leia said. "And more dangerous. It's unfair to your people for me to hold you to this without explaining more."

"What explanation can come between the Chalhuddans and their owed duty?" Occo shifted from flipper to flipper, restless with distrust of land creatures. "You dishonor us by doubting us."

Leia bowed her head more humbly than she would've to the Emperor himself and shifted into formal speech. "You doubt me, honored leader, by not hearing what I say."

One deep, exasperated croak, and then Occo said, "We will hear."

"By traveling to this system, your brave pilots put their

lives in danger. The Imperial Starfleet will soon travel to Paucris Major with the goal of eradicating everyone they find. The people there are my people, and I must save them even if it means my life. Yet I cannot transfer that responsibility onto your people without letting them, and you, know precisely what they face. Now it is known."

Occo Quentto blinked their protruding eyes, and the air sac inflated thoughtfully. Leia wondered if she'd just been so honorable she'd lost a ship—maybe even a war.

Then Occo said, "The greater the favor asked, the greater the honor. This ship will take you to the Paucris system, where you will be met by all other Chalhuddan ships in the sector. No more than four or five can we offer, but you will be transported and guarded to the best of our ability."

"That is more than recompense for my favor, Occo Quentto." Leia folded her hands above her heart, hoping the Chalhuddans' circulatory organ was located somewhere analogous. "Afterward I will again be in your debt."

"And so we will ask another favor of you someday." Occo's broad face creased in an expression that she thought might be their version of a smile. "*Now* you understand us."

As the holo blinked out, Amilyn said, "I hoped for some experience with the nearness of mortality, but I have to say, I'm getting quite a lot of it." Leia turned to her, ready to suggest Amilyn stay behind here with Mon Mothma's credit solid, but her friend was grinning. "This is *fantastic*."

Chalhuddan ships were armed—not heavily, but still. She'd managed to put together her own tiny war fleet. As pleased as she wanted to be with that, when she imagined them facing an Imperial Star Destroyer—

Leia shuddered. *Let the Force guide us there first,* she thought. *Hang on, Dad. I'm coming.*

CHAPTER 30

"Paucris system in three," said the Chalhuddan pilot, squatting in their bowl-shaped chair. Leia and Amilyn—who had in the past hour learned a lot about the greater tolerance Chalhuddans had for shock waves—immediately clambered up into the jump seat and strapped themselves into a safety harness. (If the two of them shared a harness and pulled its straps as tight as possible, it more or less worked.)

Amilyn blew aside a purple lock of her hair that had tumbled into her face so that she could meet Leia's eyes. There was no hint of her usual whimsy as she said, "What do we do if the Empire's already here?"

"Get out before they see us, if we can." The chances weren't good, but they weren't impossible; Leia doubted a droid could've gone over the odds more times than she had during this trip. "If not, we surrender right away. We plead ignorance, and we make it absolutely clear that we hired the Chalhuddans, who know even less than we do."

She didn't think it would save the Chalhuddans, but again—it was a chance. If they had even once chance in a thousand to make it through this, she owed them that.

"Plead ignorance," Amilyn repeated. "Right. I think I could be good at that."

"For our sakes, I hope so."

Leia wasn't optimistic. She figured whatever doubt she was able to instill in her questioners' minds would vanish the instant Grand Moff Tarkin learned of her arrival in the very star system he'd named to her only hours before. Neither Amilyn Holdo nor the Chalhuddans would be able to explain this away.

Either I'm saving the lives of all the rebels in the Paucris system—or I've just condemned even more people to die.

When the Chalhuddan pilot pulled a lever, the vivid blue light of hyperspace changed back into a starfield. The entire ship shuddered so strongly Leia accidentally bit her tongue hard enough to bleed. Amilyn's head knocked against hers so soundly it hurt, but she wasn't too dazed to keep staring at the viewscreen, eyes wide, torn between hope and dread—

"A fleet of planetary and civilian ships massed around repair structures orbiting Paucris Major," croaked the Chalhuddan captain. "Our own ships nearby. No Imperial vessels in the system."

Thank the Force. Leia slumped against Amilyn and exhaled hard. Onscreen, amid the distant cluster of ships, she could make out the distinct lines of the *Tantive IV*, which had rarely looked so beautiful to her. Amilyn held one fist up in the air in a victory salute.

"Don't celebrate too soon." Leia released the safety harness, hopped down from the tall bowl chair, and hurried to the communications console. At her nod, the officer there opened a channel, and she said, "To any vessels picking up this signal, this is Leia Organa of Alderaan calling Bail Organa or any other individual in charge of—anyone in charge. Repeat, this is Princess Leia Organa of Alderaan. Please respond."

No answer came. Amilyn said, "Should we fly closer?"

"We'd better not. They may have standing orders to shoot down any unauthorized intruder." Leia remembered her father's warning on Crait very well.

The seconds crawled by until her gut had begun to tighten—and then static broke through. *"Leia?"* She'd never been so glad to hear her father sound absolutely furious. "What are you do—"

"The Empire's coming," she said. "Something Tarkin said about this system tipped me off. Mom and Mon Mothma sent me. The ships may already be on their way, and you have to get the fleet out of here, immediately."

Luckily Bail Organa was a man who knew when a conversation could wait until later. "We're moving out in ten. Rendezvous with us on the *Tantive IV*."

•◆•

Once the Chalhuddan ships had taken their place among the rebel ships—each of which was being hastily restored to power and crewed with minimal personnel or droids—Leia's vessel was able to dock with the *Tantive IV* and allow her to disembark. She expected to feel more relief once she was in familiar surroundings, but they were more familiar than she'd anticipated.

"Hey, there," Ress Batten said, a rueful smile on her face. "In case you were wondering, no, I wasn't putting you on the whole time. Captain Antilles brought me into the loop not long ago—in the nick of time for some mortal danger, huh?"

"Lucky you," said Amilyn from a few paces behind, where she was wandering along, gazing at the plain white walls of the ship as though they were miraculous.

Batten frowned in consternation, but there was no time to explain these two to each other, because at the far end of the corridor, separated from her by a few crewmembers and droids dashing around, stood a tall, familiar figure in a blue jacket and cape: her father, alive and whole, as she'd thought she might never see him again.

He caught sight of her at the same instant. "Leia!"

To hell with royal protocol. She ran to him and flung herself into his arms. He hugged her so tightly her toes lifted from the floor for a moment, the way he had when she was a little girl. "I didn't know if we'd make it in time," she said. Her face pressed against his jacket muffled her words, but she wouldn't pull back or let go. Her father could hear her, and that was enough. "I thought we might find you dead."

"But for you, that might have happened." Bail Organa's broad hand cupped her cheek, turning her face up to his. "Instead, we're going to save this fleet."

"Did I finally prove myself to you?"

"Leia, no. You *never* had to do that. I've always believed in you, and I always will. If I made you doubt that these past few months, please, forgive me." The depth of the remorse she heard in his voice made her throat so tight she couldn't speak. Bail leaned closer and spoke even more intently. "Out of all the many reasons we have to fight, to your mother and me, *you* have always been the most important one. We want to make a better galaxy for you, a better future. So it's been hard, realizing that you have to fight too. That we can't simply save you—that you have to stand by our side."

She nodded. "I understand. I always did, really. It's okay."

"I wouldn't let myself accept that you were ready for this." His smile was crooked but proud. "There's no denying that any longer."

Leia hugged her father again, grateful that at last they were partners again, that no other division could come between them.

The embrace went on for as much time as they could spare. When Bail released her, he had again focused on the military operation under way; the difference was that he included Leia in his planning. "We'll be breaking up this portion of the fleet for the time being, until we can arrange a rendezvous at an alternate outpost. Self-destruct sequences were programmed into the repair stations from the start. We'll activate those before the final convoy departs."

Portion of the fleet? How many other ships were there, and where were they? But Leia could ask all those questions later. "Do you have a shuttle or hopper Amilyn and I can fly back to Coruscant?" Leia had been considering this during the docking procedure with the *Tantive IV.* "I don't want anybody to link the Chalhuddans to us."

Her father's smile was equal parts amused and impressed. "I spoke with their captain. You've made your first diplomatic alliance, and negotiated an armed convoy, at that." Then he paused. "Wait. 'Amilyn'?"

"Hi there!" Amilyn was doing some sort of elaborate acrobatic stretching farther down the corridor, maybe to allow father and daughter some privacy, maybe just for fun.

"Amilyn Holdo from Gatalenta," Leia explained. "She's a friend of mine from the Apprentice Legislature, with a knack for being in the right place at the right time."

"Those are the best kind of friends to have." Bail lifted one hand in a wave before turning his attention back to his daughter. "We have a hopper for the two of you. Should look like a civilian craft, and it's small enough that you can pilot it on your own."

Although Leia wasn't an expert pilot, she could manage. "All right. After I drop Amilyn off on Coruscant, I'd like to come back to Alderaan for a few days. Unless you'll be on Coruscant too—"

"You never need permission to return to Alderaan," her father said gently. "And after this, I think we could use some time at home together as a family."

These past many months, Leia had wished and hoped that things between her and her parents would go back to the way they used to be. Finally she understood that would never happen, because neither she nor her parents were the people they'd been before. They had to grow into the family they would become—one united to face the challenges ahead.

"Home," she repeated. "I'd like that."

•◆•

"I would've thought royal vehicles were more, well, *regal*." Amilyn peered around the tiny, gray-mesh interior of the hopper, more curious than disappointed. Her brilliant hair constituted most of the color in the room.

Leia slipped into the pilot's seat and acquainted herself with the controls. Data on a screen informed her fifty-nine ships were in the vicinity, ranging in size from that medical frigate to a few tiny single-pilot vessels. With a few taps, she was able to highlight the Chalhuddan ships; she didn't intend to leave this system until they were all safely away.

"Laying in our course to—" Returning directly to Coruscant might be risky. "To Baltizaar."

"Mirrors bend light," Amilyn said. Leia nodded, understanding her friend's acknowledgement of the need to break up their course before she recognized the odd metaphor. She sighed as she thought, *I'm learning to speak fluent Holdo.*

On the viewscreen, Leia could easily pick out the *Tantive IV* leaving orbit with the other vessels; distant as it was, its shape was as familiar to her as any other part of her home. Ships around it began to disappear, with the illusory stretch-and-pop that marked a jump into hyperspace. One by one, the sky around Paucris Major darkened as the brighter ships disappeared. Her father took the *Tantive IV* out near the very end, as she'd known he would.

Amilyn leaned over the data screen. "Only forty-two ships remaining—now eighteen—seven—two—" After a long pause, she repeated, "Two. We're still at two."

To Leia's dismay, one of the remaining ships was a Chalhuddan vessel, still far too close to the repair stations; it wouldn't be long before the self-destruct sequences activated, blowing themselves—and everything in the immediate vicinity—to shreds. "Are they damaged? Do we need to tow them out? *Can* we?"

But then the lights on the Chalhuddans' engines glowed brighter, and it, too, fled into hyperspace. Relief washed over Leia, leaving her almost limp.

"Now we have one," Amilyn said.

"Right. So we get out of here—"

"That's one *not counting us*." Amilyn's hand trembled as she brought the image into holo form: a standard, nondescript cutter, the kind of thing that could be rented at any hangar in the galaxy. It wasn't flying away from the stations; it was flying toward one.

Leia's fingers tightened around her armrests. "That ship wasn't here when we arrived in this system, was it?" Amilyn shook her head.

Stang.

Pulling herself together, Leia began running through the possibilities. The cutter wasn't an Imperial ship. Whoever piloted it wasn't an Imperial spy, either, or else they would've taken off with the others to report their findings—and even the swift glimpse they could've seen of the rebel's ships was more than enough to report. A bounty hunter, thinking to turn informant? But how would a bounty hunter know about the Paucris system? How would anyone . . .

Leia's stomach dropped. The shuttle seemed to spin on every axis at once. She hit the communications, sending a signal to the cutter and to the person she knew had to be inside—"Kier?"

CHAPTER 31

Despite what she already knew had to be true, it hurt to recognize Kier's voice.

"Leia? Thank the Force I found you." He sounded so relieved. Even grateful. "It sounded like you were in—"

"Kier! You have to get away from that station, now. It's going to blow!"

"What are y—"

If he'd hit the controls and accelerated that instant, without hesitation, the cruiser might've made it out of range. If he'd flown in closer and faster to start with, he would never have had a chance. When the blast exploded outward—ripping the station into a wave of fire and shattered steel—Kier's cutter was instead violently thrown outward. Amilyn screamed, but Leia lacked even the breath. She could only stare in horror, not knowing whether she'd just watched him die.

Their hopper shuddered as smaller pieces of debris thumped the hull. Through the metallic shards blanketing the starfield on their screen, she could make out the shape of Kier's cutter. The engines didn't glow; there was no sign of power, no way to tell how much damage had been done.

An unfamiliar stillness claimed her. When her fear or despair reached its absolute height, her mind turned crystalline—hard, set, focused, straight. Her emotions remained, but encased in a structure that would not yield.

"The Empire's on its way." She spoke to Amilyn as steadily as she'd spoken to her parents on her Day of Demand. It was as if she already knew the words. "They could be here any second. I have to try to help Kier, but if you want to dock with his ship and leave us, do it. Maybe I can get his engines back online."

"*Maybe?*"

There was no point in responding to that. Leia would accomplish that or she wouldn't. What mattered was protecting everyone she could. "You don't have to take this risk. I do."

Amilyn trembled from shock, but she shook her head. "Don't be an ass. I'm not leaving either of you."

"Then let's do this." Leia's hands went to the controls. The hopper shot forward. She adjusted their course so that Kier's cutter (dark, rolling over and over, badly dented) remained at the center of their viewscreen, larger every moment.

Luckily both hopper and cutter were such basic workhorse models that autodock compatibility was built in.

Although Kier's cutter remained unresponsive, the hopper was able to link them and pump in localized power. Leia's craft shook as the locks joined, and a warning light began to blink: The cutter's artificial gravity was inoperable. To keep its entire contents from rushing into the hopper the instant the doors opened, she immediately shut off their own gravity, hooking one leg around the base of her seat to keep her more or less in place. Then they were unmoored, weightless. Amilyn's hair rose around her head in a multicolored cloud; she stared at Leia as if unable to understand how she could be so quiet and calm. Leia didn't understand it herself.

The lock doors slid open, and Leia pushed herself upward, soaring into the cutter—or what remained of it. Every control had gone black; the only illumination filtered in through the hopper. Bits of metal spun in midair, and floating beads of water glinted as they caught the light. A droplet hit her cheek—but it was warm.

Not water. Blood.

In the center of the dark, she saw the dim outline of Kier's body, his arms outstretched, floating, loose. Her momentum brought her closer until she had to put one hand onto the ceiling to prevent colliding with him. He was near enough for her to draw him into her embrace. When she felt his heartbeat against her hand, relief flooded through her. "Kier? Can you hear me?"

The dim shaft of light from below briefly illuminated his face as his eyes fluttered open. “Leia?”

“I’ve got you. We’ll take you back to Alderaan, find a doctor.” On Alderaan, her parents could ensure he received top care in secret, a guarantee they wouldn’t find on Coruscant.

“You were—you were scared—in trouble—” Kier’s expression remained blank. He’d recognized her, but he didn’t seem to have registered anything she said. “Followed you.”

Remorse pierced Leia through so sharply she wanted to cry out, but she forced herself back into focus. Made herself crystalline. “I’m all right. It’s all right now. You came for me and I’m safe. Can you hang on to me? Brace yourself against me?”

Kier coughed, and the only thing worse than the sound of it was the terrible spasm of pain on his face. Hoarsely he said, “—memory rod—”

Consternation dissolved swiftly into her understanding that the memory rod had to be vitally important. Leia peered through the darkness until she saw it, a specialized scanner/mass-memory storage device, cylindrical and gold. Cradling Kier against her with one hand, she snagged the rod with another. “It’s right here. I’ve got it. You don’t have to worry.”

“Promise—turn it in.” He coughed again, more weakly.

"Protect them if you—but—Alderaan, for Alderaan—"

He'd heard the planning in the banquet hall. Knew about what had happened on Onoam, about the medical frigate, about the entire alliance of leaders ready to stand against Palpatine. As soon as he arrived in this system and saw the ships massed here for repair, Kier had known exactly what it meant. Once the fleet had begun to flee, he'd brought his cruiser near the stations to collect more data.

He'd recorded it all so he could turn the rebels in.

Kier loved Alderaan more than he hated the Empire. If he had to choose between the rest of the galaxy and his home, he chose his home. It was a choice Leia would never make—but she understood it.

"Leia," he whispered, struggling for breath. "Promise."

She smiled at him tenderly, caressed the side of his face, and lied. "I promise."

With a sigh, he relaxed into her embrace. His muscles went slack. Leia kept holding him next to her as his breaths became shallower and his heartbeat slowed. It was so slow, so gradual, that she couldn't tell the exact moment when he died. For what felt like many minutes afterward, she hung on to him, wanting to stay as long as she could in the last place they had ever been together.

But the Empire was coming, and Leia had other lives to save.

She let the memory rod float from her hand, then pushed off with Kier's body in her arms. Light grew brighter around them until they drifted back into the hopper; a few pieces of debris from the damaged cutter had made their way into the air too, but nothing they'd have to clear. Amilyn had used the belt from her coverall to tie herself to her seat, and she'd flipped the collar up so she could hold it against her eyes. For an instant Leia thought it was just more oddness—but then she realized Amilyn was crying, and trying to absorb her tears with the collar so the droplets wouldn't float away.

Hitting the airlock closed the link between the ship; Amilyn turned the gravity back on. Although Leia had been holding Kier as best she could, the sudden return of weight toppled her, and his body crumpled to the floor with a heavy thud.

That sound was so final—so *dead*—

The crystal shattered. All the grief Leia felt, all the fear and anger and everything else she'd kept bottled up or used for fuel—she couldn't hold on to any of it any longer. She burst into sobs, crumpling on the floor by Kier's side.

Leia had spent the past few months trying to prove she was an adult. But she wasn't this grown-up yet. She wasn't this hard or this tough. When she broke down, she fell apart, completely, as she hadn't since she was a child and rarely would again. Bending low, she let her forehead rest against Kier's chest, trying to remember the sound of his heartbeat, as though that would bring it back.

Amilyn said nothing, only took the controls, fired the engines, and took them farther from the wreckage to ensure their space was clear. Leia imagined the stations' wreckage tumbling into the atmosphere of Paucris Major, glowing with heat as it burned on reentry.

Kier's ship would be caught in the planet's gravity too, and the evidence he'd given his life for would disintegrate into atoms, lost forever.

•◆•

Leia cried through their entire hyperspace journey, terrible wracking sobs that made it feel as though the tears were being wrung out of her. When the hopper dropped out of hyperspace, she tried to pull herself together, only to fall apart when she heard the familiar chime of Alderaan's welcome beacons. Amilyn had known that both Leia and Kier needed to come home.

I'll have to lie to his parents. Leia shut her eyes tightly, as though she could block out this part of her certain future. *We'll come up with some story that explains his death. At least I can tell them that he died trying to save me. I can give them that much truth.*

Someday that would be a comfort. For now it shattered her all over again.

The comm sounded, startling Leia into looking up. From her place on the floor, she could see the face of an Imperial captain, mustachioed and stern.

The intensity of her fear, combined with her grief, was enough to nauseate her. *They were waiting for us here the whole time.*

Apparently the captain could only see Amilyn, who sat directly opposite the screen. *"Unidentified vessel, please report your—"*

"This is hopper four-zero-two-four-one-one-LN, and you can call me Lyn." The widest, daffiest grin Leia had ever seen on Amilyn's face appeared, as though nothing was wrong or ever could be. "Hey-ey."

Understandably nonplussed, the captain needed a moment to answer. *"Your vessel ionization levels suggest travel to a system under investigation."*

Amilyn nodded, slow and easy, twirling a lock of her vibrant hair around one finger. "I just got back from the Shili system. Are you guys investigating that planet too? Because I thought it was a-*ma*-zing."

Shili was a planet not so different from Paucris Major. Its star had very nearly the same size, the same properties. The ionization levels would therefore be almost identical. Leia didn't think she could've called such a similar system to mind if she'd been given an hour to think about it. Amilyn had done it instantly.

The captain exchanged glances with a junior officer standing a step beside and behind him. *"You were investigating?"*

"Yeah, because I'm into comparing the different astrological systems around the galaxy." Amilyn kept her voice even more monotone than usual, and tilted her head at an almost silly angle. "Like, whether the same stars give some of the same characteristics to people on entirely different worlds. Are you from Coruscant?"

His accent had already revealed that much. *"My origin isn't relevant. Now, young lady—"*

"See, I *thought* you were from Coruscant. What's your sign?"

"I've no idea. Such superstitions—"

"I'd bet anything you're a Genry on Coruscant, which means on Shili you'd be an Ai. And on both of those worlds, that formation of blue dwarfs nearby? It gives the people born under that sign wisdom, charisma, and"—Amilyn ducked her head flirtatiously—"exceptional virility."

A short laugh from the junior office turned into a cough just in time to ward off the worst of the captain's glare. When the captain turned back to the viewer, he irritably waved her off. *"You're cleared to go."*

"You don't want to chat?" Amilyn kept the innocent look on her face until the viewscreen went dark.

Leia's throat hurt so much from crying she could barely get the words out. "The astrology," she said hoarsely. "That's how you knew which star system to pick to cover our tracks. Astrology."

"Everything is written in the stars." Amilyn took Leia's hand, a simple gesture of comfort—but one that sealed them together as friends for a lifetime. She didn't let go until she said, "Let's take you both home."

CHAPTER 32

When Leia was very tiny, her parents had sometimes brought her up into their enormous bed, allowing her to snuggle between them as she fell asleep. Upon receiving her own "big girl bed" at age four, she had declared herself too old to sleep with her parents, a rule she'd held to resolutely, except of course when she was sick or that time she watched a scary holo about undead gundarks. Her memories of those evenings with her parents had become misty and indistinct over time, as much something she knew had happened as something she remembered happening—until the night after Kier's death, when she crawled back into that bed, curled into a fetal position, and felt as if she'd never move again.

"Do you think you could eat something?" Breha sat beside her, rubbing her daughter's back. "Or at least drink some water or tea?"

Leia wanted to shut down, to give into the treacherous misery weighing down her limbs, but she didn't have the right to do that. She had to keep going. Food felt impossible—nausea still gripped her—but she whispered,

"Maybe tea." From the corner of her eye she glimpsed her mother's hurried gesture to a servitor droid, which trundled off to the kitchens.

A soft thump and a few apologetic beeps testified to a collision in the hallway, and only an instant later, Bail reentered the bedroom. Her father's haggard face would've shocked Leia if she hadn't been sure she looked much the same. "I spoke to the Domadis." His breath caught in his throat before he shook his head and began pulling off his long coat. "To put two people through such pain—"

Quietly Breha said, "Bail. Please." One of her hands covered Leia's shoulder.

Her father caught himself. "I told them there was a small-craft accident in the upper atmosphere, and that he sacrificed himself for Leia. The droids had worked out a more detailed scenario we could use if they'd asked more questions, but . . . they didn't need it. Didn't want it." After a moment he added, more hoarsely, "I told them that we are forever in their debt, and that Kier Domadi would be recognized as a hero not only by our family, but by all of Alderaan."

Would their dead son's heroism comfort the Domadis? Leia couldn't imagine anything making this hurt less, for them or for anyone. And no matter how bravely Kier had rushed to help her, she couldn't forget what would've happened if he'd lived. "He would've reported the rebellion."

She'd told her parents that much in her first moments back on Alderaan, but she'd been too upset to reveal more than the bare facts. Neither of them had brought up the subject since. "He wanted to cover for our family if he could—he didn't understand how impossible that was—but still. He would've done it."

Bail sat on the edge of the bed, clearly weighing his answer. Breha brushed her fingers through the loose strands of Leia's hair that had fallen from her messy braids, the way she had sometimes soothed her daughter when she was a child. Leia sat there, her body too heavy with grief to rise, staring up at the centuries-old mural painted on the ceiling, where old-fashioned spaceships soared toward the sun. Finally Bail said, "Kier did what he thought was right despite incredible risk. Under Palpatine's rule, very few people have the courage to live that way, but he did. He acted selflessly, out of love. We may make mistakes when we let our hearts guide us—terrible mistakes—but I think we are never wholly wrong."

Leia didn't know if she agreed. She was weary in heart and mind, too tired to question herself, too tired to hold up her heavy head. Laying herself back down on the broad bed, she wondered when she'd be ready to get up.

But she would. When Leia rose from this, she intended to assume her rightful place alongside her parents as they struggled to free the galaxy. She'd lie here until she regained her strength, and then, she swore, she'd be ready to fight.

•◆•

Kier's memorial service on Alderaan was simple, short, and heartfelt. He'd been given full honors scarcely short of what a war hero would've received, and his parents had unexpectedly accepted their queen's offer of a place in the royal cemetery.

"It overlooks the palace," Mrs. Domadi had said. She had her son's dark eyes and sharp chin. "And the river that flows to Aldera. Kier loved this world. He'd want to rest at its heart."

"He—he wanted to study history, you know. This way he's with his heroes forever." Mr. Domadi's voice sounded so like Kier's that Leia had to struggle not to cry just hearing it. He smiled directly at her as he said, "I think he'd want to be near the palace for other reasons, too."

His words wrenched her heart—but Leia had gotten through it, with her parents by her side. She'd had days to recuperate in the palace, and endless droids and staffers eager to help in any way they could. Before Kier's burial, she had taken a lock of his dark hair and had found comfort in putting it inside her keepsake chest. She'd thought she was beginning to heal.

Then she returned to Coruscant. Walked into the Organa family apartments half-expecting to see him sitting on the low couch where they'd hung out together. Traveling along pathways they'd taken to and from the senatorial complex. Sitting in the Alderaan pod of the Apprentice Legislature alone. Her friends all tried to help her in their way, but being around them only reminded her more sharply of Kier's absence. The one person Leia could bear to spend time with was Amilyn, who took her skyfaring nearly every day; the struggle to stay aloft in the scarves pushed everything else from her mind and allowed her to exist only in her body, in the now.

On her fourth day back, she went to her father's offices to go over some proposals, only to discover his last meeting was running long. She took a seat at his desk, dreading the expanse of time ahead of her. Even if it lasted only minutes, those were minutes grief could strike.

Then the HoloNet signal blinked. Leia, used to taking messages for her father, answered—only to see the stark, pale image of Grand Moff Tarkin appear, hovering above the floor like a ghost.

"Princess Leia." He gave her his bloodless smile.

Smiling back was utterly beyond her, but she managed a pleasant nod. "Good day, governor. I'm afraid my father isn't in."

"I wasn't calling for your father. I was calling for you."

He would only have called her at this office if he'd had someone watching her, noting her movements. That troubled her less than the fact that he wanted her to *know* it. As cautiously as she would've approached a feral creature, she straightened in her seat and folded her hands in her lap. "To what do I owe the honor?"

"First I wished to offer my condolences on the death of your fellow apprentice legislator—a Mr. Domadi, I believe the name was. I understand he was a promising young man."

Tarkin had to suspect the true conditions of Kier's death, coming as it did just before the Empire's unsuccessful raid on Paucris Major. The hazy version of events given in the official report had been sufficient to convince most people, but not Imperial agents. These "condolences" were his way of twisting the knife.

"Kier was one of the best of us," Leia said smoothly. "Thank you for your kind words. I'll pass them along to the family, if you wish."

"Please do." Tarkin turned his head to study her from a different angle. "Given our conversation a few days ago, I also wished to inquire as to whether you were well. Though of course you are. I've found you to be a young woman of great . . . composure."

Translation: *I know you lied to me. I know you lie very well. I know you're a part of whatever your parents are plotting. And I know you're the reason the ships at Paucris Major got away.*

She met his eyes with ease, never glancing away. "I'm quite well, Governor. Believe me when I say I fully appreciate your concern."

The office doors slid open to admit her father. Two steps in, Bail saw the spectral flicker of Tarkin's holo and quickly moved into holo range. "Governor Tarkin. How can I help you?"

"No further help is required. Your daughter has answered all my questions." Tarkin sharpened his smile for her father. "She's become a charming young lady."

The pride on her father's face at that moment comforted Leia more than almost anything else had. "Yes, we're tremendously proud of her. Thank you so much for your call, but if you'll excuse us, we have work to do."

Tarkin's end of the call blinked out with no further goodbyes. Leia found she could breathe again. "He's watching us," she said.

"He always will be." Bail's broad hand squeezed her shoulder. "But there are ways to use his surveillance against him. Imperial agents tend to follow standard protocols, which means we have opportunities to show them what we want them to see. Give them information that leads to false conclusions. The trick is keeping ourselves protected while still making them believe they're getting usable intel."

The possibilities expanded within Leia's mind, collided and combined, taking on levels of complexity she'd never guessed at before—but they made instinctive sense. It was as though her father had begun speaking to her in a language she hadn't heard in years but had known since birth. "Will you teach me?"

Bail betrayed no sadness at seeing her plunge more deeply into the fight, only pride. "This was lesson one."

•◆•

The Apprentice Legislature session ended shortly afterward, and Leia returned home. She might've dreaded the thought of empty hours when either grief or fear could hound her—but she had important tasks to accomplish, and a challenge to fulfill.

The sun had reached its zenith just as she pulled herself up from her foothold to stagger onto the rock plateau. Sweating and panting, Leia blinked at the glare, vivid even through her protective goggles, until she'd fully taken in the view from the top of Appenza Peak. Smaller mountains and hills surrounded her, spiky and sharp, but beyond them in the far distance she could make out the green slope of gentle country. The vast royal palace, which in her childhood had seemed like a world unto itself, was too small to be more than a glint on the horizon.

We ought to have stood here together, Kier. You should've been with me.

At least she hadn't had to make the climb alone.

The scrape of boots on rock prompted her to turn. Breha pulled herself onto the summit, even sweatier and more flushed than Leia herself. Her Alderaanian subjects might've been startled to see their queen like this—wearing military-issue all-terrain gear, dusty and disheveled, but aglow with satisfaction. To Leia, this was her mother at her most essential.

"It's even more beautiful than I remembered." Breha wiped her forehead with the back of her hand before going for her water bottle. "I should've done this again long ago. Or maybe not. Maybe it's best I'm here with you."

The next question had waited with Leia for years, but the time had finally come to ask: "Where did it happen?"

"We passed it some way back. Not that I know the spot exactly. It's something of a blur, as you can imagine."

"But—it was far up enough that they granted you the summit. Said you passed your challenge."

This earned her a raised eyebrow from her mother. "*Granted* me the summit? Oh, no, indeed. I made this ascent fair and clear. What nobody tells you is that descents are even harder."

All these years later, Alderaanians still spoke of "the

accident" in hushed tones. It was the moment the monarchy nearly ended without an heir, the day when a beloved princess—even more beloved than Leia herself, as Leia well knew—had nearly died. Her mother had fallen while completing her Challenge of the Body; the resulting injuries could've claimed her life. She'd been saved through quick action by the guards observing at a distance, but some of the damage had been permanent. It was after the accident that Breha's heart and lungs had been replaced by the pulmonodes that still glowed faintly in her chest. And it was due to the accident that her parents had elected to adopt a child rather than strain Breha's body further.

Without that one terrible incident, Leia's life might've been very different.

Sitting cross-legged on the ground, Breha studied her daughter as she spoke. "We look at our challenges—at our lessons—as things we master in order to achieve our goals. But the most important lessons in life sometimes have to do with what happens when we fail. How do we know when to surrender and walk away? How do we judge our own part in our failures? Is it something to learn from, or just bad luck? And how do we pick ourselves up again afterward?"

Leia looked back toward the horizon where she knew the palace lay. She remembered standing at Kier's grave, head held high, her false promise to him heavy in her heart. The wind whipped around her and her mother, reminding them that the mountain would only welcome them for so long. Soon they'd have to descend.

"You're learning the most powerful lesson of all, my daughter," Breha continued. "You're learning how to fall."

Kier had said that. Leia had realized it was important even then. But it was one of those truths that couldn't be understood until it had been lived through, until you finally fell.

•◆•

"Normally, of course, I'd have gone with something more festive in a gold or perhaps red." 2V whirred around Leia, straightening the long skirt. "But given everything—suffice it to say, silver is formal, elegant, and flattering. You look lovely."

That was as close as her droid could come to acknowledging Leia's grief. She was more moved by the gesture than she would've thought. "Thanks, TooVee."

Glancing to one side, she saw the bare spot on her mantel where her keepsake chest had always been—until late last night, when she'd given it to her father as a sign that she considered her childhood over. Many heirs to the throne gave up their keepsake chests at the point of investiture, but the ritual didn't demand it. Leia had simply known it was time. The hardest part about handing it over had been letting go of that lock of Kier's hair, that one small part of him. At least it would always be contained within the chest as one of her greatest treasures.

"I'll take good care of this," her father had promised, in a tone of voice that made her wonder, yet again, what he'd meant. . . .

The far-off fanfare echoing through the corridors alerted her that she was running late again. Leia turned to allow 2V to fasten a broad collar necklace, then straightened. Time to go.

Once more she took the shortcut through the old armory, full skirt billowing around her as she ran. At least today the weather had decided to do its part; brilliant sunlight streamed through every window, and she knew the throne room would glow with multicolored prisms from the stained glass. She felt—not happy, exactly, but as close to it as she'd come since Kier's death.

Conflicting emotions still swirled inside her whenever she thought of Kier. She suspected they always would. In the first days after his death, she'd tried to swear she would never fall for anyone again, though the reasons for that promise shifted and twisted in her mind: because she couldn't trust anyone completely, because she didn't deserve to find love after what happened to Kier because of her, because she didn't know how to bear another loss like this.

Her promise to herself had become more realistic. *Not until my work against the Empire is over,* she told herself. *After the struggle is over, then maybe—maybe I will meet someone else I can care about.*

Until then, I fight.

When she hurried into the antechamber, the guards straightened and smiled. The way they smiled at her had changed, though. What she saw there was less like the adoration she'd been granted since childhood, more like the respect given to her parents. Leia knew to be proud of that—and she was—but in some ways it felt like a loss.

The person she'd been before, the happy young princess, was gone. A beautiful part of her life had ended. She could mourn that while still being prepared to move on.

After months of strengthening her arms and back through pathfinding, Leia found the Rhindon Sword didn't feel so heavy anymore. Holding it aloft, she waited for the next fanfare, and—

The velvet curtain was pulled aside. Leia walked into the throne room, up the long aisle, toward the dais where her parents waited. Both her father and mother were garbed in pure white, which seemed all the more dazzling amid the sun-dappled shine of the room. As Leia went, she recognized friends standing on either side of her: Mon Mothma, who gave her a small nod, and Ress Batten, who looked too bowled over to react, and Chassellon Stevis, who winked. Very near the front stood Amilyn Holdo, whose hair had been dyed glittery blue, but who wore a simple dark green dress, at last striking a balance.

Standing before her parents, though—that moved Leia in a way she hadn't been fully prepared for. The pale color of their garments highlighted the long silver streak in her mother's hair, and the salt-and-pepper tones that had crept into her father's beard. Declaring her right to the throne inevitably meant acknowledging that, someday, her parents would be no more.

The formal language of the ceremony came through in her thought: *May that day be long in coming.*

Her father started the ceremony this time. "Is this our daughter, come before us once again?"

"It is I, Leia Organa, princess of Alderaan."

Breha had the next line. "When last you stood before us, you swore to undertake Challenges of Mind, Body, and Heart. This you have done."

Leia gripped the hilt even more tightly. "How do you judge me, my mother and queen?"

"I judge that you have completed your three challenges with great strength and even greater spirit. In all ways, you have proved yourself worthy." Gesturing for Leia to step closer, Breha rose from her throne.

As Leia ascended the dais to join her parents, she held the Rhindon Sword aloft in one hand. Breha reached up to clasp the hilt along with her: two rulers, not fighting over the symbol of power but sharing its weight. Then it was time for Leia to let go and sink to her knees, bowing her head as her father stepped closer. At the edges of her peripheral vision, she glimpsed the glitter of jewels, but she had to keep her face down. Then the weight of the Heir's Crown settled on her, fitting neatly into the nest of braids 2V had prepared for it. Even though Leia had waited all her life to wear this crown, the reality of it moved her more than she would've dreamed possible.

For Alderaan, she thought, promising both Kier and her parents to take good care of what she was being given that day.

"May all those present bear witness!" Breha cried. "My daughter is hereby invested as crown princess, heir to the throne of Alderaan."

Applause and cheers filled the room as Leia rose to her feet and turned to face the crowd. Her parents stood on either side of her, beaming with pride—more pride, even, than many of their guests could know. Through the stained glass windows Leia could catch glimpses of the beautiful planet that she would someday rule.

My parents, Leia thought. *My friends. My world.*

These are the things the Empire can never take away.

THE END